KU-274-172

Deirdre Purcell

The Husband

HACHETTE
BOOKS
IRELAND

Copyright © 2016 Deirdre Purcell

The right of Deirdre Purcell to be identified as the Author of the Work has been
asserted by her in accordance with the Copyright, Designs and Patents Act 1988.

First published in Ireland in 2016 by
HACHETTE BOOKS IRELAND
1

All rights reserved. No part of this publication may be reproduced,
stored in a retrieval system, or transmitted, in any form or by any means without the
prior written permission of the publisher, nor be otherwise circulated in any form
of binding or cover other than that in which it is published and without a similar
condition being imposed on the subsequent purchaser.

All characters in this publication are fictitious and any resemblance
to real persons, living or dead, is purely coincidental.

Cataloguing in Publication Data is available from the British Library.

ISBN 978 1 444 79940 8
Cover design and typeset by www.redrattledesign.com
Printed and bound in Great Britain by Clays Lrd, St Ives plc.

Hachette Books Ireland policy is to use papers that are natural, renewable and
recyclable products and made from wood grown in sustainable forests. The logging
and manufacturing processes are expected to conform to the environmental
regulations of the country of origin.

LONDON BOROUGH OF SUTTON LIBRARY SERVICE (WAL)	
30119 027 998 40 2	
Askews & Holts	Sep-2016
AF	

30119 027 998 40 2

WA

Deirdre Purcell was born and brought up in Dublin. She had an eclectic set of careers, including acting at the Abbey Theatre, before she became a journalist and writer, winning awards for her work on the *Sunday Tribune*. She has published thirteen critically acclaimed novels, most recently *Pearl* and *The Winter Gathering*, all of which have been bestsellers in Ireland. She adapted *Falling for a Dancer* into a popular four-part television mini-series, while *Love Like Hate Adore* was shortlisted for the Orange Prize. Deirdre Purcell lives in County Meath with her husband. She has two adult sons.

Also by Deirdre Purcell

FICTION
A Place of Stones
That Childhood Country
Falling for a Dancer
Francey
Sky
Love Like Hate Adore
Entertaining Ambrose
Marble Gardens
Last Summer in Arcadia
Children of Eve
Tell Me Your Secret
Pearl
The Winter Gathering

NON-FICTION
The Dark Hunger (with photographer Pat Langan)
On Lough Derg (with photographer Liam Blake)
The Time of My Life (ghostwriter for Gay Byrne)
Be Delighted (tribute to Maureen Potter)
Diamonds and Holes in My Shoes (memoir)
Follow Me Down to Dublin
Days We Remember
Aengus Finucane: In the Heart of Concern

SCREENPLAY
Falling for a Dancer (four episodes for BBC/RTÉ)
Shine On (Vision International for RTÉ)

OPEN DOOR ADULT LITERACY SERIES
Jesus and Billy Are off to Barcelona
Has Anyone Here Seen Larry?

SHORT STORY CONTRIBUTIONS
Ladies' Night at Finbar's Hotel
Moments
Irish Girls are Back in Town

For Ciara and Hazel, who pulled me through.

Prologue

The storm outside had battered the old house for at least two hours now. Although I was wearing a heavy sweater, I shivered. The cast-iron kitchen range, rusting in parts, sighed and pinged, unable to compete with the draughts whistling through the window seals. Designed for solid fuel but converted to oil long before I came to Glanmilish, it usually produced warmth enough to comfort even the furthest nooks in the room. Not so that afternoon. The wind, having swept unhindered across my neighbours' iron-flat tillage fields, was too much for its aged lungs.

With its dresser, farmhouse table, Belfast sink, mismatched cupboards and a variety of bric-a-brac, the kitchen had not been updated, by my reckoning, for thirty-five years or more. It was still home to my late mother-in-law's collection of crazed blue and white pottery jugs and what they called in Ireland, certainly here in the depths of County Laois, 'delph' or 'ware'. Living alone as I did, the scale of everything – the table at which I sat was capable of seating ten or more with elbow room for all – served to emphasise losses and absences.

It's November now and in an effort to get a handle on events since the month of March, I've been trying to put on paper what happened in Chicago and subsequently. From such an inauspicious beginning, it's difficult to accept how such a mundane event, watching TV for a few minutes, turned out to be seismic, turned my life upside down, and led to me moving continents and living here now in this house.

My brain, although trained for journalism (get the story into the first paragraph, follow the timeline, draw a conclusion), doesn't quite work chronologically, I'm afraid; it follows winding trails and becomes intrigued with why people behave the way they do. Nevertheless, since I came here, now that I have the time, I've been determined to get something down on paper in an effort to figure out for myself why things happened and why I, in particular, behaved as I did. There are, of course, some areas where discretion dictates I mustn't become too explicit . . .

I suppose you could say that for the past few weeks I've been writing a private memoir. And the faster I write, I find, the faster the memories, some very recent, some from earlier life and even childhood, jostle each other, crowding me, baying for attention. In these dark, stormy days and darker nights, I have found the task, if you could call it that, very engaging.

I got up from the table to fill the percolator but as I passed the rattling French windows, I jumped away as a sudden arc of rain – it might even have been hail – was flung at them from the huge weeping willow in the backyard. Staying well clear, I watched the old dowager writhe, thrashing the ground with her skirts. *Daniel is dead. Daniel is dead. Daniel is dead . . .*

Since coming to Ireland and Glanmilish House from my native Chicago, I had fallen in love with that tree, not least because she had survived such storms for more than a century, bravely coming into leaf year after year.

But . . .

Daniel is dead. Daniel is dead. Daniel is dead . . .

Nothing in my life has proved to be permanent and I feared for the willow's safety now. For the integrity of the house, too, should she succumb to this storm and fall on it. My neighbours had urged me to call in the tree surgeons but I had resisted. Mindful, however, of warnings from the scientific and meteorological communities that such weather would become more frequent and intense all through this second decade of the twenty-first century, my reluctance was just for now. And while I watched the gale's continuing assault, I wondered sadly how many more years she could hold out against such ferocity.

By coincidence my current reading was Thomas Pakenham's *Meetings with Remarkable Trees*, in which the author writes that prior to a major storm he walked around his charges, hugging each individually to wish it luck during the night. Imagining the possible fate of this one, either by wind or the chainsaw, I was overcome with loneliness of a kind that, deep and black as a coalmine, signals awareness of transience, not just of the people you love but of everything you value as a companion piece to your life, even the planet itself.

Daniel is dead. Daniel is dead. Daniel is dead . . . That's now the background drumbeat to my life. I heard it sometimes in comparatively minor circumstances: seeing a couple having a pavement argument about something silly, such as who forgot to lock the front door; reading a plea for help in finding a missing dog, complete with a photo pinned to a store's message board; or watching airport reunions on TV when it was a slow news day. Each event, simple of itself, would open the floodgates and I would find myself in tears.

The storm lulled. I left the windows and was priming the percolator when I heard the clatter of the brass mail-slot, or letterbox, as they call it here. I switched on the machine so it could do its thing and went up the steps to the gloomy hallway and towards the front door.

The house faces north-east, and although the main force of the south-westerly had exerted its force at the rear, I saw at a glance from the windows on each side of the double entrance doors that the steps leading up to them were littered with foliage, small twigs and two large, splintered branches. Then, on the doormat, I noticed another of those buff envelopes among bills and leaflets advertising water softeners, grocery stores and pizza deliveries.

I gathered it all up, dropped everything onto the hall table, ripped open the envelope and withdrew the single sheet from inside. Same cheap, greyish copy paper as the first and second deliveries, same uppercase and bolded font, same placement of a single line. Only the ink differed. The sender had used magenta for the first letter ('HUMPTY DUMPTY SAT ON A WALL') and cyan for the second ('HUMPTY DUMPTY HAD A GREAT FALL'). This one, a bright, mustardy yellow, shouted, 'ALL THE KING'S HORSES . . .'

Journalistic pedantry dies hard and, for some unknown reason, I stood there and counted the periods. There were ten. Ten little Indians. Ten green bottles – until there was one.

As I stood there with the wretched thing in my hand, the gale strengthened again, squealing as it invaded the gap under the door, agitating slates on the roof of the portico, until one came loose and crashed to the top step, shattering on the granite. For a few seconds, staring at those wet shards, as if by doing so I could unite them again, I felt overwhelmed, not just by the storm, the letter, the decrepitude of the house, but by my whole goddamned life in this whole goddamned place, where I was now living in just three of the many rooms: the kitchen, the drawing room, which the family had always referred to as 'the parlour', and the enormous master bedroom upstairs.

A second slate came down and, like the first, smashed on the granite. We were under siege, the house, the willow and me. During the past months, even on the blackest of my black days, I had rarely felt as alone and insignificant as I did right then.

Glanmilish House stands above the village of the same name. Adapted from the Gaelic, its original meaning is, apparently, 'Sweet Glade', but while I was under such a barrage, the name had never felt so inappropriate. I reminded myself that, in general, I don't take fright and I'm no longer easily intimidated. So, from its place at the bottom of the stairway, I fetched the worn draught excluder in the shape of an elongated dachshund, and placed it along the bottom of the door. Then I went back down to the kitchen, scant as its comfort would probably be.

Because Daniel is dead. He was a shit, but he was my shit and he's dead.

Chapter One

My name is Marian Lescher and at the time this story opens, three days after that major storm, I was forty-two, almost forty-three years of age, recently widowed, and after my husband's death, I had come to live in the damp midlands of Ireland at the Big House, as locals called it, in the village of Glanmilish. And I was determined not to surrender to what might be an adolescent prank . . . or a campaign to intimidate me into leaving town.

It was again stormy outside, although not as violently as it had been the previous day, thank goodness – I had already cleared away some broken roof tile and had collected as much as I could from the carpet of fallen branches and twigs on the grounds in the immediate vicinity of the house until rain again swept in to defeat me. Now, while I waited for coffee to finish perking, I searched through the kitchen window for the slightest patch of blue in the sky. There was still no sign of it.

The Irish climate gets to me sometimes – a lot of the time, if I'm honest. While I accept that occasionally the gloom does lift and temperatures do rise (seeming to surprise everyone and causing widespread joy and celebration), I have gathered that for most of every year, spring, summer, fall or winter, the skies over this country can lour to a greater or lesser degree, regularly letting loose with storms. This one, if not quite as noisy as yesterday's, was forceful enough to drown out the thump and bubble of the old percolator.

Dented and tarnished, the coffee pot was one of the few articles I had salvaged from my parents' apartment when clearing it out after Dad died. I don't think of myself as sentimental and I am no longer a Catholic but for some reason, alongside the percolator, I had also saved Mom's mournful picture of the Sacred Heart that, all through my childhood, had reigned gorily over our household in the kitchen at Shangri-La, the small, rickety ranch-style we rented on Circle Pass in the suburb of Northbrook, thirty to forty-five minutes north of the city, depending on expressway traffic. After I left home, my parents had downsized to a city apartment and, along with the percolator and other household goods, it had moved with them.

I was still contemplating what to do about those Humpty letters. In a detective novel or police drama on TV, there would have been a blonde hair (complete with epithelial), a little chip of blue nail polish or a drop of calcified sweat to be retrieved with tweezers from them. It's not in my nature to do nothing when I encounter a problem so I wondered if I should bring the correspondence to the attention of the local garda.

'What do you think?' I flicked the Sacred Heart a glance as I carried my coffee mug past His position on the back wall of the house by the French windows. 'Should I go to the cops? Would you think they're from fifteen-year olds? Even a group?'

No advice was forthcoming. He remained impassive, staring sorrowfully at me from the wall while inviting me to check out His cardiac injury with a bony finger, guilting me as usual about my lapsed-Catholic condition.

It was at times like this I missed Peter's rock-sensible attitudes to life and his advice . . .

* * *

Seven years previously, Peter Black and I had met across my father's bed in the Chicago hospital where Dad was being treated following his first, relatively minor, stroke, just a year after Mom had died. Even though I had been, understandably, pretty shaken by Dad's condition, I had noticed that this particular doctor, one of several who attended, was particularly kind, radiating calm confidence. While he wasn't handsome, in the traditional sense of Leonardo DiCaprio or Brad Pitt, he wasn't bad-looking either, tall and of a type – thick, sandy hair, blue eyes, rimless glasses, somewhat like the present-day British Prince Harry. Anyhow, I immediately trusted him.

But it wasn't until after my father had been discharged back to his apartment, a second-floor walk-up on Devon in Rogers Park on the north side of the city, that I really saw Peter's best side. At the time, Dad's neighbourhood was still faithful to its old-fashioned origins, replete with Jewish delis alongside family-run Italian *trattoria*. Dad loved fresh bagels with Parma ham: I had been shopping for him and had just let myself back into the apartment when I got a call. To my surprise, Peter, as I had already come to think of him, was offering to attend to Dad in his own time. I could barely hear him because of the din from one of the L trains that, day and night, rattled past Dad's kitchen and bedroom windows, but I got the gist. 'This is too much,' I yelled. 'Are you sure?'

'Very, very sure,' he said.

Mercifully, the train had now passed and I could speak at normal volume. I hesitated a little. Then: 'This has to be on a business footing.' It would be difficult for me to find the money because I was going through a lean work period.

For more than a year, as well as providing for myself, I had been discreetly shoring up the gaps in Dad's tiny pension income while trying to ensure that his failing health did not mean he felt isolated or lonely. Without making a big deal of it ('Things are good, Dad. Got a great commission last week!'), I had tried to make sure he could pay his rent, eat wholesomely, take the occasional trip to the movies, even have the occasional 'treat meal' in Giordano's Pizza on Sheridan Road. And regularly, after Mass on Sundays, we would stop for coffee and a breakfast sandwich – eggs, cheese and ham on Texas toast – at the Dunkin' Donuts on Loyola Avenue.

Freelance journalism is a precarious existence at the best of times – you can never refuse an assignment because there are always long lines of eager aspirants, many of them seeming just twelve years old from my perspective, ready and willing to take on what you won't or can't. And having had to spend so much time looking after my father, I had, unsurprisingly, fallen off many editors' contact lists. So, even as I had made the offer to pay the doctor, I was already calculating how Dad and I could cut back in order to come up with the appropriate fee.

That good Samaritan had immediately turned down flat any suggestion that I pay him anything at all: 'Absolutely not,' he said. 'It will be my pleasure.' It was an extraordinary offer and I made a few attempts at arguing, but although more than a little guilty at what I saw as taking advantage of someone (an absolute prohibition in my late mom's lexicon of morals and ethics), I was secretly delighted.

Thankfully, my father's speech had not been affected by his stroke, and during Peter's first visit a few days later, I had left the two of them alone until I judged medical information had been elicited and needs potentially met.

Getting back into the living room, I found the doctor sitting on a stool beside Dad's ratty old recliner, listening as my father rambled on about the 'olden days' in Chicago 'when carpenters like me, son, were top dogs on Irish construction sites. We could pick and choose who to work for then, and sometimes it was the Irish working for the Irish and the Polish working for the Poles. We had a lot of them Poles in Chicago, those days. Some didn't like 'em, but I did. They were hard workers. I admired 'em.'

I sat myself quietly on the couch, kitty-corner to them, watching as Peter Black displayed a quiet patience that, to my shame, I had rarely shown during Dad's halting and repetitive trips down Memory Lane. He laughed and nodded appropriately, tolerated long, interim pauses in the narratives, even refrained from supplying prompts when memory proved elusive – for instance, as to whether it was in the Howard or Granada cinema my parents had met for the first time: 'Oh, that was a sad day when those cinemas were pulled down, kids . . .' I saw clearly that Peter would make a great family physician, should he decide to move on from the hospital to set up his own practice, but right then, it was time to set him free. 'I'm sure the doctor has to get back to work, Dad – or maybe, Doctor, you have to get home in time for dinner?

'You remember what that was like, Dad?' I turned back to him. 'When Mom would get annoyed if you were late? Remember the time she threw your lamb chops down the garbage chute?'

* * *

'That's a nice guy,' Dad said of his new friend, when I came back to the apartment having shown Peter out. 'Didn't see no wedding ring, though, Marian. Wink, wink, nod, nod, eh?'

'Don't be ridiculous, Dad!'

For years, both my parents had crusaded, jointly and separately, to marry me off. They had nagged, connived with their friends and neighbours, but nothing had ever come of their efforts, either covert or open, to introduce me to 'suitable' men. 'You're too independent, Marian,' Mom had scolded. 'And you're picky, what's more. So tell me again what exactly was wrong with Mrs Feinstein's nephew. OK, he's not of our persuasion but I betcha he'd convert. They do that, you know. The Feinsteins are good people and he has a job in that nice jewellery store on State Street downtown. And he can get discounts! Think of that, eh?'

'He's dull, Mom. And he's half my size!'

'For goodness' sake, Marian! He's a good five foot seven or eight.' She bristled. 'What are you now? Eleven feet?'

'You know what I mean – I'm at least half a head taller, maybe even more. I couldn't wear heels! I like to look my dates in the eye, Mom!' Their relentless matchmaking had resulted in the opposite of what they wanted. Like a teenager, I was stubbornly determined not to please them.

'Listen, Dad.' I was serving him his dinner of soup and tuna salad on a TV tray later on the day of Peter's first visit, as he continued, meaningfully, to sing his new friend's praises. 'Dr Black hasn't shown the slightest interest in me.' And then, blatantly lying: 'And, anyway, I'm so busy, these days, I don't have time for dating.'

* * *

At the end of Peter's second attendance, when I was seeing him out, we chatted a little and, to my surprise, discovered we had a lot in common: we were both single, and only children with one parent still living. 'Is it your mom or your dad?' I asked.

'My mom. Getting on now, living alone out in Skokie. I worry about her, but she has good neighbours.'

'Do you ever feel trapped?' I asked. It had just popped out and I immediately regretted it. He had so much on his plate – all doctors do – and we weren't on that kind of footing. 'Maybe we should do a bit of subtle getting them together,' I added hastily. 'Do you think they'd get on?'

He smiled. He had a nice smile. 'I'm assuming you do. Feel trapped, I mean.'

'Sometimes,' I admitted. 'Dad's the best in the world, but— Look, it's not your problem. Forget I said that.'

'I know the feeling, Marian. You feel you can't do anything spontaneous, that when you get an invitation, the first thing you think of is not whether you want to go but what about Dad? Or, in my case, Mom. You start trying to figure out ways you *can* accept.'

'Exactly!' He was easy to talk to.

'Well, as it happens, I'm going out to Skokie now. See you same time next Monday?' he said. Then, with his hand on the door latch: 'You don't have to be here, you know, Marian. The super can let me in. They usually trust doctors, not that that's always such a good idea!'

'I'll be here. Thank you very much.'

After I'd closed the door behind him, I stood for a few minutes in the hallway. The exchange had made me think. My reducing income and pitifully thin social life proved that, over the years, I had ceded a good deal of control over my life to the task of looking after my parents. But I had slid willingly into the role of Dad's semi-carer and, earlier, as Mom's too: after her cancer diagnosis, which had so quickly descended from 'treatment' into 'terminal', Dad had been too scared. 'She always looked after everything, Marian. I don't know what to do . . .'

I had never had much control over my life and it occurred to me, again, that perhaps not many only children do. And since my parents had been relatively elderly when they'd had me, my fate had probably been sealed on the day I was born. I didn't resent it, truly, merely accepted it as the way things were. They had done their very best for me so I had to return the compliment, and I always felt guilty when such mean thoughts arose. So, it was comforting to know that, actually, those feelings were not uncommon, and while I would be careful not to impose, I was kind of looking forward to speaking again with Peter Black.

But it was not until his third visit to Dad that the penny really dropped. I was downstairs, again accompanying him out through the entrance foyer of the block, when, instead of saying casually, as he had twice before, 'See you same time next Monday?' he hesitated, jingling his keys. Then: 'Would you like a coffee, Marian?'

'You asking me on a date?'

I had meant it jokingly, but he blushed and said, awkwardly: 'If that's what you want to call it – yes. But if it's not— ' He stopped. Another resident had pushed through the building's entrance door and was opening one of the mail lockers beside us.

During the hiatus, while all three of us smilingly acknowledged each other's presence, I thought quickly. While I liked him and had relaxed more and more in his presence, it had genuinely not occurred to me that he had any motive in coming other than innate kindness and, peripherally, fulfilling the finer diktats of the Hippocratic oath. We had our straitjackets in common but didn't know much else about one another.

But he had been seriously generous with the time he had given to Dad and, by extension, to me so I sure did owe him. 'Cool!' I smiled at him. 'Why not?'

Over that coffee date, we talked easily – as we did over dinner the next time. There followed outings to the cinema, the Goodman Theatre, and even to the Lyric Opera to hear a Mozart symphony. 'Tell me if I'm being a bore, Marian,' he said, as we travelled in on the L, 'but, to me, Mozart is supreme. Don't know why I think that – it's all subjective, of course. But *Amadeus* has a lot to answer for. Great movie, great acting, great costumes and a fantastic soundtrack – but now anyone who doesn't know about the real Mozart, much less about his music . . .' He grimaced. 'Honestly! They portrayed him as a bit of an idiot, and that's what stuck. Did you see it?'

I shook my head.

'That's great. Means that tonight you'll have an open mind. He had seven children, you know. And after all that wonderful music, the poor guy was buried in a pauper's grave. Sorry!' He smiled, a little shyly. 'Got carried away there! But I really, *really* hope you'll take to his music. It's been known – it's *proven* – to lower blood pressure and heart rate. Am I talking too much?'

'I'm sure I'll love it, Peter.'

I can't say I immediately jumped into line with Mozart as fervently as Peter Black might have wished. I knew nothing at all about classical music at the time and that concert at the Lyric was the first I had ever attended, an appalling admission to make when I was a resident of such an arts-loving city. But I did enjoy the evening, the atmosphere and the company. And that introduction to Mozart has stood me in good stead: from time to time his music has even provided consolation. On that stormy day in Glanmilish, I sincerely hoped that, wherever he was now, Peter could find similar solace.

He had been easy company, cultured, well-read, interested in politics, the environment, films, the arts in general, and had a laid-back, subtle sense of humour. Little by little, I had relaxed into the relationship. There was a bonus too. From the start, I really took to his mom, who was widowed early on, as he'd told me, living alone in the suburb of Skokie, and, unlike Dad, in full, robust health. After our first meeting, she had run out after us when we were about to climb back into his Karmann Ghia, catching my arm and pulling me aside. 'You're the answer to my prayers, honey. I don't know how my son got so lucky. Thank you, thank you, thank you! I hope we can be great friends.' She hugged me so tightly that the sunglasses I had just put on fell to the ground and broke. 'Oh, my! Oh, my! I'm so sorry, I'll get you another pair – but Peter's told me so much about you, I'm just so excited to meet you!'

After what happened subsequently, that little scene often rises to haunt me and I tear up, seeing her kind, open face under its grey cap of curls, probably shampooed and set in the beauty shop in honour of my impending visit. She had perhaps confided in the stylist what was to unfold that Sunday afternoon: *My son Peter – you know my son, the doctor? He's bringing his lovely new girlfriend home to meet me!* And all through that afternoon in her cluttered living room, behind her glasses, her eyes had glistened with sincerity, love for him and a welcome for me. These days, when I can't sleep and it's four in the morning, I'm still stabbed by guilt because of what I did to her and, of course, to her son.

Chapter Two

During our old-fashioned, decorous courtship, Peter never pushed me to go more deeply into the relationship than I wanted, and it was perhaps a couple of months before our first overnight together. The sex, when it began, was similarly traditional and remained that way. As our association continued, though, I was conscious of a deep-down niggle. Mom's favourite singer had been Peggy Lee, her favourite song the sixties hit 'Is That All There Is?'. For me, the lyric illustrated perfectly that, while I was undoubtedly very fond of Peter, something might have been missing.

That being said, after about six months with him I scolded myself for that: I had come to the conclusion that this, the longest alliance I had ever had, was probably 'it' and – this is going to sound callous – at thirty-five years of age I would in all likelihood never do better. A person could not, I reasoned, have both excitement and stability in the same relationship and, anyhow, I had become confirmed in my view that my lack of sexual adventurousness (prowess?) was of my own making and something I had to accept, since it didn't seem to bother my partner.

It was not a new revelation. As an embarrassed, gangling sixteen-year-old loner – a geek, in fact – my first strangled attempts at making out in the back of an automobile had been a disaster, and that sense of discomfort, even failure, had lingered, wraith-like, right into my thirties. Secretly, I hoped that within me somewhere, behind the fear that I might make a fool of myself, there lay a heap of ardour that would enable me to let go of my inhibitions and fling myself around, not caring about anyone else's reaction to my clumsiness.

In the meantime, while no one, certainly not Peter, had ever accused me of coldness, I had always felt a little underwhelmed by sex. And having met the man I now reckoned was my life partner, I had resigned myself to the idea that I wasn't destined to ascend the peaks of passion described by novelists. I decided Mom had been right and that I was, as usual, being picky: I should concentrate on Peter's good qualities, of which there were many.

After those first six months, I happily gave up my own apartment, with its view of an open, weedy lot from my 'open space' – the fire escape – and moved into his apartment on Oak Street. And when, almost two years later, we decided to get married, his mother was ecstatic – she wept for joy when we told her.

The ceremony, held in Holy Name Cathedral on my thirty-seventh birthday, Christmas Eve 2009, was really nice, and with so many doctors and nurses at the reception in an Italian restaurant, I didn't have to worry about Dad. A king in his wheelchair, he basked all day in attention and even found a new audience for his tales of Old Chicago.

Late in the afternoon, it was already dark when Peter's mom and I found ourselves together in the intimacy of the candlelit women's bathroom. We were titivating in front of the mirrors when she dared, for the first time, to reveal her hopes about grandchildren, blurting, 'Wouldn't it be lovely?'

She had occasionally hinted that she longed for grandchildren of her own rather than having always to rejoice in the endless production lines of her friends' kids. But now, clearly, she felt it was safe to say so. 'It would indeed be lovely, Letty.' For me, that day, the notion of having a child was still some way off, a general aspiration to be fulfilled when other matters – a suitable home, a certain level of career achievement – had been accomplished. But, yes, I did want a 'proper' family. 'It won't be immediate,' I told Peter's mom, 'but it's a priority for both of us. So watch this space!'

Articles I came across in magazines while I was waiting in the beauty parlour or the doctor's office consistently described the uncontrollable, unconditional love that unexpectedly overpowered new moms when, immediately after giving birth, they held their still-slippery babies in their arms for the first time. Maybe the same would work for me. Maybe, I thought that day, mother-love would liberate all those trapped feelings in one great dam burst, releasing my inhibitions, spilling into my love life with my husband. Perhaps it would even allow me to experience the holy grail of orgasm that up to now had eluded me (if the more detailed descriptions of the event I had read about were even remotely accurate). Meanwhile, after our lovemaking I had always assured Peter that, yes, of course it had been great for me too.

'Oh, my! Just imagine! A little baby!' In the face of my brand new mother-in-law I could see, reflected back at me from that bathroom mirror on my wedding day, that for her the next big event was now merely a matter of marking a calendar, that by my next birthday (and first wedding anniversary) we would all be having a triple celebration. 'Can't you just imagine?' she repeated, then added shyly, 'I hope you'll let me be involved.'

'You'll be sorry you said that, Letty.' I laughed, adjusting the sweetheart neckline of my gown. I hadn't worn a veil, figuring it would accentuate my height. 'You'll probably be sick of the sight of all of us!'

'Don't say that!' She grabbed my arm. 'I can't wait!'

Peter and I had actually discussed timings and had decided that before embarking on creating kids we needed a proper home for them. The Oak Street apartment was on the sixty-fourth floor and was walled with glass, affording spectacular views of the lake. When the skies were clear we could watch, below us, O'Hare-bound planes glide past on their final approaches: great for us, but for a toddler bent on exploration? With all that glass? Far from appropriate. Anyhow, the rent was as sky-high as the building and the higher the floor you occupied the more expensive it became.

By the time we got married, we had already started to save for our new home and family (well, Peter had started to save from his salary, which was quite substantial; I did the best I could), and while we had agreed to wait, our kids were plain to be seen, waving at us from the horizon.

In the meantime, during the first two years after the wedding we enjoyed, if that's the word, a stable, secure sense of mutual respect and a genuine, if quiet, acknowledgement that we did love each other. And by the time I was quarter-way through my fortieth year in the spring of 2012, we were well in sight of our family goals. We had identified a place we both liked just south of the Prairie District on the Near South Side, close to Peter's hospital and with schools nearby. We had enough money saved for a down payment, were involved in negotiation for a mortgage with Peter's bank – and I had gone off the contraceptive pill. In that regard, we had further agreed that, even if the house fell through, it would not be a disaster if we became pregnant right away. 'Pregnant and properly homed at forty' became the abiding ambition.

Looking back on it from this distance, I can no longer speak for Peter, of course, but for me, at that point, going off the pill had, out of the blue, been an urgent necessity. My baby-drive had abruptly, astonishingly, become so urgent that conceiving a child superseded all other matters – even caring for my father. It is no exaggeration to say that it consumed every waking hour when I wasn't interviewing someone, covering an event or subsequently writing to a deadline. At least during work hours I managed to retain the ability to focus on the job or person concerned.

But if there was no deadline, if the piece was not on commission and still had to be sold somewhere, I was wont to seize again on my new hobby: trawling the internet for advice on what to eat and what not to eat in order to conceive. In bookshops and libraries, I now passed up the fiction sections and walked directly to Parenting.

Poor Peter was as surprised as I was at this new state of affairs in which I had abandoned all notions of physical gratification. Sex, for me, had now become a matter of timing and thermometers, of measuring fertility. I had always seen children as being part of my life, eventually, but this compulsion, as it had become, had blindsided me. I couldn't explain it and had to accept that it was simple biology. As a doctor, he, God bless him, accepted it as Nature's way and became a co-conspirator, helping with the calculations.

One afternoon that spring, early March 2012, at ten minutes past four, I was again avidly researching motherhood and pregnancy on my creaking old MacBook, while dinner was slow-cooking on the hob in the kitchen. Like most American city dwellers, with the enormous number and variety of restaurants on our doorstep, Peter and I ate out a lot, but as one of the side effects of the baby thing, I had experienced an unusual surge of domesticity, finding myself as interested in cooking and cleaning as Mom had been. Like a bird in spring, I had clearly begun nesting. Clicking through the good offices of Uncle Google, I had half an ear tuned to the TV. As high and sound-insulated as we were, there was no sound in the apartment except the discreet hiss of the central air-con and the occasional pop and bubble from the stove. Even the aircraft glided silently by. I had turned on the set for company, tuning it to one of the local cable affiliates where it now burbled through a talk show, one of those afternoon programmes designed to fill the hours of the lonely.

The guest had apparently graduated top of his class in medical school, had been shooting upwards through the ranks in surgery, but had temporarily eschewed all of that, the anchor said, to participate in a programme researching the Ebola virus being conducted at Holy Angels, a small hospital specialising in paediatrics.

Because of Peter's work, the word 'hospital' always caught my ear. I bookmarked the webpage I was on and looked up.

The show ran like a giant hamster wheel, a new guest boarding at every couple of turns and this guy, clearly bent on making the most of the two or three minutes he had been allocated, was leaning forward in his chair, speaking in a rapid Irish brogue, words spilling on top of each other as though his tongue couldn't keep up with his thoughts. He was doing this work, he was telling the hostess, because he had become particularly interested 'in one of the most prevalent and deadly viruses of all'. Despite the low volume, the voice sounded familiar. I walked across the living room to turn up the sound and instantly recognised Daniel Lynch.

I had met him only once. I was having lunch with Peter in his hospital cafeteria – I went there occasionally when I was on an assignment in his part of town and nobody in the staff section seemed to object if I joined him. The din was always considerable.

With hygiene concerns uppermost, the floor was ceramic, the tables were metal, and at lunchtime, when the place was full, you had to raise your voice to be heard.

Without waiting for an invitation, this tall guy, physically imposing with curly dark hair, joined our group. Carrying a chair in one hand and his tray in the other, he found a place directly opposite me. As he sat down, he smiled at me with an expression in his eyes that I couldn't describe as anything other than challenging. It made me uncomfortable in ways I didn't care to examine, and I turned away to concentrate on my husband – but not before one of the nurses in the group, Cindy Kurtz, who was sitting on Peter's other side, leaned towards the new arrival, and hissed, 'Behave, you!'

That was unexpected. During the couple of times we had encountered one another, Cindy, a livewire, was usually good-humoured, and I had never before seen her irritable.

As for the newcomer's response, I couldn't say, as a novelist would, that his face 'darkened' because his smile didn't waver, but I did notice his reaction: he gave nothing more than a quick flick of his eyes towards her. I glanced at her, and she caught the movement of my head. 'Ignore him, Marian.' She grinned. 'I guess you two don't know each other. Daniel Lynch, Irish backwoodsman.' She shot him another look, waved airily in his direction, and then said, indicating me, 'Dr Lynch, this is Peter's Marian, as you may have gathered.' Having made the introductions, she went back to her lunch.

'So where've you been hiding, Marian?' Seemingly unperturbed at the exchange, Lynch took a forkful of his own lunch and then, to Peter, 'Or, more likely, where've you been hiding her, old man?'

'Marian's been here many times. You've been too busy to notice, *old man*.' Peter, unusually, had seemed nettled. 'I've got to get back,' he added. 'You ready, Marian?' He looked at my plate, on which a few bites of my chicken salad sandwich were still in evidence. 'Sorry, didn't realise you weren't done.'

'Don't worry, I'm finished.' I stood up, strangely conscious of Daniel Lynch's attention. He wasn't exactly staring at us. It was more as if he was exerting himself on us, if that makes sense. It's a poor description, I guess, but the best I've been able to come up with.

That evening, at home, I asked Peter casually, 'What was all that about with you and the Irishman, honey? Do you have some kind of history?'

'Nothing worth talking about. I just don't like him, and I guess the feeling is mutual. It happens.'

'Is there something between him and Cindy?'

'Dunno,' he said quickly, 'and, anyway, who cares? Where'll we go eat tonight? I'm pretty hungry now.'

'Let me get my jacket.' I knew him well enough to grasp that the subject was closed.

So here was Daniel Lynch again, this time sitting in front of a TV anchor, who looked pretty impressed. I could see why because this time, speaking about a cause, he seemed seriously committed, even passionate, as though determined to convince her of what he was saying, although she didn't seem to need any convincing. Actually, experienced presenter though she was, she seemed uncharacteristically dazzled.

'You probably don't know this, Peggy,' he said earnestly, 'but every year rotavirus kills hundreds of thousands of children. Up to half a million for definite, and probably a lot more, and as usual, the overwhelming numbers are in the developing world. It's a real scandal and it never causes even a ripple on the nightly news, like even the smallest hint of an Ebola outbreak does. And, Peggy, I want you to know – I want everyone to know this . . .' He turned directly to the camera, addressing it. The operator, seizing the moment, closed in slowly on his face so his eyes – a greeny-grey, although the colour on our old TV set wasn't all that accurate on cable channels – burned through the screen. 'Please,' he said, 'when you're having dinner tonight in your comfortable, air-conditioned home, big or small, think of the work we're doing at Holy Angels and open your wallets along with your bottle of Chardonnay or Bud. I want you to contrast your air-conditioning with the heat and swamps and humidity in the kind of homes where dozens of flies crawl all over the faces of the children, into their mouths, into their eyes, up their noses, and into their groins. I want you to feel the excruciating pain in their tummies as they retch and . . .' he hesitated '. . . "go to the bathroom",' the quote marks were obvious, 'in the mud. All for the want of a dollar's worth, maybe a couple of dollars' worth, of medicine.

'And if we're talking numbers, rotavirus knocks Ebola into a cocked hat! And, by the way, it's here too, not in numbers, not yet, but it's here in the good old US of A. So some day even your kid, your lovely, happy, well-nourished child, eating healthy mid-morning snacks in kindergarten, could fall to it too.'

Just then Peter came in from work, caught this last paragraph, and said, 'Hi, honey, lovely smell.' Absentmindedly, he bussed my cheek, looked towards the TV, then sat beside me on the couch. 'Whaddaya know? It's Lynch! Why am I not surprised?'

'Why?' I was still watching the screen.

'Why what?'

'Why are you not surprised?'

'You must remember Daniel Lynch, Marian. Dr Daniel Lynch? You were there at least once when he came into the cafeteria and joined us. Could always talk for the Olympics, that guy. And remember you asked me later why I don't like him? Well, as it happens, none of us does.

'I have to be fair, though,' he said then, settling more comfortably back into the cushions. 'With hindsight, the rest of us are probably blind with jealousy because we knew he'd make the big-time sooner rather than later. Sooner than us anyhow! And, to be honest, he's incredibly bright. We all thought he'd make a top-rate surgeon if he stuck at it.'

'So?' I was intrigued.

'Is he on about surgery?' He looked back at the screen. 'What's this about kids? Is he still at Rush?'

'Viruses. Research. Some little paediatric place. Angel something?'

'Holy Angels? And he's moved from Rush? That's a surprise – quite a downsize. When we were students at Feinberg, we all wanted Rush after qualification. I'm not sure but he was maybe a year behind our group.' He was thinking this through. 'He came on some kind of merit scholarship from Ireland and he did hang out with us a bit, but from day one, he was making waves. Top of everyone's party invite list until—' He stopped.

'Until what?' I really wanted to know more.

But Peter was going no further. 'He sure was entertaining,' he said briskly. 'Could charm his way into or out of any situation, and there were plenty. He has this . . .' He paused, then seemed to change his mind. 'I'm no midget,' he said, 'but he sure made me feel like one! Oh, look, this is all ancient history.'

'He's tall?' But I already knew that.

'Huge! You can't tell on TV. Come on, Marian, you must remember him! Daniel Lynch is hard to forget. Even on just a few minutes' acquaintance.'

Falsely, for some reason I didn't care to think about, I shook my head. 'Yes, vaguely – at least, the name rings a bell. Or maybe it's that Irish accent.' I turned back to the TV. The anchor, reacting to an off-set signal, had begun her wrap-up, talking to camera, smiling toothily. Her guest was now fidgeting, tapping a finger on one of his knees, both of which were jigging.

She seemed to sense this because even as she was introducing her next guest she turned to smile directly at him, with that telltale incline-the-head-sideways look from under the eyebrows. Then, as happens sometimes, the commercials cut in when she was still in mid-sentence.

'His work at Holy Angels sounds really interesting,' I said, getting off the couch and going towards the kitchen to check on dinner. 'And it's also interesting, as you say, that he downsized to do it. Want coffee?'

'Sure, hon – Colombian, if we have it, with Splenda and a splash of half and half.' Peter took care with his fat and sugar intake.

Over my shoulder, while opening the coffee canister, I called, 'Do you think you could introduce me? He wouldn't remember me, I'm sure, and mightn't react positively if I cold-called him. I'd love to do a piece on him. I'm sure I could sell it. I might even try the *Tribune*. Could be the break I need.' That was true. Dad continued to be one of my main priorities, but I had pushed myself a little to show some sort of initiative and, as a result, had begun to make strides again – well, baby steps – in my career. If as yet I had not managed to secure a staff job, which remained an aspiration, a serious, lengthy piece in the *Chicago Tribune* was the next best thing, even the first step on the golden ladder to get in ahead of the next swarm of bright, ambitious, fearless youngsters pouring out of Columbia and Northwestern to climb onto it, waving journalism degrees like banners, each bursting with eagerness and the conviction that they could *do this*.

'Are you sure you want to interview him, honey? Daniel Lynch is tricky.'

'All the better. I could do with a challenge.' That was the truth. I needed something meaty to stretch my ability and reputation, but as I filled the percolator, I wasn't thinking of that but of the challenge in Daniel Lynch's eyes that day in the cafeteria, and the way those eyes had spoken directly to me through the TV.

'Okay. If you're sure. I think I might still have his number.'

I glanced towards my loyal, steady, intelligent, kind and generous man, who continued to traipse out to Rogers Park every week to sit with Dad, listening patiently to the repetition, the worn stories and the health complaints. He was already flipping through the contacts lists on his cell. 'Won't you be careful, though, hon? He had quite a reputation around the hospital.'

'What kind of reputation?' But I already knew. It was a no-brainer.

'Do you have to ask?' Peter continued to scrutinise the screen of his cell. 'Women go glassy-eyed. You saw him there with Whatshername on the TV.'

'Don't you trust me, Peter? I'm a journalist. I can spot bullshitters and phoneys a mile off.' I was speaking to the splashback over the stove. I had the strangest feeling that I was acting in a play.

'Of course I trust you. It's him I don't trust – ask any of my male colleagues who had a girlfriend when we were all trainees. And there were even rumours that he— Ah, here it is! I'll write it out for you. I don't want to call him, though. You'll have to do that yourself.'

'OK. I think I can manage that.' I watched as he took a pen from the breast pocket of his jacket along with some kind of a receipt, turning it over to transcribe the number on the back. Peter always stuck his tongue out a little when he was concentrating, and as he checked alternately between the number on his cell's screen and the receipt, he did so now. I had always found it endearing.

'That's great. Thanks, honey.' I turned back to the bean grinder, switched it on, and the apartment filled with noise.

Chapter Three

The arrangement was that I would meet Daniel Lynch in the lobby bar of the Palmer House on Monroe, my choice. When I was interviewing people, even as a freelancer, my first choice as venue was always that venerable hotel, and specifically that bar. Decorated in creams and browns, with candle sconces, rugs and a wonderful ceiling, it exuded plushness and luxury, which always impressed those who agreed to talk to me, but in fact was no more expensive, at least for its coffee, than many of the soulless glass and ice palaces of more modern vintage. In the Palmer House, you felt a little special.

I was early, as I always was for such appointments. Arrayed in front of me on the little table were my digital recorder, with a cassette recorder as back-up, my notebook, two ballpoint pens, spare batteries and the sheaf of notes I had compiled on rotavirus, Ebola, and Lynch himself, via Google and Wikipedia; the writers of the latter entries seemed to have seen the same interview on cable as I had. Lynch had a Facebook page and was on LinkedIn, illustrated with the same photo, just a couple of degrees better than the unflattering type usually displayed on passports, and a very brief official profile outlining his education and career path. *Born in Ireland, Dr Lynch graduated with honors and moved from Rush University Medical Center to Holy Angels Paediatric, Chicago, to pursue his interest in researching epidemiology and infectious diseases as they affect children worldwide, but particularly in the emerging world.* In my rather nervous call to him to set up our meeting, I had concentrated on this, not mentioning the cable interview. 'There isn't much about you on social media, Dr Lynch.'

'Blame the marketing people at Holy Angels.'

I'd let that pass and we'd made the arrangements, I, in my nervousness, overdoing the gratitude, he seeming quite amused by it. Time ticked by. The bar staff had gotten to know me and always placed coffee in front of me when they saw me come in. It had done little to quell the uncharacteristic fluttering in my stomach. The stern command I gave myself that this man was not Johnny Depp or Brad Pitt, or even Bill Clinton, failed to control it, as did the admonition that Daniel Lynch was a serious medical man, just like Peter, and deserved to be treated as soberly and earnestly as I would Peter, had I not been married to him.

None of this helped. Even during that TV interview, a contrived situation, Daniel Lynch had transmitted something so primeval, even dangerous, that a pulse within me, previously unrecognised, had jumped to attention, engendering feelings also formerly unfamiliar. An attempt to describe it accurately is probably futile. The best I can manage is that I felt as though a kindle of kittens was jumping around in my stomach, straying occasionally into the area below my breastbone.

Our meeting had been for nine, it was already twenty after, and I raised my hand to order another coffee, instantly catching the eye of the barman, who smiled and gave me a thumbs-up.

The minutes went by. I sipped the rapidly cooling coffee.

By nine forty-five, the room had filled and I had almost finished the second coffee. Unusually, Peter had called me twice but I had rejected the call each time. I messaged him now: *Sorry, saw two missed calls. Were they urgent? All fine here. Everything okay your end?*

He responded immediately: *Just checking the guy showed up. Nearly finished?*

Not yet, I replied truthfully, and was about to embroider a little when I spotted Daniel Lynch. The last time I'd seen him in the flesh, he had been wearing scrubs, but that morning he was in a short-sleeved white T-shirt, chinos and trainers. I had time to take this in because, obviously searching for me, he had paused at the top of the flight of steps and was eyeing the room. As he did so, the palms of my hands grew warm and prickly, as though thousands of tiny needles were busy just under the skin. But he had seen me, and as he came down towards where I was sitting, I quickly hit the send button on the message to Peter, turned off the phone and stood up, as I would have for any interviewee.

Peter had not exaggerated when he'd said that Daniel Lynch was 'huge'. He had struck me as tall when he had approached Peter's group of friends at that cafeteria table, but now, as he stood in front of me, I could make actual comparisons. Not quite basketball-player height, he had to be at least six feet five, proportionally broad and long-legged, definitely built like an athlete. His dark, curly hair bloomed profusely over the collar of his sweatshirt and fell over his eyes. It seemed damp, as though he had just stepped out of the shower. 'Well, hello again, Marian!'

He held out his hand, and as I shook it, I could feel my face heating. I hadn't blushed since I was fifteen but I managed to return the greeting. 'May I order you coffee? Tea? Something stronger?'

'Tea would be lovely.' He sat down. 'Would you ask if they have leaf? I hate this American hot water and teabag on the side routine, Oh dear!' He was now surveying my equipment. 'I see you came well prepared! How many of us are you expecting? And how long do we have?'

'How long do *you* have, Dr Lynch?'

'Daniel. Please.'

'Right. How long, Daniel?'

'As long as it takes. I've got the morning off. Anything for the wife of an ex-colleague. How is good old Peter, by the way?'

He winkled away the scatter cushion from behind his back and put it on another of the chairs at the table – there were four – then folded himself more comfortably into his own seat, which seemed too flimsy to hold him. Then, without pursuing his enquiry about Peter, he said, 'Thanks, Marian. Tea would be lovely. And if they have a bun or a chocolate muffin or a cookie or something, that'd be great too.'

'A brownie, maybe? They're great here.'

'A brownie it is! Nice place.' He looked up at the ceiling. 'I'm honoured.'

Rather than sit with him, I went up to the bar to give the order: I needed to gain time and, not least, a little composure. He had arrived the best part of an hour late with no apology, and I reminded myself that I was in charge of the situation, that this had been *my* initiative.

But I was seriously discombobulated. I had never before met a man who exuded such casual self-confidence. Women, yes. Dainty preppy students, who, passing me in school or college corridors, blonde ponytails bouncing, had made me feel like a clumsy giraffe. And there had been a few female journalistic colleagues with ice-encased eyes, who wore ambition like a graduation gown, and who had intimidated the hell out of me.

The barman bustled across to me and I ordered the tea and two brownies. Then I took a deep breath, counted down from ten and, with no further excuse to delay, went back to the table where Daniel Lynch seemed as relaxed as a rag doll, one knee crossed over the other, head bent, apparently watching my digital recorder as he flipped it over and back between his hands. My unruly kittens gambolled again: those hands were long and supple, a surgeon's hands. *Stop this! You already know he has a talent for surgery. Peter, your husband, told you that.*

'Peter tells me you trained as a surgeon,' I said, as I sat back in my chair, 'and they'll bring everything over to us. Shall we start in the meantime?'

'Of course. I'm in your hands, Marian.'

'I have to be someplace at eleven.' Lying, looking showily at my watch. 'It's five to ten now.'

'Sorry about that. Late night.'

'You were working?'

'Always.' He handed me the recorder.

My fingers felt like hot dogs as I adjusted the fiddly little controls, set it running, triggered the back-up machine and somehow managed to drop into professional mode. 'So. Epidemiology? Why that? I saw your interview on cable . . . ' I was now busying myself with uncapping one of the ballpoint pens and opening a notebook.

Efficient as always, one of the bar's waiters arrived to set our table. Helpfully, Lynch picked up both recorders and held them out of the way while the man snapped out a starched white tablecloth, laid it with the creases geometrically centred and placed on it a cream jug, plates, two sugar basins, one of granulated white, the other brown lumps, a trivet for Daniel's teapot, a tea-strainer and, including spoons and sugar tongs, cutlery enough for a banquet.

'Wow! Look at all this!' His tone was ironic.

'It's just how they do it here,' I said defensively.

'It's all right, Marian. Relax. It's just so far from how I was reared.' He'd exaggerated his accent – 'rared'. He smiled at me. 'Tell me a little about you.'

'Very little to tell. A journalist, married to Peter—'

'Happily, I presume.'

'Of course.' It was true. I couldn't complain about anything – yet in Daniel Lynch's presence, I was uptight about that too. 'Very,' I said firmly. We're very happy.'

'Good for you. And good for old Peter. Any kids yet?'

'Not yet, but we're planning now.'

'Wonderful. How is the old ruffian?'

Peter? A ruffian? My Peter? 'Oh – Peter? He's fine. A very good doctor, actually . . .' I explained to him, at greater length than was strictly necessary, how my husband looked after my father. 'For a couple of years now. That's how we met. He attended Dad in the hospital after his first stroke.'

'Love blossoming across the snowy sheets? That's gorgeous.'

I stared at him but his expression was impassive. 'You called him a "ruffian". Why was that, Daniel?' The question had left my mouth before I could stop it.

'Oh, that was ages ago. He surprised me. I'd taken him for someone quite different.'

'Why?' *Why are you pursuing this?* 'Why did he surprise you? What happened?'

'What frequently happens when a woman's involved.'

That was the last thing I'd expected but his expression had closed. 'Who won?' I asked quietly, still staring at him, but he fielded me, eye for eye. 'I think it's time we changed the subject, Mrs Black, don't you? Let's talk about why we're actually here. You asked why I switched hospitals after Rush. And, of course, you'll want me to

add a few personal details. Hobbies first, naturally, to break the ice
. . .' Enumerating on his fingers, he began interviewing himself.

'Hobbies? Not many, too busy, but I do read a lot. Unfortunately,
it's mostly stuff on the periphery of work but I do speed-read the
occasional thriller for its plot, tending to miss the subtlety and
finesse of the writer's deathless prose.

'So what do I do for relaxation?' He ticked off the next finger.
'Watch a bit of sport on TV. Hate American football, steamrollers
colliding with ten-ton trucks, hate ice hockey for the same reason,
quite like baseball, love basketball. Got that?' He addressed the
two recorders, then returned to touch finger number three: 'And
before you ask your next question, no is the answer. No wife, no
girlfriend. Not right now anyhow – but, hey,' he grinned and then,
over those raised fingers, 'I could be persuaded.'

I glued my gaze to the pages of my notebook and scrawled: *Sngl.*

'Right,' he said, when I had raised my head. 'So, what else?
Let's see, don't much like walking, prefer the gym, much more
time-efficient. Used to like a bit of sailing, no time for that now,
and back home, when I was young and idealistic, I played a bit of
hurling. Was good at it, too, on the A team at school.'

I scribbled 'hrling?' and looked up. '"Hurling"?' To me that
meant upchucking, vomiting . . .

For the first time he dropped into the mode I had seen during his
TV interview, displaying enthusiasm, even passion, as he explained
the finer points of a field game, its speed, skill, continuous form
of play. 'No timeouts, no pauses, except for injuries or fouls. You
have to be really, *really* fit – try to imagine hockey or lacrosse but
with the ball constantly airborne. It's hard, like a cricket ball, but
you're allowed to run with it, balancing it on your stick, and you're
allowed to catch it with your hand and play it too. It's made of
leather, with seams, and it hurts like hell if you catch it when it's

coming at you at maybe a hundred miles an hour.' For a moment he wasn't seeing me, but harking back, gazing over my shoulder.

'Sorry. Got a bit carried away there. What else? Nothing, really, except work. I'm a pretty dull fella, wouldn't you say? Marian?' Boring into me with those eyes.

'Where do you live?' I continued doggedly, still ogling my notebook.

'Right. I get it. For completeness? City. Just off Dearborn. Basic, but it does the job and it's near Holy Angels.'

The waiter was back, bringing the beverages and brownies, and there was a further kerfuffle as they were arranged on the table. But as the man left, I saw that my interviewee was again regarding me, his eyes, a little hooded now, as watchful as those of a stalking cat. I tried to hold on to my equilibrium. 'So, I know you said that this is up to the hospital, but I'm still intrigued that there's so little about you online, Daniel.'

'I've been meaning to do something about that, just didn't find the time. I know I should have followed up, for instance, on that cable interview. You'd be amazed what a reaction that got – it was really great. You forget what media can do – at least, I do. I just find it a little . . . I dunno, trite or something. Like, Facebook and Twitter? Who actually cares whether I'm having corn flakes or Apple Jacks for breakfast, or what restaurant I like?'

'But someone in your line of work could use it for good. Get ordinary people involved? Explain why you do it? You did it so well on TV.'

'You sound exactly like the marketing women at Holy Angels,' he grinned, 'but I take the point. It wasn't bad. And they want me to do a lot more of it. "Advocacy", they call it, and certainly the sponsors would agree. I've a meeting with them tomorrow, I hear, and the hospital's very keen.' He looked suddenly gloomy. 'To tell you the truth, I'd prefer to do the work than talk about it.'

'I did find a piece about you in an Irish newspaper archive.' I sat up straight, determined to hold on to the threads of this endeavour. 'It said that you come from a small village in Ireland and have a medical background. Your father is a family physician and you have a brother in the profession.'

'You've been busy.'

'Just research. You're staring, by the way. Have I upset you in some way? Is something the matter?'

'Nothing's the matter,' he said softly, 'nothing at all. You're a very beautiful woman, Marian. The world this morning is a wonderful place and, I can see clearly now, getting better by the nano-second.'

Chapter Four

I have since checked back on my notes of that first meeting with Daniel, which lurched – that's the only word for it – on for about an hour and ten minutes. Luckily, both recorders had worked because what I found in my notebook were scribbles, hieroglyphics and doodles, the odd legible word surrounded by incomprehensible phrases:

> *diarrhea contact upch etc . . .*
> *Rotav mil XX>?*
> *scale pov stagg 3/4 wrld*

And so on.

And over two days of stop-start transcription from tape, his rapid-fire rate of speech was a professional nightmare, not least because I was having difficulty in distancing myself from the spell he seemed to have cast over me. I kept picturing his hair, his shoulders, his expressive hands, the way his eyes fired up.

For the core of the piece, I managed, eventually, to extract from this mile-a-minute word tumble a fairly coherent profile of the man that showed he was inspirational, if radical, in his enthusiasm for the work, in his indignation and even despair about the plight of the developing world, in his disdain for politics – local, national and international – where 'disgusting global choices' were constantly made that allowed for 'gold-plated yachts and diamonds on fat fingers, twenty-two-room mansions with twenty-four bathrooms and two fucking swimming pools, one for the kiddies – and the obscene pool houses, and the immigrant labour paid just pennies to clean all this stuff . . .'

Then, rhetorically: 'Does anyone else ever think about this? That the water used by any of those houses in one day would supply the needs of a rural village in Burundi, or another place like it, *and* the fields around it for a whole month or even longer?'

There was a lot more in this vein: Daniel Lynch thought big. 'I can't bear to contemplate,' he went on, 'the money spent on nuclear weapons and all the palaver and personnel to mind them and talk about them and take no action about them. Cluster bombs – and not just them but the cost of the jets carrying them, and their emissions destroying the planet, while the poor, and the sick, and millions and millions of kids wither and hang from bare trees and give up their sad, short little lives in fly-infested muck. I suppose in many ways it's thank God for them personally that their suffering is over, but what about the family grief? Believe it or not, there are some people, no names, no pack drill, who are placid about that, saying that Africans just accept this as Fate – or, like, it's Nature's fucking way of controlling the population. Like, that's going back to the fucking dark ages and slavery and that.

'Nobody in places like this –' he had swept an arm around our venue '– seems to give one sweet damn, saving your presence. Everyone in this country is too hell bent on the right to carry Kalashnikovs and assault rifles. Shit! I promised myself I wouldn't do this.'

'Do what?'

'Get up on my soapbox,' he said gloomily. 'I can't seem to help it. The only way I can sound reasonable – well, more reasoned anyway – is if I write it into a script.'

'A script?'

'Yeah.' He made a dismissive gesture. 'I do a bit of speaking, conferences and the like. The sponsors of the research team I'm on seem to like it, and as for the hospital, their holy angels are in Heaven! Sorry – again! I'm apologising a lot, aren't I? But progress in medicine, these days, seems to depend far too much on marketing. It sure is competitive because there isn't enough money to go round!'

I found it all mesmerising.

I used his quotes at length, interlacing them with his asides and my own narrative about his sweeping gestures around the bar as, in the context of his trips to Africa and the poorer parts of Asia and South America, he dismissed the ultra-comfortable upholstery, the starched white napery and, not least, our fellow Palmer House guests in their sober grey suits and conservative ties, smart 'day dresses' and Clintonesque pants suits.

He gets it, I wrote, *that every African mother, every Bangladeshi mother, is just as devastated at the loss of her child as mothers in the US*, illustrating this with the following: '*Lookit, I'm sorry if that sounds too rich for delicate palates, especially in big fat America, but it's the bloody truth. And it's not just America. It's Europe too. And Ireland, even where there're still people who can tell you, from their own family oral history, about the Great Famine.*'

Americans don't react well to criticism from newly arrived immigrants, even if they're white and from the professional classes, no matter how right-on their theories, so I was thrilled when I offered the piece and it was accepted. Then I had to hold my breath to see if the *Tribune*'s editors would let it run. (At one stage of my own editing, I had lost my nerve and removed the 'fat' references, but then, bloody-mindedly, had put them back. In general, I have to confess, I had found writing about Daniel Lynch every bit as exhilarating as interviewing him.)

Having filed, I spent the following days nervously expecting a call from the paper, but none came, and when the piece appeared, I saw that while a few cuts and substitutions had been made, to ameliorate some of the more caustic observations, the paper ran the profile largely as it had been submitted.

I had shown it to Peter beforehand, with trepidation, in case he intuited the subtext of what was going on in my addled brain. He did, as subsequent events proved – but at the time, he told me it was the best thing I'd ever written, commenting only obliquely on that aspect of it: 'You were very taken by him, that's obvious, but it's great, Marian. You should be proud. I am. Well done.'

To say I felt like a heel is an understatement. 'Are you sure? You do sound a little underwhelmed.'

'Not underwhelmed,' he said quietly. 'I'm sad.'

'Sad?' I stared at him. 'Why sad?'

'I can't imagine you writing anything as vivid about me.'

'Oh, Peter! Of course I would!'

We had been talking across our dining table and, arms outstretched, hating my duplicity, I stood up to give him a Judas hug. But he had already gotten to his feet, picked up his plate and was heading towards the kitchen. The moment passed.

Had I reached him for the hug that evening, felt in my arms the solidity, the sheer living value of Peter Black, might I have seen sense, shaken off the madness that had so suddenly – and unexpectedly – taken hold of me, body and soul? I've often wondered about that.

But I didn't go after him into that kitchen, did I?

I knew, just *knew*, that Daniel Lynch would call me. Most interviewees didn't. I never heard from them again but that was the name of the game. You write to your highest personal standards and as truthfully as you can, given time and other pressures, but unless you're entering a competition, I guess, which I never had, your aim is principally to serve the reader.

In the case of Daniel Lynch, for the first time in my journalistic life I had written an article to please the subject more than readers, editors and myself. The split was 51 for him, 49 for all the rest of us put together.

In the meantime, I was finding it hard to quell the bubbles of pleasure that constantly rose to distract me from ordinary activities. I might be paying for a carton of milk at a store counter, and when the clerk wished me a nice day, I had to work hard to prevent myself shouting, 'Yes! Yes! Yes!' Equally, though, I was having to keep terror at bay because if I pursued my instincts, which I knew full well were base, I would cause deep pain and upheaval, and would have to live with the consequences probably for the rest of my life.

No matter how many times I adjured myself that I was behaving like an adolescent, nothing mattered more than seeing that Irishman again. It was as if I had been infected with some kind of delightful joy-disease. I knew it would probably damage me, but the dance of the microbes in my blood could not be treated. I didn't want it to be treated. Daniel Lynch had spun a force field around me and I became obsessed, no other word for it.

By inserting his name on YouTube, I found an extract from his cable interview, some of the more passionately trenchant segments strung together to present him almost as though he was giving a mini TED talk that, although it lasted not the requisite eighteen minutes, just three, was nevertheless as convincing and passionate.

I played him over and over on my MacBook just to look at him. I was behaving like a deranged adolescent or, approaching forty, indulging in an early mid-life crisis. I had lost judgement, even logic.

However . . .

Save the pain and just forget it, Marian. There existed an insistent little voice somewhere at the base of my skull. I'd had it all my life, inserted perhaps by my mom, or it might have been Sister Margaret Mary, the most influential of my teachers in Holy Name Elementary. It was on a loop now, whispering that this was *wrong, wrong, wrong*, asking who or what would I have in my life when everything crashed, as it inevitably would. Asking if I could live with the knowledge that I had joined a club whose members were the most foolish women in history.

But, inevitably, excoriation notwithstanding, I would creep back to YouTube.

Twenty times I Googled Daniel's name in an effort to find anything tawdry or sinister about him that might put me off, even in publications like the *National Enquirer*, but the professional articles or interviews I found – and they were available – were just that: dry reports on speeches he had given at conferences, references to his own papers, with footnotes, cross-references and mere mentions of his name as a participant in group researches.

None gave any hint of his personality. There was a plethora of approval-laced generalities such as 'keen intelligence' or 'incisiveness', and I found, in one paragraph of a peer's conference report, that his address was *filled with Irish blarney, but that's deceptive. When you examine the substance of what Lynch, undoubtedly a maverick, is saying on his subject, we should pay attention. He is making sense and his criticisms, if sometimes overblown, are substantive. We, as colleagues and professionals, should be listening. We need more of this.*

As for personal interviews I couldn't find a single one in any online US publication, but there was the profile I had mentioned in the course of interviewing him. It had appeared in an Irish weekly, local to his county. It was a gushing paean to him, in which the writer bemoaned

this latest loss, this departure of one of the brightest young medical stars in the firmament of this brightest and best medical generation. And now he, too, is leaving our appalling health service, denuding not just it but the poor benighted Irish public who paid for his training. Our loss is America's gain. We wish Dr Lynch a personal Godspeed, of course, and lots of good luck in a career that this publication is in no doubt will be one of stellar achievement. Those of us left behind, however, have nothing to show now for training him but widow's weeds as we rake over the ashes of our hard-earned money since hopes of his return are faint. How long more do we endure this medical brain drain, Ireland's incipient twenty-first-century famine?

As an early-stage student at Dublin's College of Surgeons, he had clearly agreed with those who reviled the shortcomings of the health services in his native country, as intimated by the newspaper lamenting his departure. The writer of the article had dug up a quote from him during a student protest about medical provision being 'two-storey, the top one an excellent private health service for the rich, the ground floor offering sod-all for everyone else'.

My profile of him earned me a commission from the *Tribune* to write another: on an up-and-coming young Illinois senator, touted in Chicago circles at least as being in the Obama mode. It came with a 25 per cent increase in the fee I had earned for the one I had offered, on spec, about Daniel.

I was delighted, more because the offer indicated confidence and trust in my ability, although the money would be useful.

With regard to my mission to have a child, unease about what Mom would have called my 'carry-on' (even if it was all in my head since there had been no further contact between Daniel Lynch and me) seemed to make no difference to that drive, with one exception. Meeting Daniel had bombed to smithereens the pathway to the life I had planned with my husband, and although I hesitated to use the term and strained every brain cell to reason myself out of it, I was now dissatisfied with the blameless man who wore goodness, sense and predictability like haloes, not self-imposed or self-importantly. I really don't think he was aware of how others saw him.

I remember being in the kitchen as a child when Mom and Dad were arguing and overhearing Dad mutter, out of the corner of his mouth, 'Yes, Mrs Perfect, no, Mrs Perfect, three bags full, Mrs Perfect! Nobody ever warns you how difficult it is to live with a saint!' Treacherously, now, I felt Peter Black was too good for me.

While we were continuing our attempts to start a family (yes, that happened!), I closed my eyes because it was Daniel's face I saw above me now, Daniel's curly hair into which I wound my fingers as my husband went through his routines. He would have to have been blind and deaf, utterly insensate, not to notice the change, and he did. 'Try not to take things so intensely, sweetie,' he urged kindly. 'We will conceive eventually, we really will. But you should simply relax. That's the trick. Take that as a medical opinion. No need to try so hard.'

I was so confused during that rackety period – it was as though my brain and body belonged to two different people. I even half believed that if I could conceive with Peter the obsession would leave me, and there were times, Peter snoring gently beside me, I lying with my legs raised on pillows in the prescribed position to increase the chance of success, when I found myself fantasising about the children I could have with Daniel, a squad of beguiling, excitable little Irish kids with that smile, those hands and, most of all, that crackling intelligence, passion and articulacy. They would certainly be tall.

As though I were a high-school fresher, I even took to sneaking into the bowels of the internet, entering 'love quotes', 'words of love' even 'definitions of falling in love' into my search engines. I found that, just as there are well-documented stages of grieving after a bereavement or difficult personal event, there are stages of falling in love: passion (aka lust?) first, then intimacy, getting to know the beloved, finding the other utterly fascinating and amazing (*I've never met anyone as interesting as you*), then commitment (*You are my soul-mate: I want to spend the rest of my life with you*), et cetera.

Immured in – elevated to – the first stage with Daniel, I didn't care to research studies about why or when the force of lust could be expected to lessen, to be replaced with habit and daily conversation about daily things, food shopping, the colour of carpet tiles (see the movie *Lost in Translation*!) and the dreaded 'What's for dinner?'

Even my father had noticed my unusual demeanour: 'You're different, Marian. You get your hair done or sump'n?'

'In what way am I different?'

'I dunno. You lose weight, maybe? That a new frock you got on? You look real nice!'

'No, Dad. None of that.'

'I dunno. But there is a difference. You got roses in yer cheeks, girl!'

'Do I? Must be the wind, or a bit of sunburn. Sorry to disappoint you, Dad, but it's the same old me, I'm afraid.'

That was a lie. I was very, very far from that.

As an adult, I had always intellectualised myself as a person irretrievably corralled by the ethos of my upbringing and schooling, Catholic parents, Catholic schools and Jesuit university for my degree in journalism. It was not until Daniel Lynch came into my life (*hardly in your life? On the strength of one casual lunch, one sighting during his appearance on cable television, one professional interview? Get a grip, Marian!* My inner critic was scathing) that I gained any idea of what could actually happen in a millisecond between a man and a woman, except in literature, because that man had somehow taken possession of not just my body, but my thoughts, soul and brain.

I'm fairly well read and understand the concept of *coup de foudre* – translated literally as 'a bolt of lightning' but used by the French, and authors of romantic fiction, to describe what it feels like to fall in love instantly. In that context – to mangle the quote from *Jerry Maguire,* one of my favourite movies – Daniel Lynch had had me at 'hello'.

Chapter Five

Dear God, when I think of it from my present perspective in Glanmilish (the storm having passed, the next weather forecast being the most important broadcast of the day and, in the meantime, crows calling harshly from the trees on the boundaries of the fields outside Glanmilish House), shame engulfs me, like an incoming tide, especially when I think of the ultimate outcome.

I squirm when I remember the planning that went into my break-up with Peter: I treated it almost as though it were a difficult work assignment, separating it into its component parts. There is no defence, except the spurious one that I was undoubtedly a little mad during that period. I felt as if I had boarded a runaway express train, unequipped with emergency pull-cords to apply the brakes.

In memory, even after all that happened, sex with Daniel felt so right from the outset. From the very beginning of our relationship, I felt this was why my body had been created. And I'm perfectly aware of how trite that sounds.

On that early morning when I left Daniel's tiny apartment after our first night sleeping together (what a misnomer!), I was physically drained but emotionally dizzy with excitement and joy, a combination I had never before experienced.

Even now, even after all the terrible events of the interim, the memory of that first night, when my naked body proved not to be the stolid set of bones and tissue I had come to believe it was, can raise goosebumps. I left that morning having realised that passion had been not lacking in me, as I had believed for almost all my life, merely dormant.

The opportunity to go to bed with him had arisen because that night Peter had been away from home, staying with his mom in Skokie. She had had a bad fall – no serious injuries, thank goodness – but she was shaken and had lost a little of her confidence. He was going straight to work from there the following morning, which allowed me to go back to Oak Street directly from Daniel's studio. In Peter's airy spaces, I had all day to luxuriate in my body's recall of the night.

I couldn't wait for our next date. I had taken far more than a single step down that path, and for the first time in my life, I was being led by emotions and drives other than those dictated by a too-cautious brain, personal history or faulty self-knowledge.

Then, however, I had to wait to replicate the experience because my lover had left the apartment even before I had that early morning to travel to Paris and then on to Copenhagen. He was giving a paper to two separate conferences, detailing the latest progress of his research.

After two or three days, the strain of pretending to my husband that all was as serene as it had been between us was telling on me, and I became uncharacteristically snippy and jumpy. Peter remained patient, putting down my irritability to broodiness.

I allowed it. I was that duplicitous. In the meantime, when I was alone – at home working, on a bus or an L – I relished the opportunity to recreate in my mind the physical sensations of that tumultuous evening and night.

So, yes, I was more than a little unhinged during that period, finding colours brighter, breezes from the lake more refreshing, smells more pungent. I took every chance to be aroused. Even shopping for groceries, my eyes lingered on shapes I had never noticed before: the curves and bulges of bell peppers, the solidity of cucumbers, the open mouths and rude tongues of calla lilies . . . As I said, unhinged.

To go back a little, after my interview with Daniel, I had managed to restrain myself from contacting him again for three whole weeks, within which, as I've already said, I continued to make love with my husband in an effort to conceive a child but also in a sort of desperate effort to satisfy a new appetite that was threatening to become all-consuming and, in fact, already was. I was dissatisfied with the way I lived alongside Peter, through no fault of his – I cannot emphasise that enough. He was solicitous and gentle and good company, but now that wasn't enough.

In my own (feeble) defence, during those first three weeks I was on tenterhooks, waiting for him to call me. Despite my conviction that he would do so after publication of the profile, he hadn't. So I tried to pay heed to the urgings of whatever common sense I had left, even reminding myself of the admonitions of Hippocrates, Kurt Vonnegut, the Dalai Lama and countless gurus about doing no harm if you can't do good.

But, after those weeks, I caved in. Under the pretext of apologising for a typo in the piece, which had Daniel aged forty-five rather than thirty-five (yes, he was almost five years younger than me), I called him.

He hadn't noticed the error. Or so he claimed, although he had liked the way I had written the thing. 'Who'd have thought,' he said, voice silky in my ear, 'beauty *and* brains? So, where do we take things from here?'

'How's the rotavirus research going?'

'You didn't ring me to ask that question.'

'Why else would I call?'

'Fine. If you say so.' He let a pause develop. He was at work: I could hear a low buzz of workplace conversation as I scrambled around for what to say next, trying to convince myself I could deal with this. I was a mature woman, askew a little at present, but I could handle myself. I was about to say something, anything to break the tension, when he broke in: 'Do you think I came down with the last shower, Mrs Black?'

'Of course I don't,' I said, hoping I'd sounded brisk, 'but you're right. I do have an agenda. Believe it or not, the *Tribune* has asked for a follow-up. The features editor really liked the piece. I've got no guarantees of publication,' now that I'd started, I couldn't stop over-egging the lie, 'and I know you're busy, but I promise I won't take up too much of your time.' A deep breath. 'This means a lot to me, Daniel. But if you can't . . .'

'Of course I can.'

I could almost hear the grin.

Before each of the three subsequent meetings for coffee I had with Daniel over a period of ten days, I had to repeat the falsehood to Peter: I was meeting Daniel, I said, because the follow-up commission from the *Tribune* was to be part of an occasional series it was doing on the positive side of alien immigration. This time, I said to him, the features editor had asked me to try to elicit richer personal details, family background, education, why he had chosen medicine, what he had done in Ireland, why he had come to the

States and chosen Chicago in particular, 'that kind of stuff'. I was earnest. I had to believe my own stories.

'Why does it take so many meetings?'

'You wouldn't believe it, honey! On the surface he's voluble – he can talk for the Olympics about his research – but otherwise he has a hard shell. Difficult to get under it. But I'm making progress.' I had found that once I had started lying I had become quite adept at it. Anyhow, the substance of this assessment of Daniel Lynch was no lie.

For all three occasions during which he and I had met following my initial call, I had again chosen the Palmer House. Not knowing who else might turn up there, though, I had my reporter's paraphernalia with me each time, not switching on the recorders but keeping the notebook open on my lap and a ballpoint in my hand. He was initially amused by the artifice, but by the end of the third meeting, eyebrows beetling, he had said, 'That biro must be red hot. Why don't you give it a break and put it down?'

'You know why I'm holding it. You may have nothing to lose, Daniel, but I do.' He said nothing, which spoke volumes.

I put the ballpoint back into my workbag. 'Happy now?'

'Somewhat.' He looked at his watch.

So, before that, what did we talk about during that one morning and two afternoons? I was in the phase I've described before, where everything about the other is fascinating and the sexual current runs very strongly under general chat.

Now and then, though, I got the impression, whether true or not, that I might be boring him – and he also made clear, without saying so directly, that he sure didn't like being pestered with personal questions.

'What was your mother like, Daniel?'

'She was an Irish mother. Period.'

'Yes, but was she beautiful?'

'I suppose so – do you want another cup of coffee or what?'

I was under no illusion as to who was actually in control. We could be talking about the quality of the coffee or the muffins, or why the Palmer House persisted with using all the unnecessary silverware – 'Think of all that cleaning, Daniel!' – and with one look, acknowledging that we were not talking about cakes or cutlery, the kittens at the base of my stomach would be tumbling over each other.

Meanwhile, any time I broached anything he didn't want to talk about, around feelings or relationships, for instance, he clammed up and changed the subject.

It was clear he didn't like it at all when I ventured a question about past liaisons. 'You know everything about my so-called love life now, Daniel,' I said, with a skittishness I wouldn't have thought part of my make-up. (Throughout that period, like an addict, I continued to pretend to myself that I could stop this at any moment, despite the overwhelming physical rush.) 'So, what about yours? Tell me all about the ladies in your life.'

'That's nobody's business except my own.' The tone remained as before but those hoods had come down on the eyes. 'They aren't relevant. I'm here now with you, aren't I? Actually, maybe this is a good time. Let's talk about reality – about where you and I go from here.'

'I beg your pardon?' I faltered.

'I've enjoyed this.' He leaned back in his chair, regarding me with narrowed eyes. 'Otherwise I wouldn't have taken time off, three times now, to come back here. I'm here because, to tell you the truth, you intrigue me. It's like, forgive me if this offends you, you're the little princess who's never been kissed. I'm always up for a challenge, Marian,' he said slowly. 'I want to get both my hands on that lovely butt of yours as you have made perfectly plain you want to get your hands on mine.' Abruptly, he abandoned the lazy act and leaned across the table. He was so tall that those eyes were now just inches away from my face. 'And here we are. We might as well be talking about the village fete.'

'What do you mean?' Blood hurled itself through my every vein and artery. 'We weren't talking about any village fete.'

'You know damn well what I mean. Cards on the table, Mrs Black.'

'I'm just being practical. You know my situation. What are you suggesting?'

'You know what I'm suggesting.'

I swallowed. 'An affair?'

'Whatever.'

'That's not really an answer.'

'It works in California,' he said, with a glimmer of a smile, then leaned forward again. 'You're up for it, Marian. The only question now is, will it be with or without Peter Black?'

That shocked me. His tone had been matter-of-fact, as though he had asked if I wanted my coffee with or without Coffee-mate. 'Because you're a very smart woman,' he went on, 'you can tell, I'm sure, that I'm not a half-measures merchant. And in our case, I'm now through with this baby-steps flirty stuff. I've enjoyed it, as I know you have, it's great fun, but it gets to the point we're at today. So, Mrs Black, my preference would be that you're fully on board, if you get my meaning. If you're not, no hard feelings.' He waited.

I got it. Up to that point, I had been so deeply carried away by the flush of new feelings, the excitement of it all – except for the occasional dart of fear about being found out – I had not contemplated the future in any serious way. The game itself had consumed me, imagination colluding with desire to get into bed with him, and I had seen no further than that. Or had not wanted to see.

On the other hand, in the darkest recesses of my mind, there had been a glimmer of knowledge that this moment would come. This was now far from a game. Brain had emerged from its sleep but Body persisted in its efforts not to pay heed. Filled with confusion, I looked around the bar, in which all the tables were occupied, to see who was staring at us, which spy had witnessed this momentous event in my life.

But the low buzz of conversation rose quietly from the usual array of businessmen and, it being late afternoon, a good many tourists. If in company, they were absorbed in each other, if alone, each was messaging, reading or looking earnestly at a laptop with earbuds firmly in place. Nobody, as far as I could see, had paid the slightest attention to what had just happened; nobody had recognised its magnitude. I looked across at Daniel Lynch who, expression inscrutable, seemed at ease. Unlike me. 'You're asking a lot.'

'Of course I am, and you wouldn't have it any other way, would you?' His voice, usually full on, was lazy. 'To those who give a lot, a lot will be given.' He smiled. 'But you must be sure about this.'

'I'm sure.'

What had I said? I hadn't recognised my own voice. But the thought of cutting short this new sense of vibrant life, of shooting dead the wild, galloping horse I rode, was intolerable.

'No doubts?'

'None.' A lie. Of course I had doubts. I was the one who had driven this endeavour – but I had met the man just four times. And now he was asking – for what exactly? I gazed at Dr Daniel Lynch, who was clothed in an attraction so powerful that I couldn't understand why every other woman in the room hadn't been drawn in. For a second or two, I hesitated as a thought of tangible substance flickered: *Will I regret this? Am I now just one of those moonstruck, wafting heroines of romantic fiction?* 'I'd like to know what's involved here,' I said shakily. 'How do you see things?'

'I think you know that.' His smile didn't waver. 'You don't need to ask and I don't need to answer.'

The flicker of sense died and I nodded. It felt good to surrender.

Just three days later, Peter's mom suffered her fall so he went to Skokie for the night and, well, you know what happened.

Chapter Six

All in one day, I went to visit Peter's mom, then Peter himself at his hospital, then in late afternoon, my dad – I was emotionally in bits after the first two encounters and I skirted that fence, taking the easy route to the finish. What kept me going was the conviction that I shouldn't let things drag on until someone, probably Peter, discovered what had been going on. That would have been grossly unfair. This, I recognised, was a medieval, dancing-on-the-head-of-a-pin kind of deceit, but at the time, I felt I had to salvage at least a shard of good behaviour: if I were to betray Peter, it would not be covertly. In so far as there was anything honourable about any of this, at least, I thought self-servingly, I could always dredge up the consolation that I had only danced once and was owning up. I wasn't a serious two-timer.

Nevertheless, all during that period, short as it was, guilt constantly flipped places with excitement, and I continued to ask myself why, if guilt was such a prominent part of the package, I was acting like that. Hell-bent on – what exactly? And what was wrong with my marriage to Peter? Was this merely to be a short aberration, a fling, and if that was the case why blow up such a storm, hurting everyone dear to me?

Our marriage was not loveless, if marital love can be so loosely boxed. He had done nothing wrong. We had co-existed well, each giving the other space, respect, all the traits I should have valued, indeed had valued up to then.

But somehow, so quickly it was frightening, I had become critical of Peter's decency. I couldn't even call it dullness because he wasn't dull. His intelligence, work ethic, intrinsic kindness, even cooking skills, all of which I had admired, had not diminished.

Baldly, what was lacking was passion. There, I've said it. Daniel Lynch's vivid, flaming appearance on the pitch had somehow faded Peter's to sepia and I was aware that this wasn't fair. But for the first time in my life I was stepping willingly into fire.

* * *

Daniel was due back from Paris on a late flight that evening and, as a surprise, I planned to be at O'Hare to meet him. I had also booked us a room at the Palmer House. Where else?

That early summer – technically still in spring – was in line to be one of the hottest for decades for the time of year. Chicago is always humid in summer, but the indicators from forecasters were that, right now, the current heatwave was to deliver temperatures of at least 100° Fahrenheit in mid-afternoon, with the humidity approaching 90 per cent. In other words, the outside air would be barely tolerable, and it was already sticky that morning by seven thirty when, with exhaust fumes from traffic snarls in the downtown Loop area rush-hour further adding to the heat, I entered the cool depths of the Palmer House to leave my overnight bag and laptop case in the luggage room, prior to my arrival that night.

I cannot adequately describe the depth of the distress I felt when, a little later, I climbed into the bus to Skokie to give Peter's mother the last news she would want to hear. All that prevented me getting off and jumping on the next bus home to take a more cowardly delivery route, such as the phone, was that I knew I was doing the right thing. (And, in a way, by seeing Letty Black before I broke the news to Peter, I was confirming a rather odd suspicion that I was breaking up with her rather than him.)

Like any arch-traitor, I had carefully planned my treachery. My husband was attending a seminar that morning so his cell would be off: his mother would not be able to warn him before I arrived at the hospital at lunchtime to tell him. At least I would always be able to say that I'd given him that much consideration.

But there was nothing seemly about any of this and on the bus, stifling and getting hotter by the minute, I felt dreadful about the methods I was using to reveal my multiple betrayal. Given what I now felt for Daniel Lynch, the cocktail of feelings and excitement I had never felt for poor Peter, I now doubted I had ever been in love with anyone before, least of all my husband. Or had I? In the confusion, I couldn't even say for sure that I was 'in love' with Daniel Lynch either.

I did know that love came in many forms, including my regard for my dad and for Peter, but being 'in love' was, I guess, unexplored territory for me. Whichever term – compulsion, obsession, lust – applied to what I felt for Daniel, it would not be denied, but I had neither the upbringing nor the stomach to test it by having a mere clandestine affair. Step too far. And I was so driven by this that, to me, it really didn't matter whether or not Daniel Lynch felt the same. All I wanted was to be with him, even if I was the one to make the compromises so we could get together. At the time, I wanted him so badly I believed that.

To this day, I'm sure Peter's mother guessed why I was there within seconds of my unexpected arrival, hot and flustered, on her doorstep at ten past nine in the morning. Her initial expression of delight, as I accepted a hug and her invitation to step inside, faded very quickly when, rather than going straight to the kitchen as I usually did – 'Sorry, Letty, but unfortunately I have to get back to the city. I can stay only a few minutes' – I simply stood there, with Peter's high-school graduation picture grinning down at us from the wall as she closed the door behind me. I had debated whether to bring flowers for her, but in the end had not. It would, in a way, have been an insult.

'What is it?' she asked now, clearly knowing this was something big but not an announcement that I was pregnant, which might have been her first thought on seeing me. She tried nonetheless, hands clutched together. 'You came all the way out from the city! And the coffee's already on.'

She was wearing a headful of rollers under a hairnet, and her housecoat, tied tightly around her body, was strongly pink and patterned with monkeys, flowers and bananas. It was made of cheap, thin nylon or some such, her house was not air-conditioned, and I was close enough to see staining under the armpits and that the edges of the garment where it crossed her chest were now visibly pulsing. My instinct was to run, but I had to hold my nerve.

She still did not give up, attempting to take the cotton jacket I carried over my arm but I held tightly to it, removing her hand as gently as I could. 'No, honestly, Letty, I really can't stay.'

She dropped both hands in defeat, tears standing in her faded blue eyes. 'This ain't great news, is it, Marian?'

I had to use up whatever reserves of strength I had left so that I didn't throw myself at her and renege on my decision about the whole thing. 'No, I'm afraid it isn't. I'm so, so sorry. I really am.'

Even as she wept, she continued to beg me to come into her kitchen so we could talk about it over the coffee and the excellent cookies she knew I loved. 'You might change your mind. There's mediation, a counsellor, family therapy . . .'

'I can't, I really can't. This is hard, Letty, but I've made up my mind. And I can't tell you how sorry I am. It's nothing that Peter did – he's a good man and I know there's a good woman out there for him but, unfortunately, she's just not me.'

'But you kids, you two were like peas in a pod, I was so hap—'

She couldn't continue. I was very close to breaking down myself, and all I could do was to hug her. 'Just one more thing,' I said shakily, when we broke apart. 'I'm meeting Peter at lunchtime to tell him in person. So I'd really appreciate it if you wouldn't call him before I do. He deserves that.'

'But why, Marian? Can you at least tell me what happened? What about that lovely little house you've found? You'd be so cosy there. And everyone was so thrilled about your plans for a family.'

'I know, I know. They were my plans too, genuinely. But I'm the one who has changed. I'll always be grateful to Peter for his concern for me and, of course, his kindness to Dad and – and –' my voice cracked '– I'll never forget you for taking me into your little family, Letty. I hope you know how I feel about you – that hasn't changed.'

Lips and chin trembling, she nodded. 'But then why . . . There's someone else, isn't there? You've met someone?'

'No. Of course not. It's nothing like that.' I ducked it. 'It's just . . .' But I couldn't continue to lie to her beloved lined face, even in an attempt to save her more hurt. I tried to say something more, something of comfort, but I couldn't. Neither of us could. We hugged again. 'I'm so, so sorry, Letty,' I whispered again, and I doubt I've ever before or since felt like such a heel.

When we disengaged, instead of letting me go entirely, she held on to me with one hand, dashing away tears with the other. 'Life is so complicated, these days. But we can still be friends, Marian? I could go into the city and we could have lunch . . .' Again she faltered. She and I both knew that was not possible. That Peter would never forgive her for what he would believe was her betrayal of him. And that she and I would never see each other again.

Somehow I found the strength to give her a last brief hug and, hand scrabbling at the inside button of the Yale lock, to get back outside.

Not even during my own mom's last illness had I had to call on such reserves as I did that morning. I could barely imagine how Letty would take the news that I had lied about there being a third party. And the main encounter, with Peter, was still to come.

The house was fronted by a small yard behind a picket fence and, half blinded by tears as I closed the inset gate, I risked a look back and, seeing this, Peter's mother raised her hand in farewell. I became so emotional that I very nearly ran back to accept what she had suggested and to tell her that of course we would meet again. But that would not have been fair to any of the three of us so instead I bolted. And when I looked back finally from a few yards along the sidewalk, she had remained standing there, in her ugly hair accoutrements and cheap housecoat, absurdly gay in the circumstances, arm still raised as though it was frozen.

I couldn't get that final image out of my head as I waited in the dusty, sweltering heat for the bus to take me back to the city and the meeting with Peter. Luckily, I was the only one at that stop, and by the time the bus actually came, I was back in command of myself. Sort of.

But all the way into the city, holding one of those tiny battery-operated fans inches from my face, I was haunted by that picture of Peter's mother, and deliberately filled my mind, or tried to, with

the kind of easy phrases that people in circumstances such as mine
– not just guilt-ridden women like me – use to rationalise their
actions. I had heard them from colleagues in similar situations. I
had certainly read them or their equivalent in the agony columns
of even the stuffiest publications:

> *You have one life.*
> *Life is short.*
> *You deserve this: you're choosing life rather*
> *than death by small cuts.*
> *Rather one glorious day in the sun than a*
> *lifetime of grey.*
> *No human being owns another human being.*
> And, of course:
> *CARPE DIEM!*

'Et cetera, et cetera, et cetera': the wheels of the bus, running over
a set of rumble strips before an oncoming junction, sardonically
echoed Yul Brynner's rhythmic intonations at Deborah Kerr in the
old movie version of *The King and I*. But if you think I'm making
light of this, I'm not. I despised myself for what I was about to do
– had done already. I hated myself. I didn't recognise the woman I
had become – overnight, it seemed.

And yet – and yet I was going ahead with this because even
that day, on the bus, the face of Daniel Lynch, bright as a rising
sun, hung magnetically in front of me. And as we trundled along,
stopping and starting as people got on and off, I tried to shoot down
the image but failed. Then, coward that I was, I tried to convince
myself to put everything off until the following day because I'd
been through enough trauma already.

But the damage was done. I had already told Peter's mother, who certainly would not hold off beyond today in telling him, and the words I had said to her could never be unsaid, even if I never saw Daniel Lynch again. They would contaminate all future visits.

Which words could I employ to tell Peter himself? *You're a wordsmith, dammit*, I told myself – but where was the vocabulary when I needed it? Still under Daniel's golden grin, I tortured myself by picturing the shock, scorn and, yes, contempt on my husband's face when I told him, privately, I hoped, and as hurtlessly as I could, that I was leaving him and our marriage.

That last bit was crap and I knew it. I was, simply, *dumping* my husband, a blameless, good man I had vowed to love and honour for the rest of my life. And anyhow, I thought sourly, 'hurtless' wasn't even a real word, as far as I knew. The bus was taking me to a killing field where I would murder a man's self-esteem and peace of mind.

Would he weep? I wouldn't be able to bear it if he did. But it would be just punishment for me because I would never forget it. I might even recant if he wept – he and his mother might forgive me in time, but he, like his mother, would never fully trust me again.

I knew one thing for sure: Peter was too dignified to make a scene so I'd be spared yelling, thumping and threatening. That was a comfort, which I did not deserve.

The bus was coming up to the stop at the hospital. It was difficult even to stand up from my seat to get off, to behave as though this was an ordinary day and I was doing something ordinary.

A minute later, I was standing on the sidewalk in front of the glass-encased mini-skyscraper that was John Berchman's Hospital, on concrete so hot that, through the thin soles of my sandals, my feet felt as though they might burn. As people hustled past me through the doors, I looked at my watch. Still only eleven thirty – Peter had told me that morning that he would call me at about noon when the seminar was due to break up for lunch.

There was still time to change my mind. Not to put him through this . . .

I could call Letty, too, apologise for upsetting her, tell her that everything was okay now, that I had suffered some sort of weird aberration but was now back on base. But there it was, Daniel Lynch's bright sun-head, eyes daring me to go right ahead and be a wuss, to turn my back on what every nerve and fibre of flesh dictated.

I saw heads bobbing about inside a section of the vast swathe of plate glass. I'd forgotten there was a coffee area to one side of the main lobby – coffee would be good, I thought.

No, camomile tea would be far better.

No, it would have to be iced tea: I needed to cool down. Sheathing my little fan, I walked through the revolving glass doors into a blast of wonderful frigid air inside the quadruple-height foyer, busy and echoing with voices. I checked the noticeboard. Peter's seminar was being held in the main auditorium, the entrance to which was at the far side. I looked at my watch again – just eleven thirty-three. Still time to think, to plan, to choose the right words and rehearse them to find the right tone, somewhere between genuine care for Peter, humility, contrition and determination.

But as I crossed the marble floor, aiming for a vacant table, I saw my husband, ashen-faced, standing directly in my trajectory.

Chapter Seven

'It's Daniel Lynch, isn't it?' I had never heard such ice in Peter's voice – and it had nothing to do with the Arctic air-conditioning in the lofty, echoing atrium of John Berchman's Hospital.

'Your mom rang you?' It was as though the skin on my face, the backs of my hands and on my forearms had been plunged into snow and the sweat on my forehead had frozen. I felt lightheaded and feared I might actually throw up. 'She promised she wouldn't. I wanted to tell you myself. I'm sorry, Peter, but I have to sit down.' I skirted him and headed for one of the empty tables in the corner, hoping I'd make it before my rubber legs let me down.

I pulled out a chair and sat, keeping my head low.

'Well, thank you. That answers one of my questions.' He had followed and now towered over me. 'But she told me she figured there was a third party, although you wouldn't admit it. So there clearly is or you wouldn't look so guilty. Is it him?'

'Please,' I begged. 'Please sit down, Peter.'

'I'm fine standing here. I don't want to sit. And I'm certainly in no mood to talk. All I want is an answer to what I asked you.' His stance was rigid, the light wool of his best suit – an Armani I had bought him as a birthday gift from an online discounter – stretched between his shoulders, and still he stood there. I had never seen that in him, never would have believed him capable of such anger. 'You're scaring me, Peter. Why don't you sit? We have to talk.'

'That's facile. Unworthy of you – unworthy of both of us.'

But incongruously, now that the crisis was directly upon me, I began to feel calm. I was in the wrong, very definitely the perpetrator of a horrible deed, but for some reason, I was no longer nervous.

Eventually he sat in a chair opposite, before scooting it away and, tellingly, leaving a gap of three or four feet between himself and the edge of the table. 'So let's talk. Tell me, Marian.'

'What do you want to know?'

He responded with an expression of such contempt that I couldn't bear to see it and hung my head again, staring at the table. 'Cut the act,' he said levelly. 'Just tell me. And, by the way, you might have had the courtesy to inform me first. You left my mother in a terrible state, but you know that, and what do you care about her?'

'Don't say that.' I lost my composure. 'You know I love Letty.'

'Odd way to show it, wouldn't you think?'

There was no possible answer to that, but this time I managed to hold his gaze. 'Yes, it is him,' I said. It now occurred to me that Peter and I had never before had a row. Not one. 'But he doesn't know I'm here, Peter. Don't blame him. Blame me. It's all me.'

'Don't blame him? *Spare* me.' The harshness of his laugh resounded against the marble floor, all the hard surfaces around us, and could probably have been heard beyond the balconies on each tier of the multiple mezzanines above. The heads of the couple hugger-muggering at the next table had swung towards us. He glared at them and, shrugging, they resumed their conversation. 'So,' he turned his gaze to me, 'that piece you wrote, that – that *hymn* to him, all those so-called follow-up interviews, there's no follow-up commission from the *Tribune*, is there? You took me for a mug and you were right.'

'I didn't mean to, Peter. I'm sorry. I'm so sorry. I do know it's no consolation but I really want you to know—'

'*Spare* me, I said!' One hand had been holding the edge of the metal table. He clenched it now so the knuckles turned white.

'Sorry,' I repeated. We fell silent. How many more times would I have to say it before I felt as though I had expressed it adequately? 'May I buy you a coffee? Please, Peter?' I could no longer bear this. 'I really do need one.'

He was holding it together as he nodded, but his face was as pale as the marble underfoot. 'OK.' I got up. 'Splenda, half and half?'

'Black,' he said tonelessly. 'Espresso, double shot.' He looked at his watch. 'I have plans to meet some others for lunch. I intend to keep them.'

'I'll be quick.' I walked to the self-service coffee machines on the counter and placed a pair of paper cups under the spouts, watching closely as they disgorged water that changed from silver to brown. Even in the midst of an appalling situation such as this, I thought, the banalities pertain. Is it a sort of protective reflex? I threw a few single, as I thought, dollar bills by the till. One was a five, I noticed then, but left it.

'Have you told your dad?' he asked shortly, when I came back with the two cups. I shook my head. 'I'm going there this afternoon, when I leave here.'

'Be sure to say goodbye for me.' The depth of his bitterness was hard to hear but I deserved it. And more. Tears threatened but I had no right to let them spill over. 'I will,' I muttered. 'You won't believe me, I know, but I genuinely wish it was different, Peter. I wish I could turn back the clock. I wish I'd never seen that cable TV programme.'

'No, you don't. For God's sake, Marian, what do you take me for? At the very least, do me the courtesy of being honest.'

'I'm sorry. Again. I'm so sorry.'

'I sort of pity you, actually.' He sounded as though he was working it out as he spoke. 'I don't forgive you, I never will, but, you know, that guy—'

'I don't expect you to forgive me. If the situation was reversed—'

'But it isn't, is it? And never would be. I would never do something like this to you. I believed in those vows we made. I even got married to you in a Catholic church. We're Presbyterian. I don't know if you appreciated that at the time.'

'I did, Peter. I really did.'

'Well, it's academic now, isn't it?' Suddenly he sounded defeated. That was almost the worst of it. I had been counting on his even temper but now discovered I would actually have preferred him to yell. 'Anyone but him,' he was saying, so softly that I knew it was for himself only to hear. Despite the situation, it was on the tip of my tongue to ask him what had transpired between them to make his dislike of Daniel, in particular, so intense, but he had lapsed into silence, examining the knuckles of the hand still clutching the edge of the table. He released it. 'So what's the next step?' he asked, voice low. 'What happens? Attorneys? Removal vans? I'm not budging out of that apartment.' He looked at me directly, challenging. 'And what do I do about that house? All that saving . . . I even *told* people at work we were buying it.'

'We just don't go ahead with it. And of course you won't have to move out of your apartment. It's yours, Peter, your name on the lease. Hardly anything of mine there, except my clothes.'

'Fine, fine. I don't want to talk about this any more.'

'We'll have to talk about it sooner rather than later.'

'When, then?'

'I don't know. I can't come home tonight. I'm sure you accept that. You wouldn't want to see me anyhow, not after this, not after—'

'How considerate of you. And, by the way, you may have noticed that I'm not pleading with you to change your mind. But I will say one more thing. You're a bloody fool, Marian. If it was anyone else . . . I could give you a list of about ten people I might have worried about over the years, but that – that *King Kong*? You disappoint me, Marian. I thought you were better than this. I don't care how wonderfully talented he is, how persuasive, how magnificently *important* he is in his field. As far as I'm concerned, you're welcome to each other.'

And before I could think of anything appropriate to say, he had stood up. 'And you can stop with the sheepish "I'm so sorry, Peter" act. Mewling doesn't suit you, and please don't say you understand how I must feel – you could have *no idea* how I feel. Save your sympathy for where it's needed, and that will be for yourself. You're going to need it. And I hope you'll remember I said this—' His voice broke. 'I have to go now.'

'I'll call you in the next few days.'

'You have my number.' He swallowed. 'I won't be there when you come to collect whatever you believe is yours so I would appreciate it if you'd give me some notice. By text message or email, if possible.' He walked away without looking back. And without having touched his rapidly cooling double espresso.

Something in me died as I watched him go, obviously trying for a dignified exit, but his head drooped and his shoulders, usually straight, slumped. I held onto the table with both hands, squeezing until it hurt. There was now no sign of the totemic golden sun that had been my companion between Skokie and here.

* * *

During the following quarter-hour, my own coffee went cold while the lunchtime crowd took more and more tables, and all around me, like a rosy cloud, happy chatter, about movies, the price of groceries, the heatwave, ascended to the heights of the atrium. I felt more wretched than I had ever felt before.

Eventually, I managed to get myself out of my seat, away from the café and through the revolving doors to be hit again with what felt like an assault by a hot, wet sheet. Probably because of the contrast with the hospital's chill, the energy-sapping combination of high heat and humidity seemed to have intensified while I had been inside. The thought of getting into another bus or, worse, the L was too daunting so on impulse I hailed a passing cab, a luxury in which I rarely indulged, except when taking Dad to see his doctor or to a hospital appointment.

The driver was delighted at getting a cross-city fare and would have gabbed throughout the journey had I not ostentatiously put in my earbuds, turned on my iPod and closed my eyes. I had turned the volume way, way down and didn't even recognise the playlist. I felt wrung out, enervated, and deeply guilty about the two encounters of the morning, which was only a small fraction, no doubt, of the upset and shock I had inflicted.

I was Judas, Lord Haw Haw. I was every disloyal and unfaithful woman in a long line of concupiscence. Big word, 'concupiscence'

. . . But I've always been grateful to Sister Margaret Mary, who was English and a stickler for 'proper' pronunciation (we had left her classroom in no doubt that it wasn't 'addidoode' but 'attit-yude'; we didn't watch the 'evening nooze' but the 'evening nyooze'). As for 'vocab', as she called it, I've had reason to thank her for insisting that 'her' girls would leave her well equipped with words. She kept a huge copy of *The Oxford English Dictionary* on a lectern in her room, and we spent the first ten minutes of every day learning a word she chose by opening it at random, closing her eyes and stabbing the page with her ruler. Having read out the word, then written it with its meaning on the blackboard, she made us recite it in rhythm with the tapping of her ruler on her desk: 'Con-*cu*-pi-scence!' we chanted. 'De-*sires* of the *low*-er *app*-e-*tites*, and *do*-ing *things* that are for-*bid*-den!'

I hadn't understood it then – none of my classmates had. She hadn't explained in too much detail, but had given the impression it sort of meant the equivalent of stealing cookies from a neighbour's jar or eating too many Easter eggs at one sitting.

I sure understood it now. Deep in the trench of sinning, my behaviour in coming clean to Peter had, in the abstract, sounded like the right, even honourable, way to go. Right now, the reality of the human distress I had caused felt like butchery.

There was no glossing over it. Daniel had given me an ultimatum. I had jumped. I had to take the consequences. Even the prospect of seeing him that evening – what we might do together – felt flat.

As the cab entered Lake Shore Drive and headed north for Rogers Park and Dad's apartment, I lay back in my seat, turned up the sound on the iPod and, against the retro sound of The Eagles, tried to prepare myself for breaking the news to Dad, who always looked forward to Peter's weekly visits. It was going to be hard for him to understand that he could no longer expect to see his medical friend.

* * *

Heat-wise, the small apartment on Devon proved not too uncomfortable. During Mom's last illness, to augment the cooling in the bedroom, along with the window air-conditioner in there, I had invested in electric fans for it and the living room. Although they were not nearly as efficient as central air-conditioning, the combination did the job well enough to make things tolerable, but was very noisy. When I let myself in, everything was chugging furiously. In addition, with Dad's hearing having deteriorated, he was watching TV at almost maximum volume. Mom had been devoted to her 'stories' in the afternoon, and while he had scoffed at this, he had taken them on after she had passed away and now would not have missed them, especially *Guiding Light*, *General Hospital* and *Days of Our Lives*.

'Hi, Dad.' Gently, I took the remote control from his lap and reduced the volume a little. He looked up at me, eyes a little vacant for a second or two – he hadn't heard me come in. Not for the first time, I wondered if he was suffering from the early stages of Alzheimer's or dementia. I'd had him tested but he had been in the clear then. In his eighties now, his general health was not great and maybe it was time to have him tested again. 'What's happening, Dad? Have you had lunch?'

'Of course I have.' He snapped the remote out of my hand and again raised the volume. 'I'm not a baby. And I'm watching this. I wasn't expecting you until this evening.'

Definitely not Alzheimer's, I thought, as he went back to his stories while, dismissed, I moved towards the kitchen to load the dishwasher and clean up. 'I came this afternoon because I'm not able to come this evening, OK? Will you remember that, Dad?'

He didn't look up from his TV realm – he probably hadn't heard me – and as I worked on bowls, spoons and food-encrusted pans, I decided, with an (indefensible) measure of relief, I didn't have to bother him right away. I would tell him at the first opportunity. For now, though, he was happy enough and I could postpone my disclosure. As long as I kept up the routine of visits and monitoring, of taking him to doctors' appointments and so on, there was a remote possibility he might not notice Peter wasn't around. If he quizzed me about his absence, I would tell him then but, right now, I took myself off the hook.

* * *

I got to the Palmer House shortly after five in the afternoon, checked into my room, pinned up my hair and took a long hot bath, basking in water scented with oils provided by the hotel.

I dressed carefully but simply in a navy boat-necked shift dress and black ballerina flats. I hesitated over my wedding and engagement rings – too early to remove them? But I had irrevocably betrayed my marriage so it would be dishonest to wear those symbols of fidelity. I took them off and put them in the room safe.

Although I knew I couldn't escape the lifelong psychological consequences, my shame about the outright cruelty and damage I had caused to two blameless and loving human beings, I could park it for now because the worst was probably over. There was no going back. Like Mom's old friend Scarlett O'Hara, I would consider the implications tomorrow. If I thought any longer about them now, I'd probably wreck tonight, which was why I'd created such havoc in the first place. Even on such short acquaintance I knew that Daniel Lynch was not the type to indulge regret, that he was a 'move-on' guy.

But it was only when I was leaving to go downstairs and wait for him in the lobby bar that, on passing the room's full-length mirror, I realised that, without meaning to, I had dressed like a nun.

Chapter Eight

Day three after the 'Great Storm', as they were calling it in Glanmilish (day two having been billed as 'Baby Storm'), dawned so bright and blue it felt like a miracle, like waking up in a different country. The master bedroom in Glanmilish House spans the depth of the building from front to back, with dual aspect, and that early morning, sunlight poured from the windows set into the front. I don't close the drapes except to block out vile weather.

I sprang out of bed and opened all of the windows, front and back, immediately letting in a cacophony of coos and caws from pigeons, crows, rooks, jackdaws and magpies, with the fluting of two blackbirds, twitters and tweets from smaller birds and, from a distance, the intermittent trumpeting of a farmyard cock. They were singing quite late this year – well, the crow species shouted all year long, but it was unusual, certainly it had been in Chicago, to hear blackbirds in autumn.

I hadn't yet managed to finish tidying the grass, still covered with leaf and twig litter some of which lay around my willow and had become entangled in her foliage. That would be the first task after breakfast: I'd do it while the sunlight held.

Normally when I wake up, the awful events of the early-summer months assail me within seconds. That morning, however, it was impossible not to be gladdened by the sounds outside, the promise of a glorious day to come. But then, turning away from the windows, I caught a glimpse of those three letters on my bureau. They were not spooking me necessarily – in some respects they were laughable – but right now they were profoundly irritating. Enough was enough. It was time to engage with the Gardaí.

So, first thing after breakfast, again postponing my leaf-litter patrol, I got into the Camry, Daniel's ancient car, which he'd never got round to selling when he'd left for the States, and headed for the nearest cop shop. With the one in Glanmilish village closed for ever, the nearest, I'd been told, was now in Durrow. Beside me on the passenger seat, the three envelopes were in Daniel's medical bag, of that old, roomy type called the Gladstone after the British prime minister of that name. Daniel's father had used the bag, originally black but now brown with age, and I guessed his grandfather before that.

The Camry, right-hand drive, of course, and too fast for the little country roads, shot around a lethal blind corner and got away with it because there was nothing coming against me. Heart thumping in light of what *might* have happened, I again promised myself that, some time in the near future, I would trade it in along with thinning out a lot of the clutter in the house.

When I got to Durrow, the Garda 'station', as it's called in Ireland, proved to be firmly shut, and despite the Garda insignia over the blue-painted door, there was no sign of any physical presence in the sturdy, rather stately house. There was, however, a note in the window beside it:

If you have a non-urgent matter and wish to speak to a local garda, please write your name and telephone number down and put it through the letterbox and you will be contacted when they return on duty to the station.

Beneath, a separate sticker gave the phone number of a suicide helpline.

Now that I had started on this project, I didn't want to quit and so, quite cross, I got back into the Camry and headed for Portlaoise. What was going on in this country? Mail offices, police precincts, drugstores, little fashion boutiques, mom-and-pop grocery stores, even pubs, were shut and shuttered in all these little rural places. Who runs this country? Wake up, people!

The Irish electoral process, proportional representation with multi-seat constituencies and transferable votes, remains impenetrable to me, although it has been explained many times. In the States, by contrast, everything seems far more cut and dried. You diss your opponents, loudly, you get elected, you take your seat. Or maybe that's too naïve of me. Maybe you understand totally only what you're used to.

Coming into Portlaoise, I had to stop to ask directions of a guy walking his dog, then couldn't find a parking space so I was in a thoroughly bad mood by the time I walked through the imposing stone archway leading into the Garda station courtyard.

The public area inside the building was rather less grand, to put it mildly. A very small lobby, with slatted wooden seating arranged in an L shape, faced a glass-fronted counter. It hosted at least a dozen people and one enormous stroller accommodating a restless baby in the care of a woman who might have been an African tribal princess, clad as she was in a vivid full-length robe. There was no space left for me to sit and so, holding my purse and my little folder, I tried to make myself as inconspicuous as possible while standing just inside the door.

It was a silent congress, the only sounds being a slight rustling as people shifted position, and the fussing of the baby. Most of the people I could see were clutching forms, eyes intently fixed on that glassed-in area behind the service counter as if they could magic up attendance.

After about five minutes, without warning, the baby's mother jumped up, clopped noisily over to the glass and pressed the bell beside it. She kept her finger on it for thirty seconds or more, until a uniformed garda finally appeared from behind a wooden screening wall. Even before he had completed the couple of steps to his side of the counter, she let rip. 'What kind of a country is this?' she yelled, so loudly that she caused the baby to raise his or her decibel count. 'We've all been here since half nine,' she went on, in what I could recognise now as an Irish midlands accent. 'He won't stop cryin' and now I'm after missin' me bus home.' It was past ten thirty.

Then, not waiting for the garda's reply, she brandished her forms an inch in front of the glass partition, as close as she could get them to his face, tore them to bits and threw them into the air. Before the first shred had reached the floor, she had grabbed the stroller, wrenched it around and was manoeuvring it towards the door. One of the younger men in the room, greasy blue-streaked hair confined to a long braid, leaped up to open it. If he hadn't been so quick, she might have driven the baby straight through it. 'Good luck to yiz all!' she cried, over her shoulder, bumping the stroller past him. We all looked at each other. It had been a magnificent display, and I guess we all wished we could have been so assertive.

The cop behind the glass shrugged. 'Who's first?'

My turn came up surprisingly quickly since most of the petitioners simply needed to show ID and have their forms signed or stamped. When I presented my envelopes, the garda listened to my story, then took them from me, read the contents and replaced them in their envelopes. 'Four weeks this has been going on? Since you came to live here? You should have reported it sooner.' He picked up one of the envelopes again, holding it carefully by its corner between thumb and index finger.

'You're thinking fingerprints. DNA, that kind of stuff?'

He sighed. '*CSI*, I presume.'

I nodded, a little shamefaced. 'Sorry!'

'Don't be.' His grin was infectious, stripping years from his age, which I had reckoned to be in the early fifties, but now thought, maybe mid-forties. Of middle height and what they called hereabouts 'stout', he wore stripes, so was obviously a sergeant. 'You might be more on track than you think.' He glanced down. 'None of these is self-seal. I don't want to get your hopes up, but if he licked them . . .'

'Could be a she?'

'Indeed. But he or she would have to be on file for any DNA or even fingerprints to be of any use. We don't have a database of "perps" yet.' Again he grinned at me. 'Sorry, but apparently we're getting one. Soon. Everything to do with the force is "soon", these days, but to tell you the truth, and maybe this will give you a bit of comfort, these things here,' he tapped the envelopes, 'don't look like they're the work of anyone with a criminal record. But they're nasty. Anyone you know,' he asked casually, 'might have a grudge against you or your husband – or even his family?'

'Not that I know of – but, then, I don't know that many people around these parts. Not yet anyhow.'

'Sure. Not to worry.' He took a plastic bag from under the counter and carefully put all three envelopes inside. 'I don't mean to be flippant. Don't think I'm not taking it seriously.' Setting the package aside, he propped his elbows on the counter as if settling in for a chat. 'Stop me if I'm being too personal – I get slagged for that around here – but how are you managing out there on your own, Mrs Lynch?' He extended his hand through the gap to shake mine. 'Jack Cantwell,' he introduced himself.

I might have been imagining it, but there was something in his eyes, a flash I couldn't interpret, but before I could think about it he was interrupted by a colleague, jacketless, a young woman, blonde hair tied up in a loose ponytail, who looked from my perspective to be about fifteen years old. She had come out from behind the wooden screen. 'Have you got a minute, Jack? Need you back here.'

'Sure, be right there, just give us a sec.' Cantwell returned to the Humpty envelopes, visible through the plastic. He tapped them. 'You could do with this kind of thing like a hole in the head, I'd imagine. Look, the very minute you get the next one, assuming there'll be one, give us a call. Don't hesitate – the sooner you tell us, the sooner we can do something about it. And you might consider getting CCTV. Any idea who it could be?'

'None. But with those inks and fonts, he must have a computer.' I felt stupid now – everyone had a computer, a tablet or a smartphone. I was 'wasting police time' – wasn't that the phrase? Just because I was being spooked about a few lines of a nursery rhyme. 'I'm sure you have more urgent things to do and I shouldn't be bothering you with this. It's probably some kid getting his kicks.'

'Please don't apologise. As I said, we do take something like this seriously,' said the sergeant, being tactful, no doubt. 'There's one or two little villains around here, but this is probably too subtle for them. There's stamps on these envelopes. Too much trouble to lick 'em and get to a postbox. The ones we know get their kicks more instantly.'

He took a small notebook from his pocket and scribbled in it for a minute or so. 'Right. We know where you live!' He grinned. 'Sorry! Couldn't resist that, Marian. Mind if I call you Marian?'

'Of course not.'

'OK. Do you have a mobile phone by any chance, Marian?'

I gave him the number, then my email address.

'That's grand, grand. We'll hold on to these for a while.' He held up the plastic package. 'Who else knows about this by the way?'

'Absolutely nobody. I've told no one at all.'

'You're a strong lady.'

'Not that strong.'

'You're living alone.' He looked thoughtful now. 'We'll send a car round by your place now and then,' adding sarcastically, 'if we have one . . .'

His cell rang. He pulled it out of its holder and looked at the screen. 'And, again, you might consider that CCTV. Excuse me for a moment.'

As he turned away, the lobby's main door opened and a man clutching a sheaf of papers came in and took a seat. Cantwell's call lasted just a few seconds, and as he broke it, he turned back to me, peeling a business card from a small set he rooted out of his pocket. 'My mobile's on there as well as the general number. The mobile's probably the best way to get me.'

I left the place feeling physically lighter than I had for weeks. At some level I had been listening out for the rattle of the mailbox.

Most comforting, though, was that the cops had not treated me like a ninny, telling me (or thinking) that the letters were nothing to worry about.

Chapter Nine

The photographs I took with me to Ireland, from Dad's apartment, framed in silver now, are dutifully lined up on my bureau. My parents' wedding portrait. Me, squinting into the sunlight in the garden of Shangri-La. Me holding my Mickey Mouse lunch pail as I left for my first day in kindergarten. A framed snapshot of Mom, face shaded under a straw hat as, on her knees, trowel in hand, she smiles up at the camera from the margin of her zucchini patch. I also saved one of Dad sitting proudly in the driver's seat of their ancient motorhome, a shot of them both standing in front of the World's Biggest Ball of Twine in Ohio, and a professional one in which they're sitting on a boat under Niagara Falls during their honeymoon. They had evidently been happy that day. The photos reign over my bedroom in Glanmilish, at the centre of Ireland, in the only Irish county that 'does not touch a county that touches a coastline'. Claim to fame, say some. Marooned, say others.

Daniel always said that Glanmilish House was not just in the centre of Ireland but at the centre of the world. 'Look, Mar, look!

If you hold this map of the world at a certain angle' – he would adjust the atlas – 'there's the States, there's Russia and all the rest of it. Look where Glanmilish is. Aren't I right?' To please him, I always nodded agreeably, refraining from pointing out that there was an entire southern hemisphere he was not taking into account.

I should probably tell you about my first impressions of Ireland.

I've talked earlier about the weather and it didn't disappoint during the first four days of our six-day honeymoon: my first visit to the country. It lashed, to use the local terminology for heavy rain, blew, misted and fogged, sometimes simultaneously.

Daniel and I had married quietly with, as witnesses, Dad and his Filipina carer, whom I had hired to help me look after him during the final months of his life before he was ultimately hospitalised. Luzveminda was wonderfully capable and patient, Dad liked her and, after her first few weeks with us, I had trusted her completely to cope while we were honeymooning.

My divorce from Peter, at his instigation, came through in less than six weeks. He used an online service, and as it was uncontested and I had sought nothing from him, it was relatively painless for me as a legal process, although I can barely imagine how it played out for him and Letty.

We never met after that last bruising encounter in the atrium of John Berchman's. As he had requested, I had messaged him to say when I would go to the Oak Street apartment to collect my belongings.

Daniel's apartment was tiny, with just one bedroom and one closet, so fitting my stuff in with his would be a squeeze, even though I took only what I could pack into one large travel bag and a carry-on, mainly clothes, the more expensive of my toiletries and the few pieces of jewellery I had, nothing valuable. Peter had given me a gold locket as a wedding gift to wear with my white dress – it had belonged to Letty ('She gave it to me to give you so that's the "something old", Marian. Her mom gave it to her on the day she married my dad.'). Search as I did, however, I couldn't find it.

Natural justice.

I put everything else into garbage bags and sent them to Goodwill, in the hope that someone, or a few someones, might get some benefit from them.

I had brought my rings with me. I'd intended to leave them on the kitchen worktop where Peter would find them with my keys, but at the last minute had decided that was insensitive, so I put them back into a pocket of my purse.

Being in that beautiful Oak Street apartment again, even for such a short time, had resurrected all the guilt and sadness, but I had to face facts. I knew that treachery, like a personal demon, was destined to ride on my shoulders, prodding me with its trident, for a long time to come. I would have to deal with it privately because I knew I could expect no sympathy from my new boyfriend.

So, how long did it take Daniel Lynch to ask me to marry him? His proposal, surprising me with its suddenness, came quite quickly, in a matter of weeks, and had been far from romantic. He had been away at yet another of his conferences and I had missed him in every possible way. On the night he got back, I couldn't wait to tumble him into bed with me. Unusually, when he did get in, he had protested tiredness – the shindig had been in San Francisco so the flight had been lengthy, and even for him, he was unusually tetchy. I had become accustomed to his rapid mood swings – if you want to know me, come live with me – but had learned pretty fast that one way to get him back onside was to push the sex button.

Earlier that day I had fallen for a saleswoman's outpourings in Saks, Michigan Avenue: 'That blonde colouring! That height! Those legs!' But as I checked myself out in front of the store's deliberately flattering mirrors, letting the silk billow, then settle around me, I was picturing how Daniel would react to the feel of my body through it. The dress was highly inappropriate for meeting a boyfriend at ten o'clock on a Wednesday evening in the kitchen-diner of a place so small it was probably illegal everywhere except Japan. It was pale grey, sleeveless, falling in wide, loose pleats from a high silver collar that exposed most of my shoulders, and under it that night, I wore no lingerie, so when he came through the apartment door, all I had to do, I knew, no matter his demeanour, was to hug him. And that proved to be prescient.

Having woken together the following morning, we were barrelling around getting ready for the day – he at Holy Angels, me back in the Palmer House where I was to interview the CEO of a cancer charity. I was brushing my teeth in his minuscule one-person bathroom when he came up behind me. 'So, how about it, Mizz Lescher? Shouldn't we make this permanent? We could get the licence during lunch-hour today. Saturday good for you?'

'But that's only two days away!' I was watching him in the mirror. In my solar plexus, it felt as though my stomach and heart had collided.

'So?' He raised an eyebrow.

But while every nerve silently screamed, 'Yes! Yes! *Yes!*' I managed to sound like Marian Lescher: 'What brought this on?'

'Do you have to ask?'

'And what's the rush? Two days? And my divorce isn't through yet. You know that.'

He had been pressing against my rear end but pulled back. 'You don't want this?'

'You know I do, Daniel – that was nice! Do it again.' I backed against him.

That time he was less than enthusiastic, complaining a little:

84

'Talk about spoiling the moment! What's the point of putting it off?'

'Oh, come on, don't be a curmudgeon. You know I can't get a licence until I can show them the papers.' I reached behind, took his arms and brought them around me.

'I mightn't be in the mood then. I'm in the mood now,' he said sulkily, but I pressed backwards, hard against him and he took the lobe of my ear gently between his teeth.

I managed to hold off a little longer. 'What I mean is, honey, wouldn't you like your dad, your brothers and sister to be at your wedding? Shouldn't you give them time to make travel arrangements and so on?' I was still watching him in the bathroom mirror. My reflection, white toothpaste foam around my mouth, hair unbrushed, greying tee bearing the legend 'GO CUBS!' was not quite bridal.

'Who's this wedding for?' His big gesture thwarted yet again, he was frowning. 'Whose business is it, except yours and mine?'

'The state of Illinois's for one! I get it, Daniel.' Still processing this development I wiped foam from my mouth. Although this was fundamentally way past exciting, I had a vague niggle that it was all too sudden or that I was missing something.

'All right, I take your point,' he said grumpily. 'I'm just trying to circumvent the ridiculous side of weddings, I've been to lots of feckin' weddings, where there's the bride, smug as hell, tottering around like a big puffball on shoes that are a complete health hazard, with money utterly wasted on booze and inedible food. And there's the bloke, sweating in his tux, drinking his head off because he's looking at all these women around the bride chuntering away, absolutely delighted that another guy's gone for a burton, so he's worried about what he's got himself into – and don't get me started on speeches.'

'Daniel!' I remonstrated. 'If that's your attitude—'

'However . . .' holding me around the ribcage now, he tightened his grip so my breasts rose, exposing cleavage above the neckline of the tee '. . . you didn't let me finish!'

He lowered his head and bit softly. 'And will there be cream for tea?' He turned me round then, pulled me to him, and all my half-baked cavils flew to the four winds. That little voice did try to break in – *Is this guy really husband material?* – but I shut it off before it could get into its stride.

* * *

But, of course, we had to wait until my divorce came through, and four days after it did, our wedding took place privately in a very small meeting room at the Hilton Hotel in Northbrook, chosen not just because my dad had suggested it but, prosaically, for its proximity to O'Hare. With the help of Luzveminda, I had bought my father a new suit from Sears, complete with a gaily patterned pocket square, but was taken aback at how the pants pooled over his shoes and the jacket, well cut though it was, hung so slackly from his thin, stooped shoulders, his hands protruding like claws from the cuffs.

'That's great on you, Dad!' I said, hoping I sounded sincere. 'You look swell, a million dollars – isn't that right, Luzveminda?'

'Wonderful!' The carer played along. 'Mr Lescher, you are like a movie star.' She had never called him by his first name, and when I had asked her why, she had told me that it would not have been respectful. 'Don't worry,' she said quietly to me, as she saw me out. 'I am good with the needle. I shall make him George Clooney.'

On the day, she helped him shuffle through the door of the hotel room, decorated with the white flowers that had been included in the price of hiring it. 'Your mom would have been so happy,' he said, formally shaking hands with me, and then, to Daniel: 'You're getting a great wife, Peter.'

To his credit, Daniel made nothing of this. 'I am indeed, sir,' he said quietly. 'I'm a lucky man.' Although he had wanted to meet my father for a while, I had believed it might fluster Dad and hadn't thought it a good idea. As it turned out, that had been a wise call. For the first couple of weeks after I'd left Peter, Dad had asked plaintively why he wasn't coming any more, but then Luzveminda had entered the picture and there had been no further mention of him.

Although Cook County does not require wedding witnesses, Dad and Luzveminda both signed the register proffered by the court clerk, a portly, happy-looking woman who clearly loved her job and beamed professionally throughout. I was intrigued to see how Daniel signed it: *Donal B. Ó Loingsigh*. 'I assume that's Gaelic?'

'Give the girl a gold star!'

'And what's the B for?'

'Bartholomew. After my great-grandfather.'

Not to be outdone, I signed myself 'Marian A.T. Lescher'.

'M-A-T? "Mat"? I don't believe it!'

'Marian Alice Therese. Alice for Mom's mother, Therese for my confirmation.'

'I wanted to take Elvis for mine but no one would let me!'

The clerk thought this was hilarious but poor Luzveminda, uncomprehending, looked from one to the other of us and Dad was busy fumbling with his hearing aids so the joke bombed. The clerk shook hands with all four of us, wished us well and left us to it as Daniel called down for our room-service lunch.

When it came it was adorned with napkins tied with white ribbons and a complimentary bottle of champagne. Daniel hates champagne. Because of all his medication, Dad could have only a dribble and Luzveminda did not drink alcohol. So that left me. I love the stuff, and waded into it during the meal, which in general was taken in a stilted, rather silent atmosphere. Luzveminda, intent mostly on sorting out her charge with menu choices and protecting his new suit with napkins, uttered only the occasional word. The anodyne Muzak that played discreetly in the background somehow interfered with Dad's hearing aids so he had to take them out. That left Daniel and me to keep the conversation going and it was hardly appropriate that we should chatter like schoolkids.

Anyway, I thought happily, as I ate the starter – a warm goat's cheese salad with pears and walnuts – we had the rest of our lives for chat. Meanwhile, I continued to indulge in the champagne.

As our waiter was serving the main course, Daniel's cell pinged. He checked the screen and then, face like thunder, pressed the button to respond, rose from the table and turned his back to take the call. Even from across the table I could hear a shrill female voice at the other end. The call certainly sounded urgent. 'You're breaking up,' he said loudly. 'Hang up, I'll call you back.' Pressing the off-button, he turned back to us: 'Sorry, folks, I have to find a better spot.'

'Something wrong, honey?' I put down my glass. He hesitated for a beat as though reluctant to tell me, but then: 'There's been an RTA, a big pile-up on Eden's, multiple casualties. Every hospital in the area is involved in a major disaster plan, even Holy Angels. I guess there must be children involved. But obviously someone's got wires crossed here – I'm on vacation and that's official. But I have to sort this – can't have it on record that I'm playing hooky!'

'Don't worry,' I said, 'take your time, but don't let them boss you around! I'm getting on that plane whether you are or not!' I had meant it as a joke but he didn't laugh, just left the room.

I shrugged apologetically at Dad and Luzveminda. She smiled back. Dad, oblivious, did not raise his head, but at some level I was annoyed. Sure, I hadn't been on for the big dress, the veil, throwing the bouquet and that stuff – been there, done that – but this was our celebration, Goddammit, and I'd made an effort. I'd bought another nice dress in Saks, green silk this time. When I'd tried it on, the salesperson (same woman who had sold me the grey one) had again flattered me, saying it brought out the colour of my eyes. At the salon that morning, the hairstylist had insisted on clipping a spray of lily of the valley into my hair and I was even carrying a small but lush bouquet of white roses.

And, yes, by contrast to my wedding with Peter, which had been traditional and sparkling, his mom weeping happy tears all day, this one was not just low-key, it was hovering near no-key, but it was an important occasion, or supposed to be. I know it was selfish of me but I had determined to ditch the guilt demon for that one day and surely I was entitled to my groom's undivided attention.

When he came back from making his call, Daniel was flushed and his mood had darkened.

'Did you have a row with them? Was it a mix-up?' I was feeling no pain. With no one else imbibing, I was on my fourth glass of champagne. It was good stuff, I thought, a shame to waste it.

'Mix-up?' He picked up his cutlery. 'And some. Let's get this done, and get out of here.'

I was a little shocked at his abrupt tone, but Dad was there, and so was Luzveminda, so I held my tongue. All in all, though, I was glad when my new husband and I were able to see off my father and his carer, and were alone in our cab on the way to O'Hare. There was a news-stand in the hotel lobby and I had wanted to get a paper: 'We should check if there's anything yet about the pile-up on Eden's.'

But he'd pulled me away. 'Are you crazy? It just happened! Those papers were published this morning – you, of all people, should know that! The taxi's outside.'

'Right.' I'd allowed myself to be led out.

He looked quizzically at me as the vehicle moved away from the kerb. 'That was weird.'

'What? You being called in?'

'Your dad calling me Peter. I suppose we shouldn't really have had him there. He's clearly not capable—'

'I wanted him there. And it was my choice that he didn't meet you before the wedding. He loved Peter. I figured he'd just get confused if I brought you into the picture too quickly. It would have been different if he'd had time to adjust, get used to the idea of Peter gone and you coming in—'

'So this is all my fault, is it? You didn't consult me. It was my wedding too.'

'We're not going to have a row about this, are we, Daniel?' I hated it when he frowned. 'This is our wedding day, Goddammit! We've been husband and wife for – what is it? – an hour and forty-five minutes, and here we are, spatting about one little mistake made by a feeble old man. Not a good omen, eh?'

Instead of responding, he turned away to stare at the industrial landscape speeding by his window. I realised I hadn't handled that cleverly. No doubt it had been the champagne talking. Time for damage limitation. 'Oh, for God's sake, Daniel.' I searched for his hand, brought it up to my lips and kissed it. 'So it wasn't a traditional ceremony with hearts and flowers and big frilly dresses. I gave you that much, didn't I? And so my dad got a bit muddled, but he's an old man and here we are, married, Mr Lynch, really married, licensed by the state. Isn't that the main thing? Let's not fight about what's not important.'

'Not important to you, you mean?'

'Christ!' There was only one thing to do now. Working against the constraint of the seatbelt, I grabbed him and kissed him passionately on the mouth. 'I love you, you big, silly, touchy old lunk of a blarney-filled Irishman. Let's not fight. A few hours from now we'll be halfway to Ireland. Isn't that great? Aren't you looking forward to it? Seeing all the family? Showing me around?'

'Three hours from now we'll still be queuing to get through security.'

'Whatever.' I wouldn't be put off and kissed him again. 'Don't be such a grump! Today was one of the highlights of whatever remains of Dad's life so be nice, give him that much, and get over whatever's bothering you, okay? What is bothering you, by the way?' I searched his expression. 'You haven't been the same since that bloody phone call. I should have insisted we all, including you, turned off our cells.'

'You're right.' At last he came round. 'You're absolutely right. Sometimes I think the kids in that hospital have taken over the running of it. I did get a bit grouchy, and I'm sorry.' While the cab driver studiously avoided looking in his mirror, he kissed me hungrily, then murmured, eyes glinting, 'I'm so sorry, Mrs Lynch. You can show me later what a bad boy I've been.'

'Be sure of it, Mr Lynch.' I kissed him back.

Chapter Ten

Despite the early hour, we got into the arrivals hall at Shannon airport to be met by a group of Daniel's relatives, fifteen or twenty of them, waving banners and flags, balloons and handmade notices to welcome us. On sighting us, some started singing, a little confusingly, in what sounded like Spanish (*olé*, *olé*, *olé*) as they pressed around us with outstretched hands, backslaps and hugs.

We were impeding other passengers coming through and politely, with great good humour, a security man asked us to move outside the barrier, which we did, and once there, before we could be engulfed again, Daniel managed to grab me, saying into my ear, 'I didn't know this was going to happen. The only person I told that we were coming on this flight was Jerry.'

It would have been impossible not to recognise Jerry as Daniel's brother – height, hair, eyes – and I knew he was well into his training as a doctor. 'Dad sends his apologies,' he said, above the hubbub of flattering comments about me ('God, she's lovely, isn't she?'; 'Fell into it there, he did, eh?'). 'He sent these. ' He thrust flowers into my hands.

Then someone called, 'Speech! Speech!' and they all took it up, 'Speech! *Speech!*' clapping their hands. Other people in the concourse were watching us now, but although I would normally be shy about such overt attention, it was impossible not to be taken up in the warmth of this welcome.

'All right so, but I've nothing prepared,' Jerry began.

'Thank God!' shouted one man. 'Me cows aren't milked yet and it's a good road home.'

'We're all here today to welcome Marian,' Daniel's brother continued, having waited for the laughter to die down. 'Meeting her now for the first time, I can see why my beloved brother looks like the Cheshire Cat, and I want to say to him, most sincerely, "Daniel, you can wipe that complacent smile off your face because you are clearly, *clearly* punching above your weight!"'

More laughter.

'So that's all the jobs done now,' he continued, 'bouquet handed over, welcome given, but,' he turned to address me directly, 'on behalf of the family, I want to say that while this fella here is like an old penny, always turns up no matter what we do to keep him away, you, Marian, are an adornment to the family. I can already see that, and I don't know how he managed to persuade you to marry him. You are very, very welcome to Ireland, we're delighted to see you and I hope we'll be seeing you often. And, by the way, thank you for taking him off our hands.' He gave me a bear hug, creaming the flowers.

The next few minutes were almost overwhelming as, clutching my flowers, I tried to keep up with the introductions, especially as two other men were called Jerry and three of the women were Mary, while almost everyone present seemed to be surnamed O'Sullivan,

Harrington or McCarthy, with just Jerry (and Daniel, of course) being Lynch.

My new husband had filled me in on his origins. On both sides, they were from west Cork, specifically the Beara peninsula. 'I don't really know if it's still the same – I haven't been there since my early teens – but families were very large there. My mother was one of eleven and she always' said she probably had between eighty and ninety first and second cousins. And when you add third cousins and cousins once or twice removed she said she couldn't count them. So stand by. When we're there we'll be meeting them all. Word has probably spread – it's that kind of place.'

It was a great welcome to Ireland, but right now my energy, sapped by the long flight and the earliness of the arrival – and not helped by drinking more champagne on board – was ebbing and I was looking forward to getting to our hotel, some sort of castle: Jerry had organised a two-night stay for us as a wedding gift. We could go straight there and to our room. To sleep.

Over the next four days we took in the sights on the famous west coast, or part of it – or we would have, had we been able to see it through the mist and sheeting rain. Instead, I had to rely on Daniel's graphic descriptions of the Cliffs of Moher, the Ring of Kerry, the Lakes of Killarney and the Beara peninsula – our arrival there timed to coincide with the Castletownbere Regatta. We could sense rather than see the participants through a veil of horizontal rain.

In general, progress was slow on this part of our tour because we kept being asked into cousins' houses for tea and scones 'or maybe something stronger'. And I was frequently presented with gifts, local craft or produce. 'Don't open it now, Marian! It's just a little piece of Beara to bring home with ye to Chicago!' The two McCarthy sisters, who ran McCarthy's Bar in Castletownbere, were adamant that the drinks we had there were on the house. 'First time here, Marian! Congratulations! We hope to see lots of you now.'

Daniel was defensive about the weather: 'I promise you, if you could have seen it, you'd have been blown away, but the good thing is that this scenery's not going anywhere. We'll come back. And by the way, I also promise you that we'll have a "proper honeymoon"' (he made the quotation marks with his fingers) '– by that I mean a little less socialising with relatives – very soon.' That was on the afternoon of our last touring day, when we were on our way to check in for a family party at the Eccles Hotel in Glengarriff.

I hadn't realised how big this would be until I came down from our room at seven thirty that evening to find that the group who had welcomed us at Shannon were all there, augmented by, I guessed, a hundred more of all ages, from babies and toddlers to the elderly, all facing the door to cheer when we appeared in the room, as though we were at a surprise party, which, in a way, it was. 'What's going on, Daniel?' I was dazed.

'Haven't a clue. I didn't set this up – I warned you it would be a big affair, though, didn't I?' He looked gleeful as, taking my hand, he led me towards a round of new introductions. The names, a euphonious river of sound, flowed past and there was no point in trying to remember them all because I knew I wouldn't. Back in our room in the early hours of the next morning, I noted as many as I could recall in my journal. In geography class, Sister Margaret Mary had taught us to recite sets of towns of England, tapping them out on her desk with her ruler. (Leeds, Bradford, Halifax, Huddersfield, Dewsbury, Wakefield and *Barnsley*. I can't remember whether they were famed for cotton or wool – I could Google them, I suppose!) Using the same method I made a recitation of family names, whispering them under my breath to embed them in my mind. I can still reel them off: McCarthy, Sullivan, O'Sullivan, Harrington, Lynch, O'Neill, Leahy, Healy, Crowley, O'Driscoll and *Donegan* . . .

Almost last in line for greeting me, my husband's close family watched from a table in a far corner of the room, and by the time we got to them I really needed a drink. They stood up as we approached. 'You're very, very welcome,' said Daniel's dad (also Daniel but known as 'Big Doctor Dan' to differentiate him from his son, aka. 'American Doctor Dan'), who was officially our host. A big man with a big smile, carrying weight but as charming as his eldest son, he took my hand in a warm, enveloping grip. 'We could have had this in Glanmilish House,' he explained. 'It's big enough, God knows, and was famous for parties when Daniel's mother was alive, but the space is finite, and with all these people denied a Big Day Out because this fella,' he flicked a glance at his son, 'kept it all to himself in Chicago, too many people would have had to be left out!' Another flick. 'Anyway, the house is all steps up and down and, as you can see, there're quite a few in wheelchairs. They deserve a party too. See that woman over there?' He indicated a bright-eyed lady in one of the wheelchairs, glass in hand, back straight as a ballerina's as she held court in a corner of the room. 'She's a hundred and three years old. Nothing really wrong with her except old age. Sharp as a tack and still living at home, alone in her house, never married, likes her drop of brandy. She can walk, but the wheelchair is safer. She's a good example of the people we couldn't leave out.' Then, taking my arm, he introduced me to Daniel's three siblings and their spouses.

As schooled by Daniel during the flight, I had already memorised pairings, names, offspring, and where they lived. Eleanor, 'a housewife', according to Daniel, lived in Limerick City with her husband, Martin, an auctioneer, and they had three children, Colm, Finn and Patricia. Jerry, the trainee doctor I'd met already at Shannon, and his wife, Aoife, an Aer Lingus stewardess (they were 'hostesses' on the Irish airline, he'd said), lived in Dublin with their baby son,

Tom. 'And we think Aoife's pregnant again.' He added that this was still a secret. Eamon, 'the financial guru of the family – I think maybe he's a financial adviser, or an insurance broker, something in money anyway,' and his wife, Sharon ('likes to shop'), lived in Nenagh, County Tipperary, not far from Eleanor and Martin. 'No kids.' I would have known Eamon immediately: he was roughly the same height and physique as Daniel and Jerry but fatter than either. By contrast, his wife was a thin, brittle blonde but her bony handshake was strong and her expression lively. Aoife, Jerry's wife, an elegant brunette and almost as tall as myself, was lovely. Smiling, with candid eyes, she held my hand for a few seconds, and I knew instinctively that we could be friends, should the opportunity arise. Sometimes in life this happens, and when it does, it's wise to note it.

By contrast to those of her sisters-in-law, the welcome and handshake of Eleanor, Daniel's sister, were as listless as her ash-blonde hair, which hung about her pale face in limp strings. She had the family eyes but they were lifeless. Indeed she seemed withdrawn, entirely the opposite of the rest of her family. I'm no medic but I'd been around doctors long enough to wonder, as her gaze slid away from mine, if she might be on medication.

'Well, now you have the full deck,' said Daniel's father, smiling at me. 'How on earth did you manage to get this man to see sense and settle down, Marian?' He grinned. 'We thought we'd be stuck for ever with an oul' bachelor.'

'And have you discovered yet that he's a sociopath, Marian?' In her pallid face, Eleanor's eyes had come to life, whether with malevolence or mischief it was hard to tell. 'Ellie!' Her father remonstrated. 'Behave yourself!' But he laughed as he turned to me. 'Daniel and Ellie are close in age – I guess they never got over early sibling rivalry.

'As for our Daniel, their mother threw up her hands and said she didn't know what to make of him, that she'd never know from one day to the next whether he was the Omen or a poster child for Disney. Said he was her mystery child. She adored him, of course, he was her golden boy, but, then, he was her firstborn. Mothers, eh? What are we all drinking, family?'

He started taking orders and while the others sat down again, telling him what they wanted, Daniel said softly, 'You all right, Marian?'

'Sure,' I responded. 'Although I don't think your sister likes me. But it's early days—'

Jerry interrupted: 'Come on, the two of you, sit down with us. We've kept seats.'

'In a sec,' Daniel said. 'Order me a pint, there's a good lad. We'll be back, but there's still a whole table of people over there who haven't met Marian yet – I'll take her over for a couple of minutes.'

'Hang on.' Daniel Senior (I just couldn't get my head around calling him Big Doctor Dan) touched my arm. 'What'll you have, Marian?'

I asked for a glass of white wine, and then Daniel was steering me towards the tableful of people smiling expectantly in our direction. On the way to them, speaking quickly now and having to raise his voice so I could hear him over the cheerful babble that was rising in volume, he reverted to the subject of Eleanor. 'Tell me honestly what you thought of her.'

'Why?' I said. 'It's early days – why her in particular?'

'Dad and Jerry – me too – we all think she might be self-medicating. Benzodiazepine maybe, wherever she's getting it. That's a bitch to come off and Dad thinks she's been on it a long time. Too long.'

'It did occur to me that she might be on something.'

'Why?' He seemed abruptly apprehensive. 'Has she said something to you?'

'We've just met, Daniel! Of course she hasn't! We hardly know one another!'

'Ah, don't worry about it,' he said quickly. 'Forget I asked. Hello there, Teresa!' He raised his voice as we got to the target table. 'Isn't this a great night?'

And on we went. I made a special effort to keep in contact with Daniel's family, who were all utterly charming, with the exception of Eleanor, whose smile under her dead eyes was mechanical and who, when addressed, continued to respond in monosyllables.

Once or twice at the family table, I looked across to see her, head to one side, studying me. She didn't smile when our eyes met and I decided not to try to force things with her. You couldn't win them all, I thought, and I was in danger of being loved to death by the other six. Daniel's dad, the two brothers, their wives, even Eleanor's Martin could not have tried harder than they did to make me feel welcome. Six out of seven wasn't bad, I thought.

The party hadn't thinned out much when, at about two in the morning, I was genuinely enjoying myself – entertained by the group around the 103-year-old woman, not least herself, fresh as a daisy, it seemed, and a fount of good stories about the area and its people. Abruptly, however, I crashed, struck by fatigue, an overload of chat, and an ache in my entire face from too much smiling. I decided to go to bed.

I looked around for Daniel but could see no sign of him so I said my goodbyes and slipped away.

On the way to the room, however, I heard his voice, intense and in full flow, coming from above me on the landing at the top of the stairs. I was too far away to distinguish what he was saying but when I got to where I could see him, he was deep in conversation with Eleanor, who was staring at the carpet, head lowered, so I couldn't see her expression. Nevertheless, her body language might have been characterised as mutinous. They heard me approach and simultaneously both heads turned. I hesitated, but felt I had to continue. 'Sorry, I didn't mean to interrupt anything.'

'You're not.' Daniel seemed to relax. 'Ellie and I haven't had a chat for ages. Isn't that right, sis?' His eyes bored into hers, and I couldn't help feeling he was sending her a signal.

She turned away from him and headed towards the stairway. 'Good night, Marian,' she said, passing me, eyes averted, tone without nuance. 'Hope you had a good time. It was nice to meet you.'

'Nice to meet you too, Eleanor,' I called after her, and then, to my husband, 'What was that about? Is she all right? Is everything okay between you?'

'Far from it, I'd say,' he replied. 'I was giving her a brotherly lecture and she didn't like it.'

'Was it about coming off that medication?'

'Oh, look, this is nothing for you to concern yourself with, Marian. I'm not being rude, not telling you it's none of your business, because it is your business since you're officially part of my family now. But the truth is, we'll be gone out of here in less than two days, she's a big girl, and there's plenty here who'll look after her, including her husband.'

He gave me a one-armed hug around the shoulders, but despite his easy tone, I could tell he was tense. 'So it's nothing to do with her resenting me marrying you? Nothing like that?'

'Of course not. Just give her time. She'll love you just like all the rest of them do. What's not to love?' He let me go. 'You're going to bed already? The night is but a pup.'

'I'm whacked. But you go back down. They're your people and you should be with them.'

'Have you enjoyed yourself?'

'Greatly.' I reached up to kiss his cheek but he turned it into one of full-on passion.

Then, pulling away, he said, 'I don't know what I'd do without you, Marian. You do know that, don't you?'

'You know I do.'

'Yeah.' He looked over my shoulder. 'But I will go back down, if you don't mind. God knows when I'll see them again and I haven't been with all the family together like this since – since . . . Would you believe it's so long I can't put a date on it? Ma's funeral? I didn't make it for Jerry and Aoife's wedding. We sure don't live in each other's pockets, or maybe it's me not living in theirs, eh?'

'Go ahead. And I hope things work out with Eleanor. Sibling rivalry, your dad said. Isn't it time you both had a look at it?'

He was taken aback. 'He said that?'

'Yeah. He also said your mom reckoned you were her mystery child. And you're my mystery man,' I said affectionately. 'Come on up to bed soon and I'll show you!'

'Yeah,' he said flatly, for once not rising to the innuendo. 'Don't be worrying about Ellie. She's just like that. Console yourself with the fact that I can see you're definitely Top of the Pops with the rest of the family – with everyone. Tonight, in fact, you're officially a hit, wife, and why am I not surprised?' He flashed me one of his dazzling smiles. 'I won't be long, promise! Keep that bed warm for me.' He went off towards the stairs, which he took two at a time.

I leaned over the banister. 'Where do you get all that energy?'

'You'll see,' he called back. 'It's all that good living!'

I went into our room and, having hastily scribbled my name-recitation aide-memoire, virtually fell into bed where, for the first few minutes, I was strangely conscious of a sort of journalistic niggle. I can't say I was ever a Woodward or a Bernstein, and never would be, but I had been on the fringes of journalism for a long time. The profession facilitates not just an essential natural curiosity but growth of a set of antennae, and there was definitely something going on with Daniel's sister. My instinct was that, no matter what her family thought, there was more to her reaction to me than medication dependency. Her attitude had been polite but fixed, and my hunch said that this had preceded my arrival.

What had she been told, and by whom? Who could it have been but Daniel himself, because who other than him knew anything about me?

Like Daniel's, my activity on social media was almost non-existent, unless I was researching a topic or person of interest; I followed a few top reporters on Twitter, while never tweeting much myself, just the odd retweet. After a few of my more high-profile interviews for the *Tribune,* including Daniel's, I'd gained a few 'friends', so-called, on Facebook, but in the absence of meaningful engagement with me they had fallen away. Now I was rarely targeted directly, except for greetings on my birthday, prompted by Facebook's 'Wish Marian a Happy Birthday!' exhortation. How on earth had Eleanor formed any impression of me without meeting me?

I had always scolded myself about my lack of effort on social media since, as a freelancer, hiding, even in plain sight, was no way to get jobs. Because of my upbringing and Catholic schooling, I had been imbued with the conceit that 'blowing your own trumpet' was immodest, boastful and dislikeable. And somehow it had also been dinned into me that the quality of the work should speak for itself, not because I was drawing attention to it.

Maybe her obvious antipathy (or indifference, it was hard to tell) to me had something to do with her personality and I'd just have to suck it up. I'd been accepted by everyone else. I hadn't the energy right now to work it out. It was hardly a tragedy, but that niggle meant I had to keep trying. It would be hard to do it from the other side of the Atlantic, I mused drowsily, and then, despite the gales of chat rising from downstairs, I thought no more.

Chapter Eleven

I dozed on and off during the journey to our final stop, Daniel's home, waking fully only as we passed through a pretty little village called Durrow. 'Hi, sleepyhead.' Daniel was in a sunny mood. 'Not far now!'

To tell you the truth, although the welcome from his dad could not have been warmer, my first impressions of Glanmilish village and the family home were . . . disappointing. In the village's main street, where once there had been a row of businesses, there were now mostly shutters and hoardings, with just one grocery store, a veterinary practice, a small drugstore and what might have been a tiny pop-up clothing business. It shared a fascia with a premises that sold buckets, feeding troughs and featured, bizarrely, a manikin in a tutu, which stood behind a stack of children's buckets and spades, a net of beach balls and several hurling sticks – as the art and science of the hurling game had already been explained to me, I knew what they were. The sign overhead declared the joint enterprise to be 'ALL THINGS BRITE AND BUCKETFUL'.

There was a small rundown hotel at the end of the row, which bore signs of life: a sandwich board outside it advertised 'Full Steak Dinners 2 Courses and Coffee €10.95'. As far as I could see, that sad street represented the sum total of Glanmilish's commercial centre.

Daniel had sensed my reaction: 'I know it looks bad but things are bound to improve – are improving, actually – and we'll rise again, I'm sure.'

When we got to Glanmilish House, the omens were not much better. With farms, tillage and dairy on either side, it stood on a little hill above and apart from the village, its weedy gravelled driveway flanked by overgrown shrubbery, its lawns running wild. Set over wide granite steps that led up from a very large turning circle, its double entrance doors and portico must have been impressive in their day but the doors were now showing mostly bare wood, with streaks of brown where once there had been varnish.

'That's the surgery to the side there.' Daniel indicated a single-storey extension, faithful to the style of the house. 'And, by the way, nobody round here ever uses the front door. They go in through the back.' He accelerated, spraying gravel, as we drove around the corner of the house. 'Dad doesn't notice what the place looks like – he never did. My mother took care of that side of things, décor, furniture, even the gardening, all the good stuff women do.' He smiled across at me as he braked to a stop. 'It left him totally free to be a proper doctor.'

Something about his tone alerted me. Did he see me as slotting in here eventually to take over his mother's role?

* * *

'I'll leave you to it.' Daniel Senior, having welcomed us with a cup of tea and some cookies in the kitchen, had departed within fifteen minutes, saying he had to visit a patient fourteen kilometres away.

'You give her the grand tour, eh, Daniel?' Then, to me: 'You'll have to make a few allowances, Marian. I'm like a lot of my patients, these days, ancient, alone, and letting the house fall down around me.'

My husband grew progressively morose as he conducted me through the house. 'God, I know it's years since I was here.' He surveyed the drawing room. 'Maybe it was because everywhere was filled with people for Ma's funeral and I just didn't notice.' Large and finely proportioned, with a high ceiling and sash windows, the room's ornate wallpaper was peeling, couch and chair upholstery had seen far better days, and the side tables were dusty, their legs hung with cobwebs. 'Look at this!' He waved at the brass fender and fire irons around the marble hearth, all black with neglect. 'Ma kept this place like a convent parlour. If she could see it now . . . How could he have let this happen?'

'He probably never comes in here.' I didn't want to add to his distress by being critical. 'It's all surface, cosmetic, Daniel. There's nothing here that a good cleaning and decorating company couldn't sort in a week.'

'Dad's too busy, these days. His practice stretches over a lot of the little villages around here. The health service in this country is fucked, pardon my French. None of the new crop coming out of the colleges wants to become a rural GP – they're all going abroad, to Australia or Canada, the way me and some of my classmates fled to the States, and who can blame us, or them for that matter?' We had moved up to the master bedroom where the lightshade, of peach fringed silk, hung wonkily from the ceiling and the hems of the matching drapes were stained and spotted with black mould. 'This is dreadful,' he said, picking one up and releasing a cloud of dust.

'Don't say anything to him, Daniel. I'm sure he does his best.'

But that night I could actually smell the damp in the bedroom, despite the fume-laden heat issued by what Daniel had referred to as a 'Super Ser' gas heater placed between two of the three tall windows. Beside me, I knew that he was also having a bad night but neither of us acknowledged the other's wakefulness. I guess we didn't want to admit how we felt about his ancestral home.

I felt sorry for his poor father, clearly a cultured and intelligent man, but was aghast that he had actually considered holding our wedding party there. Despite the fun and warmth of the Irish welcome, I was now secretly looking forward to getting back to civilisation, as I saw it.

* * *

I was exhausted, almost on the verge of collapse, when at noon the next day, in Dublin airport, we embarked for Chicago and found our seats on the plane; there wasn't a single vacant one. Nevertheless, despite screaming babies in two of the rows just behind us, the lack of legroom and general discomfort in the packed economy cabin, I slept quite a bit during the flight, which took almost nine hours. 'Headwinds,' said the captain, in his slow, laconic drawl, as he apologised for our late arrival while we were taxiing to the terminal at O'Hare. I stretched my legs as far as they could fit under the seat in front of me whereupon one instantly and agonisingly charley-horsed.

It was forbidden to stand while taxiing so Daniel, realising immediately that I was in trouble, released his seat belt, extricated my foot and, with one hand, dragged it up at right angles, grasped the affected calf with the other, then squeezed and massaged it as hard as he could. Despite the limited space, the procedure worked. The muscle relaxed and the pain eased. 'Thanks,' I gasped. 'Thanks, Doctor!'

Two hours later, as we got back into his tiny, stultifyingly hot apartment, I was still limping with residual pain. While he went to the bedroom to turn on the window air-conditioner, I threw open the screen door, leading from the kitchen to the fire escape, hoping against hope that there might be a slight breeze despite the stillness of the summer's day. Instantly, the clammy hand of humidity reached in to raise perspiration on my scalp and face, under the light cotton of my chinos and between my breasts; it even dripped from my eyebrows.

I closed the door again and went into the bedroom, where the air-con had not yet become cold but was at least causing a small movement of air. I sat on the side of the bed, holding my face to it. There was no pleasing me, I thought. I'd been looking forward to getting away from cool, rainy, misty Ireland and back to the Chicago summer, conveniently ignoring the fact that I suffered badly in heat. 'We need to move to a better apartment,' I said. 'One with central air-con.'

'Just wait until this kicks in.' Daniel pushed the machine's control to max. 'I like this place – it's only a four-minute walk to work.'

'Well, I don't. Like it, I mean. And I've got to work here.'

'It's only like this during a couple of summer months.'

'I mean it, Daniel. We have to move.'

'We're near the L here. You could take your Mac to Lincoln Park. Work in the open, under the trees.'

Disbelieving, I looked at him. 'That's your solution? Behave as though I'm homeless? And you know I'm allergic to mosquitoes.'

'I'll get you a gallon of Jungle Formula – maybe something stronger. I'll ask around my colleagues.'

'We have to *move*, Daniel! I'm stifling here. You're not here all the time – you're in Seattle or Canada or San Francisco or Paris!'

'I understand your frustration, Marian,' he said levelly, 'but are you pre-menstrual? Actually menstruating?'

That did it. 'I'm going to Tommaso's,' I said. 'At least it'll be cool there.' I leaped off the bed and limped the few feet into the kitchen-diner where I collected my purse. 'Join me if you like. If you don't like, I don't care.' I slammed out of the apartment.

Tommaso's, on the next block, was our neighbourhood 'Italian' although, shrewdly, the restaurant also offered a limited American menu of lamb chops and Italian-dressed burgers, both served with its version of fries, cooked in olive oil. The place was a throwback to the type of establishment once familiar in Rogers Park where Dad still lived, with Chianti bottles for table lamps, red-check tablecloths and subdued Neapolitan songs playing softly in the background. My parents, thinking them the height of sophistication, had patronised them in their healthier days, right up until Mom's cancer became so painful that she could no longer walk even as far as the door of a cab to go to any restaurant at all.

I looked at my watch: it was five thirty, a little early for the dinner rush, but I was welcomed like an old friend by Tommaso himself, in his eighties, presiding proudly over his new-fangled – to him – digital cash register just inside the door. 'Table for two, Signora?' he asked, short only of springing up to give me a hug.

'For one, please. But my husband might be joining me if he can get away.' Despite the pizza oven, the place was blessedly cool and, as I took my seat, I could already feel my temper subsiding. I had lived with Chicago summer weather all my life and it wasn't Daniel's fault. Should I call him? Apologise?

But how could I apologise and still make the very valid point that his place was inadequate, way too small for two large people, a half-apartment, really, with a 22-inch shower-stall and that single closet in the bedroom. Using the oven even for a short while on days like this was beyond contemplation, and being crushed together in a standard-sized double bed at night was no longer romantic but intolerable.

I had to convince him. The only place I could safely hang my two silk dresses without them wrinkling was on the back of the bathroom door. We had to share an underwear drawer, which had been fun for a while, and even sexy as we pretended to make the wrong choices, but the novelty had quickly worn off, especially when we were both rushing to get out in the morning.

Even Dad's walk-up on Devon was Paradise by comparison, I thought, but the demon on my shoulder pricked me with its trident: *just deserts*. It hadn't needed to for it had occurred to me before, rather starkly, that I had chosen to leave the lofty, airy spaces of Peter's Oak Street home.

Bleakly, as I considered the situation, I couldn't see my husband making a big move unless I could persuade him that he had come up with a solution that suited him. His father's words, 'We thought we had an oul' bachelor for ever on our hands' or something similar ('stuck with an oul' bachelor'?), had been apt.

I examined my conscience. Had I fallen out of love so quickly? Purely because of our living arrangements?

Of course I hadn't. Those little hairs still stood up on my forearms when I recalled aspects of our nightly, sometimes daily, lovemaking. I still admired him, not just for his passionate interest in his work and in the developing world, but also for his intelligence, articulacy, even his medical instincts – I hadn't forgotten the speed at which he had detected and dealt with my charley horse earlier that afternoon.

But for too long, I thought, my new husband had been unanswerable to anyone else for his actions. He had been his own boss, mobile, no discussion necessary about his frequent travel plans, his life and work enabled in a way that had suited him and him alone. All he had to do was to fling a few things into an overnight bag and flag down a passing cab for the airport.

But if I took all this into account and didn't push too hard, it should be possible, I thought, to come up with a solution to reflect his changed status, which would accommodate both of us.

Maybe, a new idea dawned, in the interim, it would be possible for me to accompany him to some of those conferences and meetings in the more attractive locations. The more I thought about this, the more I liked it, and not just for personal reasons (those huge, terrific bedrooms with spa baths, the rooftop swimming pools). I would have great journalistic opportunities too – many of the people who attended those things lived, surely, at the cutting edge of medicine and science. Couldn't my husband call in a few favours? Arrange interviews for me? In any case, I was perfectly capable, given the opportunity, of setting them up for myself.

I cheered up. I couldn't believe I hadn't thought of this before. The waitress came and I ordered *penne all' arrabbiata* with a half-carafe of house red, then took out my cell and speed-dialled Daniel's number.

It was busy.

I tried the number on and off for the next ten minutes until the food came, then left the cell on and visible beside my plate. He might have been trying to call me while I was doing the reverse.

But all evening the number remained unavailable. He didn't call and I went home, tail metaphorically between my legs. He was not in the apartment and there was no note. We had been married for seven days, plus an eighth spent flying back to Chicago.

I tried the general Holy Angels number but it didn't have a twenty-four-hour switchboard and the voicemail that kicked in offered a direct line for 'emergencies only to do with patients in residence, but if you do have an emergency, the fastest route to immediate help is to dial nine one one'.

Chapter Twelve

By early next morning I was frantic. On the nightstand beside the bed, my cell was on charge because I had run down its battery by using it every ten or fifteen minutes during the night and the early hours trying to contact Daniel. I picked it up again now in case I hadn't heard it ring, even though I knew that was not possible. I had time-checked the digital clock beside me every few minutes.

23.40 . . .

23.56 . . .

00.14 . . .

. . . right up to 05.20, twenty minutes ago. It was 05.40 now and I was due to meet Mollie Lehman, managing editor of a new bi-weekly 'magazine for the savvy woman', at eight o'clock in her office on LaSalle Street. Out of the blue, she had called me on the evening before the wedding. I was actually having my nails French-manicured at the time and, to the obvious displeasure of my nail artist, I had picked up – as freelancers always will on seeing an unfamiliar number. We're always on standby for work.

I had heard about and had read puff pieces about the nascent publication – as had, no doubt, every other journalist in the country – so was thrilled to get the unexpected call. The managing editor had been impressed, she said, with my 'take' on 'that Irish doctor's crusade' in the *Tribune*: 'It's exactly the kind of thing we're aiming for here at *Femme*. We want our readers to use their brains and widen their worlds, to be compassionate but not mawkish. We'll feature an interview section but not just the usual "I survived bulimia" kinda stuff. We're focused on solutions rather than problems at *Femme*. Geddit, Marian? Mind if I call ya Marian?'

'Of course not. That sounds wonderful. And thank you for thinking of me.'

'Not a problem, Marian. So . . .' I could hear the riffling of papers '. . . ten thirty tomorrow morning? That good for ya, Marian?'

I had read the woman's profile: she had a reputation for not suffering fools and, for a millisecond, I actually wondered if I could take the meeting offered and still be fancied-up in time to get to Northbrook for my wedding at noon. I dismissed the notion as impractical and explained the situation. 'I'm really sorry, but I'm sure you can understand. Perhaps if we could meet earlier tomorrow morning or even this evening?'

'No can do, Marian.' She was clearly not best pleased. 'I'm packing up for the day now and tomorrow we're interviewing from seven thirty because I have to commute from the boonies and I can't get in much before that.' This was followed by another pause. Then: 'Ya going on honeymoon too, Marian?'

'Yes, but I'll be back in action a week from tomorrow.' I held my breath.

Another pause. More riffling of paper. Across the table in the salon, the manicurist, looking stern, was checking her watch. I nodded at her, shrugging apologetically.

The editor came back and, while saying all the right things, congratulating me and so forth, I was left in no doubt that she was annoyed. She did, nevertheless, agree to postpone until eight o'clock on this fraught morning. If I wanted this gig, which I sure as hell did, I had to get my act together: Mizz Lehman was clearly not the type to show understanding about a 'domestic' on top of a postponement for something as trivial as a wedding *and* a week-long honeymoon. She was originally from New York.

That early morning, however, the stress caused by Daniel's vanishing act, combined with jetlag and lack of sleep, meant I didn't know how to count my fingers, much less gather my thoughts about an important interview. How was I going to turn up on my top game at the offices of *Femme* less than three hours from now?

It was ironic, I thought, as I dragged myself out of bed and into the shower, that it had been the interview with Daniel that might have changed my luck in pursuing a career when my distress about him this morning might kill it off. The demon on my shoulder smiled and licked its paws.

Somehow, after turning the water in the shower to cold, several coffees laced with sugar, and breakfast consisting of a high-protein 'health bar', washed down with a dissolved Berocca tablet, by the time I left the apartment later that morning, I had managed to shake off the fog and make myself presentable in a black pants suit, white shirt and kitten heels. I was carrying my portfolio in a briefcase and a raincoat because, blessedly, the heatwave had broken during the night. The wind was already getting up from the direction of the lake as I kept stride alongside the waves of workers moving towards the L station. Above our heads, lightning crackled intermittently behind swelling clouds – we were in for a storm.

I actually found a seat on the L but I was having to employ all my mental resources to keep Daniel Lynch and his continuing absence caged at the back of my mind so I could focus on my interview. I mentally repeated my mantra as we jolted along, collecting and discarding passengers: *You can do this. You can do this . . .*

Luck remained with me in one respect: when the L disgorged me at LaSalle and Madison, although the cloud had thickened and the temperature had noticeably dropped, the rain was still holding off. *Femme*'s offices at 30 North LaSalle were just a block away and I clipped along as fast as I could. I could see it – well, you couldn't miss it: forty-four storeys, curtained from top to street level entirely with black glass, it seemed to have landed unexpectedly on that street otherwise filled with traditional and rather gracious old buildings.

Anyhow, it was just a couple of yards away when, as though taking a cue for curtain-up on a stage play, multiple lightning flashes lit the clouds and I heard a crack of thunder so loud that the storm had to have been almost directly overhead. Simultaneously, as if someone had emptied a gargantuan bucket, monsoon-like rain deluged the entire building, spilling down its obsidian façade to stream across the sidewalk and my shoes into the street canyon.

I was just feet away from the doors, and escaped inside, suffering only superficial wetting and a small dent in my dignity as my heels skidded on the marble floor. I would have fallen, had my arm not been grabbed by a woman. 'You OK?' she asked but then, without waiting for an answer, let me go and hustled off towards the elevators.

I found a set of washrooms on that floor and went inside to dry my shoes. Everything else about me was as it should have been. I combed my hair, applied fresh lipstick, then went to join the throng waiting around the bank of elevators.

* * *

Less than an hour later, I was leaving my new boss's office. 'So we're clear now, Marian.' She had escorted me to the door but was keeping one hand on the handle. 'It's four thousand words for the main interview every two weeks, subject to be cleared with me in advance. Suggestions for additional pieces to be brought up at editorial meetings on Thursday mornings at seven thirty sharp. You should have your contract by tomorrow morning and, as we discussed, it will have a no-compete clause. Twelve months, no writing for the competition, if for any reason this doesn't work out. Got all that, Marian? Anything else?'

I shook my head. 'Thank you very much, Mollie. I don't think there's—'

'Good. Nice meetin' ya, welcome to the team, bye!' Firmly, she ushered me out and shut the door.

When I got to the first floor and the entrance atrium, I could see through the windows, dark as they were, that it was still Weather Armageddon outside. The heads of passers-by were ducked inside collars and the hoods of raincoats, as rain hopped off the metal of automobiles. But watching for lightning, I saw none so it appeared that the main storm had passed.

The adrenalin that had fuelled my survival for the past couple of hours drained away abruptly, to be replaced by a heavy wash of tiredness. If I was to get home without falling asleep on the train, I needed another boost. This was the heart of the Loop district and there was a plethora of Dunkin' Donuts shops within three minutes' walking distance. If I was going to transgress, I thought, I might as well go the whole hog and not stint. It was five minutes after nine so the breakfast rush would be long over. A chocolate doughnut with extra sprinkles and a double espresso should do the trick. But before going out into the deluge, I took my cell out of my purse and tried Daniel's number. It went to voicemail.

I tried to convince myself he had now to be at Holy Angels: he always turned off his cell when he was absorbed.

In the darkest part of the previous night I had pictured my husband mummified in some ICU, horribly disfigured because of a mugging involving a knife. Now, however, I was able to reassure myself that, vast though the numbers of hospital professionals were in the city, he was a famous, even notorious member of their tribe. If he had been carrying no ID or was unable to speak, reason dictated he would have been recognised and someone would have known where he worked or lived. So I would have heard.

I donned my raincoat and, braving the rain, went out to refuel.

By the time I got back to the apartment, my heart was banging in my chest and I had a headache, from fatigue, of course, but also because I'd had a ton of caffeine and sugar since getting out of bed almost six hours previously. As I let myself in, I was jumpy and hyper-aware.

The entrance foyer of the minuscule apartment led directly into the kitchen-diner/living room, so that from the front door, that area was visible. The door to it, though, was closed, which I had never seen before.

Heart beating even faster, I opened it carefully.

Back to me, Daniel was sitting quietly at the table, reading, or reviewing, a set of documents at the side of his plate, on which sat his customary lunch when he took it at home: a cup of Campbell's tomato soup and a self-made sandwich, on white, spread with salted butter from Ireland and crushed banana. It was extraordinary to me that anyone could eat that mishmash, but for his part he could never understand the logic of having jelly and peanut butter on rye, with a can of Dr Pepper's, or even maple syrup with bacon. 'You're back,' he said quietly, without turning around, as though I had merely returned from a trip to the grocery store.

I wanted to explode. My head, filled with relief and anger in equal parts, felt as though it was being tumbled in a cocktail shaker. I needed to think. 'I'm going to the bathroom,' I said, choking on the words as I went past him. Once inside, with the door shut, I turned on the hot faucet, not really knowing why, and let the water run while I stared at my reflection as it dissolved in the rapidly fogging mirror.

I switched on the light to fire the extraction fan, then shut off the faucet, watching my face gradually reappear, outline first, then detail – part of one ear, pearl sunk into the little hollow at its lobe, eyebrows, chin, mouth, nose and eyes – until I was looking at myself, eye sockets darkly shadowed, mouth clamped in a straight line. A lot had happened in the fourteen and a half weeks since I had first seen Daniel Lynch on cable TV, I thought, staring at this less than attractive, dour portrait of myself. I had fallen for Daniel, horribly betrayed my husband, destroyed the joy and hopes of my mother-in-law, got divorced, got remarried, met, it seemed, a goodly proportion of the population of Ireland, or at least some parts of it, a slew of new in-laws, the personality of one being ripe for fictionalising, all the while continuing to look after my dad's temporal needs. And now, this morning, bringing events up to date, I had been offered the first exciting job of my career. Oh – and my husband, calmly sitting a few feet away at our table, had not come home last night.

Some trip. The questions now were, what to do? What to say? How to say it? How to behave? Why was it necessary to feint like this? And yet I knew it was.

For the very first time, I was allowing myself to square up to an inkling about what my life with Daniel Lynch would entail. It would be neither an easy nor a calm ride – the price to be paid, I supposed, for what was arguably the most exciting and passionate relationship I could ever have envisaged. Peter's good sense and placid sensibilities had receded from my consciousness – but there were times, like this one, when I let myself wonder. I had loved Peter Black, but in a very different way.

I hated to admit it so soon but, in contrast to the life I'd led with my second husband, the life I'd had with my first had been a slam dunk. As I watched my face come back into sharper focus, I wondered why I wasn't experiencing profound relief that my husband was *not* floating in the Chicago river or tied to intravenous lines in some intensive care unit. Far from either, there he was, a few feet away, coolly engaged with his spread of documents and his ridiculous lunch, as was normal for him at this time when he was at home. As if nothing untoward had happened. It was understandable that I should be angry, and I was.

Then, through the bathroom door, I heard him call a cheeky 'Goodbye'. He was gone again, dammit, just when I could have done with a good row.

I turned on the shower, setting it at low temperature. I took off my damp pants suit and everything else, left it all in a heap on the tiny floor space and stepped under the cool water.

Chapter Thirteen

Dimly, I became aware of a church bell. It was ringing from somewhere very far off. Oh, God! Was I late picking up my dad to take him to Sunday Mass? Consciousness was slow to crystallise, but as it did, I realised that the ringing was coming from my cell. As I reached for it on the nightstand, it stopped.

I wiped sleep and sweat from my eyes, then looked at the screen. The missed call had been from Daniel. Without thinking, I pressed the callback button. He responded immediately and cheerily: 'Hi there, just wondering if we have any plans for dinner.'

'What time is it?'

'Six thirty.'

I had slept for five hours, I thought, but then, like a returning flood, anger swamped my stomach, overflowed and rose into my chest. I sat bolt upright. 'Where were you last night?'

'Where do you think? I was at work.'

'You didn't consider leaving a note? Answering my calls?' I was clutching my phone as though it was a little javelin.

'My cell was off. I was busy.' His tone was one of patient reason.

'Busy where?'

'Holy Angels. Where else?'

'And when you saw all the missed calls, you couldn't have called me then?'

'I knew about your interview this morning. I didn't want to disturb you – I assumed, quite naturally I think, that you would call me this morning to tell me how you got on.'

'But on my way home I called again and—'

'What's this about, Marian?' he interrupted.

'What this is about,' I raged, 'is that I couldn't sleep last night worrying about you and imagining all kinds of things. I was so wasted when I got up this morning I didn't know my own name, never mind being in good shape for an important interview. I could have blown it!'

'Well, did you?'

'Did I what?'

'Blow the interview?'

'No. I got the job.' I felt deflated. In ordinary circumstances that achievement would have seen me shouting from the rooftops but the good had been taken out of it, as Mom had frequently said about Dad when he objected to some scheme of hers and then gave in. I didn't seem to be getting through to Daniel how upset I'd been by his behaviour, which, at the very least, had been careless.

'That's great, Marian. I knew you would. I have news myself, actually.'

'What is it? What's happened?'

'It can wait. It's kinda mixed. And I'd prefer to tell you face to face. How about you put on one of those silk dresses of yours and I take you somewhere really nice so we can celebrate your new job?'

This was impossible, like fighting with a cloud. If I refused to accept his offer – which might, at a stretch, be seen as an apology of sorts – I could legitimately be accused of sulking, or of being the type to hold a grudge. 'Okay,' I said quietly. 'But it's too hot to dress smart. Can we go somewhere in the neighbourhood, please? I'm still tired and Tommaso's will do fine, for me anyhow.'

'No problem. I'll be home in jig time. I need to shower away the day. And, by the way, congratulations.'

A few minutes later, taking yet another shower, the third in thirteen hours, I let the water run and run in an effort to salve my feelings of dissatisfaction. For sure, our relationship was still new and we had never before had any reason for a knockdown, drag-out fight of serious proportions. But this one had been a doozy and his reaction to it rather disturbing. I was beginning to see how Daniel Lynch, his mom's golden boy, had thus far been able to sail through life, accustomed to valuing only what he chose to value. His commitment to work was uncontestable, the work itself illustrious, but right now I wondered where his marriage figured in the pecking order.

I was just dog-tired, I told myself, so I shouldn't start analysing right now. All this could wait until the spark plugs were firing properly in my addled brain. We were just back from our honeymoon, dammit, brand new to marriage, so there were bound to be glitches and smoothing of rough edges for a while. I also had five years on him and that counted in the maturity stakes.

In addition, I had been married before and was therefore more cognisant of the compromises involved when two people cohabit. He was just a learner, and it would probably take a few more fights for him to grasp that he was no longer an 'oul' bachelor'.

On the plus side, I told myself, he was bloody generous: since we had gotten together, he had not once cavilled about money. He never bothered to suss out what I spent, wouldn't hear of my contributing to the rent – 'It's peanuts. When you get the Pulitzer, we'll reorganise things' – and when I was maxed out on my credit card, he had no problem in giving me his and telling me his PIN.

So he sure was not mean. The diamond on my engagement ring was a hefty solitaire and both wedding bands were platinum – although I'd noticed he didn't wear his much. 'I'm just not used to having anything on my hands, Mar. Even this watch,' he looked disparagingly at his wrist, 'feels like an encumbrance. I'll wear the ring for formal occasions, like if we're going to someone else's wedding, or a dress dance, anything that requires the dreaded tux. Anyway, didn't I wear it all through the trip to Ireland? And isn't it the spirit that counts? It's new-fangled, this thing about men wearing rings. Da never wore one and he and Ma were perfectly happy together until she died. So let's not make a big thing of it, eh?'

I'd been able to find no real answer to that and didn't try.

* * *

I was belting on a pair of jeans over a sleeveless white tee when he came through the door and, as though the fight had never occurred and he had nothing for which to answer, threw his arms around me. 'Great! You're ready! I'm starving. Tommaso's is the right choice. I was just being silly saying we should go posh, because actually I couldn't face fine dining tonight. I couldn't face even the L.'

He let me go and patted my butt. 'Mm-mmm! Nice! Those jeans should be banned.' Then, kicking off his shoes, he went into the bathroom.

* * *

To say I was taken aback by Daniel's 'news' as we settled in at Tommaso's is a serious understatement. We had ordered our food –

a burger each – and when our waiter had left us, taking the menus with him, I sat back in my seat. 'So what's this news you have?'

Calmly, as though I was a patient he didn't want to distress too much, he told me that his dad had been diagnosed with pancreatic cancer.

'Daniel!' I was shocked. That big, warm, handsome man, who had so genuinely welcomed me into his family? 'That's awful. When did it happen? The diagnosis, I mean.'

'Funnily enough, apparently on the day we got married. It was why he didn't come to Shannon to meet us. He was undergoing tests that day and had been kept in overnight.'

'That big party – they *must* all have known in the family, Daniel. Having tests to diagnose cancer is not the kind of thing you can hide – I went through all that with my mom.'

'The story was he was being checked for a duodenal ulcer, and maybe he actually believed that at the time, we'll never know, but Jerry's the only one he told when that proved not to be the case, and he was sworn to secrecy. No one else in the family knew any of it.'

'Not even Eleanor?' It occurred to me that this might explain her strange behaviour towards me. If she'd known, maybe she had fought her father against putting himself through the party, thinking, correctly as it turned out, that it would be too much for him. I mentioned this now but Daniel was having none of it.

'She didn't know. How many times do I have to tell you, Marian? None of us knew, except Jerry.'

The waiter arrived with the hamburgers, and when he had left, Daniel bit into his. When he had swallowed his mouthful, he said, 'Okay? You got it now?'

'Your poor dad.' I was still thinking about him. 'He went through all that organising even though, as a doctor, he must have suspected something major was going on. But, Daniel, he'd had that diagnosis for a *week* and didn't tell you even though you're a medical man too. And the eldest of the family.'

Daniel Senior's son, unlike me, seemed quite calm. What drove these Lynches?

'I know, but that's my da for you, Marian – and as far as Jerry was concerned, that day in Shannon, it was just the ulcer.'

'How did you find out?'

'Eamon rang me this morning.'

'Did you know this when I came home from my interview at lunchtime?'

'I'd just received the call.' He treated me to what I was beginning to know as the Stare. It signified: *Back off!*

'And you were just sitting there,' there was no stopping me now because I was so taken aback, 'eating your lunch and working. Daniel, why didn't you tell me straight away?'

'You didn't seem in the mood for bad news.' He raised a cynical eyebrow. 'You'd stormed out, if you remember.'

'And you were punishing me for that by giving me the silent treatment – by holding on to this devastating news about your dad until now.'

'How dramatic! How very *Femme* of you, Marian! I'm not punishing you. I had a tricky piece of writing to finish before New Orleans.'

'You're going to New Orleans? When? This is ridiculous, Daniel! It's the first I've heard of it.'

'Day after tomorrow, early flight. And, no, it's not the first you've heard of it. I have mentioned it—'

'If you did, fine, I'll let that go – but . . .' I took a deep breath '. . . you have to cancel, honey. *Pancreatic cancer*, Daniel!' Even I knew that the odds of recovering from that were low. 'You're the eldest, you have to go now. Tonight if possible.' Without noticing,

I seemed to have shaken off every last tendril of resentment about my husband's behaviour during the previous twenty-four hours. 'What are we doing here as though nothing's happened?' I seized his hand. 'Can I do anything? And there must be something you can do to postpone that trip. Everyone would understand . . . '

But he frowned and then patiently, as if I were a particularly dense pupil: 'We have a lot riding on this. You should know that. I've told you often enough. For months now we've been very close to a breakthrough with the new vaccine. If you can recall what I said just two nights ago, we've applied for a trial. And all that's missing now is the cash for one last big push. We have meetings set up with three foundations starting with the first one in . . .' he looked at his watch '. . . thirty-four hours' time. They're all small-scale philanthropists, but cash-heavy and looking for places to spend. This is really important to me, Marian, and I would have hoped you'd support me.'

'Of course I do.' I was still finding it difficult to believe that he wouldn't immediately, right this minute, rush to O'Hare. I tried one last time. 'This is your father, Daniel, and here we are, eating hamburgers and going to New Orleans as though nothing's happened.'

'He's not going to die in the next few days, is he? And we're just back from Ireland. We saw him – what was it? – forty-eight hours ago. He was hardly flat on his back. And we do have to eat. And, by the way, what does it matter when exactly I told you? Aren't you being a little unreasonable here?'

'Oh, Daniel.' I looked across the table at the man I loved. Maybe he was in shock. Or suppressing his grief for my sake. 'I'm so sorry, honey,' I said. 'You must feel terrible.'

'Save the psychological insights for your magazine,' he said, 'and, if you don't mind, I will go to New Orleans. And I'll go straight from there to Ireland.' With an expression of distaste, he lifted the top half of the hamburger bun and removed the gherkin. 'I hate pickles,' he said. 'They should know that by now – we've been here often enough.'

'Will you connect through O'Hare?' I wouldn't give up. 'You shouldn't be on your own – I'll go out there tomorrow night and come with you. The hell with Mollie and her magazine.'

'Thanks but no thanks. Anyway, it's easier to connect through London. Direct flights from New Orleans, millions of flights to Dublin from there.' He continued to act as though his dad's lethal illness was an empty tick box on a list. Yet with my own project-management approach to dumping my first husband, who was I to criticise?

His tone softened: 'Look, the timing couldn't be worse, for you too, for both of us. I have to follow through with my job, you have to look to yours or lose it. Based on what you told me, I doubt that dragon would hold it open for you if you abscond again to Ireland having been there for a week just a couple of days ago.

'And of course I'll go, but from New Orleans. I don't know how long I'll be gone, that's *if* my presence is warranted, but medically speaking, based on what Eamon said, I don't think it'll be more than a few weeks.'

He was right about one thing, I thought, and that was Mollie Lehman's reaction if I jumped ship again to go to an Irish funeral. I could already hear the shock-horror in that rasping voice: *You're just back! You haven't even started with* Femme *and now you're going again? Just to be with your husband? Not even for your own father but for his?*

Since I'd been told I had the job, I had been casting around mentally for potential interviewees for my series, and I had to start with a splash so they'd better be pretty top-tier, instantly recognisable, to warrant four thousand words. That might not sound a lot but academic papers, including some of Daniel's, were presented at half that length. And now that I'd calmed down a bit, I really didn't want to let that job go.

'You're a peach, Marian Lescher, do you know that?'

As though he'd heard my thoughts, my husband, with another of those rapid changes of mood, squeezed my hand. 'A lot of women wouldn't understand how important my work is to me. And, lookit, I have a few seminar and conference commitments I've already signed up for over here. Believe it or not, cancer services have been brought up to scratch by the scruff of the neck in Ireland so Dad will be in good hands, and at every opportunity I'll make sure to connect through O'Hare so we can see each other. That's a promise.' He flashed one of those smiles, sunny and charming as all get-out. 'I'll make sure you won't forget me, wife!'

'You're taking your dad's illness very calmly.' Treacherously, in the circumstances, the thought occurred to me that he was being so nice to me because, to quote Mom again, he had once more gotten 'his own way'.

'What else can I do? Jeez, another one.' He removed a second slice of gherkin from under his burger, now half consumed. 'It's inconvenient that I've to go back there again so soon, I know that, but Jerry's doing exams and Aoife's definitely pregnant, Eamon is involved in some huge liquidation thing in Dublin, and Ellie . . .' he hesitated '. . . well, she's Ellie. That leaves only me to offer moral support. He'll be very anxious about the practice – he's old school and so are most of his patients. His partner's good, but a lot of the old-timers insist on seeing him. So I'll really have to step up because, as you so elegantly pointed out, I'm the eldest, the heir apparent. However, as we all know, but are probably afraid to say, it won't be for that long. Doctors make bad patients and he left it too late to do something about what he must have suspected. That's not uncommon. Anyway, he's a very independent man. He won't want mollycoddling so he won't mind if I I'm not there twenty-four/ seven.'

'I'd be climbing the walls.'

'And what use would that be to anyone?'

I gave up, and our meal that evening progressed so quietly even Tommaso noticed. 'Whassa matter, you kids? Cat's got your tongues this evening?'

And when Daniel explained, he brought us two more glasses of wine. 'On da house.'

'Thanks, Tommaso.' My husband waited until we were alone again, then leaned forward. 'By the way, about this new job of yours, I'm asking you for one favour. Stay away from the medical profession. Okay?'

'What? But why, Daniel?'

'Because it would be embarrassing. They're my colleagues and, anyway, it wouldn't do you any good. You'd be leaving yourself open to the accusation of nepotism. You wouldn't want that, now, would you?'

'But, Daniel—'

'Sports stars, media figures – there are other cities within reach. I suppose you can charge travel expenses.' Not waiting for a response, again counting on his fingers: 'Indianapolis, Milwaukee, Madison – plenty of IT specialists there – Minneapolis . . . There's more to Minnesota than the Mayo Clinic in Rochester. See what I mean? Loads and loads of opportunities and interesting people for you to talk to and for these "thinking women" to think about.'

'Are you already making fun of *Femme*?'

'Do you love me, Marian?'

'You know I do – but this is important to me. And this fatwa is a blow. I was actually hoping to ask you if I could go with you to some of your conferences so I could make contacts there – I'm sure other delegates bring their wives. Aren't there dinners?'

'Thanks, Marian. You'll do this one thing I ask, and with what I've shown you, just off the top of my head, I'm sure you can see you won't have any problem. You're a star.' It was as though I hadn't spoken.

* * *

Early the next morning the phone rang. Groggy with sleep, still readjusting to the time differences, I realised it was Daniel's and made the small reach to the other side of the bed and his nightstand. 'Hello?' I croaked, then had to clear my throat. 'Hello?' I said again. For a second or so, there was no response, just the sounds of distant traffic. I cleared my throat again. 'Hello?'

'Hi.' It was a woman. 'That Marian?'

'Yes, but this is Daniel's phone – he's gone out for a run. Who's this? Can I take a message?'

'Sure. Will you tell him Cindy called? You and I met at the hospital but you were with Peter at the time. I just heard about Daniel's dad. I called to say I was sorry for his loss.'

'He's not dead, Cindy, well, not yet. But the news is bad.'

'Oh. I was misinformed. Cancer, is it? How's he doing?'

'Yes, it's cancer. The worst kind, I'm afraid, but Daniel's taking it well, I'd say. Quite calm. Philosophical more than anything else, but it was unexpected. We saw his dad only a few days ago at a party he gave for us in Ireland during our honeymoon and he was in fine form. So I can't say I know him, but he's a nice guy and it's very sad.'

'Big party, huh?'

'Amazing. I'd say more than a hundred people, half of them related to Daniel's family! You ever been to Ireland, Cindy?'

'Not in this life!' Her chuckle was harsh.

'Anyway,' I said, 'I'm sure he'll give you all the details himself. Does he have your number?'

'Yeah. Is he going over to Ireland now to see his dad?'

'Yes, he is. Leaving shortly, I guess. I'll give him your message and I'm sure he'll call you before he goes.'

'And tell him I said there's anything I can do – be sure to say that to him, Marian, yeah?'

'Thanks, Cindy. I'll do that, and thanks for the call. I'm sure he'll appreciate it.' We broke the connection.

I remembered her. Lively, petite, even doll-like, with large blue eyes and, among the bobs, buns, loose French pleats and ponytail hairstyles of the rest of the nurses and other female staff, she'd stood out because hers had been cut half and half, one side shorter than the other, which had been folded over it, like a little white-blonde blanket. It gave her face an arresting, almost angular look, as though she was a subject in a Picasso painting.

And, of course, she had cemented herself into my memory because she had dared to reprimand Daniel that day in the hospital cafeteria. Brave of her, I'd thought at the time, but I guess most of Peter's group, those with whom I was acquainted anyhow, were pretty feisty, Peter being a possible exception. They all knew each other so well, and their jobs were so emotionally difficult that I supposed when they got together they were like a big family, prone to squabbles, as all big families are – or so I'm led to believe.

Dressed and ready for the day, I was pouring coffee for myself when Daniel, hot and sweaty, came back from his run. He was heading directly for the bathroom when I told him, over my shoulder, about the call.

'Cindy? Cindy Kurtz? What did she want? Where did she get your number?'

I was topping my coffee with cream and explained about answering his cell but when he didn't respond I turned – and surprised a look of anger on his face. His voice was even: 'No one answers my phone, Marian, not even you. I don't like it. But maybe it's not your fault. Maybe I should've made that clear.'

'I was half asleep when it sounded and I picked up automatically. Anyway, to get to the point, she called because she'd heard about your dad, but got it a bit wrong, I guess. She seemed to think he was already dead. She's asked you to call her back. I said you would. Was that out of order too?'

'That was why she rang? But, yeah,' he was taking off his trainers, 'I guess the medical profession here is just a big tribe. Nothing said in passing gets left out of the broadcast.'

'She wanted to express sympathy, Daniel. No harm done. Asked me to make sure to tell you that if there was anything she could do . . . Why don't you like her?'

'Who said I don't like her?' He frowned. 'I never said I didn't.'

'Well, it's just your attitude – you don't seem too happy she called.'

'Nothing against her personally,' he growled, 'but I've left that bloody training hospital behind, thank God. You're right, though, it was nice of her to call. As you say, she's well-intentioned so I'll call her later. I'm hungry. Have we eggs?'

'In the refrigerator. Want me to fix—'

'Nah. I'll manage.' He went into the bathroom.

'So what side of the bed did *you* get out of this morning?' I muttered, then remembered I'd have to make allowances. Worry and grief come in different guises to different people. Daniel and I have a lot to learn about each other, I thought, but we'd have a whole lifetime to do it. Right now, I couldn't waste time ruminating: I had to get going on my new job. At the thought, my stomach turned.

Gulping coffee, I took the eggs from the refrigerator and left them on the table, top of the carton open, along with mixing bowl, spatula and his Irish butter beside them, then put two pieces of Wonder bread into the toaster – Daniel always referred to it as 'sliced pan', which I thought very funny.

How do you slice a pan?

With a buzz saw . . .

He was still in the bathroom when I was leaving so I scribbled him a note:

I'll be thinking of you and your dad. Let me know re developments. Should be home late afternoon. Have a good time in New Orleans and don't forget to call Cindy. Love you, your helpmeet – I think! (joke!) Mx

Chapter Fourteen

By the time I got back to the apartment later that morning, Daniel had gone and I didn't hear from him again until, two days later, he Skyped me from Glanmilish House when he got there at around noon Irish time, six a.m. in Chicago. He hadn't called me from New Orleans but that wasn't all that unusual and, of course, he had a great deal on his mind. As it happened, so had I. I was at full throttle, on phone and email, trying to set up my interviews for the first few editions, at least, of *Femme*.

The Skype connection cut out three times, and by the time we had reconnected for the fourth, he was angry and irritably abrupt as he responded to my concerns about him looking after himself: 'You look real tired, Daniel, have you eaten?'

'Don't mother me, Marian!' he snapped. 'I'm fine.'

I took a deep breath. 'So how's your dad doing?'

'He's out riding a bicycle. What do you think, Marian? He has fourth-stage cancer.'

I let that pass. But as the silence continued for thirty seconds, he saw he had stepped over a line. 'Sorry. Look, this isn't working for me. I'll call you again tomorrow, but on the phone. I hate this thing.' He swiped at the little camera at his end, obscuring his image for a second or two. 'I'm wrecked.'

'We'll talk tomorrow, then,' I said quietly. 'Take care of yourself, won't you? And please tell your dad I'm thinking about him and wishing him well.'

'I will,' he said, sounding defeated. Quickly, I cut the link and sat for a few minutes staring at the blank screen.

I was learning very quickly that my husband, gorgeous and sexy though he was, could be a 'handful' – my mother repeating herself. There were times during the honeymoon, for instance, when he hadn't gotten his own way in small things, like him being in a hurry to get to the next relative's house while I insisted on taking advantage of a rare weather clearance to get out of the car for a photo. Or my asking to stop in some town or village because I needed the bathroom. ('For God's sake, Marian, we've only been driving for an hour. You went during our last stop, what's wrong with your bloody bladder?')

The skirmishes – and they were small – were usually short-lived. I found that if I didn't argue, he would, initially with bad grace, give in and then, after another few minutes, it was forgotten. I decided it was part of a natural adjustment to marriage after such a short courtship and that I had been spoiled by Peter's calm equanimity.

The main attractions of my husband remained undiminished – the sex, of course, but also his sharp intelligence. When he was on form, even cynical or critical of colleagues, many of whom, in his opinion, were not up to his standards, his words were magnetic, his knowledge formidable about all sorts of eclectic subjects.

Although I was wont to blab on about my own parents, upbringing and early life, and was avid to know everything about

Glanmilish and his formative life with his family, he did not reciprocate ('I'm not one of your interview subjects, Marian. I'd hope we've moved on from there') and would change the subject. That served merely to increase my curiosity. He had introduced me to all and sundry when we were in Ireland so I didn't believe he was deliberately hiding anything, but where this new husband of mine was concerned, I was learning the truth of the old saying that information is power and to withhold it is more powerful still. With the exception of my life with Peter, of relatively recent vintage, he had shown very little interest in my past. And even where Peter was concerned, with the exception of a few minor flurries, he hadn't trespassed in the way some other men might – 'Is he better than me in the sack?' – but I guess Daniel Lynch felt pretty secure on that score and with good reason.

His approach to asking about my first marriage was subtle, more a tone of voice than any actual question. 'You told me Peter introduced you to Mozart,' he said one evening, while we were watching the TV news. 'Why would he have done that, d'you think?'

The question sounds innocuous, and perhaps it's silly to bring it up. However, because of the way in which he asked, I felt obliged to defend a long-dead composer, who needed no defence, my first husband, who didn't either, and myself. Did he believe I didn't deserve to be musically educated? I replied carefully: 'I'm a musical dunce, honey, or was, but I'm always eager to find out about new things. And Peter, if you really want to know, was like that too, anxious to learn—'

'And I'm not?' he had interrupted.

'Of course you are, honey. I didn't mean anything like that. Your work, your whole life is spent trying to find solutions and to learn new things . . .'

Trying to explain this now is like trying to grasp a handful of air.

And later that night, as I tried to figure out this latest little kink in the way we related to each other, something about it had reminded me of Peter's slumped, defeated shoulders as he walked away from me for ever in that glistening cathedral of medicine.

I have a ragbag brain, common in writers and journalists. We tend to store seemingly irrelevant snippets of information that would speed through the attention span of most people. I had watched Woody Allen's *Hannah and Her Sisters* several times and various snippets of dialogue in it had lodged in my mind. While I was mulling over Daniel's quirks, I remembered a phrase used about Hannah, played by Mia Farrow, describing her personality as 'passive aggressive', and had decided that this was a useful trait I could watch out for when interviewing someone (not that I would use the phrase, but if I could report casually on a particular behavioural tic or attitude in my subject, I could alert readers to it).

That morning, after Daniel's Skype call, I sat back on the bed, opened my laptop and, to refresh my memory, typed 'How to spot passive aggression' into the search engine. Much of the information the question evoked was entirely irrelevant to what I was trying to formulate about my husband, but two phrases that popped up, 'off balance' and 'silent treatment', struck a chord in me. Did my husband, subconsciously or otherwise, like to keep me off balance? He certainly believed in the silent treatment.

So what? asked the little voice at the back of my brain. *You chose him.*

I had indeed. And when I looked at him sometimes, while he was absorbed in a book or working on his papers, I still felt like pinching myself. Flaws notwithstanding – who didn't have them? – how had I landed such an interesting, handsome and extraordinary person?

In any event, life with Daniel would never, ever be boring. And I'm almost embarrassed to mention the next thing because it seems so shallow, but what had grabbed me from the very start, even through the medium of a TV camera, was that whiff of danger, the nakedly carnal aura he gave off. It still held me and, I was sure, would bind us until one of us died.

I closed the laptop.

* * *

Over the next few days I started to find my feet at *Femme*. After all the scrabbling around in the solitary work-world of the freelancer, I already loved my job – *loved* it – not least because I had colleagues now, and the atmosphere around the office was one of exhilarating collegiality. We were all pushing a start-up, everyone determined to play a part in the success of our effort.

Mollie, along with her backers in the new venture, had not scrimped either: there was decent square footage for each of us individually in our open-plan, rather elegant office, with a separate desk for everyone, each with a shiny new iMac. We had a small kitchen, with fridge, sink, microwave oven and Mr Coffee machine, and off it, not just a decent, well-lit powder room but, joy of joys, a spacious walk-in power-shower, with lockers and two hairdryers. Rather than continue to use the diminutive bathroom in the apartment, I took to arriving before the others to shower at work. Bliss.

As well as Mollie herself and her Japanese deputy, Ryoko, who was equally terrifying, on the journalism side we had two good all-rounders, graduates from Columbia and Northwestern, an issue-driven bluestocking from Brown, an Englishwoman with a doctorate in literature from Oxford, whose brief was wide but mainly in the arts and literature, and a generalist, a friend of Mollie's, headhunted from *Ebony*, which was also based in Chicago. There was a social diarist: 'We mustn't forget the city socialites, people!' Mollie glanced around us all: 'We might think we're above them, but remember, their dollars are as good as anyone else's and we are going to have picture pages. And as for photographers, you ask,' none of us had, 'we'll be working with freelancers.'

And then there was me, expected to blow everyone away with my insightful interviews.

With publication just three months off, the first of our meetings was a general one, attended by all. We journalists, the show ponies of the outfit, were ordered to get ahead by six weeks to facilitate the publishing schedule. So, with one piece to run on P-day, I had to have six of my interviews ready within that time. 'More if you can, Marian,' Mollie dictated, 'and, by the way, I don't see why not.'

Additionally, keeping the rest of us on our toes, we had two highly ambitious young interns, with our boss making no secret of the fact that they could compete on equal terms for space in the magazine. 'Everyone, and I mean *everyone*, is on probation here and has to earn her place. Sorry, Larry.' She grinned at our beardie, the chief sub-editor and the only male on the staff, big, grumpy and wheezy from too many cigarettes, but very good at his job. 'You know what I mean.'

We had two other subs, one of whom also had the job of fact-checker. We had a designer, a graphic artist, a marketer and her assistant, four advertising 'executives', a secretary, whom Mollie and Ryoko shared, and two sales staff. There was a temporary hire, a PRO, whose job was simply to get us as many publicity opportunities as possible and on the public's radar. We had a financial controller and, last, a very nice, rather matronly receptionist named Cherry to whom I took instantly and who, by sleight of hand it appeared, seemed able accurately to supply us all with our individual choices of lunch sandwiches without writing them down. 'I've been a waitress all my life. This, ladies, is a no-brainer.' We were expected to take lunch at our desks unless we were out on a job.

As she wrapped up that meeting, Mollie's smile as she looked around the room, taking in all of us, reminded me of Kaa, the treacherous Indian python in the Disney version of *The Jungle Book*. It didn't affect me all that much because, after my first few days in the office, I was confident that the list of seventeen possible interview subjects I had submitted was pretty strong and, despite my patchy CV, I felt I could deliver at least ten of them, even if I was aiming a little high with my 'top four', as I had labelled them. I knew that every other hack and hackette in the US, and possibly the world, had them on his or her list too.

Mollie had taken a hand in making the initial cold calls on my behalf (she was doing the same for everyone, journalists and salespeople). She was the one who trailed a sky-high reputation for turning failing publications around. This start-up was her first foray into Chicago, and while distribution would be initially in the Midwest, the plan was to extend to other regions and, all going well, nationwide. So everyone in the trade was watching what she'd do and how, as were those who courted publicity and their handlers.

It was only as I watched her in action that I could see what a privilege she'd accorded me in asking me to work on the magazine – and it was largely due to Daniel: I'd had calls from other publications on foot of that *Tribune* interview – journalism likes new names – and had been considering their offers when *Femme* came along. That had proved too exciting to turn down.

I followed up on Mollie's calls, and by the time of that first meeting, I had contacted those 'people' surrounding ten of those on my list, including the top four. To my secret astonishment – and thanks largely to our editor as way-maker – none had summarily rejected the overture.

We were pitching *Femme* as a different type of women's magazine: 'Think *Vanity Fair* crossed with the *New York Times*.' Our boss had hammered home that message, not only to everyone's 'people' including those of my personal top four (Tim Cook, CEO of Apple, Oprah Winfrey, Tina Fey and Michelle Obama, the last three of whom had Chicago connections) but she had made sure everyone at the magazine was on message.

Having perused my list and my progress so far, she said in the meeting that if I landed all of the top four for our first four editions, I could expect a raise. 'But no cut-and-paste, ya hear? We're lookin' for somethin' way, *way* beyond that lazy shit!' Conscious of a few hard stares from around the table, I blushed.

Realistically, she and I were hopeful of snagging at least two of the top four. It does happen, and sometimes for the most unexpected reasons, including the way you ask. I've found that the high achievers, who no longer feel they have to throw their weight around, are the most amenable.

As it turned out, even in the short time I was to spend at *Femme*, the editor, despite her biting manner, proved a good influence on me. She seemed to sense that, while money mattered to me, it was the work, its standards and quality that really drove me.

It would be pushing things too far to say she was inspirational, although in a way she was. She didn't treat me, or any of us, as anything approaching her equal, and certainly believed in an equality of disdain. However, I intuited early on that, while she would probably continue to make things uncomfortable for us all, she would stretch our capabilities and not just mine. Second best was not enough for her.

With Daniel absent, I could concentrate solely on work. That doesn't mean I didn't miss him, I sure did, but for those first weeks prior to the launch, I worked very hard, wheedling and schmoozing for a 'yes' with potential subjects, then researching as though they had already agreed. I found that our hired-in PRO was doing her job effectively in that we were already attracting interest. Mollie was appearing on all the local chat shows, giving pithy, acerbic quotes to gossip columnists, and there was even talk of her getting a slot on *The Today Show* on launch day.

Anyhow, within ten days after that first big meeting, I already had two profiles in the bag, ready for Mollie, the fact-checker and the subs.

The first profiled a nun who had worked, unheralded, around the drug dens and homeless shelters in deprived areas of the city for most of her life and was now approaching her eightieth birthday. The second concerned a rising star in the IT world: he had just sold his start-up into Silicon Valley and, at the age of twenty-two, had become an overnight multi-millionaire. News of his ascent had appeared in newspapers but he had not given any interviews and had agreed to talk to me because he had attended my high school and his sister had been in my class at Elementary. Of such small coincidences are journalistic opportunities mined. We don't hold back on using any contacts, no matter how tenuous or long lost. I enjoyed the hunt.

There was a personal aspect to my life, though, that I simply could not keep at bay, and even with Daniel absent, the ticking of my pesky biological clock continued insistently to rise in volume. It was a sound I had yet to discuss with Daniel – I suppose, if I'm honest, sex for its own sake was so exciting that I didn't want to wreck the buzz by reducing it to numbers, as I had during the last months of my sex life, comparably muted as that had been, with Peter.

Also, I hadn't broached the subject because I didn't know yet how my new husband would take it. So, for the moment I continued to allow the protection and left the thermometers and charts to mutter to themselves at the bottom of one of the bags I had moved into his apartment. That overactive Catholic conscience was also at work: had I been dishonest in not revealing my longing for a baby before Daniel and I married? He had never mentioned kids.

One evening, physically sated after an afternoon of wonderfully fulfilling activity in our bed during one of his 'transit visits' between Ireland and a conference venue (I'd told colleagues I was 'researching at home'), we were munching takeaway pizza. Perhaps this might be a good time to bring it up, I thought. It was just after five thirty and he had to leave in less than a half-hour for O'Hare and a nine-thirty flight to Cleveland. Although he was relaxed, the time window was small.

'Daniel,' I began, 'there's something I'd like to discuss with—'

His cell pinged. 'Hold that thought, Mar.' He picked it up and examined the screen. 'It's from Ireland,' he said slowly. 'It's Ellie. She never calls and it's almost midnight over there. I have to take this, OK?'

And so I was privy to the news that his dad had slipped into a coma, was in the ICU of a Dublin hospital and, according to his sister, was not expected to survive the next forty-eight hours.

With exquisite timing, my own phone buzzed while he was talking to his sister – or, rather, listening to her: we were so close to each other I could hear her voice and, although I couldn't make out what she was saying, she was clearly yelling.

I picked up my own phone: *number withheld.* Journalists, especially freelancers, cannot afford to be pernickety or lofty about this, and although I don't like it I always pick up.

The caller was one of Tim Cook's associates, although I didn't immediately catch the name. The instant I heard 'Tim Cook' and 'Apple', everything else faded.

I sat up straight. The corporation, the woman said, *might* be interested in my 'project' for the new magazine but would insist that it should be in the first edition (that meant for the launch, gaining potentially maximum attention). 'Tim', the woman said, would be in Chicago sometime in the next couple of weeks. In the meantime, if I could come out to Cupertino at my earliest convenience, we could all discuss the 'necessary parameters'. 'He is interested,' I was told, 'but we'll want him to be on the cover.'

I managed to prevent the words 'Will Tim be there himself?' popping out of my mouth as I scrabbled for a ballpoint in the drawer of my nightstand. Instead I said, airily, 'Oh, I'm sure that'll be fine. I'll get back to you tomorrow morning.'

'Tonight would be better. What time do you guys have there? About five forty-five?'

'That's right,' I said, hoping against hope that the boss would still be in the office. As yet, none of us journos had her cell phone or home number. 'I'll check in with my editor and call you within the hour so we can make arrangements.' Then, ballpoint poised over the inside of my left wrist, 'Could I have a direct number for you, please? And I didn't quite catch your name.' I inscribed both, thanked her and we clicked off. I looked at Daniel, who was holding his cell inches from his face as his sister's voice continued to issue forth.

Yes. Timing is everything.

Chapter Fifteen

Daniel was as good as his word about a 'proper' honeymoon, although its provenance was not that romantic! Just three weeks after his dad's funeral, we picked up an RV, in the town of Great Falls, Montana. It was emblazoned with technicolour lettering advertising the rental company, and all over its rear, a huge, three-times life-sized picture of two kids, boy and girl, joyously waving. I had been a little surprised that we had taken this vacation so soon after his dad's death, but Daniel's attitude was: 'Life is for living, Marian.'

Although we were due to take just a week in Glacier National Park, entering through its west entrance, we had provisioned the vehicle for at least ten days. The area was huge and patrols scanty. All the literature had emphasised that we had now entered a remote wilderness area with minimal network coverage, usually none at all, and had counselled we should be prepared for all emergencies, including carrying food and water for three days more than we planned to stay.

Our stratagem was to take full advantage of this rare opportunity and to wander at will, crossing into its Canadian area if we had time, gradually making our way towards the east entrance and to spend our last night in the campground at St Mary.

How had we come to be there?

It's a long story but I'll summarise.

Daniel had boarded his flight to Cleveland that evening when we had both taken calls, he from his sister, I from Cupertino, but next day, having given his conference address in the afternoon, he flew to London, thence to Dublin, but found his father had died while he was in Ohio. In Glanmilish, they postponed his dad's 'removal', as they called it over there, from his home to the church, until he arrived. The service was set for the following morning. And while I felt guilty that I wasn't with him, I did ask myself if he would cancel one of his trips to look after me if I fell ill. He was more focused on work than anyone else I'd ever encountered.

Best not to go there, I thought. We had vowed to take care of each other 'for better for worse' – or had we? Had that been Peter?

So, when I'd called the magazine, Mollie had been still in her office, but when I'd attempted to raise the subject of another trip to Ireland, she'd refused to countenance any talk of my going to the funeral. And, of course, she was delighted about Tim Cook: 'They called? That was quick,' immediately sanctioning the trip to Cupertino. 'We gotta strike before they change their minds, hon, so call them back, then call the airport, see if there's a red-eye tonight. Put everything on your credit card. Don't know about Cook as a cover, though – this is a women's magazine – but don't tell 'em that right now. Fudge it. What can they do if we already have the interview? You can definitely tell 'em we'll use him in the launch edition.'

When I relayed all this to Daniel, he understood immediately. Although I was a little put out that he wasn't begging his wife to be with him at such a sad time, this was what my mom would have called 'contrary': I guess the words 'pot' and 'kettle' came to his mind as they had to mine.

Ironically, by the time I had returned Apple's call, Tim's 'people' had changed their minds about my coming out to Cupertino. They'd had a chat and it had been decided that a 'face' was not necessary, that we could negotiate by phone and email.

Then . . .

When Daniel came back to Chicago after the obsequies for his father, he dropped a bombshell. Within minutes of his arriving home, he told me we were moving to Ireland, he to take up his dad's practice, I to do— 'What exactly, Daniel?' I interrupted, but faintly: I just couldn't believe this. It was off the scale. 'I've just started a new career. I really like it. I've an interview with Tim Cook lined up, possibly, for next week, if the man is in Chicago. When do you see this move happening? Is it not to be a subject for discussion?'

That had brought on one of those one-sided lengthy special pleadings into which it was impossible to break because he was speaking so fast: 'We're discussing it now, aren't we? It's the age of the internet, email and the mobile phone, for God's sake. *Femme* magazine can take your articles from anywhere, even Ireland. There are important people there and more important people passing through, even Hillary – she visits frequently – and we've had Barack, and he said he'd come back, and apparently Gerry Adams is really big with Americans.

'Anyway, Dublin's only an hour from London, an hour and a half from other European capitals. You'll have no shortage of people to interview. This rag of yours purports to be for the thinking woman, isn't that right? There's a lot of thinking people in Europe, you know – I'll help you do a list. You want me to meet this dragon, explain the situation?'

At last he stopped for breath. I looked at him. The thought of an encounter between Mollie Lehman and Daniel Lynch was almost funny, especially if he was explaining that I was to tag along with him and he'd sort me out with Important Europeans. The earth would move, and not in a good way.

'Have you forgotten I have to look after my dad?' I asked. 'What about him? Whatever about my job, I certainly can't just leave him. Not now. Please understand that. Who'd look after him? He would have to be placed in a facility and we can't afford that.'

'He has Blue Cross on top of his social security. We pay enough for it.'

'Come on!' I almost laughed. 'You can't be serious – for God's sake, you of all people, a medical professional. We're having to supplement for his meds even as it is, and the last time he was in the ER, they couldn't wait to discharge him.'

I changed my tone, became conciliatory. 'You know I'm talking sense, honey. For me, this is not just out of the blue, it's absolutely out of the question. It's not long since you thought you might want the two of us to join Doctors Without Borders and go out to do field trials in some Godforsaken place in the African desert or somewhere – remember?'

We went round the houses like that for two whole days, on the phone and at home, I resisting the move, he finally accepting that I would have to stay to look after Dad, while insisting that he would go to Ireland because the Skype-and-transit routine had worked fine for us the last time. 'I know that on paper it doesn't look great, Mar, but other couples do it.'

'What other couples? Name two.'

'Film stars . . .' He couldn't do any better than that, of course: we were both so busy we didn't do couple-on-couple socialising. In fact, still in the first embrace of a ravishing sex life, we did little socialising of any consequence.

I lost the main argument, but the eventual compromise was that we would set up additional care for Dad for a week and the two of us would take a seven-day honeymoon before Daniel left for Ireland. It was I who had proposed a trip – in the abstract – to be taken before he had to leave, and I had been agreeably surprised that, without too much resistance, he had consented. I left it to him to make the arrangements, while I accelerated my work rate to the extent that, having actually met the impressive Tim Cook (business acumen to burn, positive attitude to work-life balance), by the time we left, barely a week after Daniel had come home, I had completed the piece and two others, so Mollie couldn't complain.

As she had warned me previously, Cook's wasn't to be the cover piece (that honour had been accorded to Hillary, profiled by our editor-in-chief herself), and I wasn't looking forward to conveying that information to Cupertino, but it was to be strapped – given an advertising banner complete with thumbnail photo. I had poured every ounce of insight and previous experience into writing all three pieces.

Daniel and I differed on our choice of holiday location. Whereas I had envisaged us lolling about someplace like Hawaii, he had come up with Glacier National Park in Montana: 'I've been in the US for years, Mar, and all my travel's been work-related and to cities. Maybe, I thought, it's time I saw a bit of the country.'

So, with three pieces delivered and six weeks still to go to launch, a further two interviewees confirmed for the week after I got back and Michelle Obama considering, my editor admitted she couldn't complain, although not in so many words. She did go through the motions of being exasperated, but this time, confident of the quality of my work, I argued, 'It's only a week, Mollie. I'm tired, I need to recharge, and I'll come back all fired up to hit the ground running. You have to admit that at the very least I'm pretty well organised.'

She did. Sort of.

Montana is not an easy place to get to, and as Daniel and I boarded our flight from O'Hare, the first of a sequence, I resolved to wipe everything and everyone to do with work from my consciousness for the duration.

For his part, the venue having been his choice, my husband was forced to accept all the warnings in the literature that cell coverage in Glacier National Park was patchy at best but overwhelmingly non-existent.

We had a truly memorable week. As only to be expected, there was lots of sex, but the experience itself withstands adequate description, and I defy anyone with half a soul to resist Glacier's magic. Unlike Yellowstone and Yosemite, which, I have gathered from those who have been there, are far more highly populated, especially in the summer, during our time at Glacier, we rarely encountered, or even saw, another human being.

We rose with the dawn, went to bed at sunset and, in between, travelled through monumental vistas of mountains, tumbling rivers and pristine lakes, of plains undulating with grasses, and all under a sky so vast it seemed physically to shrink us.

In the past, the slogan engraved on Montana state vehicle licence plates had been 'Big Sky'; by the time we got there it had been changed to 'Treasure State', reflecting its abundant mineral reserves and gemstones, including amethysts and sapphires. But as an instant description of the most relevant attribute the state enjoys, the former is by far the most appropriate for any licence plate I've ever seen.

It's all very well to try to describe Glacier, but to be as wonderstruck as I was, I think you have to be physically there, with soft wind on your skin, the sudden cry of a bird in your ear, those ever-present Rocky Mountain peaks jagging the western line of that sky. Regardless of how skilled they are, no cinematographer can do justice to the overall package, that sky, the variety and beauty of the landscape, its sheer scale – at the risk of sounding Californian, the *awesomeness* of it all.

We saw a couple of black bears, a lot of big-horned sheep, hawks and majestic eagles riding the thermals – and while eating lunch one day on the stoop of the van, we caught a brief glimpse of a lynx in the distance. The sense throughout was of space, light and emptiness, but you always knew you were sharing it with creatures perhaps just feet or even inches away in the grass or behind a rock nearby.

Many times, we halted the RV right in the middle of one of the roadways to take a photo or just because there was no other traffic and we could. This Eden was ours alone.

And when it came to our second last day and Going-To-The-Sun Road, aptly named by the resident Native American Blackfoot tribe, what can I say? RVs are banned now, but on a little red bus, which took a few of us up there, even the Japanese on board employed the pause buttons on their video cameras, tablets and smartphones. And as we came off the bus back at St Mary campsite, our last stop of the whole trip, one of the two Japanese women on board tapped her chest and said to me, in English, 'Too much beauty. I have pain in my heart.'

We exceeded even that experience later that same day as we drove the RV into the park again. We stopped for coffee on one of the flatter, plains-like areas and were eating our sandwiches, scrunched together on the steps of the van, when Daniel suddenly grabbed my arm. 'Ssh!' he whispered urgently. 'Don't move, look straight ahead . . . ' He nodded almost imperceptibly towards the sea of tall, sere vegetation in front of us.

There it was, a grizzly, unmistakable, and only about thirty feet from where we sat. We hadn't noticed it when we pulled in because it had been foraging, head down, back camouflaged by the grasses. It had now raised its muzzle to the sky, sniffing the air – the day was so still we could hear the snuffles. And then, a sight I will carry with me for the rest of my life: it heaved itself to its full height, slowly swinging its head, scanning from right to left, and saw us.

It was so close I could see the movement of its eyes, small in relation to that massive head and, under the thick fur, could even make out a slight flicking of the ears. I had to resist the urge to go right over and pet that animal as though it were a very big dog. Perhaps sensing this, Daniel, still holding my arm, tightened his grip so it hurt a little, and I could feel the fast beat of his pulse.

For perhaps thirty seconds, that bear continued to stand, eyeballing us, front paws hanging like hog hams in front of its chest. Then it gave its great head a little shake, as though to dislodge some irritant, glanced again at us, almost disparagingly – *they're not worth the trouble* – dropped to all fours and more or less vanished back into the camouflage of the vegetation, although now that we knew it was there, we could make out the curve of its back.

'Did that really happen?' I asked, voice hoarse, when we were safely back in the van with the door closed. But I needed the bathroom, and while my husband sat in the captain's chair on the driver's side, I skipped like a child down the aisle. I, Marian Lescher, daughter of Bill and Maureen Lescher from the city of Chicago, had had a close encounter with one of nature's giants.

I was still jubilant when I got back to the front of the RV and, instead of sitting directly into my seat, threw my arms around my husband from behind, chair and all. 'Oh, Daniel! Wasn't that just wonderful? Can you actually believe it?' In my enthusiasm I dislodged his cell, which was in the breast pocket of his sport shirt. 'Oops! Sorry.' I caught it just before it fell to the floor of the camper and saw the screen was lit. 'Hey! Look!' I said excitedly. 'We have coverage here. Someone's called you and got through.' I held it out to him.

He took it, almost snatching, then peered at the screen. 'Shit!' he said, under his breath.

'Who is it?'

'Private number,' he muttered. 'I really hate that. Get belted up, Marian. The sun's going down and I don't want to be driving this trail in the dark.'

'Who do you think it was?'

'I said it was a private number, Marian. Are you deaf?'

But I was high on adrenalin, serotonin and every happiness-inducing hormone on the spectrum, and before sitting down, again I wrapped my arms, this time even more tightly, around him, nuzzling his neck. 'Oh, Daniel. It won't take long. Let's make love right here, right now. Let's make a—'

Roughly, he detached my hands. 'Did you not hear me? Sit *down*, dammit! It'll be dark in half an hour.'

Dismayed, feeling foolish now, even a little resentful, I did as he asked. I had been about to ask that we make a baby, right here, right now, because on that day of all days, our last full one there after such a wonderful week, we'd had such an extraordinary experience together. Apart from a few small spats of no significance, we had coasted easily in each other's company, so to me, this had been a Heaven-sent opportunity to ditch the Durex and make a start on our family. It had even flashed through my mind how great it would be to tell the kid, when it was old enough, where and how its life had begun and in what circumstances. I could see its thirteen-year-old face, eyes wide: 'Mom! I don't believe it! You're makin' it up – a real live grizzly bear? Right there? Standin' up?'

I fastened my belt, my seat rocking from side to side while he, again muttering under his breath, manoeuvred the unwieldy vehicle forwards and backwards, making a difficult U-turn on the narrow track. It sported giant mirrors but no rear window. I glanced across at him. His expression was grim as he checked each mirror over and over and then, finally straightening us out, set off, too fast, in my opinion, staring ahead through the dusty, insect-encrusted windshield. I decided it mightn't be diplomatic to say anything about his speed, but I was puzzled by his reaction to the call. 'What's the matter? Were you expecting a call, Daniel?'

'Oh, God, here we go again. The third fucking degree!'

I shut up. I refused to let him take me down from my high – even though his *volte-face* was inexplicable. During our vacation, we had made love almost as frequently as we had eaten breakfast and dinner, even once, at lunchtime, in the open, by the side of a cobalt-coloured lake. What had happened to make him close up like that when all I'd wanted, initially anyway, had been a hug?

As the van trundled noisily along the rough trail, crockery and cutlery rattling loudly behind us and the door of the shower cubicle banging to and fro, I reeled back in my mind, trying to figure out if anything I had said or done might have caused his mood-change but could find nothing. He'd seemed to be just as taken by the encounter with the bear as I was. In fact, he'd been the one who had pointed it out.

It had to have been that bloody call. Instant communication and a permanent state of being accessible, I decided, was the curse of modern civilisation. It's not a new complaint but, having experienced the profound quiet of Glacier, I now understood it. *Screw it*, I thought, and, determined not to let that blot diminish the whole experience for me, stared through the window on my side of the RV and didn't open my mouth for at least a quarter-hour.

But I couldn't stand it, and in a conciliatory tone: 'Hey, honey? I notice you're not using the cell cover I bought for you.'

'I apologise,' he said, sarcasm dripping from his tongue. 'The reason it's not on the mobile right this minute is that it's too big and awkward to fit into the pocket of this shirt. I'll put it back on the bloody phone the very minute we get home if it means that much to you.'

'I was only making conversation.' I hesitated. 'What's wrong?'

'There's nothing wrong. I'm simply trying to get us to the campsite before dark.'

'What are you thinking about, then? Something's definitely changed. You were in fine form when we saw that bear, but the minute we got back into the van and that call—'

'*What are you thinking about?*' he mimicked. 'Why do women always ask that?'

Bent on sorting out the spat, I ignored that. 'You're real tense, honey. Please talk to me.'

'Dear God in Heaven! Will you stop nagging, please? I'm not tense. I'm just fucking driving!'

I gave up and we spent the rest of the journey in silence. I had judged the cell cover to be a relatively safe topic of conversation, a passage back to marital harmony. I had bought it for him. A horrendously ugly object sporting masses of little rubber bobbles, I had chosen it because he was always dropping his phone, or it was falling out of his pants pocket. 'They use these cases on construction sites,' I'd said, when I'd handed it over, 'and it's waterproof. You can dive with it to forty feet and still make a call when you get back to the surface.'

'Thanks, Mar, but I don't dive.'

For someone so clever, Daniel could be dense. 'I know that, for God's sake, honey! I'm just telling you so you'll appreciate that this wasn't bought in Target or Wal-Mart. This is high-end gear. It would survive a nuclear explosion.'

'Oh! Really? That's good. Thanks. It's lovely. Thanks, Mar.'

'I made that last bit up . . .'

The silence in the RV lasted until we got back to the St Mary campsite, grassy and sloping, with a high mountain ridge to the east. He pulled up at the reception office to collect our bill for next morning, but before he killed the engine, he looked across at me. 'Sorry, Mar. I'm sorry. I'm just a bit grumpy, that's all. I'm not one for psychoanalysing myself but I suppose I hate that the holiday's over. Am I forgiven?'

'Of course you are,' I said, and meant it. I still wanted to query the mood-change, but knew better than to ask right then. After he had parked up and gone into the office, the niggle remained, but I knew it would be fruitless to pursue it any further. He had made an apology and I had accepted it, so the accusation of nagging would be justified if I kept on at him, especially when it had been only a small glitch set against a perfect week. And we still had the night to come. I shivered in anticipation.

My libido, curled up like a caged dormouse for decades of my life, had been liberated by this man; my physical desire for him was now, it appeared, limitless. I sure was lucky, I thought, seeing him come back, the setting sun lighting his dark hair, which he wore unfashionably long. For about the millionth time, I asked silently how the hell someone like me had gotten to marry someone so physically attractive.

Sometimes, though, deep in some secret place of my psyche, I continued to wonder if I would ever fully relax with him.

Chapter Sixteen

On our last morning in Montana, I woke in the position in which I had fallen asleep, head and knees hard against the van wall. Daniel was a bed-hogger. A spread-eagler.

Our vehicle had been given a north–south pitch, and as I sat up to peer through the east-facing bedroom window, I could see that there had been quite a bit of rain during the night but that right now, in the mid-distance, with the sun rising behind them, as it had for millions of years, the mountain peaks rejoicing in the names Single-shot, East Flat-top and Red Eagle stood in dark, ragged relief against an exuberant sky painted in an array of colours – salmon, peach, coral and tangerine.

I glanced down the aisle. Daniel, his back to me, a cup of tea in his hand and wearing only his boxers, was standing in the open doorway holding his face up to the brightness. There was an unusual stillness about him and I didn't want to disturb him so I lay down again, making a big, stretchy X with my arms and legs, luxuriating in having the length and breadth of the big bed all to myself.

St Mary, one of the very few campsites inside the boundaries of Glacier to offer hook-ups – to preserve the 'pristine wilderness experience' within the park – had been a godsend after a week of washing only with a damp cloth, dipping toothbrushes into an inch of our precious water supply and cleaning tableware and cutlery with paper towels.

At St Mary, we could empty our 'dirty' tank, take long, hot showers and have all the water and power we needed to clean the interior, then wash off the dust and the carpet of small dead creatures from the vehicle's mirrors and grille. *Return it clean, or pay for cleaning* was one of the provisions of our contract with the rental company.

And as there had been virtually no network coverage for almost all of the wilderness trip, it seemed odd to have my cell ping with four messages, two hang-ups from *Femme's* number, two from – who else? – Mollie Lehman, who wanted to talk to me about queries from my Cook piece, which was on the subs' desk. 'For God's sake, Marian, they've been trying to contact you for hours. Have you fallen off the fucking planet?'

Then, a half-hour later: 'Forget it, Marian. It's dealt with. Don't blame anyone but yourself if you don't like what they've done.'

The previous evening, before it had gotten completely dark, we had spent some time cleaning parts of the exterior, then a half-hour packing, not a huge task since we had travelled light. All that remained, prior to the arduous return journey to Chicago, was to complete both tasks.

And then what?

I still hadn't told Mollie about the planned move to Ireland.

In a way, I thought now, staring at the ceiling, the vacation had indeed been our real honeymoon. Although I had enjoyed the one in Ireland, it had been so exhaustingly social, memory had mushed it all into a loud carousel of volubility and changing faces, with the odd glimpse of sodden scenery thrown in.

I raised my head to look down the aisle again. My husband was still contemplating the rapidly brightening dawn sky, so I got up and went into the shower, loving again the comfort and luxury of having the pressure of hot water over my head.

The towels we had rented from the RV company lay in a damp, threadbare heap on the floor outside the shower cabin. I did not fancy using any of them on my nice, warm body so I stepped over them and put my nightgown back on. I was planning to dump it: it was old, the cotton had worn thin, and as sleepwear, it was uncomfortably short, tending to ride up during the night.

I went to join Daniel, still in the open doorway, sipping what I presumed was tea. 'Morning!' he said quietly, without turning around, so I stood just behind his shoulder, having to shade my eyes with both hands against the brightness, the sun's disc now glaring from between two of the mountain peaks, bringing into high relief many of the individual rocks, painting them with hues of rose gold.

'Do you think we'll ever come back here, Daniel?'

'Who knows? Who ever knows anything in this world?'

'Very deep.'

'Thanks! By the way, the guy in the office has recommended a restaurant for our last dinner tonight in Great Falls. I've booked it for eight o'clock so make sure to put on the old glad rags, OK?'

'I don't have glad rags with me.' I was still standing behind him.

'Well, just put on the best you have.' He took a last look at the sky, then turned to come inside. 'Jesus!' His expression froze.

'What?' I looked over my shoulder to see what had frightened him. '*What*, Daniel? Oh, God – is it a rat? I can't see anything.' I glanced back at him.

He was still staring. 'It's you.'

'What's wrong with me?' Looking down I saw that quite a lot of me was showing through the thin, worn cotton as it clung to the damp skin of my breasts, stomach and upper thighs.

I tugged at the garment but he grabbed my hand and wrenched it away. 'No! Leave it.' He reached with his free hand to cup one of the breasts to which the fabric, despite my efforts to pull it off, had stuck. 'Daniel! People'll see. And we've a lot to do.'

'There's no one around. And we've plenty of time.'

'Give me a break – I've just had my shower!' I tend to be goal-oriented and my concentration was now on getting to Great Falls, but those treacherous ripples were already in play as, seizing my shoulders, he began walking me, bare torso to damp one, backwards into the body of the van, then down the short aisle. When the back of my legs hit the bedframe he let me go briefly, pulling loose the drawstring of his shorts with one hand, while reaching with the other under the nightgown to stroke my ass, raising shivers in places I would prefer not to name. 'You can have another shower. You can have two showers. I'll wash you, it will be my pleasure.' He lowered one of the straps of the nightgown, bit softly into my breast, and all thoughts of opposition wafted away as, succumbing, I arched to facilitate him. Swiftly, he placed both hands under me, lifting me, as though my bones were as hollow and light as a bird's, and we fell together onto the long-suffering bed, rocking the vehicle and causing crockery to crash through the open doors of the overhead lockers. 'Leave them,' he whispered, as I reacted, squirming to get out from under him to assess the damage. 'Leave them.'

'But we have to pay for breakages . . .'

I heard myself saying other words then, but didn't know

what or why, because he was kissing and licking the exposed breast, the hollow at the base of my neck, the delicate skin of my earlobe. 'Indeed we do have to pay,' he murmured. 'I'll pay for all breakages. It's what husbands do.' His hands were still under me. He squeezed, then raised me a little, adjusting me to where he wanted me. 'I'll pay,' he murmured, 'whatever it takes, I'll pay,' while, expertly, with his doctor's hands, slipping on the prophylactic.

* * *

An hour or so later, we were back outside, cleaning the van. 'Listen,' he said, without expression, concentrating on sloshing soapy water over the rear window, 'when you were in the shower that second time, I turned on my phone. There's coverage here, as you know. There was this voice message from one of the speaking-agency women, I think, although I'm not sure because she was breaking up. Anyway, I made out the word "Dallas". They might want me to go to Dallas – and I was thinking, we're going through Denver on the way home and I could easily get to Dallas from there. What do you think? Would you mind taking the last bit of the journey by yourself?'

'Oh,' I said. 'Why can't they leave us alone for one goddamned week? Was it them called you yesterday evening?'

'How do I know? I told you that was a number withheld. Anyhow, I'd better call back, eh? So here you go.' He handed me his sudsy cloth. 'Won't be a sec.' He took his phone out of the pocket of his shorts.

'Come on! Let's at least finish this part of the—'

'Signal's only halfway up this morning. Probably better where there are no trees. We've plenty of time. See you anon, kid.' He chucked me under the chin and, before I could say any more, was striding off, flip-flops sucking at patches of mud left by the overnight rain.

I looked at my watch. It was just twenty of nine; no point in being crabby about this. He was right, we did have plenty of time.

But then I thought about him using that damned condom earlier. Once we got home, I decided, I would fight. I would offer proper grown-up reasons for us not to delay having kids any longer – especially as we were again about to fall into our Skype and hello-goodbye routine. Who knew for how long that would be?

Something else, a journalistic tic, nagged at me. 'Private number' or 'number withheld'? He had said both but which was it – or could they be the same? If not, what was the difference? I'd had both showing on my own cell but it was something I had never before considered. I made a mental note to check it out. I think I mentioned previously that I have the sort of brain that loves detail and stores it. Had Daniel had two calls?

Speaking of which, I had to start directing my mind towards real life . . . I should reassure Mollie that I'd be back in the office bright and early two days from now. I picked up my own cell but got Cherry's chirpy voice message telling me all the lines were busy. After the tone, I relayed my own message and cut the connection.

I filled a pan with water and switched on the little hob under it to make coffee. While I waited for it to sing, I finished my own packing, then set a mug and two cookies on the table beside the wretched bobbly phone case. He was still not using it, dammit . . . Ah well, his loss, I thought, then poured my coffee and settled with it on the steps in the open air to wait for the return of my husband, turning my face up to the rapidly warming sun.

* * *

By nine thirty I was irritated, believing that Daniel was delaying his return so that most, if not all, of the cleaning would be done by the time he got back.

By nine fifty-five, irritation had turned to fury and I set off in search of him. What the hell was he playing at? On the off-chance he had met someone compatible, maybe another doctor, with the two of them now gabbing and comparing notes in the little site office, I went in there. The only visitor, a guy who liked his beer by the look of him, was asking the man behind the desk how he was supposed to access the 'free wiffie'. I went back outside.

The office straddled an elevation, from which most of the camp was visible. I walked its length. No sign.

For the first time, I began to worry.

* * *

I have scant recall of the intervening days, just a sense memory of pressure in my chest and behind my eyes, faces coming and going, mouths uttering consoling platitudes, everyone urging me not to lose hope.

Try not to worry. This happens and they show up right as rain . . .
We've found people after six days . . .

I have no idea what my side of those conversations sounded like. Dimly, I remember hearing someone scream, the noise seeming to go on and on, coming from the trees, or from behind one of the mountains. It couldn't have been me, could it?

By sunset on the third evening no trace of Daniel had been found, although I was told the search had already covered a widespread area radiating from the St Mary site.

On day four, a spotter plane droned overhead, while two power RIBs slowly patrolled the surface of the water for up to five miles downriver, their two-man crews using poles as probes in the water, clear again after the previous heavy rain had muddied and rushed it.

By this time, the Irish media had learned of the story and, after several bouts of questioning along the lines of 'How do you feel? It must be very emotional for you. How are you coping?' it came to the point that, other than the numbers belonging to Daniel's family, anytime I saw a number with a 353 prefix on my cell screen, I handed the phone to whomever was with me at the time. I could no longer speak coherently.

Both Jerry and Eamon had offered to fly to Montana. I would have welcomed Jerry's presence, but he was in the middle of exams crucial to his medical qualification, and I wouldn't hear of it. I had also convinced Eamon not to think of coming. I couched this in terms of cost, distance and perhaps futility – but promised that if I felt I needed him I would call immediately.

Aoife, Jerry's wife, also made daily calls, during one of which, coming to my senses for a few minutes, I gave her the name of the agency who had supplied Dad's carer, asking her to liaise and to explain the situation.

There had been just one call from a copiously weeping Eleanor. She didn't offer to come and, careful not to say anything she might construe as encouragement, I was glad. In the midst of my own distress, I still had enough sense to know I couldn't have handled hers.

'We have lots of boots on the ground too, ma'am. We'll find him, you bet.' This from one of the two kind men – I think they were from a local volunteer group – who had been detailed to look after me. After finishing the call with Eleanor, I was gazing up at the spotter plane.

But my memories of those five desperate days of searching for my husband are sporadic and I can't seem to arrange them in chronological order. Some are just sensory grabs: the new *thuckety-thuckety-thuckety* of a helicopter overhead, a dark ungainly insect buzzing against the bright sky as it, too, arrived to become another element of the search; the visual of 'our' van bumping slowly towards the entrance of the site, slaying me not just for the resonance it carried with it, but for that technicolour illustration of the two cheery children on its squat, square back. Waving goodbye.

I was seeing omens and symbols everywhere, and one of those kind-faced men, the one who, earlier, had moved me and my bag, Daniel's too, into a chalet on the site, misinterpreted my stricken expression as I watched the van leave. 'You don't give that ole wagon another thought, ma'am. It'll get home. That's no longer your concern.'

During that period, I couldn't eat proper food but I did snack, and drank all the liquids – coffee, cola and herbal teas – brought to me in an endless stream. I retain a mental snapshot of the table in my cabin, covered with soda bottles, half-sandwiches, half-drunk cups of coffee, and potato chips spilling out of open bags. I remember the bearded face of the doctor who came in and gave me an injection so that I knew nothing for hours afterwards. I certainly remember the comedown when I woke up, groggy, and there was still no sign of Daniel.

And then there was the man, dressed in a suit, standing by me one morning telling me that the Irish government was there to help me 'whatever happens'.

By the morning of the fifth day, I was literally without the means to think but, somehow, managed to pull myself into a sitting position to climb out of the bed, then get myself into the bathroom where a person with hollow eyes and hair like a furze bush stared back at me from the mirror.

I stepped into the shower and let the water get icy, standing under it, shuddering and scrubbing, until my skin felt raw and I could no longer bear the cold. I wrapped myself in one of the towels supplied by the site, wound my hair in another, and stepped back into the bedroom. Through the connecting doorway into the living area I could see that, while I had been in the shower, I had been supplied with yet another pot of coffee, a pail of ice, two bottles of water and two Hershey bars.

I downed a cup of the coffee, followed by some ice water and, while drying my hair, ate both candy bars. Then, dressed in a fresh tee and a pair of jeans, I tied my still-damp hair into a ponytail. Having brushed my teeth, I stepped outside into the sunshine. Somehow or other I had to find the moxie to be the woman Daniel loved instead of that fluttering moth of a person she had become. My husband, alive or dead, was out there somewhere, and I was going to carry him home one way or the other.

Then, on the breeze, a peal of female laughter drifted towards me. It seemed to be coming through the open door of the RV that had replaced ours. A man and a young boy stepped out and, on the grass, began hand-batting a football between them. A woman, probably the one who had laughed, followed them to sit quietly on the steps and watch. That hurt.

Otherwise, all was quiet right now, no whirly-bird in the air, no RIBs or canoes on the river, as far as I could see. Feeling queasy and a little unsteady after so much lying around, I turned away to flee from the reality that the world had continued to revolve without me and my husband.

I walked to the far side of the site, aiming for open, flat terrain where I could see all around me. Stupidly, I was wearing neither a hat nor sunglasses and, under the high, hot sun, had not gone far when I started to feel lightheaded. So I sat on a small hillock to rest. The only sounds permeating the profound, empty stillness were faraway twitterings and nearer, in the grass, a sort of soft ticking, probably made by an insect. It was very peaceful. I closed my eyes.

I must have dozed off because the next thing I knew the site manager was looming over me: 'There's news . . .'

Chapter Seventeen

They moved Daniel to a hospital morgue in Great Falls by helicopter but they wouldn't let me accompany him for insurance reasons, so the site manager kindly drove me to the city. Like a cloud of white feathers, a muffled sense of calm had descended on me. Sight, speech and hearing continued to function, but legs, hands and feet were puppet-like, as if jerked around on strings.

The manager was reluctant to give me details but I overrode him: 'I need to know.'

Daniel had been found downriver, almost five and a half miles from the campsite and, given the heavy rainfall and the water pouring off those mountains, that wasn't surprising: the river, which was pretty wide and contained rapids, had been in spate. I was overwhelmed by the thought of him struggling in that water for so long.

'Was he injured? He must have been, battered around like that – and those rocks in the rapids . . .'

'As far as I know— Are you *sure* you want to know all these details, Marian?'

'Of *course* I do! This is my *husband* we're talking about. Sorry!' Without meaning to, I had yelled at him.

'No apology necessary, Marian. It's completely understandable. We have to wait for the autopsy of course, but it appears – and don't quote me on this, please – that his right knee was very swollen and bruised, and because of the malformation of the joint, the immediate assessment from the scene of the first responders was that it was pretty badly smashed up. There was probably another break on the tibia but that hasn't yet been confirmed.'

His car purred along beside a wide stretch of water, as calm as an inland lake. 'Is this the same river?'

'It's been five days, Marian . . .'

It had not been helicopters, divers or riverbank searchers who had come across him, but a vacationing wilderness hiker, who had, fortunately, been on the fringes of one of those patches of network coverage and had therefore been able to make the 911 call.

He had found my husband lying in a small hollow, almost invisible under a thick covering of prairie grass stretching in all directions for miles. It was fourteen feet from a trail running parallel to the riverbank, but 154 yards inland. Daniel had somehow managed to walk or crawl that far.

He would probably not have been found for a lot longer, if ever, had the hiker, plagued by a stone in his running shoe, not paused to remove it and, sitting on the ground, seen something flash in the vegetation and gone to investigate.

After Daniel Senior's death, his family had shared out his personal possessions. His medical bag and his watch, an analogue Tissot on a worn leather strap, had been the only items Daniel had wanted for himself. The watch was not particularly valuable: although its case was gold, it was battered and dented. Crucially, though, on its dial, the makers had placed a diamond, so small it was normally imperceptible, under the numeral '12'.

My dead husband had been found lying on his side in the foetal position, knees drawn up, hands wrapped around them, his watch hand uppermost. And at the precise moment that the hiker had sat to take the stone out of his shoe, the sun overhead had sparked a bead of fire in the jewel. 'Are you OK?' the site manager asked, when he had finished. 'Too much?'

I was still cocooned in my white feathers, light but dense enough to keep invaders, such as difficult scenarios, at arm's length. Mostly. I already knew it would return to haunt me. 'Thank you,' I said quietly. 'I appreciate it.'

I will gloss over the identification process in the hospital morgue, except to say that the attendant unveiled just Daniel's face, which, to my relief, was not grimacing or creased into an expression of suffering. Even though the skin on one side had burned to a deep dark brown, the face was that of the real Daniel in repose.

The next couple of days in Great Falls were rife with officialdom, not just to do with identification but with police, who, polite as courtiers, asked carefully phrased questions, clearly designed to elicit my husband's 'state of mind' immediately before his death. I had to restrain myself from shouting at them as I had shouted at the campsite manager. 'My husband's state of mind was that we had enjoyed a perfect, wonderful vacation. We were making plans for dinner that night. We had spent good money on tickets to go back to Chicago, so for sure he was suicidal!' I remember saying to one guy, who hadn't deserved such sarcasm. Then I had to apologise to him too.

I was asked to sign innumerable documents for funeral directors and air carriers, who would conduct the casket across the various aircraft that would come into play.

Daniel's brothers were calling me daily. Eamon, God bless him, had assured me that I was not to concern myself about the cost of all of this, which would be substantial. 'It's likely, Marian,' he'd said, 'that because of what you're going through out there, this mightn't have occurred to you until you were presented with bills, but whatever it is, repatriation flights, coffin, anything, we've had a chat over here and we'll cover it. That site manager is across it, and I'm in touch with him and the Irish consulate. It's all in hand so you just take care of yourself now, OK? And we'll see you soon.'

After the autopsy, I was told that Daniel's death was deemed accidental, a legal term, it was explained to me, that is used when there isn't enough evidence to give a definite reason for how a person dies an unnatural death.

'Did he suffer? To what extent?'

'That's impossible to know.'

'But I was told that he had a broken leg, his knee and his tibia—'

'Yes. That was confirmed.'

'Well, that must have been very painful. And he dragged himself a hundred and fifty-four yards from the riverbank?'

'It appears so. Please, Mrs Lynch, you mustn't upset yourself.'

'I'm upset anyway. Is there anything you're not telling me? One side of his face was almost black with sunburn.'

'We do know that your husband survived the water. He didn't drown. He must have been very strong to get himself into that little creek where the water was quieter – and then, with a leg so badly broken, to drag himself up to where he was found.' The official who told me all this said then: 'It's not much comfort, unfortunately, Mrs Lynch, but it may be of some consolation to you, in time to come, to know that your husband was certainly a man of spirit and determination. I wish I could offer more than that . . . And as for how he found himself in the water, if you were to ask my opinion,

I'd say that having gone too close to the water – remember, the river was very high and the overlap on to the ground might have looked shallow – he just lost his footing, slipped on the bank and got caught in the current, which was considerable.'

'Where did he fall in?'

'Impossible to tell, Mrs Lynch. The water began to recede from the bank into its usual course later that same day. We'll look for evidence, I promise you that. I understand he had his cell with him. Apparently there was quite a search – divers, dragging – but there was no sign of it. Someone will find something of him – his cell, some clothing – perhaps when we least expect it. Of course we'll contact you immediately.'

The story seemed to be that Daniel had died from dehydration combined with exposure. My only consolation, which was insignificant when set against the enormity of his death, was that he had tried to save himself, which must mean he had planned to come back to me.

I was not able to visit him until the mortician had fixed him up for his trip home. When I did, I found that most virile and vigorous of men lying with most of his body covered with feminine creamy-white ruched satin, fingers daintily entwined on his chest. He was wearing the only jacket and formal shirt he had brought with him on the trip. When he'd been packing, folding them roughly into each other to shove into his rucksack, he had said, as he frequently did when going away from home even for a few days, 'You never know, I might have to go to a funeral!'

I had argued, 'You're just adding weight. We're supposed to be travelling light!'

I hated what had been done to him, especially his hair, smoothed and gelled, drawn back from his ears and forehead, exposing a deep widow's peak. In fairness, I guess the morticians had done their best with his sunburned skin, but the make-up was caked on and unnatural, as were the rouged cheeks.

Worst of all, for me anyway, was the mouth. In life, Daniel had had a wide mouth with full, sensuous lips, but they had been dragged into a thin, straight, mean-looking line, slightly crooked at one end and, ludicrously, coloured a pale pink.

The funeral director had been watching me. 'I'll leave you to have a few moments alone.' He withdrew discreetly. He was under time pressure as the hearse and accompanying limo were on their way to take us to the airport.

Right then I saw no point in sitting alone with the rouged, dressed-up doppelganger that resembled Daniel but was very far from being him. The husband I knew was absent from that funeral chapel, with its over-sweet odours, soothing neutral colours, candles, soft lighting, impenetrable silence – and one tissue pulled discreetly through the slot of the white china Kleenex holder. No religious symbols, and no flowers because we were due to travel, Daniel and I, but in different areas of the three separate aircraft we would occupy intermittently over the next thirty hours or more.

I felt strangely compelled to do something appropriate to signify that solemn occasion. I had been left alone for a purpose: there was an etiquette around this that I must follow. After a few minutes I stood up from my chair and did what was expected of me. I approached the casket, taking my last viewing, as it were.

'Goodbye, Daniel,' I whispered, then forced myself to touch the cold, waxy cheek. 'Please don't forget me . . .' The actuality of what I'd said hit me and tears, hot geysers, erupted uncontrollably.

The funeral director chose that moment to re-enter the room. 'Is it time?' I snatched a handful of the tissues and wiped my face.

In soothing, respectful tones, he told me that the hearse and the limo were waiting outside. 'But they're early so there's no rush.

Everything is in order. A man from the Irish consulate has come to be with you. I have given him your airline tickets and all the necessary documentation, including the death certificate and the coroner's report. You will have no difficulties at any of the airports. I have also included the name and telephone number of the Irish funeral director who will meet your plane in Dublin.'

Then, seeming to vanish within himself, he added, 'So, please, take all the time you need. I'll just leave this here with you.' He placed a small black cardboard box on the table beside the Kleenex, then withdrew again.

Inside I found Daniel's watch, his father's Tissot, its second hand still loyally sweeping around the dial, its little diamond, the one that had brought about his discovery, barely visible until I took it up and inclined it towards a table lamp so it caught the light. There, too, was his wedding band. He must have been wearing it. The tears erupted again. What had possessed me to harry him about it?

I fastened the watch on my own wrist, pulling the leather strap to its innermost hole, but it was still too large and the face immediately slid down to dangle under my wrist.

The wedding band was too loose to stay on any of my fingers, even my thumbs, so I put it back into the box and closed the lid.

Chapter Eighteen

Coming off the Boston flight, the third of three during the previous thirty-six hours, I was not just dizzy with exhaustion but half dead with repressed emotion. The first person I recognised was Aoife, in uniform, her baby bump substantial, standing beside Jerry. They were waiting for me on the jet bridge just outside the exit door of the plane. She burst into tears when she saw me and opened her arms. As for me, I suffered a complete meltdown as I fell into her, holding on tight as all restraints sprang loose.

She had brought me a black pants suit and dress shoes, and when we had both calmed down, she took me into a little room to help me dress for the funeral, using her own make-up kit on my face in an effort to deal with the tired lines and shadows. 'So you won't be worrying about how you look,' she said, studying me critically when she had finished. 'That's grand. You won't care about things like this today – you'd probably say, "Who cares?" – but you'll be glad later. Trust me.'

It was still raining when we got to the church where for an

American, accustomed to the modest group of relatives and perhaps a few friends who attend funerals in the US, the turnout was amazing. Under an overlapping canopy of umbrellas, Glanmilish's little Church of the Holy Family was flanked on both sides by a huge crowd.

And as we drew up, a troop of men, women and children, all clad in the red and yellow of the Glanmilish Gaelic Football Club, came out from under the umbrellas. They lined up, stoically bareheaded, getting drenched, making an honour guard. Their dad, Jerry whispered, had acted as team doctor, and they had been expecting Daniel to follow suit.

Ahead, I could see the immediate family and a number of other men sheltering in the little porch in front of the church door. The casket was to be shouldered by eight men: Jerry, Eamon, Martin, someone from the football club and four cousins.

Along with the undertaker, as funeral directors are called in Ireland, Eamon, Sharon, Eleanor and Martin came forward to shake my hand, then the man gave us our orders: I was to walk immediately behind the casket, with Eleanor, Aoife and Sharon just behind me, followed by a grouping of the cousins. I nodded like an automaton, but all I could see was the casket being slid out of the hearse on to a gurney.

The crowd went completely silent and still. Aoife put her arm around my shoulders. Except for the rain pattering on all those umbrellas and the murmured directions of the undertaker, there was no sound while the eight pallbearers heaved the casket on to their shoulders, steadied themselves a little and, with the undertaker in front setting the pace, began slowly to move. The boys and men of the honour guard bent their heads; some of the younger ones, overwhelmed by the gravity of the occasion, wept.

For the time being, I had wept myself dry and, for Daniel's sake, kept my head up, shoulders straight, eyes on the swaying casket as the men walked slowly in step while carrying my husband on his penultimate journey along the earth.

As was customary in Ireland, when the service ended – it had passed in a blur for me – the priest announced from the altar that, after the burial in the family plot, the entire congregation was invited to have sandwiches and soup at the Heritage Hotel in the village of Killinard – the nearest place, Jerry whispered in my ear, that could, in comfort, seat the numbers expected.

Outside, the rain had stopped and there was a brief hiatus while the pallbearers switched, a second troop of eight carefully taking the burden, literally, from the first. While we were waiting, two men, one with hair braided Rastafarian-style, came up to condole with me and, to my astonishment, introduced themselves as two of Daniel's colleagues from Holy Angels. 'Thank you so much.' I was flabbergasted. 'You came specially? That's really nice of you – you will join us at the hotel?'

'Unfortunately we have to run.' The Rastafarian guy spoke with the musical cadences of the Caribbean. 'We've rented a car and we're going straight back to Dublin airport to catch an afternoon flight.'

'It was really great of you, thank you so much. I can't tell you how much I appreciate it.' I knew I was going to be saying this a lot that day, but it would never be more sincere than now. I was really moved. 'Does anyone else in the family know you're here? I should introduce you.'

'No, thanks,' said the second man. 'We really do have to run. You've had such a huge attendance here, ma'am, and we're impressed, but it's no less than he deserved. He was such fun.'

'If you could get him on his own.'

'Yeah, he was very popular, but such a big loss. He wasn't just a thinker –'

'– outside the box –'

'– he was also a great colleague.'

'Oh, man! We'll really miss him.'

Over their shoulders, as they spoke, I saw that the substitution of pallbearers was complete and that Eamon and Jerry were coming up to join me. 'You should at least meet his brothers,' I said, and since their names had already escaped me I made a generic introduction: 'These are two of Daniel's colleagues who came from Chicago just for this. These are Daniel's brothers.'

'Man, he was the greatest, we're so sorry for your loss,' said the Rastafarian guy, pumping first Eamon's hand and then Jerry's. I introduced Eleanor then, and both men shook hands with her, too, repeating their condolences, then quickly left, just as the cortège began to move.

The cemetery adjoined the church, and that part of the ceremonial, at least, was relatively short. As the priest, using a tinny PA, intoned the final sets of prayers, I stood at the grave, Jerry close to me on one side, Aoife even closer on the other. I couldn't watch. That huge storehouse of bright, disputatious vigour, that brainpower, that incorrigible carnality, what happened to it now? Where was it going? I closed my eyes and Jerry and Aoife, probably thinking I was going to faint, grabbed me.

* * *

'Oh, God, I never asked how the exams went!' I had been so engrossed in my own problems that I had forgotten Jerry's finals. I had also forgotten that I had no special lien on mourning. He and Daniel had been close. 'Not too bad.' He smiled at me.

We were walking back to their car during an emotional rebound, quiet but obvious, that had seemed to spread through the gathering of those who had attended the graveside. People had gathered informally in little groups, chatting, smiling, even chuckling as they caught up on local news and gossip before they, too, walked back to their vehicles. I guess the sunlight now bathing the cemetery helped the air of general loosening up.

'Don't mind him. He did great!' Aoife thumped her husband in the ribs. 'And, Marian, you should take a second night in that hotel. You really need to breathe a bit before you decide what to do. I'm not rostered for the next few days so I can stay, too, if you'd like company – that okay with you, Jerry?'

'Of course.'

Before we got into Jerry's car, he glanced at his wife, and then, to me, said, 'I don't know how you'll feel about this, Marian, and now may not be the time to say it, but in case someone blurts it out inappropriately, I thought I should tell you that the administration of Da's estate came through last week. It was quick enough because it was simple, or seemed so on the surface. We thought you should know but didn't want to tell you while you were going through all that stuff in Montana. Quite some timing, eh?'

I didn't give a fig about the testacy. What I wanted was quiet and oblivion in that order. But, showing willing, I looked from one to the other. 'That's good, isn't it?'

'Jerry,' Aoife said, in a low voice, 'tell her. Just tell her.'

'Tell me what?'

'Better coming from us. Just say it!'

'Not really the place?' He looked uncomfortable but, signalling, she widened her eyes at him.

'He left various individual financial bequests,' he said quickly. 'Apparently he had built up quite a substantial portfolio of shares and bonds, things like that – who knew? We certainly didn't. But he left Glanmilish House and the practice to all of us in equal parts, including Daniel. I don't know who was advising him, but that's a bit of a nightmare – it means we all have to agree on everything. Only three of us now, of course, with Daniel sort of looking over our shoulders . . .' Hesitating, he watched for my reaction, and when none was forthcoming, he didn't relax. 'Do you know if Daniel made a will?' he asked quietly.

'Well, actually, I don't think so. If he did, he didn't tell me.' I couldn't believe this question was being asked on such a day. Yet as I spoke, I was remembering something . . .

* * *

Having just got into bed one evening, during the period of negotiations about the move to Ireland, I found that Daniel was in an unusually playful mood. So I asked, in the same vein, 'What's in this transatlantic upheaval for me? What guarantee do I have that you won't just go off with a twinkling Irish *Riverdance*r and leave me stranded? My job isn't that secure, you know.'

'Equally, Mrs Lynch,' he pinched my bottom, 'how do I make sure you won't go off with a Chippendale? Hey – I know!' He jumped out of bed and came back quickly with two pieces of A4 paper and two pens, handing me one of each and scribbling quickly on his, intoning as he wrote, 'As a token of my fealty, I hereby bequeath to Mrs Marian Lynch this legacy of all my worldly goods. Well,' he added merrily, 'most of them anyway! Can you put that in a will? The word "mostly", which would let everyone fight it out afterwards?'

I played along. 'I think you have to be specific! So we're writing wills, are we? I suppose I could leave you all my back issues of the *New Yorker*.'

'Thanks but no thanks,' he said, flashing his paper at me. Then discarding it on the floor, he grabbed me. 'C'mere, you . . .'

Afterwards, brain loosely connected to body, limbs languorous, I watched him pick up the paper. 'You know, this isn't a bad idea,' he said thoughtfully. 'People should have wills, shouldn't they? My father certainly had one – I must get on to Eamon. He spoke to me about it when he was making it, and as I'm the eldest, Da wanted me to be his executor. Naturally, I pointed out I wouldn't be much use from the far side of the world. I'm kind of sorry now. Has your father made one?'

'Don't know. I should ask him, I suppose. Although that won't be easy. He'll think I believe he's at death's door.'

'Yeah. But the thing is, you don't want the bloody state of Illinois to get whatever little bits and pieces he has, do you?'

Then, 'Ah, shit! This is getting too heavy.' He crumpled up the sheet of A4 and stuffed it into the drawer of his nightstand. 'That was supposed to be fun!' He kissed my forehead, and grinned down at me. 'So, now we have *our* succession rights sorted, that's the *real* Irish wedding under our belts, and all we need to do to top it all off, Mrs Lynch, is to consummate it, buy the grave and we're all set!' I had seen Daniel in all kinds of moods but that height of gaiety in him was rare and, for once, in case I ruined it, I refrained from asking him why.

* * *

'Could he have had that paper signed and dated?' Jerry asked, when I had finished telling the story, at less than half the length, naturally, in the graveyard on that day of days.

'I don't know,' I said. 'I doubt it. I didn't get to see what was actually written on it. He was in great spirits that night and all I saw was him putting it away.'

I thought it odd to be talking about all this, even with my deliberate omissions, in a place where, only yards away, earth was being shovelled on top of the main character in the play. I guess I was lightheaded but no one can do top-level grief 100 per cent of the time. The body and brain bring their own defences to bear.

'There's no hurry about this, Marian,' Jerry said then, 'but after you go back, you really should try to find that bit of paper. It could save an awful lot of hassle down the road.'

'I'd know where to start looking, anyway. And I seem to remember Daniel saying that your dad did talk to him about his will, giving him an outline of his wishes and wanting him to be executor, that kind of thing.'

'He did? That's news to me.' Jerry seemed taken aback. 'Anyway, come on. Most of the people who were in the church are probably already at the hotel now. We should get a move on.'

Once in the car, however, I wondered if Daniel had removed that piece of A4 paper from his drawer. I'd been busy organising extra care for my dad while we were away in Montana, preparing for the trip and shouldering the demands of *Femme* magazine, so it hadn't featured in my thoughts.

Right now, I couldn't deal with it, at least not intelligently. 'Maybe Daniel didn't say that, Jerry,' I said from the back seat. 'I really don't know. I don't know my own name at this stage and maybe I just imagined it.'

'Not to worry. But do check.'

'I will.'

I was exhausted, and this was merely an interval in today's three-act drama. I still had to go to the hotel to face Act Three.

Chapter Nineteen

When we got there, the room allocated for the funeral reception was already humming with chat as waves of mini sausages and hot soup were borne around the room to augment piles of sandwiches and jugs of something called 'orange squash'. It was free seating, but I was again protected: Jerry placed me between himself and Aoife at one of the tables occupied in the main by a jolly group of Beara cousins, all of whom knew each other, but were obviously treating this as a great chance for a reunion.

When they saw us approach them, though, as if at a signal, the merriment subsided and they reiterated a chorus of their very sincere sympathy to all three of us, then resumed their chat at a level respectful of us as chief mourners.

There were at least two hundred people in the room, including several children, and I noticed that Eleanor's three, Colm, Finn and Patricia, were sitting with another three in the care of a woman I recognised as Olwen Moore, Daniel's colleague and partner in the medical practice. I can't say that I knew her well. I had been introduced to her very briefly during the honeymoon. Anyhow, all six of the kids, hers and Eleanor's, were hunched over cell phones or other devices, staring intently at the screens, thumbs flying.

I also recognised a guy from the village, although it took me a minute or so to sort out the context because I had been into Glanmilish only once, walking down to the grocery store on the morning after the single night Daniel and I had spent at his family home during the honeymoon. I had needed to get away from the gloom of the place even for a few minutes. Daniel had been still asleep, and his dad was gone, presumably to the surgery next door.

I was surprised to see the man here: when last I'd seen him, he had been dressed in a filthy black winter coat even though it had been a rare hot summer morning. It was hard not to stare at him – and not just because of the inappropriate attire and wild black hair, greying a little, but because he had been marching to and fro on the sidewalk outside the store, conducting a murmured conversation with himself; at intervals he had waved his arms and scanned the sky, pausing only to bow courteously to shoppers, myself included, who were going in and out through the glass doors.

For today he had dressed, or someone had dressed him, in an ill-fitting navy suit. He was a tall man and the pants were too short, exposing white ankles above a pair of down-at-heel but highly polished black shoes. The jacket was off and his shirt, blindingly white, was still creased from its wrappings. His tie, still tightly tied, narrow, unfashionable, was also navy. His hair, sticking up in tufts now, might have been cut with secateurs.

I brought him to Jerry's attention – 'Would you know who that is?' – indicating where the man was sitting, gesticulating and talking with some animation to the men on either side of him, one of whom I recognised, including context, even though he was not in uniform. He was Sergeant Cantwell, the nice cop.

'That's Billy Murphy,' Jerry said, of the guy using his arms. 'He's absolutely harmless, as they say around these parts. He's a kind of institution in the village.' Then: 'Look, you might as well know this too. Apparently he's some kind of cousin of our mother's – there are legions of them, as you've probably gathered – but we were a bit surprised to find him singled out in Da's will, where he's referred to as "my dear wife's cousin, Billy Murphy". Da left him twenty thousand euro. None of us knows why, but we're guessing it's because he and the mother were both patients, but otherwise . . .' He shrugged. 'None of us'd begrudge it to him, mind. We're all pretty well set up.

'And those other men with him? There was the stipulation in the will that the cash was to be administered on his behalf by the St Vincent de Paul. Those two are from the local branch. One's a garda, used to be in Stradbally station, in Portlaoise now, I think – I know him slightly, good guy. I'm not sure they're aware of the legacy yet, or the poor fella himself. It's a windfall, but that amount would certainly not secure anyone's future in this country. I suppose Da, who knew him probably better than his own mother, wanted to do something for him rather than give the money to a dogs-and-cats home. It was good of him. The only other charity he left anything to was Concern, and that was maybe because of Daniel's work – well, *potential* work on behalf of kids in those areas of the world. He'd admired that. Now, anything else you want to know about anyone here?'

'Thanks, Jerry.' Despite exhaustion, ragged emotion and everything else, journalistic curiosity had kicked in. 'Was Billy Murphy born like that?'

'He had an accident, apparently. The mother was a bit simple and apparently she let him fall out of his pram when he was a baby. There was brain damage. Da had treated them both since then.

They had medical cards, of course, but there are always other costs involved so I'd say Da probably did a bit of financial juggling there. That poor divil hadn't a bean, and nor did his mother when she was alive. Any time they had a few bob, like on dole day, it'd be spent on ice cream . . . or drink, in her case. But I'm glad to say everyone in Glanmilish pitched in for a decent funeral for the mother when she died a couple of years ago.'

I was intrigued. Should I follow this up? But common sense kicked in: I had enough on my plate right now. Anyway, my surroundings were receding again and I had to fight the temptation to fold my arms on the table and rest my head.

I resisted, I think, but I doubt I made sense with anything I said from then on. At one stage I stood up, seeing, somewhat gratefully, that some of the tables had been vacated and the waiting staff had begun to clear them. People were leaving in ones, twos and family groups.

My neck still hurt from the previous day's sleepover in an airport lounge – it might have been Denver, it might have been Boston – but rather than having to twist it to look upwards as people stopped by to reiterate their condolences as they left, it was easier to talk to them at their level. Standing, I found, did nothing for my staying power. But within fifteen minutes of the teas and coffees being served, the crowd had diminished to maybe seventy or seventy-five, including immediate family members, and I felt I had held myself together for long enough. Daniel could not have asked any more of me. I needed the bathroom and excused myself. Seeing me get up, Eleanor's husband, Martin, rose from his seat and intercepted me: 'You're not leaving?'

'No, just the restroom.'

'I won't detain you so. I just want to say that I'm sure you've noticed Eleanor isn't exactly firing on all cylinders today.' He reddened.

'She's grieving like the rest of us, Martin.' I looked across at his table but his wife wasn't there.

'She's gone to the Ladies,' he said, causing an instant revision of my own restroom plans. 'I don't know what she feels or thinks, these days,' he added sadly. 'But I just wanted to talk to you, to ask you to – to make allowances . . .'

'Of course. No worries, Martin. Anyway, I'll be going to bed very shortly now and back to Chicago in the next couple of days – work, you know.'

'You know about the house and everything?'

'Jerry and Aoife mentioned it.'

'I just wanted to explain. Has she talked to you today?'

'I can't remember, to tell you the truth.' That was not strictly accurate. After our arrival with the casket, while Eleanor, Sharon and Aoife were forming up behind me to follow me up the aisle in the church, Aoife had given me a warm hug, Sharon had touched my shoulder with obvious empathy, and Daniel's sister had merely said, 'Hello, Marian.' You do remember these things.

'This really has little to do with me, Martin,' I said now, trying to find a middle way between brushing him off and sounding sisterly. Fatigue was threatening my balance: I felt dizzy, as though the room was rocking, like a ship in choppy waters. 'I'm sorry she's upset, Martin,' I said quickly, 'but, truly, it's nothing to do with me. I'll have some reason to return here in the near future, I'm sure. I'll talk to her then. Have you any idea what it's about?'

But something had caught his eye over my shoulder. 'She's coming back,' he said. 'Please don't tell her that I've said anything to you.'

'Of course not.' In the event, however, Eleanor didn't come near us but went straight back to her table. Grateful for small mercies, I thanked him and headed for the restroom.

Shortly after that I left, fielding all kinds of solicitous wishes on my way to my room. Once there, I called down to Reception to extend my stay at the hotel for a second night. I needed to take a breath, to sleep and swim in the hotel's pool – somehow I'd remembered that my shabby old swimsuit was in my carry-on, the one I'd taken to Montana – and get used to the idea that I was now a widow, although I knew I wouldn't fully grasp the concept for a long time.

Before I passed out, I managed to get through to the agency looking after my dad during the day – Luzveminda was staying with him at night. They told me that things were going okay – or what passed as okay, these days – and I extended his care for a further twenty-four hours, explaining what had happened. After her night duty, Luzveminda, whom I'd kept up to speed from the campsite after Daniel had gone missing, was probably still asleep and I didn't want to wake her.

I did feel somewhat guilty about taking the extra day, but I definitely needed to catch my emotional breath. I was finding it hard not to feel that I was being deliberately targeted by disaster and death and, briefly, succumbed to feelings of self-pity and victimhood. But such feelings, I knew, were destructive and not helpful.

Tomorrow would be better. There's always a clean sheet next morning – that, of course, had been drilled into me by my mom, who, as I've already mentioned, was wont to quote Scarlett O'Hara. Arrogant, manipulative and deeply flawed, yes, but magnificent, Mom thought, purely because she never gave up. Suffering setback after setback that frequently she had caused, she always picked herself up and kept going.

When I was a child, whether I had fallen from a tree I had been forbidden to climb, or had trailed home from high school, miserable and drooping because I had been snubbed yet again by one of the cool kids for some non-cool thing I had said or done, Mom would ladle out a cupful of the chicken soup she maintained in her stockpot, originally made from a recipe favoured by Mrs Feinstein, our Jewish neighbour. Eight years old or eighteen, Mom would put the cup in front of me, with a cookie and milk to follow, and channel her Scarlett: 'Learn the lesson and don't forget they put erasers on pencils. One foot in front of the other, Marian, one foot in front of the other.'

Beat as I was, I changed my mind about getting into bed. The best thing to do to clear my head, I thought, and to help with lifting that self-pity, was a bit of physical exercise. So I extracted my swimsuit from my bag, put it on, with the terrycloth robe supplied by the hotel, and made my way to the pool.

Unfortunately, it was filled with teenagers, having a marvellous noisy time, so I went back to my room, where I found that my cell was now out of battery. I didn't bother rooting around for the charger and, in addition, removed the receiver from the room phone. Then, remembering I had consigned my old cotton nightgown to the garbage in Montana while cleaning the RV, I climbed naked into bed and slipped into a sleep so profound that, for the first few seconds of semi-consciousness, it was as though a heavy black blanket was falling slowly from the ceiling, gently and mercifully covering every inch of me and the cool, clean bed.

* * *

The next morning I woke up to a persistent knocking on the bedroom door and, for a glorious moment, had no idea where I was or why. Then I heard someone calling my name – 'Mrs Lynch? Mrs Lynch?' – and more knocking.

I stumbled out, snatched up the robe from the floor, put it on and went to answer. The girl, in a receptionist's uniform, had the sculpted cheekbones of Eastern Europe and slightly too-perfect English: 'There have been many telephone calls for you, Mrs Lynch. They are from America.'

'Thank you.' I took the slip of paper from her. Sure enough, the area code was 312, Chicago, but I didn't recognise the number. I sat on the bed.

Dad.

Now Dad had died too? I couldn't take it.

Slowly I got up again and walked across the room towards the window. In passing, I saw that the red message button on the room phone number pad was flashing.

Backing up, I replaced the receiver, took it up again and, holding my breath, pressed the button. The calls hadn't been about my father, thank God, they were from Mollie Lehman. Four calls, increasingly angry, the most recent incandescent: 'Where the hell are you, Marian?' she yelled. 'You had a week's leave and taking that was bad enough with the launch coming up. It's been *two* weeks now. It's two in the morning, you're coming between me and my sleep because, by the fucking way, I worked my ass off with the Michelle Obama interview and she was actually considering doing it but I couldn't confirm it because I can't fucking find you and I just can't find the time to do it myself! That was nearly twenty-four hours ago. Your cell goes straight to voicemail and when I call I get the international tone telling me you're probably in fucking Ireland again. Call me today, ya hear, Marian? If I haven't heard from you by the time I get into the office by seven thirty this morning, don't bother. Consider yourself fired. *And what the hell are you doing in Ireland again?*' This was followed by the sound of a crash. It was impossible to tell whether she had slammed down her handset or fired it across the room.

So much for the dream job. I glanced at Daniel's watch. It was just after four in the morning in Chicago. It wasn't that I hadn't thought of calling *Femme* while I was going through all that trauma, I just couldn't face it and, in any case, while I was waiting for news of Daniel, nothing else had seemed important. I regretted now that I hadn't asked someone, Jerry perhaps, to call on my behalf, but I was so accustomed to doing everything for myself that it hadn't occurred to me to do so.

I decided I had time for a swim before I faced the music.

* * *

The pool was calm, restorative and free of teenagers. I had it to myself. I've loved swimming since the endless summers I spent in the public pools complex in Northbrook when I was a teenager.

Lapping quietly up and down, with just the sound of my own movement, helped me to think clearly, and I decided that the best way to manage the next set of dramas, around my dad, around *Femme*, was to take each segment individually as it arose. And while I wouldn't be able to keep grief about Daniel at bay, the best way to cope with it was not to resist but to let it come and go, engulfing me, then washing away to leave me temporarily in peace. All very well in theory, of course, but it did feel good to have taken back some sort of control. Or, more accurately, to have planned it.

In the meantime, as part of getting and keeping myself together, there were a few practical details I had to organise. I was still operating with just the bag I'd had with me in Montana, so sometime soon, today if possible, I had to deal with that. I had both my own and Daniel's credit cards. Miraculously, I remembered his PIN.

And I had to call the office.

In the meantime, I didn't know how Aoife was fixed, but maybe she could drive me into the local town to buy a few things. It was not my usual practice to ask for help but, right now, I had no choice.

Cherry answered on the first ring. I told her what had happened, as succinctly as I could, trying not to become emotional. 'And please tell Mollie that after he was found, the official stuff was horrendous, the form-filling and coroners and all that. Would you mind explaining it wasn't that I didn't think about calling, I just couldn't do it. I spent the whole time waiting for the next crisis.'

'Oh, sugar, you poor thing. What a horrible thing to happen. Are you okay? Is there someone looking after you?'

'Daniel's family has been marvellous.'

'Where are you now?'

'The funeral is just over.' I figured that in the hierarchy of sinning, given what I had been through, this was venial. 'I'm too late to catch today's flight,' I said truthfully, 'so it'll be tomorrow, I'm afraid.'

'Try not to worry. I'll tell her the whole story. I'm sure she'll understand.'

'Thanks, Cherry. Thanks very much.' But as she went off the line I felt that her optimism about Mollie understanding my problem, at least the depth of it, was probably misplaced.

Having something practical to do, even something as basic as buying a few bits of underwear and a new pair of jeans, was the way to go, at least for today. Someone, probably a Hallmark employee, had coined a bit of doggerel about yesterday being history and tomorrow being a mystery but today being the gift we have right now. And, right now, I'd take advice wherever it presented itself.

Having made these decisions – even knowing they would probably derail themselves – I felt calmer. And a little better able to face the wrath of Mollie Lehman.

* * *

Thirty-six hours later, I was taking my aisle seat on the Chicago-bound plane. It wasn't completely full. When the door of the aircraft was being closed, the guy in the window seat and I exchanged a smile, delighted that the middle seat in the row was not occupied, but before the plane started its run, one of the flight attendants came down the aisle with the manifest in her hand, eyes upwards as she checked seat numbers. To my surprise she stopped at mine. 'Mrs Lynch?'

'Yes?'

'My sincere apologies, but there's been a mistake. I'm afraid you're in the wrong seat. Would you come with me, please? I'll help you with your bags.' Not waiting for a response, she opened the overhead bin. 'Is this yours?' She pulled out my soiled, worn canvas carry-on. Daniel's was even worse, and I was glad I'd checked it in.

I was slightly annoyed at the interruption because I assumed I wouldn't have the same space to spread out in my next seat and also found it embarrassing meekly to follow her with all eyes upon us and on my bag – she held it in front of her as though it were the Turin Shroud – as we passed row after row towards the top of the plane. Astonishingly, she kept going, until we were well inside business class. 'There you go,' she said, indicating my new seat. 'Enjoy! And Aoife says hello!'

I was so astonished and grateful, I was almost in tears. Again.

Chapter Twenty

Although its presence loomed in the background, some hours into my flight back to Chicago grief had temporarily covered its face. I was stretched out on my fully reclined seat, having dined well and indulged in a large gin and tonic. My mind was freewheeling.

I had left the country, ears ringing with expressions of sympathy, appeals to me 'not to be a stranger' and assurances that if there was anything, 'anything at all, Marian', that anyone could do to relieve my 'troubles', all I had to do was to ask. 'Even a cup of tea and a chat can help, Marian. We're all here for you.' It was very moving and the memory of all those virtual strangers who had taken me into their hearts was comforting.

And then there was Aoife, whose care and warmth had been exceptional. On top of that, she'd been pretty informative, and parts of our conversation at a coffee shop in Portlaoise had been quite something, and continued to vibrate now, like one of those annoying mechanical tin toys: wind up the postman and he flaps his little arms.

My sister-in-law had introduced the notion that, whether I liked it or not, I might end up as part-owner of a half-derelict house. On the morning after the funeral, she had happily made herself available to drive me to Portlaoise and help me shop for replacement clothes since all I had with me was laundry and what she had lent me.

Once there, she had guided me towards Penneys and Dunnes: 'They're both very reasonable, the quality is fine, and we're not exactly looking for an investment wardrobe, are we?' So we bought jeans and a denim jacket, several sets of underwear, three tees in different colours, a pair of white sneakers and a wool-blend sweater. 'It may be cold on the plane and the journey's long.' To my astonishment, the cost had totalled less than the price of a single pair of fashionable trainers from Bloomingdales, Nordstrom or any of the department stores trading on the so-called 'Magnificent Mile', Michigan Avenue, in downtown Chicago. But I was well into Daniel's credit card, having drawn cash out of ATMs to a degree I didn't care to think about. Because he'd travelled so much, though, he'd always boasted that his credit limit was very high.

Ignoring her objections, I had insisted on buying her a cute multi-coloured tote she had admired, to thank her for everything, and by the time we went for that coffee, I realised I had managed to survive for a whole hour without weeping or feeling sorry for myself. Isn't the human spirit resilient? I thought. Then came the usual self-putdown: *Or am I just shallow?*

My sister-in-law was very good company, her personality ideal for her profession, and I knew instinctively that, in other circumstances, she and I would have become friends. 'Can we keep in touch, Aoife? Would you mind?'

'Not only would I not mind, I'd love it. After my maternity leave with Buster here,' she tapped her bump, 'I'm due to go on the transatlantic route. We'll definitely meet in Chicago. You can show me places us hosties have never been to before. We tend to sightsee in Filene's basements, out-of-town outlets and, at a stretch, Bloomingdales and Macy's for the carrier bags. They have . . . What do you call it?'

'Cachet?'

'That's it!'

Buster. 'You think your baby's a boy?' I was conscious of jealousy's brief stab and hoped it hadn't shown.

'Haven't a clue.' She smiled. 'Tom wants a brother, and I suspect Jerry loves the notion of having two little boys.'

As the plane whispered on (from up there in the posh quarter, engine noise was minimal), physically I was as relaxed as I could have been but, of course, off and on, the difficulties I faced – Mollie Lehman, my dad, not least how I was going to cope without Daniel – continued to intrude. Recalling that conversation with Aoife, the ease of it despite the revelations, I realised how much I missed having a close woman friend. Aoife was younger than me by about ten years, but the gap meant little to me and, I suspected, had not crossed her mind during the hours we had spent together.

But she had broached the subject of her father-in-law's will: 'What did you feel about that house business, Marian? You can be honest – I won't even tell Jerry.'

I had shrugged. 'Why should I feel anything?'

'Well, if Daniel made a will—'

'Oh, come on, Aoife! I told you. We were just playacting that evening. Neither of us was taking it seriously. I was leaving him my stash of *New Yorker* magazines – that kind of thing.'

'Look,' she said slowly, 'forgive me if I'm being too nosy or prying here, but if there was a will, *if*,' she repeated, 'what would he have left you, d'you think? Did he say anything that night?'

'I don't know.' I thought hard, visualising my husband waving his sheet of paper in the air. He had certainly said something – Irish marriage? A grave? The latter I had thought to be rather peculiar – before he'd jumped on top of me in the bed again. I could certainly remember the air being knocked out of me, the width of his grin as he looked down at me. 'Maybe,' I said. 'I can't be sure of this, Aoife, it was all a bit of buffoonery, remember, but he might have said something about "worldly goods". That seems to ring a bell because of the word "worldly". But of all the people I've ever met, Daniel Lynch was the least worldly in that sense, certainly where money was concerned.' I added sadly, 'We weren't together long enough to get down to the nitty-gritty of who owned what or, more likely, who didn't own anything. But what does it matter? Why are you so interested?'

'It's really Jerry who's latched on to this. Daniel was never straightforward about anything, Jerry says. And even I remember that when their mother died, and Sharon and I were helping clean the house for the wake, we found money, quite a lot of it, banknotes, stuffed down cushions, under mattresses, behind pictures on the wall, even at the bottom of a box of teabags. We mentioned this, naturally, to Daniel Senior, who was quite upset about it. Apparently, he believed that this was money Daniel owed to his mother to repay her for various loans she'd made him over the years but, for some reason, he wanted to make her work for it.'

'But she didn't get it?'

'They're both gone now so we'll never know, will we? We found a fair whack, but who knows now if there was more? That day we were tidying, not searching. There could still be some there. There are a lot of bedrooms in that house, and most were unused even when Jerry was growing up. All the kids had their own rooms, so that's five at least when you count one for the parents. And there were definitely spares for visitors and relations.'

'So there's no proof he did that, then?' I felt I had to stick up for my husband.

'No.' She shook her head. 'Just what we found and what Daniel Senior said to us – but he would have been in a position to know stuff like that, Marian.'

'That's really weird. Are you sure there's not another reason? Like the mother herself hiding the money? I never found Daniel to be mean.'

'It's nothing to do with meanness. It's just a quirk, is my guess. Their mother, from the little I knew of her, had a brain as sound as a bell. If she was hiding money, wouldn't she simply hide it all in one place? Inside a book or at the back of a drawer, rather than distributing it like some kind of confetti? But, look, I've said too much. I'm sorry. It's not right. I don't want to upset you.'

'This started off with you asking about that stupid jokey will exchange – I made one, too, at that time, if you remember?' I didn't want to go any further down that very weird rabbit-hole she had shown me. Money under cushions? That wasn't the Daniel I knew – but she persisted, leading me to believe she was under instructions.

'If Jerry's right, and you can find that bit of paper, it's quite possible that Daniel's leaving you his worldly goods is no joke. We'd hate to think that because, from your point of view, as you said, it was just a bit of fun, you mightn't even read it and casually throw it out. We felt you should at least search for it.'

'But, Aoife . . .' I tried to digest this. I guess I hadn't been thinking like a wife, I had probably not been one for long enough. We had been still in the newbie induction phase – at least I had. I had lived with Peter before we had taken the big step and I'd had an opportunity to make the switch from cohabitant to wife(there is a difference – honestly!). I'd been able to ease myself into my first wifehood. 'He had nothing of value.' I visualised the contents of

Daniel's studio apartment, not a big task. 'His banjo, maybe? He said it was an antique.'

'Daniel played the banjo?' She was astonished.

'I know it sounds funny, and I think "played" is a bit of an exaggeration. He acquired it at a charity auction apparently and twanged at it occasionally, when he said he needed to "unknot knotty problems". I think that was the phrase he used.' I stopped.

That instrument, in its beat-up case, presumably still leaned against the wall of the bedroom in the tiny apartment. Would I continue to live there now? For the first time I realised I was going to have to deal with a lot of this kind of stuff when I got back to the States. What the hell was I going to do with an old banjo, no matter how venerable?

I was going to have many such 'realisations', both practical and emotional, I thought, swallowing hard and managing to control the treacherous stinging behind the eyes as an image rose in my mind: my husband, curly head bent over the strings of the instrument, as slowly, note by note, he picked out a tune, 'Oh Susanna' being a particular favourite.

Aoife had seen I was getting upset: 'Are you all right, pet?'

'Whatever you do, don't be nice to me,' I blurted. 'I won't be able to stand it.'

'Oh, God, I've made things worse. I'm so sorry, Marian. I'll stop talking about it.'

'I'm fine, I'm fine,' I said. 'Honestly. Look, this is going to happen to me. I'll be emotional for the foreseeable future, I guess.

'And, by the way, I don't mind talking about this. I'm just surprised, that's all. But I do know he didn't own anything substantial. He took a big drop in his salary to transfer to the hospital he worked in because of his commitment to what he clearly saw was a cause – he loved the research work. And . . .' something else occurred to me

'. . . I guess he loved to travel, too, and that job gave him endless opportunities. You know, Aoife, if he'd wanted it he could have been away twice a week – and the fact that two of his colleagues came to his funeral from so far away on what was essentially a day trip goes to show . . .'

'Impressive, all right,' she said, before I could find the right words to describe what the presence of Daniel's colleagues had shown. 'You know his ultimate ambition was to get a job at NASA? Even to get up to the space station? He confided this to Jerry, who thinks that was why he switched away from medicine proper to doing so much research on bugs and— What do you call it? Epi-something?'

'Epidemiology?'

'That's it. But,' she added quickly, 'in case you think he wasn't committed to the job he did have, he really was. He cared about improving the life expectancy of those kids in the developing world. That was genuine. But . . .' she hesitated '. . . I'm not sure I should say this, Marian, it's not really my place.'

'Go on.' I was sitting very still.

'I think that while the commitment was real, his interest had more to do with how the drugs and vaccines would behave than in the actual fate of the children. Hope I'm not out of line.'

Rather than go down that road, I referred back to something she'd said earlier: 'He never said anything to me about NASA.'

'Jerry says he seemed quite serious about it.'

Now, in the comfort of my airline seat, I thought about all of that, and out of the blue something else occurred to me. I began to wonder if all those conferences had indeed been fully paid for, as Daniel had claimed – or if the actual travel, an innate wanderlust, had attracted him so frequently to airports. By my reckoning he had been away from home, cumulatively, for at least a quarter, even a third, of the very short time we'd been together.

Stop this, warned the little voice at the back of my brain.

So I did.

It was only a side issue in any case. I would never now discover what his true motivations had been. Or would I? Although I felt uncomfortable about them, my journalist's instinct – curiosity – kicked in as usual. I had the opportunity now to go through his things quite legitimately. Dear God, I thought then, here I am, thinking like a harpy, my husband just fresh in his grave . . .

Quickly, I forced myself back to remembering the discussion I'd had with my sister in-law: 'As for what else might be a "worldly good",' I'd said to her, 'I already have his watch. See?' I'd exhibited it. 'It originally belonged to Daniel Senior. Both Daniels gone in the space of a few weeks, and now I'm facing the death of my own dad. What have I done in a past life, Aoife?' I had meant to add my own little bit of lightness to the discussion, but the question had backfired because my voice had cracked.

'Oh, Marian, Marian . . .' She put a hand across the table to take one of mine.

I clutched hers but carried on, trying to keep the topic of worldly goods on the rails: 'Daniel's apartment was rented, his car was an old Camry, which stayed here when he moved to the States, he'd have known I had no use for his medical books, and his clothes were crap. So, you see? What could he have left me?'

'You keep forgetting about Glanmilish House,' she said gently, relinquishing my hand.

'What about it?'

'It's partially his, or was. His father left it to all of them, as Jerry told you in the graveyard, along with the practice. Although he didn't specify anything like this in the will, our guess, Jerry's and mine, is that Daniel Senior clearly hoped that the two doctors in the family would at least keep the practice going, and by leaving all four of his kids the house, that at least one of them would live in it. He loved the place. So one thing's sure out of all of this. Daniel owned a quarter of that house and the practice for the period between his father's death and his own, even if he didn't know it. The solicitor involved was away on holidays when Daniel Senior died, and what with one thing and another, Eamon and Jerry didn't get around to seeing him until after you left for Glacier. The two of them are named as executors.

'And listen, Marian, under Irish law, even if Daniel didn't leave a will, you have inheritance rights of his share. On the other hand, if there is a valid will, and if your husband bequeathed you all his worldly goods, it's not just the crap clothes,' she had smiled, 'but his share of the house and the practice too. Last word on this, and then we'll change the subject because I can see you don't really want to deal with it. It's probably far too soon.'

'But . . .' I had trailed off. I didn't want Glanmilish House, not even a bit of it. And I certainly didn't want part-ownership of a medical practice. I played for time: 'I'm genuinely sorry to hear what you think he put his mother through with that cushion business, but *if* he did it, it was probably when he was very young.'

'Probably.' She spread her hands in surrender. 'You're right. I shouldn't have mentioned it. Any of it. But I was glad I could be the one to talk to you about all of this. Jerry's a man on a mission – he can be forceful when he gets engaged. He's calm and gorgeous and all that – those looks run in the family but so does that drive. Jerry's dogged.' She smiled again, this time fondly. 'His middle name is "Fair Play"! Anyway,' she added quickly, 'is there anyone alive who doesn't have his or her little foibles? So, tell me about your job, Marian. It sounds very glamorous. Oh, and by the way,

I nearly forgot, Ellie asked me to slip these to you. In case you're having difficulty sleeping or find the next few months too hard.' She passed me a small blister pack of pills. I looked at the lettering on the back: Xanax.

'From Eleanor? But she doesn't like me.'

'Ellie's, well, a bit complicated but, believe me, she wouldn't have made this gesture if she didn't like you. I know it's only a small one, but you can stop thinking she has anything against you. Daniel and she were as thick as thieves all their lives, according to Jerry, but in the time I've known her, I've noticed that she hasn't a good word to say for him and maybe in some way this transferred to you. I've no idea what happened between them but, poor thing, she must be really suffering now. You know what they say about a bereavement following unresolved issues . . .'

I nodded. I had no intention of taking a Xanax tablet, and as the plane glided on, the little pack, unopened, was nestled in a pocket of my battered leather purse. My father had given it to my mother on their twenty-fifth wedding anniversary ('Bought it himself, Marian! Went into a real shop and picked it out!'). If someone had tried to snatch it, I would have bludgeoned them to death with it. Although after I got back to the apartment in Chicago I was planning to give it a rest for a while and employ the Gladstone bag that Daniel and his dad had used.

I continued mentally to forage through all of this. Those images of Daniel stuffing banknotes behind cushions rather than give them to his mother? They were bizarre. And yet, obliquely, in spite of my instinctive dismissal of it in his defence, some part of me thought they might be real.

And what had happened between him and his sister? I had been witness to a row between them during our honeymoon.

And why hadn't he revealed his interest in NASA?

What else didn't I know?

Actually, I thought now, deeply unsettled, I had clearly been wronging Eleanor. The pills had been an olive branch, but why had she behaved like that? What was the origin of her falling out with her brother?

How much did I know at all about my dead husband?

Chapter Twenty-one

Without Daniel filling its tiny spaces, the studio apartment seemed counterintuitively to have shrunk. It was stifling, and I left the entrance door propped open to get some air circulating. Then (temporarily not caring either about humidity or the mosquitoes and flies this action brought in) I opened both the door leading to the fire escape, and the tiny window in the bathroom since the one in the bedroom housed the air-conditioner. Finally, I turned this on, even though, with so much of the apartment gaping, much of its cooling effect would be wasted in the humid air.

Perspiring heavily, I sat on my own side of the bed, hyper-aware of the physical gap he had particularly left there. His death in Montana, a faraway state, burial in a country even further away, the gales of chat in the hotel and good humour in the cemetery, even Aoife's stories about him, all seemed to have coalesced into one enormous hallucination. I know it's a cliché but I kept glancing towards the open entrance door, expecting to see him bounce in, full to bursting with talk. Boy, would I have some questions to ask.

Just a few feet away, the air-con, still not cold enough, wheezed a little as I began to open the mail. There were some greeting cards, and five letters. I recognised the handwriting on one instantly and my heart flipped. It was from Peter.

I was nervous about opening it although I knew Peter was too decent to write anything mean. Nevertheless, I set it aside and tore open one of the others instead.

It was from Peter's mother, formal and short.

Dear Marian,
I was so sorry to hear of the death of your dear husband. Please know that although we are not of your religious persuasion, I am having a Mass said for the happy repose of his soul. It will, I am told, be celebrated in Holy Name Cathedral in the near future although they could not give me a date yet. I have given them your cell number and they have promised to call you in good time.
With best wishes,
Letitia Black

The other two handwritten notes were from the heads, respectively, of Northwestern University Feinberg School of Medicine, from which Daniel had graduated as a doctor, and from Holy Angels Paediatric Medical and Research Facility, both writing warmly about him and expressing condolences to me.

The cards, seven of them, were carefully secular, illustrated with sprays of foliage or sunrises, the senders allowing the printed verses to speak for them. Six had been signed by people whose names I didn't recognise. The seventh, which had no verse, was from Cindy Kurtz, who had written a couple of personal lines: So sorry, hope you're okay, please give me a call if you want to talk. It was signed: Cindy and Junior and Peppy the dog. Underneath, she had scrawled her telephone number.

That had been nice of her, I thought, although I was hardly likely to call her, was I? While I did remember her, we'd only ever had that brief encounter in the hospital and short conversation on the phone.

I steeled myself, then opened Peter's.

Dear Marian,

I am sure you must be dreadfully upset right now and I am very sorry for your loss. Although you and I did not part on good terms, I was sad to hear what happened, and so, of course, was my mother, who will, she says, write to you herself. Daniel Lynch was one of those exceptional individuals who comes around rarely and much was rightly expected of him. He will be greatly missed, not least, I'm sure, by you. Please accept my sympathies.

Sincerely,
Peter

That lovely man – my mom would have killed me if she'd known what I'd done to him. I certainly knew what she would have said about it.

I couldn't be so sure about Dad's reaction. We had never discussed it in detail, and it seemed to have passed him by (despite his having mistaken Daniel for Peter at the wedding) because in some part of his drifting brain, he might have been pleased that Luzveminda had replaced his former buddy. Instead of having a visitor just once a week, she came every day.

I read Peter's letter a second time and this time, in a strange, rather unsettling way, my guilt was tinged with regret. Had I not left him for Daniel, I wouldn't be in my present predicament, and – whisper it – I might even have been buying baby clothes . . .

Scandalised, I brushed away the thought. How could I think such horrible things? And anyhow, I reasoned, if it hadn't been for Daniel, I wouldn't have discovered the real me, a person not deficient in passion, unlike what she had believed for most of her life.

I checked the time: almost six thirty – only hours until I had to face Mollie Lehman tomorrow morning. Better to get it over with. I should call right now to make an appointment. I even picked up the phone – and put it down again. Right now I couldn't face the rant: *What is it with you, Marian? Are you under a Mayan curse or sump'n?*

What a mess – I threw myself backwards onto the bed. If there had been any alcohol in the apartment, I'd have poured myself a very stiff drink, but neither Daniel nor I was a big drinker. Wine with meals in restaurants, or 'restrongs', as he called them – *had* called them: I had to get used to the past tense when I thought or spoke of him – a few glasses had been about the height of it for us.

Then I remembered I had Eleanor's Xanax in my purse – I'd hardly get addicted if I took one for this one night.

I was so tired my eyes were closing. I was sure Dad could wait. The agency looking after him knew I was travelling and probably wouldn't be in touch until tomorrow.

The cost of my father's care was now another worry. Daniel had been heavily subsidising it – as in paying most of Luzveminda's salary and the agency fees for the time we were away. I'd have to find some way to sort out my finances. Hopefully, when I checked, I'd find I was entitled to some sort of widow's pension or that he had life insurance. Another discussion we hadn't had . . .

And what about searching for his will, so-called? I glanced at the nightstand on his side of the bed. Did I really want to know?

Tomorrow.

But, said that insistent little voice, *you promised to call Jerry about it when you got back.*

I will, I will. Tomorrow, tomorrow . . .

I extricated the Xanax from my purse and swallowed one of the pills without benefit of water. Then, too tired to undress fully, I turned off my cell and got straight into bed in my underwear. It had been quite a couple of weeks, I thought drowsily, then dropped off.

* * *

I was surprisingly alert when I woke the next morning at just after five thirty. I had slept for almost eleven hours. No more procrastination: time to get busy.

After my shower, I turned on my cell. There had been two missed calls from the care agency and one from Luzveminda. I called the agency first: 'I don't want you to worry, Marian,' said the night-time phone minder when he came on. 'Our lady, as you know, leaves at six after serving dinner to your dad and clearing up, but when Luzveminda came in at eight to spend the night there, she found him not too well.'

'What does that mean?'

'He was unconscious in his chair.'

'What? And you call that "not too well"?'

'If you check your cell you'll see we tried to call you after she spoke to us. Naturally, we told her to call an ambulance.' He gave me the name of the hospital.

* * *

When I got there, my father was in a deep coma, tethered to his bed with drip lines and an oxygen mask, lying quite peacefully, now and then opening his eyes or sighing, which I was told was quite normal but, unfortunately, did not mean he was coming round. Since he had arrived by ambulance, he had 'so far' not regained consciousness.

This was from one of his doctors, who spoke to me in the corridor outside the room, his soft voice admirably suited to this kind of discussion. 'Even if you'd been here, there isn't anything you could have done, Mrs Lynch. His carer did absolutely the right thing in calling nine one one. And twenty-four-hour care, as it's called, can't be that. It's more like twenty-three, or even less. People have to take coffee and toilet breaks, even in a hospital situation. So there's no one to blame. Not yourself, not your father's carers . . . '

'I might at least have had a chance to say goodbye.' I was desperately upset – and furious with myself for having taken that extra day in Ireland while ceding my father's care to others when I, his primary carer, was responsible. I had been away from Chicago for almost three weeks, with minimal contact. So, it was my own fault that I might now be too late.

'But you don't know whether he would have heard you or not.' The doctor reacted to my distress. 'None of us knows that for sure. What we do know is that his body is going through a process, making the journey we all have to take before the end . . . ' He went on to explain how, one by one, the organs gradually fail until there is no longer any meaningful activity. 'It takes weeks in some cases, but in your father's, it has already started. Perhaps a week? We'll look after him, of course, and keep him comfortable, but he's already in God's hands.'

The hospital, originally founded by a Catholic congregation of nuns, almost all now either dead or themselves invalided, still maintained threads of the religion among some of the staff, since they still owned it and, in theory, ran it; they certainly kept an eye on its ethos.

Initially, I found the fatalism discomforting, but I had no choice other than to accept it. After two days of keeping vigil at Dad's bedside, trying to concentrate on whatever book I was reading while listening for changes in his breathing, I came quite quickly to find the regime rather consoling.

But that first day I had another urgent task. 'I'll be back, Dad,' I whispered into his ear, before I left, but there was no response.

It was hard to shed the image of my father in his sterile bed, but by the time I got down to LaSalle Street, I was already thinking ahead to what was to come, and bracing myself for the inevitability that Mollie would not countenance any further absences on my part. I could have called rather than gone all the way down there, but I felt the need to stand up and be counted. As I went up in the elevator towards *Femme*'s floor, however, my imagination already had me coming down again.

In the foyer, Cherry was talking to Mollie's deputy, Ryoko, whose back was to the door. On seeing me enter she widened her eyes in warning. Ryoko, spotting this, turned round. 'Well, well, well!' she said, in her high, lethal voice, placing her free hand on one of her teeny-tiny hips. 'I have to admire you. You have balls!'

'Is Mollie in?'

'No, she's in Timbuktu – what do you think, four weeks before we launch?'

'Can I see her?' Suddenly I was no longer nervous. Compared with what I had been through already and what I faced in the next, relatively uncharted, period, Mollie, Ryoko, actually *Femme* in general, were peanuts. I glared at the deputy editor, for once glorying in my height. Measuring hers from a distance of about ten feet, I reckoned that the top of her head wouldn't reach any higher than my third rib.

'I'll tell her you're here.' Cherry punched her desk phone.

'Good luck. You'll need it!' Ryoko, after one last venomous look, went into her own office.

'She says you'll have to wait, Marian.' Cherry quietly replaced her handset. Then, taking a quick glance at both closed doors, she pulled off her earpiece. 'Are you okay, sugar? Have you found out yet how it happened? Let me give you a hug.' Quickly, ignoring the insistent ringing of the phone, she came out from behind her desk and held me tightly.

'Nobody seems to know how he ended up in the water, Cherry,' I said, when she let me go. 'I really think, and so it seems does everyone on the scene, that it was just an awful accident. Something maybe attracted him in the river and he may have gone to look and lost his footing. There'd been a lot of rain and the water was very high. When he was found his leg was badly broken. There's no way, Cherry, no way that he took his own life, although I was asked a couple of times about his "state of mind" recently.'

'Of course not,' she said staunchly. 'Is there gonna be a formal investigation?'

'I have the coroner's certificate, so I think that's the end of it. No one will ever know exactly what happened, I guess – but now, Cherry, you probably won't believe this, I hardly believe it myself . . .' I brought her up to date on my dad's condition.

'Oh, Marian,' she said, when I'd finished. 'That's truly awful, and so sad.'

'Yeah. I'm inclined to believe that the gods have decided this job is not for me! I was so excited about it but, hey, it's not the end of the world. There'll be other jobs.'

'Sorry, sugar.' She reacted to yet another ringtone: 'I gotta answer these damn phones.' She hurried behind the desk and, having put her earpiece back in, chirped her greeting, asking each caller in turn to hold on. By the time they were all dealt with, her console was blinking red, like a Christmas tree. 'I told her you're here,' she said quietly, 'and I have to warn you, I know it's not fair, but you're gonna get a rough ride.' Her phone rang yet again, but before she took the call, she whispered, 'Don't let them kick you around. Where the hell do they think they are anyway? New York?' She pressed a button, carolling, 'Good morning, *Femme* magazine, Cherry speaking, how may I help you?'

I crossed the foyer to sit in one of the uncomfortable but terribly modern steel chairs in the shape of spiders, the seats being the bodies. What was *Femme* anyway? Despite the self-important aspirations, it was just another mag to take its place with *Vogue*, *National Geographic* and *Reader's Digest* on coffee tables in the waiting rooms of doctors, dentists, podiatrists and therapists, to be thumbed, surreptitiously divested of its more interesting pages and special offer coupons, until it was so ragged and unreadable it was replaced with *Car and Driver*.

I picked up the magazine's glossy launch brochure, its cover in shades of iridescent blue, and leafed through it. Money had been spent on it: it was actually very good.

Cherry's desk phone never ceased ringing, but after ten minutes or so, her internal phone buzzed too. 'Yes, fine, I'll tell her,' she said quietly, then looked up. 'Mollie's ready for you now.'

I'll bet she is, I thought.

As I passed her desk, Cherry asked her latest caller to hold the line for 'just a moment, please', and then, to me, in a low voice, 'Don't forget, honey, we're Chicagoans. We're from the city of big shoulders.'

* * *

'Close the door, Marian,' Mollie said, over her shoulder. Standing at her (darkened) window, she had taken the classic movie pose, back to me, moodily looking outwards at another (darkened) skyscraper. 'I'd be interested to hear your side of the story.'

'I don't think that's true, Mollie,' I said steadily. 'I actually don't think you're in the least interested in what I have to say. So, please, let's get this over with. I've got to get back to the hospital.'

She pivoted. '*You're* sick, now, Marian?'

'No, I'm not, thank you for asking. My dad has about a week to live.'

'Well, my God.' She sank into her seat. 'You got a dyin' grandmother upstate too?' Suddenly she banged her desk. 'Whatsamatter with you? You had everything going for ya here. I *trusted* you, Marian. I gave you my *trust*! And this is how you repay me? We got four weeks, just four weeks, to go, and where's Marian Lescher? She's nowhere. I call her.' She gestured, right palm uppermost. 'Michelle's people call her.' She palmed up the left. 'But she's nowhere – and now I hear on the grapevine that Michelle's doin' *Martha Stewart Living* for Thanksgiving. *Martha Stewart* fucking *Living*, Marian, when she could have had *Femme*. I had her pegged for *our* Thanksgiving edition but, no, she'll be on the cover of *Martha Stewart Living*. Thanks a whole bunch, Marian.'

'I don't suppose you'd be interested in *why* I've been missing? And *why* I'll have to be absent again for at least this week and maybe longer?'

'You gotta be kidding.' She stared at me, so angry I could see that the downy hairs along the side of one of her cheeks, gilded by the light angled at them from her desk lamp, were trembling.

'Let's get to the point, Mollie,' I said quietly. 'Based on your attitude, how angry you are – and, of course, that's quite understandable—'

'Cherry tells me your husband went missing.'

'Yes. In Glacier National Park. He died of exposure and wasn't found for almost a week. By the way, there's little or no cell coverage there so even if I'd wanted to call you, which I actually didn't, Mollie, it was impossible. Daniel, my husband, was Irish and had to be repatriated. There was a lot of paperwork and delay before the set of flights to get him back to his Irish family and his funeral. Funerals in Ireland are pretty immediate but not that quick.'

'I'm sorry for your loss,' she said. At least she'd said it but immediately got back on message. 'And now, you say, your dad too—'

'Yes, and now my dad.' I glanced up at her ceiling, at the ultra-*ultra*-modern steel chandelier that had probably come from some Nordic country and cost thousands. Then, before she could get in again: 'You know what, Mollie? I don't really want to go through it all. You talk about trust? That goes both ways. I got you Tim Cook – and if I hadn't been up to my eyes in tragedy, Michelle Obama too, it seems. Do you really think I'd go AWOL without proper cause?'

She opened her mouth to respond but I stood up, pulling myself to my full height, and, like a traffic cop, held up a hand to stop her. 'Save it, Mollie. I'm assuming I'm surplus to requirements. I know you're busy and I'll save you the trouble of saying it, but I'll have to be paid for the interviews I've given you already, including Tim Cook's. I'll be in touch with— Who signs the cheques?'

'I sign the cheques,' she said levelly.

'I'll call Cherry and send in my invoice. She knows I can't be in this week because my dad has no other relatives. That's genuine, Mollie. You have a good day now, and I do wish you and all your colleagues here the very best of luck with your new magazine. That's genuine, too. And so is my gratitude to you for hiring me.'

I didn't slam her door. That would have been childish.

'How'd it go?' Cherry whispered, as I swept back into the reception foyer.

'Don't ask, Cherry, but you can take a wild guess. Can't stop now, I have to get back to the hospital, but I'll give you a call.'

Her phone rang again. 'Good luck, Marian, talk soon. *Femme* magazine,' she sang into the phone. 'Cherry speaking, how may I help you?'

I went into the common area to clear out the few belongings I had left at my desk – pens, a few bits of makeup, a pair of flats, a 'good' coverall jacket suitable for interviewing someone unexpectedly. I kept my eyes focused, trying not to react to the surreptitious looks of some of my colleagues. It was almost as though to consort with me might be contagious and they, too, would be dumped. And as I went back out through Reception, Cherry, again on the phone, listening to someone, mouthed at me, 'It was nice to know you. I mean that.'

'Me too,' I mouthed back.

Outside again on LaSalle, I was surrounded by waves of office workers carrying takeaway coffees as they pounded towards their day's work: *Outta my way, I'm busy. I'm important. I'm employed.*

There was, too, a sprinkling of early-rising rubberneckers, who were getting in everyone's way as they deployed cameras and camera-equipped devices up and down the street. With the Chicago Board of Trade building, one of the stars of Chicago's art-deco period, straddling its end, LaSalle, a box canyon, is not just a financial hub, it's part of what has been officially designated one of the city's Historic Districts.

How did I feel? After the battering I had taken in recent days from events outside my control, I felt brilliant that I hadn't allowed myself to be pushed around.

That wouldn't last, I knew, so before going to the hospital, I decided to make the most of it and have a proper sit-down cup of coffee and maybe a Danish.

But then, mug in hand, as I took my seat in Starbucks: *What have I done?*

Chapter Twenty-two

Next morning, I wasn't even dressed when a courier arrived at about seven thirty with a letter from *Femme* magazine. I assumed it was my formal severance notice, threw it aside and went into the kitchen to make coffee.

It was only after my shower that curiosity overcame me and I tore it open.

Cherry had come through for me, and Mollie, who had signed the cheque inside, had also included a note, sweet and sour in equal measure:

Marian, It was on the cards. You're a good writer and a hard worker, but you really need to get your priorities straight. The Cook piece was good, not exceptional, but I could see potential in you and I did believe that with us you could have become one of our stars. After our meeting yesterday, there was no way back, though, was there? As

*you know we don't pay until after publication so
I'm bending the rules with this (encl). As you'll see,
I've doubled up on Cook, which means halving
the other two, and those payments will be sent
on as each is published. Pity it didn't work out. M*

I accepted that, from *Femme*'s point of view, with regard to priorities, she certainly had a point, but it was the other phrase that rankled. The Cook profile had been 'good but not exceptional'? That nearly killed me. I had worked so hard and carefully on it . . . Perhaps, after all, I was not cut out for journalism at that level.

But I'm the type who simply cannot resist proving people wrong about me. I'd show Mollie Lehman . . .

First things first, though. I lodged the cheque.

* * *

Four days into my vigil at my father's bedside, I had nodded off, book still open on my lap, when I was gently shaken by one of the nurses: 'Mrs Lynch? Mrs Lynch! You need to wake up now.'

'Wha—' I blinked, briefly forgetting where I was.

'It won't be long,' he said. 'Would you like to say a prayer?' He, or someone, had lit a candle on the locker beside my father's bed. Its flame flickered as he pulled up a chair and quietly sat beside me.

I looked towards the bed. Dad's breathing was sporadic now, with long intervals between breaths. His head was thrown back a little, showing the creases on his neck and the tideline between the pallor of his chest and the faded builder's tan he had somehow retained, despite almost two decades of retirement.

His mouth was open, breath rasping a little, each time he took one. I had believed I'd prepared myself for this, but I hadn't. This was my dad, contrary, spatting with Mom, full of opinions, but always steadfastly just *there*. But now he looked so vulnerable, meekly offering his throat to the inevitable. Unaccountably I was flooded with desperate love. The nurse put a hand gently on my shoulder. 'Not long,' he murmured. 'Shall we say a Hail Mary?'

'Is there a priest?' Stricken, I looked at his kind face. 'I'm sure he'd want one.'

'Unfortunately, Father is not with us this afternoon. But he was here when Bill was brought in and gave the last rites then. You should take his hand, perhaps.'

But I seemed to be unable to move. Gently, he picked up my hand and placed it on Dad's. I took it then, so much lighter than I had expected, so much not my father's hand. It twitched, just once, like the paw of a dreaming cat, against my palm. The candle flame was steady, seeming to enclose the three of us in its light as, beside me, the nurse made the Sign of the Cross: 'Our Father Who art in Heaven . . .'

Once embedded, those words never leave. '. . . hallowed be Thy Name . . .' Shakily I joined in, only half believing that this was to be the final act.

We had got through the second decade of our Rosary and were into its Gloria, when instead of starting with the next Our Father, the nurse stopped leading, placed a hand on my arm and leaned forward a little. 'Your dad's gone to God,' he said quietly. 'May he rest in peace.' He turned to me then. 'No need to take your hand away yet,' he said. 'I'll leave you for a few minutes alone with him.' Very quietly, he got up from his chair and slipped out of the room, closing the door without a sound.

* * *

As for poor Dad's funeral, it was sad, short, and very lonely for me. In no way did it do justice to a life of work ethic and fidelity to parish, family and trade.

In fairness to them, Daniel's two brothers, Jerry and Eamon, had tried to get to Chicago, but the whole of Ireland and Britain, it seemed, had been stormbound and all flights had been cancelled. 'We've been offered alternatives to fly from Amsterdam or Paris,' Jerry yelled, as he tried to speak over the roaring of wind in the background, 'but the high-speed ferries have been taken off and the slow ones are very slow, and then we'd have to spend hours and hours on cross-country trains. I don't think we can make it, Marian. I'm very sorry. We're very sorry, Aoife too. She sends her love by the way.' Still having to shout, he told me that the disruption was to continue tomorrow, so there was no point in holding off the funeral until the next day.

'I understand perfectly,' I said. 'Please don't worry about it.'

But as I closed the call, I found I was upset they weren't able to come. I'd known my in-laws for such a short time, but already they felt like family. Certainly Jerry and Aoife did.

I felt very conspicuous in my solitary occupancy of the top pew in Holy Name Cathedral, rendered even more cavernous by the sparse attendance at Dad's obsequies. Other than myself and the handful of 'ordinary', mostly elderly, Mass-goers in the back pews, there were eighteen people either serving or observing in the spaces of Holy Name Cathedral that morning: the priest, two altar servers, three neighbours from his apartment block, four parishioners, six of the funeral director's staff, a ninety-four-year-old priest, who had presided over the parish years ago and had known both of my parents, and Luzveminda, who was actually very upset, more visibly so than I, who felt quite dizzy throughout. And, although this is going to sound very odd, I was too tired to cry.

No relatives, because neither Mom nor Dad had any left, not even in-laws because, few enough in any case, they had all passed, too. I did have two cousins, whom I barely knew except from signatures on Christmas cards, but one lived in Florida, the other was married, with family, in South Africa. I had not gotten in touch.

The officiating priest was new to the parish and hadn't known my father, but he did his best with the eulogy, based around the information I had given him. But he got the name wrong, calling Dad not Lescher but Laski. It happens. But you do remember such little details and hearing that erroneous name boom and echo, several times, through the PA system, was maddening.

To my surprise, two of my former teachers from Holy Name Elementary, Sisters Margaret Mary, gnarled hands now on a walker, and Consilio, the principal, both seeming ancient yet simultaneously ageless, turned up with Holy Name's retired secretary at the crematorium.

For me, that whole day, including the cremation, felt weird. I was light-headed with exhaustion. This was not happening, was it?

But it was. There was my wreath of white roses being removed from the casket at the crematorium, there sounded the almost imperceptible hum of the mechanisms as my dad's casket was slowly taken from our sight, and now here were the final handshakes and shoulder-pats from mourners, including the gentle touch of my two former teachers and their secretary, who now lived with them 'in community'. 'We're too old to go all the way into the city now,' said Sister Consilio, 'so we couldn't make the cathedral, but we're not too far from here. So it was handy. We're praying for you, Marian.'

No one from the high school, of course, but the presence of those elderly stalwarts illustrated perfectly that, when I remembered my schooldays, it was Elementary I thought of almost exclusively. 'I'm so grateful you came,' I said to the trio, meaning it.

And while her companions looked on, Sister Consilio gripped my hand. 'God bless you, Marian, and God speed your dear daddy to his reward in Heaven.'

I was touched, but as I walked alone to flag down a cab, I was depressed. The contrast between the huge, friend- and relative-laden ceremonials at Daniel's farewell and this sad, small affair was stark. It was on occasions like this, I thought, that a person needed siblings or a close friend.

The traffic was very heavy all the way into the city, and I was completely exhausted by the time I was letting myself back into the apartment that evening. Without making myself a meal, or even coffee, I shed my formal clothes and sat heavily on the blanket box at the end of the bed. The reality started to kick in. Never again would I have to organise my calendar around visits to my dad, or snoop through his icebox to check on his food supplies, or chivvy him into keeping a hospital or dental appointment. Sitting there, I would have taken any counsel, any information, any comfort. But there was no one who actually *had* to be in my corner now. I hadn't appreciated him when he was available. I'd never told him I loved him or run to him to confide. Too late now to say anything because my dad had drifted away from the bonds of gravity in search of stars.

Chapter Twenty-three

There had been a few downpours during the night, and on the morning after my dad's funeral, although the sun was about to come up, the air was temporarily cool outside and I could shut off the window air-conditioner in the bedroom.

Getting back into bed that morning, I was accompanied not by its noisy breath or, sadly, by the breath of my husband, but by the sounds of the waking city, the trundling of the L, car doors slamming, a snatch of conversation on the sidewalk between two kids – *Well, I don't think so. She's definitely hot* – and, approaching and then fading, the sound of hip-hop from someone passing with what we used to call a boombox. I don't know what they call them these days, but since the advent of iPods and all that sophisticated technology, it was rare to hear music on the streets among a population silently going about its business with earbuds inserted and plastic wires trailing over their chests into pockets, purses or money belts.

I felt wrung out – there are no other words to describe it – and, having nothing actually scheduled that morning, no hospital visiting, no interviewing or writing (and no funerals), I decided not to get up just yet. I knew, though, that I was facing into a day of paperwork and phone calls to see where the land lay in terms of my future. I had to sort out a place to live, since I now assumed I had no right to stay on at the apartment, even if I wanted to. I had to call someone – I had no idea whom – at Holy Angels to ascertain if Daniel's accounts were up to date. I had to contact federal and state tax offices to make sure he was legal with his taxes. I had to find out how to go about registering my father's death – Daniel's family could take care of his, which was yet another thing to mention to one of his, and my, relatives. Another wrinkle: perhaps I had to do it because he had died on American soil.

Then, on my own behalf, I had to call Cherry. Oracle as she was, she would also be able to tell me whether they were planning to include my profiles in their forward publishing plans and, if so, when: freelancers, even those on contract, and of course that no longer applied to me, were paid only when the stuff appeared in print.

Where did I have to go to find out if, as Daniel's widow, I had any social-security entitlements, given that right now I hadn't a single commission to do any work?

And that reminded me. I had to contact the two unfortunate interviewees I had lined up for *Femme* for this week. Could I persuade the *Tribune* to take even one of them, a high-profile attorney?

I groaned as the list of tasks continued to grow, and the more it did, the more irksome it seemed and the more self-critical I became about how much I had to learn about the mundane aspects – and the attendant paperwork – of civic life. Along with my second marriage I seemed to have shucked off this awareness. Peter and I had discussed everything. I could have put my hand instantly on any of his files, even – dare I say it? – on his will. And he had frequently urged me to make my own.

Don't dare think about what might have been. I threw off the sheet and got out of bed.

In the shower, normally an enjoyable part of my daily rituals, even in that shrunken cubicle, the parade of negatives continued to march past in lockstep. On paper I had no major assets whatsoever. My small cache of rings, my own, Daniel's wedding band and Mom's, her little ear studs and a few bits and pieces I had accumulated over the years didn't amount to much. If I included my engagement solitaire, I estimated that, when purchased retail, the entire cache might have cost, cumulatively, ten thousand dollars.

But pre-owned, or 'pre-loved', as sellers say when trying to seduce you on eBay or Etsy, the prices they would fetch were paltry. Somewhere it had lodged in that hotchpotch brain of mine that, like cars, jewellery devalued the moment it left the store but a lot more dramatically, perhaps by as much as 60 to 75, even 80 per cent. That is, unless it had been a statement or heirloom piece valued because its previous owner had been an Elizabeth Taylor, a Duchess of Windsor, a Princess Diana or one of the new icons, an Elton John, a Beyoncé or even, for some people, a Kardashian. So, I'd be doing well to get, maybe, three thousand for the lot. And that was being optimistic.

As for the Camry, it was almost ten years old and in Glanmilish. Who'd be interested there? I supposed someone might give a thousand euro for it. And even if I could sell it, there'd have to be more bloody paperwork, change of ownership or whatever.

So, let's say less than four thousand dollars in total if I managed to sell everything – added to whatever fees I could finagle out of *Femme* magazine. That was the full extent of my fortune.

Not much to show for my decades on this earth, I thought – and my credit card was no doubt lining up to give me a slap.

But at least I was healthy. And I could leave aside that grim agenda of tasks for now – because who'd know what I was up to? Who in Chicago would ask? Cherry, maybe, for a while anyway but, inevitably, she would move on.

But on the bright side I had a roof over my head for today and hopefully tonight; the bed was comfortable; outside, it was a cool day and I had some cash in my wallet – enough to have pancakes for breakfast in a honky-tonk and to buy a few groceries for my dinner. Right now, there were no demands on my time from anyone else. So for the present, for this one day, that surely was enough to ask of the universe.

Above the blackboard in our classroom at Holy Name Elementary (yes, we're back there again), there was a sampler. Its embroidered wording, once navy blue on a cream canvas background, had aged to blue-grey on dun. *Consider the lilies of the field*, ran the cursive script, the initial capital C a little wobbly, *how they grow; they toil not, neither do they spin: yet I say unto you, even Solomon in all his glory was not arrayed like one of these.* It was only a few years ago when I was reading again and again about the 'new' concept of mindfulness that I saw what an old approach to living it actually was.

Anyhow, that was me for today.

It seemed as though I had been perpetually in motion since meeting Daniel Lynch – or, more accurately, going after him. There had been spikes of excitement, sometimes extreme (actually meeting Daniel, properly discovering sex), sometimes less so but pleasurable enough (our wedding day, that sociable honeymoon), delight (seeing the bear in Glacier, recognition, at last, by the *Chicago Tribune*), and the job offer from *Femme*.

On the other hand there had been conflicted emotions when I'd left Peter and Letty, acute agitation during those five days of waiting for Daniel's body to be discovered, those two terrible sets of mourning in quick succession, first for Daniel, and then, moving right up to date, for my dad.

And now there were all the dilemmas which had arisen from my decision to pursue the man I conceived to have been the love of my life.

On balance, had I won or lost?

That's semantic. I shouldn't be asking such questions. Life wasn't about winning or losing, or placing happiness on a scale of one to ten. Life was, is, what it is – to use that phrase. My mission for today was to consider the lilies.

I had lost. No question.

But lilies be damned. As I stood in the bedroom, now cocooned in Daniel's oversized robe, trying to decide which predicament I would face first after I'd dried my hair, my gaze fell on Daniel's nightstand. Was that piece of paper still in the drawer?

I decided that, as a matter of urgency, I had to dry my hair.

Then I decided to dredge the last of the coffee grounds from the tin.

Then I had to perk them.

Then I had to drink my coffee, although there wasn't even a slice of Daniel's famous 'sliced pan' to have with it.

Then I had to wash the mug, dry it and put it away.

Then I had to unpack my bag and package up my laundry for the laundromat.

Then I had to unpack Daniel's bag, a task I had been dreading. One option, I thought, was simply to discard the lot, bag and contents, without opening it. But suppose there was something in it that shouldn't be dumped with the normal garbage but could identify Dr Lynch as its owner? The city was fussy about its litter laws, over-fussy, some would say, and might come after me, as his widow, with its sanctions and fines.

Before I could overthink that rather remote concept, quickly, like pulling off a Band-Aid, I undid the straps of the rucksack and turned it upside-down to shake the contents onto the bed.

Out tumbled his spare pair of jeans and a couple of T-shirts, sandals, trainers and two plastic bags from the shopping mall at O'Hare. Neither had been tied and the toiletries from one, his socks and underwear for the laundry from the other scattered everywhere. (The shirt and jacket about which I had argued when he was shoving them so roughly into the backpack were missing, of course, having gone with him to the grave.)

I fetched a second garbage sack from under the sink and began shoving everything into it, even what looked clean. He had folded each sock into its fellow, but inside one pair, I felt something hard.

It was a black velvet ring box. Heavily folded and stuffed into it, with some difficulty, I imagine, were two pages, one a receipt from Macy's on State Street, the other, torn from a prescription pad, covered with Daniel's execrable handwriting with which even I had difficulty.

Before taking the ring from its slot, I read this, more than once having to pause over a particular word to decipher it.

Mar, I know it's not your birthday or anything, but I was passing Macys where we bought the wedding rings and it just occurred to me that I should buy you something. Anyway, the saleswoman persuaded me to buy you this eternity ring. I'm enclosing the receipt if you want to change it for something else but you have nice fingers and I thought it would look good on you. After what I hope has been a memorable holiday in Glacier, topped off with a memorable meal in Great Falls on our last night in Montana, I hope you like it. Enjoy.

D

PS You can thank me in the usual manner!

A poet he wasn't.

That glad-rags dinner he had booked, but never eaten, in Great Falls? That had been the reason for carting a jacket and shirt with him – and the discovery that someone like him, not given to the grand gesture, had gone to such trouble for me made all of this almost unbearably moving.

When man makes plans, God smiles. I sure got to understand that concept of Mom's. I also understood the word 'heartbreak'. The ring itself, platinum like our wedding bands and inset with a half-circle of small diamonds (totalling .67 carats, according to the receipt), fitted perfectly.

Like an automaton, I finished packing the second garbage sack for the laundromat. Then, when I could postpone it no longer, I approached the nightstand and opened the drawer. It contained pens, a notebook, nasal spray, spare spectacles, an unopened pack of Bufferin, nail clippers, a spare toothbrush, an address book, a few torn-up bits of paper with his scribble on it, a prescription pad and his Holy Angels ID, on its lanyard. I looked at the torn-up bits and found just telephone numbers with names on them. No A4 sheet of paper.

Well, I thought then, so much for Jerry Lynch and his theories! I closed the drawer and went out to the kitchen.

While waiting for the coffee to heat up again, I remembered that under the silverware drawer, there was another Daniel used for paperwork. I had never opened it, believing it was private and that I had disrupted his bachelor life enough as it was, but I had glimpsed its contents – bills, tax returns, that kind of thing – when he had.

I opened it now, feeling like a thief, hesitating before examining the contents. Then I put on my journalism hat, telling myself that Daniel was dead now and his privacy was really of no consequence to him. Perhaps I could find something, a bank statement maybe, which might be of benefit to me, his widow. Before I could overthink this, I took everything out and piled it on the table. There were the receipts and tax documents I had expected, a few letters from Daniel's bank, all unopened, his apartment lease – which, to my dismay, turned out to be short-term, week-to-week. There was no single sheet of A4 paper. But there was an unopened letter from J.L. Ruttger and Associates., attorneys at law, with an address on Clark Street.

Taking a deep breath, I opened it.

The letter inside proved simultaneously innocuous and intriguing and had been dated three days before we left for Glacier.

Dear Mr Lynch,

Thank you for your telephone enquiry yesterday and we confirm, as of this morning, receipt of Certain Documents you have sent to us. As discussed, should you wish to proceed with matters, it would be our pleasure to serve your needs. Please call at your convenience to make an appointment with me or one of my associates.

Thank you for choosing to contact J.L. Ruttger and Associates. We appreciate your business.
Yours sincerely,
John Lorimer Ruttger

The letter was signed personally, the name followed by a bunch of qualification initials, and the masthead proclaimed that the firm's practice lay in general, family, criminal and tax law.

The light in the kitchen was relatively dim so, leaving the letter on the table, I went out on to the fire escape for some fresh air and, once there, held my eternity ring up to the light, angling it this way and that, watching how the rising sun sparked tiny flashes of red and green in the little diamonds. Miniature traffic lights. *Two roads diverged in a yellow wood . . . And sorry I could not travel both . . .*

I went back inside to get dressed, and when I was ready, delicately, as if the attorney's letter was made of spun sugar, I put it back into its envelope. I needed to think.

Chapter Twenty-four

I was having pancakes with extra maple syrup, bacon, an egg sunny side up and wheat toast in a local eatery. A local radio station was giving the temperature for Chicago this morning to be a 'cool' 81 degrees Fahrenheit with humidity at just 60 per cent. Pleasant, in other words.

So where now for me? Sometimes the best thing you can do is nothing, was another of Mom's adages. And, yes, that was fine and dandy for Mom, whose life had been bounded by regular mealtimes, Dad's salary cheques and her weekly game of canasta with Mrs Feinstein, our neighbour after the downsizing. It was usually just the two of them at the green baize card table, although sometimes Mrs Feinstein's sister, a 'fierce competitor', according to Mom, joined them. My mother dressed up for those evenings whether it was to be for two or three, dabbed herself liberally with her lavender cologne and always took with her a basketful of homemade chocolate chip cookies.

With the exception of the five years I spent with Peter Black, my life has not been so regular, I'm afraid, certainly not since Daniel Lynch had thrown a bomb into it. It seemed there had been nothing but drama for me since we had gotten together, the culmination being his death – followed so closely by Dad's. Doing nothing was no longer an option. I had been washed around by seas of reaction and indecision long enough. It was time to take charge of my life. I opened my purse, pulled out the attorney's letter, then my cell.

* * *

At ten fifteen I was sitting in a windowless but well-furnished meeting room in front of one of John L. Ruttger's associates on Clark Street, a person listed among the 18,220 (believe it or not) attorneys in the Chicago area. I had chosen her from this firm's sixty-eight attorneys because she was a woman, and because, in her online photograph when I had Googled the firm, she had looked kind – but mostly because her calendar had been clear this morning.

In person, she was nothing like her photograph. Hatchet-faced, much thinner than I had been expecting, her hair scraped back into an untidy bun, she was quite intimidating, I felt, although her Southern drawl, lush and beguiling, somehow ameliorated the severity of her appearance.

When I had called the firm to make the appointment, the receptionist I had spoken to was understandably circumspect about why or even when Daniel had contacted them, and wouldn't divulge what documents he had lodged there. So, when I arrived, I had with me everything I could think of: social security ID, marriage licence, Daniel's death certificate, even our two passports, Daniel's Holy Angels ID and both our driver's licences. Further to prove my bona fides, I had even taken along Daniel's note about the eternity ring.

'Wow!' said the woman, I having related the gist of events leading up to why I was there. 'An' your daddy, he died just a few days later? Dear God in Heaven, how awful for ya! And we're sorry for your loss.'

She confirmed that the firm had checked Daniel's submission and, chuckling, added: 'That original document was one of the shortest I've ever seen in my life! Kinda like a soldier's in wartime. It wasn't quite what we'd call here an 'all to mother' will but near enough. We didn't change anything of the substance but it's all proper now and good to go. That will be two hundred dollars, one hundred for the consultation, one hundred for makin' good the document.'

'But your listing says the first consultation is free.'

'Honey, this ain't the first consult. Your late husband's was.'

Fortuitously, among the papers in Daniel's business drawer, along with the other documents, I had found an envelope containing 565 dollars and some change, probably, I thought, some travel expenses. I still had more than three hundred left and I gave her what she wanted. She left me for a few minutes and when she came back, she had with her one of those transparent document wallets, just like the one in which I had put the Humpty letters to give to the Gardaí.

There was a yellow Post-it stuck to the plastic. 'Just one thang,' she said. 'I've a note here to ask you to confirm if your husband's daddy's dead.'

'He's dead,' I nodded. She removed the sticker. 'That's fine!' She pushed the wallet across her desk.

'Can I have a receipt, please?' I eyeballed her.

She gave it, but with bad grace, scrawling her signature and stamping the document rather too firmly.

* * *

Back in Daniel's studio, on studying his lease again I realised I could stay in it only until the end of that awful week of mourning, of losing my job (or, more accurately, of not fighting to keep it – what had possessed me? Right now I couldn't believe I had acted so foolishly. I guess I had momentarily lost all reason). Anyhow, I had no choice but to move. On finding the lease I had been surprised at the type, but not for long. I told myself it stood to reason: the place could never be a home. He had probably felt he needed only a bolthole so he could, in a heartbeat, up sticks and move to another country, whether it was back to Ireland or onwards to Bhutan. Pick a place and go. Wanderlust knows no bounds, especially if, as his brother had insisted, his ultimate goal was outer space.

And, it seemed, Jerry had had it right. In the drawer where I had found the lease, I had also found two completed application forms for a residency programme in aerospace medicine, one for the Mayo Clinic, the other for the University of Texas. My mind had boggled briefly – but, then, nothing about Daniel Lynch could surprise me now, I'd thought. This was just another thing I hadn't known. Was he going to tell me? Maybe call me from his new location? Where did I fit into all of this?

The more I thought about his plan to stay in Ireland to look after his dad's practice, starting immediately after our vacation, and for me to join him, the more I figured that this was a figment, a fantasy. Daniel Lynch wouldn't – couldn't – have stayed for long before we were on the move again. Such a small place couldn't hold such a big personality . . .

At any rate, there was no benefit to be gained from speculating. Daniel was dead, dead, dead. He had taken his secrets with him.

Dad's lease, I found, was long-term, renewable annually, and when I probed, I discovered that a full seven months remained on it. And because the building was old, filled mostly with relatively permanent tenants, like my parents, the rent, for Chicago, was modest. That suited me, gave me a decent pause to consider what the hell I should do next and I moved in, taking from Daniel's place only my own bags and what would fit into the trunk of a cab.

My husband's apartment had been rented furnished and equipped. Dad's place was overstuffed with his and Mom's furniture and accumulated clutter, but after the confines of the studio, it felt as spacious as a palace.

Later that day it was a wrench to meet Luzveminda for the last time. She had genuinely cared for my father and not only in her professional capacity. She certainly deserved a bonus payment but I simply hadn't got it to give. She understood, I think, and because I was now wearing Daniel's watch full time, I offered her mine as a gift: 'Just to say thank you, Luz, and to remember us by. It's a Seiko and that's a good brand. I've noticed you don't have a wrist watch, only your upside-down nurse's one.'

'Thank you. But I was wondering if, instead, you have no use for Mr Lescher's walking frame. My grandmother needs one but can't afford.'

'That's terrible, Luz, where does she live?'

'Quezon City,' she said simply, 'with my parents,' as though I should know that families, all families, look after their own.

'But is there anything else, portable, of course, that she or your parents need that we could give you rather than that bulky old thing? There's very little here,' I waved an arm around the apartment, 'that's of any use to me.'

'Only the walker, please.'

'But how would you get it home? Shipping it would cost a fortune, far more than just buying a new one.'

'Screwdrivers!' She smiled. 'We take everything apart here and someone going home will take a piece and someone else will take a piece, and then my brothers will put them together again.' To say I was taken aback is an understatement. 'Of course you can have it.'

I gave her 150 dollars from Daniel's stash and a cheque drawn on my own bank, where I had lodged my payment from *Femme*. This all seemed so final – she seemed to find it emotional, too, and tears stood in her eyes. 'I will never have a patient again like Mr Lescher.'

'Thank you so much for everything, Luzveminda. I'll always remember you.' My own tears weren't far behind hers as we hugged.

From the top of the stairs, I watched her, the last human link with my family, as she hefted the unwieldy walker down the stairs. I had appreciated her for what she did, for lifting a lot of day-to-day responsibility off my shoulders, but, lumpenly, I had been so caught up in my own life I had known nothing about hers. I had never even tried to learn.

At the bottom of the stairs, she turned and we waved to each other. Then it was over.

I've often heard someone say, 'I don't know what to do with myself', when they're confused, perhaps directionless, or even using it as a bridge to a better story. It describes my mood perfectly after Luzveminda left.

I went back into my parents' apartment but could find nowhere I wanted to sit. I didn't favour watching Dad's 'stories' as he would have done around that time of the day, didn't feel I could call anyone – and, anyhow, I had no one in Chicago to whom I could make a personal call. Cherry at *Femme* seemed to like me and I definitely liked her, but on such short acquaintance I could hardly call her to bleed my troubles all over her ample bosom.

It may sound strange that, out of a population of more than two and a half million in the city, I hadn't one close friend, but that was the case. I'd had buddies in Elementary but they, along with the geeks I'd hung out with in high school, had dispersed widely, to other states, to Europe, even to Japan and China, while I had been the only one in either group to follow journalism and go to Loyola. I might have made friends there but, unfortunately, my mom's cancer had by then become a serious problem and I had gotten caught up in that, particularly in trying to cope with my dad's panic. There hadn't been much time for socialising. I guess a work-life balance had been an alien concept for me. Then when Peter and I had married, I was still dealing with Dad although, of course, Peter was helping. I suppose, during that period, Letty had stepped into the friendship role, which was perhaps why it had been so hard to 'break up' with her. Or maybe I had simply fallen into the habit of my own company.

Lately I had certainly welcomed my time with Aoife. We had clicked, relaxed in each other's company in a way that had shown up my dearth of real friends.

But, as I knew from experience, long-distance friendship, while it can work in fiction and in movies, one friend flying coast-to-coast to comfort the other who is in trouble, would be difficult to sustain in real life and usually petered out. Well, I believe so, and in my case, despite my initial efforts to message college friends or send birthday cards, communication became less frequent, then ceased. Maybe I should try to fix this, I thought. Facebook is apparently a great help in reconnecting with people.

Actually, I mused, not for the first time, with both Dad and Daniel gone, what was holding me in Chicago? I could go anywhere . . .

Too much navel-gazing, too much speculation. I put my CD of the Mozart double violin concerto into Dad's old player, but then, because it reminded me too much of happier days with Peter, ejected it again.

One of the reasons for my restlessness was that on my way back to the apartment from the attorney's office to meet Luzveminda, I'd had an SMS message from a 'number withheld' (that again!) signed 'Mollie L', short, succinct, Lehman-style: *Marian, please be at Femme offices at 6.30. Thank you.* I was, to say the least, astonished, but held back any feeling of celebration that she might be about to offer me my job back. Given Mollie's personality, I thought that was rather unlikely (although she had been generous – more so than I would have expected). I could have called Cherry to find out what was going on, but in case she didn't know anything – and the last thing I'd want, or need, was to set everyone in the office on fire with speculation – so I held off. But what the hell did she want?

In the meantime, it was now still only two o'clock. How to fill in the hours between now and then? Should I sweep the floor, start the process of culling some of the contents of this apartment? But even Goodwill, I felt, wouldn't countenance a lot of the stuff – I did a quick visual survey of the kitchenware: burned pans, a colander with only one handle, several cracked jugs, silver that was clean but so blackened with age and harsh detergents that it would only be someone desperate who would offer it a home. The L rattled by, serving to emphasise the silence in the apartment.

Enough.

I spent the next few hours getting ready for that meeting with Mollie, mentally and physically, carefully choosing my outfit. I had to be ready for whatever, good or bad, it might bring.

Chapter Twenty-five

I walked into Reception at *Femme*, right on the dot of six thirty. Cherry was not at her desk, which surprised me, as the launch was rapidly approaching, and Mollie's door was open – also unusual. I crossed to it and knocked. 'Hello, Mollie?'

'Come in. Have a seat.' She continued to tap on her keyboard. I couldn't read her expression as I sat opposite her, the machine's soft clicking sounding quite loud in the odd silence. There were no phones ringing, no one was crossing the plush carpet in Reception. 'Is everything okay here, Mollie?'

'Just a sec . . .'

She clicked for another thirty seconds or so, then stopped. 'What time is it, Marian?'

'Nearly six thirty-five.'

'Mm-mmm.' She seemed to think about this. Then: 'At midnight tonight *Femme* magazine is officially closed. The backers have pulled out.'

'But—'

She held up a hand. 'You've had your tragedies all piled up together. This is mine. This magazine was my child, my baby. Nothing like this has ever happened to me before so, if you don't mind, I won't go into detail. I'm sure you'll be reading and hearing about it.'

I looked at her and suddenly, weirdly, felt sorry for her. She was so subdued and I missed the New York bravado. My tragedies, as she'd called them, were personal and private. This was public humiliation on a grand scale. 'So why did you want to see me, Mollie?' I asked.

'It felt like the right thing to do. I wasn't very fair to you, I think – after all, you didn't kill your husband or your father. This is not an excuse, Marian,' she glared defiantly at me, 'it's an explanation. For the last month I've been under stress with this project in a way I've never been with any other one. I jumped too fast into it and took money from shit people whose expectations were too high and who made impossible demands. Three months was not long enough as a lead-in but I agreed to it. I was foolish. I take full responsibility. There. I've said it.'

I scrambled around in my mind for something appropriate to say. 'I – I appreciated the way you paid me up front, Mollie. That was very fair, and thank you for that.'

'You were lucky,' she said wryly. 'I had to let good people go today without having paid them anything. Ryoko, for instance. She's worked for nothing these last three weeks because she trusted me. She has a little girl who's autistic, did you know that?'

'No.'

'Anyway, any money left in the kitty will go on the lease. We're tied in, unfortunately. I hope you cashed the cheque.'

'I did, and I've been drawing on it. So it's fine.'

'Unfortunately, despite what I said in my note to you, there won't be any more.'

I really couldn't think of what to say next, except the formulaic 'So what'll you do now?'

'Oh I won't let this keep me down.' The old Mollie surfaced. 'It was a good idea in the wrong city. New York is where it's at and I can't wait to get back there. Chicago ain't called Second City for nothin', honey! But, look, during her so-called "exit interview" – how I *hate* calling it that – before she left, Cherry gave me hell about the way I treated you and she was right. Here.' She opened a drawer in her desk and took out two files. 'Take these back. They technically belong to the sharks because they're assets, but what they don't know won't hurt 'em. So get 'em outta here pronto and try to place 'em somewhere else.

'Take a bit of advice.' She sat back in her chair. 'They're good, Marian, these two. They're real good. They show your strengths: compassion, empathy, observation of the telling detail. Cook? They'da loved it in Cupertino,' she smiled cynically, '*loved* it. But in essence it was an extended puff piece. Very well written but there was nothin' new in it, and although you hid it pretty well, it was obvious he snowed you. Stick to what you do best, honey. Leave the shiny folks to their PR.' She stood up. 'So that's it. The adventure's done. Now it's over to the fucking lawyers.'

'But it happened so fast.' I stood too.

'Welcome to my world.' She shrugged. 'This is how it's done. Tomorrow morning there'll be nothin' here but dust.' She gazed up at her smart chandelier. 'God, I do love that thing, and if I had a ladder . . .

'As I say, this is a first for me,' she said briskly, picking up the files and holding them out to me. 'These are why I brought you in at a time when no one could see I was goin' soft. I've a reputation to maintain! So we're quits now? Okay?'

I hesitated. Would it be on the cards to hug her?

Nah.

* * *

It was standing room only on the L on the way home. And –
wouldn't you know it? – my cell pinged.

'Marian?'

Although I could tell it was Jerry, even with the noise on the train,
his voice seemed to be at a strangely high pitch. For a millisecond
I flopped back into panic mode – had something bad happened to
Aoife? 'Is everything OK, Jerry?'

'I'll put you on to Aoife,' he said, still shaky. Was he weeping?

'Hi, Marian.' Aoife's voice, too, was weak, but at least she
sounded like herself and my panic subsided a little.

'Is everything OK, Aoife?' At least she hadn't died.

'You're an aunt again,' she said. 'The baby came early and she'll
be in an incubator for a few days but nobody's worried about her.
She's beautiful, Marian. She's perfect. Jerry and I would like you to
be her godmother, if you agree?'

I was instantly beset by a swarm of mixed emotions: joy for
Aoife, gratitude for the privilege she and Jerry were according me,
fear that I would not be able to fulfil this awesome responsibility,
but also, I admit, jealousy. This should have been my baby with
Daniel.

'Are you still there?' Aoife sounded anxious.

'Sorry, Aoife, I'm on a train. That's wonderful news.
Congratulations – a million trillion congratulations. And she's a
girl?'

'Yes, can you imagine? The perfect family, a boy and a little girl!'

'And I'd be extremely honoured to be her godmother. It's just . . .'

'I know what you're going to say.' She sounded stronger now. 'Whether you go to Mass or whatever is not our concern. As long as you're there for her baptism and confirmation, that'll be fine. Otherwise, religion doesn't come into it for us and, as far as I know, the Church doesn't conduct inquisitions any more. As I've said, we've discussed this and what we want is someone to care for her and to be in her life. To remember her birthdays and Christmas and to be there for her when she can't talk to us because she hates us. Poor old Jerry can't speak right now. He's too emotional because he's the daddy of a daughter, with all that entails for a man . . .' I could hear the love in her voice, which faded briefly as she turned towards him. 'But I have to tell you,' she came back, 'that one of the reasons we've chosen you is because Jerry loved his brother and his brother loved you, and we know you'll love our little girl. From his perspective, you being her godmother is perfect. It keeps the connection. Like a chain.'

I was still processing this, and I still had doubts. Despite their faith in me, this was huge, an enormous responsibility. What kind of godmother would I be? In my present state could I – should I – be one at all?

'Are you still there, Marian?'

'Sure, sure. When was she born?'

'Two hours ago.'

'Was it tough?'

'Tough enough. I'm tired, but she's here now and, oh, Marian, she's a dote and it's all brilliant. They say we'll be able to take her home in about a week or ten days. So you agree?'

'With a heart and a half.' What choice did I have? Could I throw this honour – and it was an honour – back in their faces? 'Thank you very much for asking me. By the way what's her name, or do you have one yet?'

'Rose. Rose Marian . . .'

That took my breath away.

'Is that okay, Marian? You still there?'

'I'm here.'

'I'm guessing it'll probably be run together as "Rosemary" at some stage, but she'll always be Rose Marian at home. So, you see, you have to say yes!'

Jerry had taken the phone: 'Marian, it's me again. We've hit the right note – she's like a little curled-up rosebud right now, all wrapped up and snug in her incubator so it had to be Rose. Oh, Marian, you'd want to see her—' His voice broke again and he passed the phone back to Aoife.

'See what I'm dealing with here?' She laughed.

'I'd better let you go. You've a lot of other people to call. Congratulations and thanks again.' We said goodbye.

Gosh! I must tell Daniel! The thought, as swift and merciless as one of those eagles he and I had seen so often in Glacier, swooped and struck me a severe blow. I had even started to punch in his name . . .

I put the cell away. The man standing beside me smiled. '*Mazeltov!* Long life to enjoy – a little baby girl?'

I nodded. 'A little baby girl. Rose Marian.'

Life went on, not only in Chicago but everywhere. If I hadn't thought so before, I sure as hell thought so now. Life would go on for me.

Chapter Twenty-six

Next morning I couldn't resist buying the *Chicago Tribune*, the *Chicago Sun-Times* the *New York Times* and the *New York Post*, scanning each quickly for news of the magazine's demise. All had covered it, but only in a couple of paragraphs, buried in the financial and business pages. But over the next few days the story would probably get more prominence in the gossip columns. Poor Mollie.

I had looked again at the giving-with-one-hand-and-taking-away-with-the-other note she had sent me. Those words of hers – 'good, but not exceptional' – in relation to Cook had wormed their way very effectively into my psyche. Which journalist or author wants to be merely 'good'?

But the cheque had been a great bonus, a kind and surprising gesture on her part. At the time I had wondered if she wasn't one of those people who were all teeth outside but butter within, and although the latter had been difficult to detect, I was beginning to believe my instinct had been correct.

Rather than dwell on that, and filled with fresh resolve, I took my two interviews to the woman I had dealt with before at the *Tribune*. Being inside the famous Michigan Avenue Tribune Building, a historic landmark, was exciting. It housed not just the newspaper but a radio station and CNN among other entities, and to watch the deceptively casual gait of reporters, executives and auxiliary staff – *We belong to this place; we're cool* – was fascinating. Even the delivery persons, temporarily part of the action, seemed to handle their boxes differently as they made their missions known.

While I was still, obviously, hugely emotional about the double bereavement, my description of what had happened – to Cherry, to Mollie – rang in my ears. I was almost, dare I say it, in danger of boring myself.

And in this place, peopled with those who looked outward, sometimes to enormous tragedy in countries thousands of miles away, my personal story would be just that: personal. On a slow news day, Daniel's being missing would have rated a few paragraphs, but next day his space might have been given to the discovery of a new moon circling a distant planet.

So, when my contact came down to see me in the lobby and asked how I was, I simply said I was fine, and explained that the reason I was there was that the two pieces had been written on commission for the magazine and, of course, like everyone in the media, she already knew what had happened there. She took them from me and, as I'd expected, said, 'I can't promise anything, but you know that. And you probably also know that these are far too long. But we'll see. Give me a few days. I'll call you.'

I offered her the interview I'd already arranged with the noted Chicago attorney and which had been destined for *Femme*. But she said, 'Let's get these two under our belts first. Eh, Marian?'

At least I'd put the work out there and I was lucky she'd seen me first off. That Daniel interview was working its magic again.

* * *

Next stop was Holy Angels. I had called in advance and been put on to the financial controller's office. When I got in there it was quite a surprise to find that the officer himself was the guy with the Rastafarian hairdo, one of the two who had made the day trip to attend Daniel's funeral. He was exceptionally helpful.

Daniel, it turned out, had been paying into a pension fund but he had not been in it long enough for the payout to be substantial. Actually, it would be derisory. There would be a 'minimal' lump sum, but the monthly payment had still to be worked out by the actuaries, and I would be entitled to half of it, but that, he said, would probably amount to something between twenty and twenty-two dollars a month. 'However,' he added, 'there is good or, at least, better news.' I would be receiving a one-off 'widow's benefit' payment of ten thousand dollars. 'It's not huge, but it was originally designed to help with funeral expenses and cash flow until a pension came through. I'm trying to expedite it for you. The plan is to FedEx you a cheque if that's OK. I have your cell number now and I'll call you to let you know when it's on the way. You still at Daniel's address, yes?'

'Actually no . . .' I gave him my dad's and he clicked it into his computer. 'This is delicate, Marian,' he said then. 'You had no children, perhaps from a previous relationship? Your husband didn't have a stepson? Or even any natural children from any previous relationship?'

'No. I'm afraid not. And, of course, we were married for only a few months. Why do you ask?'

He hesitated, wrote something on a pad, then looked up at me. 'Because if there were any children, each of them under the age of eighteen would be entitled to an ex-gratia payment of two thousand dollars on the loss of a parent.' He took a card from a little stack. 'My number's on here.' He gave it to me. His name was Ajay, and he was from Bangladesh, he told me, when I asked, not the Caribbean. (Wrong again, Marian!)

'You have my number now. I wish you luck. And, as I said, I'll be working hard to get you that money as soon as possible.'

I thanked him and left.

* * *

Back in the apartment after that flurry of activity, I sat down to take stock. The previous few weeks had been an emotional hurly-burly in which I had reeled from event to event. It was time to draw breath and consider how I'd conduct myself from now on. No more yo-yoing around, reacting as events dictated. I needed a steady, progressive action plan. My mourning would be put into context and I would suffer in private. And if I had to seek grief counselling I'd do it.

All my adult life, it seemed, I had been bound to others: my parents, as their carer, and my successive husbands. Paid work had featured in parallel but regularly, where my parents and Daniel were concerned, it had come off second best. In other words, although I had resented Mollie Lehman's pointing out that I hadn't sufficiently prioritised work it was now obvious that there had been truth in it. And my walking out on *Femme* without putting up a fight showed I hadn't been as committed as I should have been to my career. (That word, 'career', seemed too harsh and single-minded to me. Instinctively, I had always preferred to use the softer, broader embrace of 'work'. It probably had something to do with my rather sheltered upbringing.)

Now was my opportunity to change all that. Even to try my hand at a book. I certainly had the material for a memoir. The problem was that, while it would certainly be packed with incident, would I be interesting enough as a person? Had I enough to say?

On the other hand, if I committed more enthusiastically to journalism, I would have to change my lifestyle drastically – get out and about, socialise, identify interesting people and get to know them, update my contacts book . . .

Develop a circle of friends . . .

I flattered myself that I could write – even Mollie had confirmed it. I had the instinct, the curiosity, the discipline to succeed as a journalist when I put my mind to it. What I lacked were the habits and the behaviour, the wherewithal to pick up leads – and the gossip that might develop into them.

Despite my urgent curiosity about what was in Daniel's will, I'd felt it would be unseemly to rip into it straight away – as though I were a scavenger – and had left the lawyers' document wallet unopened overnight. To start the process of building my future, I fetched it and opened it now to see what pathway my late husband had sketched for me. But whatever he thought I should do, I was now in charge, and could handle virtually anything. If I liked what Daniel saw for me? Fine. If I didn't? That would be fine too.

And what if Jerry and Aoife had been right and moving to Ireland was part of it?

To be considered, of course: nothing should be ruled out at this stage – especially until I saw whether or not my, ah, career would sustain me there. But, no matter what Daniel had laid out, it was far too early to make such a big decision.

As Miss Southern Belle had indicated, the document, sealed into a heavy-gauge brown envelope, seemed at first glance to be admirably short and to the point: two sheets, an amplification of what my late husband had said about all his worldly goods on that night of his playacting.

As she had remarked, he'd had it 'legalesed', or translated into appropriate language, then signed it in front of witnesses: two people in the offices of J.L. Ruttger. It was dated two days before we had left for Glacier National Park.

He had three executors: his three siblings.

After stating who he was, his date of birth and where he lived, that he was of sound mind and so on, he revoked 'all previous wills and codicils', then stipulated, first, that all legal debts and taxes due be paid out of his estate.

Then, instead of that 'all to mother' simplicity she had mentioned, he had listed his bequests to me, starting with the copyright to all his authored papers, whether published or unpublished, in which he, at the time of his death, held such rights. He left me his belongings, including 'any and all' property, jewellery, clothing, vehicles, art and artefacts, 'which are, at the time of my death, lawfully owned by me, whether in my possession or not'.

On reading that, despite the bittersweet emotions it had engendered, I almost laughed out loud. It must have been an insertion by the lawyers. Jewellery? Daniel? What jewellery? I had never seen Daniel Lynch wear any jewellery, except his watch and, sporadically, his wedding band. As for art, I doubted he had ever set foot inside a gallery, any gallery, even the Art Institute, one of the most glittering gems in the city's crown. He had certainly exhibited no art in his studio apartment.

I read on.

I bequeath to my wife, Marian Lynch, the right of residency for her lifetime in the property known as Glanmilish House, situated at Glanmilish, Co. Laois in the Republic of Ireland, a quarter-share of which I own, it having been bequeathed to me by my father, also known as Daniel Lynch, along with equal shares to my three siblings, Jeremiah Lynch, Eamon Lynch and Eleanor Shanahan, née Lynch, this right of residence not to be unreasonably withheld by my three siblings as named and my share to revert to them, unencumbered, after my wife's death.

To my brother, Jeremiah, I bequeath my quarter-share interest in a medical practice in Glanmilish, Co. Laois, also inherited equally with my three siblings from my father, Daniel Lynch.

And I bequeath the entire sum of what shall have accumulated, at the time of my death, in a savings account held in my name at . . .

I gaped. Believe it or not, Daniel's bank was on LaSalle Street.

. . . to my living child, Daniel Lynch.

Rebound.

I bequeath the entire sum of what shall have accumulated, at the time of my death

. . . bank . . . South LaSalle Street . . . account . . . name . . . to my living child . . .

Living child. Very, very carefully, I placed the document on Dad's kitchen table and smoothed out a small crease in the corner of the paper. I felt quite calm as my mind utterly refused to take that on board. The kitchen was semi-separated from the living area by a wide arch and I looked through it towards my father's recliner to ask him for a second opinion on whether or not I had read it wrongly but, of course, he wasn't there.

Nobody was there. Nobody at all.

So, I decided to behave logically, to work towards my own second opinion and went right back to the beginning of the document, this time reading it slowly but straight through, concentrating, without reacting to individual sentences, without stopping to smile at the notion of Daniel Lynch wearing jewellery or going to art galleries.

And then, when I got to where it said, 'to my living child, Daniel Lynch' I again paused. Beneath the name of the bank on LaSalle Street there were some more lines, which had now blurred because, behind my eyes, the blood was pumping so hard.

I performed the three-three-six: inhale for a count of three, hold for a count of three, exhale gently for a slow count of six. I did it three times and still my heart banged about against my ribs. Apparently the living child, Daniel Lynch, had been born on 19 March 2012. (About three years before I had seen Dr Daniel Lynch on cable TV.) In the event of the living child not having reached his majority at the time of the testator's death, ran the next piece of text, the money in the bank at LaSalle Street was to be kept in trust for him by his mother until he did.

The address for both the living child and his mother was given as Cherry Street in Park Ridge, Illinois.

The mother's name was Cynthia Kurtz.

Cindy.

Chapter Twenty-seven

It must have been an hour before my thoughts halted their circular gallop. Despite my trying to control them, I couldn't. My brain insisted on finding a flaw in the wording of the will. Daniel, my husband, did not have a living child also named Daniel. He couldn't have. He didn't. But . . .

I had the address of the living child's *alleged* mother now and, unless her number had been recently unlisted, I would have no problem calling her – after all, on her sympathy card she had invited me to call her. But to say what, exactly? *What were you doing with my husband before I met him?*

Didn't scan. Not quite.

But one memory now made sense: that of the day Daniel had sat opposite me in the hospital cafeteria when Cindy had made the introduction to him, calling him, I think, something like an Irish woodsman. No. 'Backwoodsman': that was it. I recalled her tart admonition: *Behave, you!* Even at the time it had occurred to me, very briefly, that it had been the response of someone who had been more than a colleague, or even a friend. Even a close friend.

And then there was Peter's response to seeing him on cable TV when my own reaction had proved so fateful. Peter had warned me about him, even as he'd scrolled for Daniel's number so I could contact him for interview. And my then husband had also said something about 'rumours' but hadn't specified.

I sprang up from where I was sitting and went to Daniel's Gladstone bag in which, since his death, I had stored the sympathy cards and letters I had received on my return to Chicago after the funeral, drawing a little comfort from them each time I saw the little bundle around which I'd tied a red ribbon. (I'd deliberately selected that colour rather than black. Red, I believed then, was far more appropriate to my husband's vibrant character.)

I untied it and removed Cindy's card. Unlike the others, with their careful illustrations of trees or sunsets giving subliminal messages of comfort about life continuing after death (the sun will rise, the tree will survive another season), hers bore a picture of a small cottage.

And, yes, inside, under her message, she had given me her telephone number.

I looked at Daniel's watch, still dangling under my wrist, its strap still too large. It was just after three in the afternoon.

To whom would Daniel have confided this news? The only person I could think of was Eleanor. Repeatedly, I had been told that the two of them were close, but then something had happened although no one else in the family seemed to have any idea as to what it had been.

I scrolled through my contacts – yes, her number was there, with Eamon's, Martin's, Jerry's and Aoife's. Like most journalists, as I've said, I usually registered the name of anyone who made contact with me. The only one missing was Sharon's – although she too had called me.

Sharon would have been my second option. She and Eleanor were friends, according to what I had seen.

What time was it in Ireland? Three o'clock here – nine in the evening over there.

I dialled Eleanor's number but got her voicemail, her tone as colourless as I remembered: 'I'm away from my phone. Please leave your name and the time of your call and I'll get back to you. Thank you.'

'Hi, Eleanor, this is Marian.' Then I improvised: 'I never got to thank you for giving Aoife those pills for me. They were life-savers. I don't know what I'd have done without them, so thanks a whole bunch. Listen, nothing that important, but would you give me a call when you get a chance, please? My number probably came up on your screen, but if it hasn't . . .' I called it out slowly, emphasising each digit. 'Thanks again, talk soon, I hope. And love to all . . .'

I paced the small space, weaving through the excess furniture in the apartment. I made myself coffee and a tuna sandwich but neither ate nor drank. I turned the TV on, then off again. I shouldn't call her a second time because that would indicate eagerness on my part and, based on what I knew of her personality, I'd frighten her. But I was now regretting the casual tone I'd laid down on her voicemail . . . Maybe I should have said it was urgent.

I waited another five minutes and called her again.

Still the voicemail.

I thought about it for a while, then dialled Eamon. He answered, obviously driving: 'This is a surprise, Marian. How nice to hear from you. Is everything all right?'

'You're driving, Eamon. Should I call back?'

'I'll call you. I'm just on my way home from a consultation with a client. There in ten minutes. Okay?'

Those ten minutes stretched to fifteen and then twenty. I found them unbearable. The original feeling of calmness had long ago evaporated.

When the cell actually pinged I almost jumped on it, but, forcing myself to sound normal, answered as though I wanted merely a pleasant routine catch-up. 'Thanks for calling back, Eamon – nothing urgent, but do you have a number for Sharon, please?'

'Of course I have. Not being nosy or anything, but is there something I should know?'

'Not at all,' I lied, hopefully with conviction, 'and I'm sorry to bother you. It's just that I promised to call her after I got back to the city here but it slipped my mind until now and I can't find her number. You know how it is.' I attempted a chuckle but it misfired horribly.

There was silence at the other end, and I worried that he had caught me out but he said eventually, 'It's on my phone . . . tricky to find when I'm actually using it. Ah, here we go . . .' He called it out. Having written it down, I recited it back to him.

'That's it. How are you doing, love, you managing okay? Is there anything we can do for you?'

'Not a thing,' I said. 'I won't hold you up – what's the weather like over there, by the way?'

'It's really gorgeous, if you can believe that. I hate the idea of going into the office. It's actually beach weather. Everyone's in great humour too . . .'

I couldn't wait to get him off the line but had to continue: 'That's great. It's not bad here either – not too hot. Which is nice. Well, bye, Eamon, and thanks very much.'

'Don't be a stranger now – and on that note, when do you think you'll come back to pay us a visit? Are you sure you're all right? It has to be difficult for you. I know you were married only for the blink of an eye – but in a way that kind of makes it harder. It can't be easy – even I miss the old bollocks, pardon my French, and that's saying something, so I can barely imagine what it must be like for you.'

'It isn't. Easy, I mean. But I haven't hit the gin bottle yet.'

'Well, chin up and take care of yourself.'

'You too. Thanks again.'

'God bless!'

At last we broke the connection.

But in case Eleanor had woken up in the meantime, or come home or whatever, I tapped her name into my Contacts but kept making mistakes, my hands were shaking so much.

This was ridiculous. I opened the door to Dad's fire escape, went out and took several deep, calming breaths of the muggy air.

One last time.

Back inside, I punched in Eleanor's numbers, all fifteen of them, prefixes included. My next phone bill was going to be something else. The hell with it. I got the same result and broke the connection before the voicemail could kick in properly.

I was just about to give in and call her a fourth time when the cell went off. I pounced on it. It wasn't Eleanor but her sister-in-law. 'Marian?'

'Sharon! This is a surprise! I just called Eleanor – I was going to call you too.'

'I know. She rang me. She's in a terrible state.'

'What's wrong?'

'Look, I'm in a supermarket in Limerick. Will you be by your phone for a while, Marian?'

'I will, sure.' I tried to sound cheery. 'Any time, Sharon, I'm at home all evening. But is Eleanor okay?'

'She will be. I'm going over to her house when I'm finished here – she's only ten minutes away. Talk to you soon, Marian. Bye!'

In the absence of any other distraction, I turned on the TV again while I waited. If you were to ask me what I was watching – a wildlife programme? A soap opera? CNN or Fox? – I couldn't have told you.

* * *

Two hours later I was on a bus, packed with home-going commuters bound for the suburbs north and north-west of the city. Park Ridge, according to the schedule, should take me just over an hour via Greenwood and Busse Highway.

Following a map, I disembarked at a mid-block station on Busse and (reluctantly) resisted the temptation to stop at a Burger King for a coffee – something inside me didn't want to do anything that might postpone my arrival on Cindy's doorstep. I pressed on, crossing North Knight and North Western, onto Cherry. Then after a few more minutes, following the house numbers, I had reached her block.

Park Ridge, hometown of Hillary Clinton and Harrison Ford, is a heavily wooded, modest suburb. Cindy's house, when I found it on Cherry Street (yet another coincidence? I took it as an omen), was a small, wood-framed ranch with a single garage attached and a yard with a lawn, in the front of which were an upturned child-sized wheelbarrow and a ratty football. The driveway sported a red Honda Civic that had seen better days. Unless it belonged to a childminder, Cindy was home.

Chapter Twenty-eight

I had set out for this encounter like a galleon in full sail, but instead of rowing straight in, cannons booming, I stood for a few minutes on the street opposite Cindy's house, pretending to take a call on my cell, while I tried to formulate what exactly I would say to her when she answered the door.

Was it possible I was going to funk it for fear that she would run rings around me and that my last state could be worse than my first?

When Sharon had gotten back to me that day, she had done so from Eleanor's home, and every so often, I could hear her sister-in-law prompting her, confirming what I already knew. 'Eleanor actually suspected he was having an affair some days before your wedding. She rang him when he was at a conference in a hotel somewhere and a woman answered his phone. And when poor old Ellie asked who she was, she answered, bold as brass, that she was Daniel's lover. You and he were together by then.

'He'd already rung the family to say he was going to marry you. She and Daniel had had terrible rows about that discovery of hers. He admitted the affair but told her it was over. She might be lots of things but, like everyone in that family, she's far from thick. She didn't believe him. And she confronted him again at your wedding party. Apparently you came up the stairs and heard it. Didn't take a feather out of him but she was really upset.

'It's awful, Marian, I've just heard all this in the last fifteen minutes. It was going on right up to the end.' Sharon sounded as shocked as I had been, although it was hard to quantify what I felt just then. *Right up to the end?*

Abruptly, I had remembered the phone call in Glacier when we had happened on a sliver of network coverage – and Daniel's very quick change of mood.

All those conferences, none of which he had wanted me to attend, even insisting on going to Cleveland on the night his father had slipped into a coma – so that they'd had to postpone the Glanmilish funeral mass for him. What kind of a man opts for a tryst with a mistress over his father's serious illness and even death?

I tried to concentrate on what Sharon, still talking, was saying: '. . . too upset to talk about it to you right now. She's been carrying it all on her own. She knew it before you got married and not just because of that phone call because – guess what? Cindy had got hold of her mobile number and rang her to try to persuade her to get Daniel to call off the wedding – and she told poor Ellie why exactly she wanted this to happen. It was to do with money. She was pissed off that, with a wife in tow now – that'd be you, Marian – Daniel's income would have to be shared out a bit more. Hold on a second, Marian, Ellie's saying something.' It sounded like she covered the mouthpiece but I could hear her sister-in-law's muffled voice.

'She confronted him with it, she says, and they had another huge row and he said he'd never speak to her again if she told anyone. Yes, love?' Again it seemed like she covered her phone. 'He threatened, apparently,' she was back on the line, 'that he'd make absolutely sure no one would believe her. What, Ellie?'

'Can she not talk to me herself?' I was getting impatient.

'Ah, here, Ellie.' In response, Sharon's voice dimmed, although I could hear her clearly. She must have been holding the phone on her extended arm. 'Come on, love, talk to Marian. I promise you she'll understand.'

'Hello, Marian.' Eleanor's voice was low. 'So, now you know about my brother. What you must think of this family – even of me, dripping around, afraid of my shadow. I shouldn't say it, but it's a real relief to get this off my chest. I was so ashamed and guilty – how could I have told you? The only times I saw you were at the wedding party and then at Daniel's funeral. Neither was suitable for laying all that on you. I can't apologise enough for all of us, Marian. Can you forgive me? Forgive us, I mean.'

But Sharon had grabbed the phone from her and said we would all talk next time we met. 'Look, when will you be back? We need to have a proper talk about the house. Of course I can't speak for all the others, but as far as Eamon and I are concerned, you're as welcome to Glanmilish as the flowers in May. If you decide to come. In my book, you'd be a great addition to the family and none of us has any use right now for that big pile of stone so you could move in.'

'Thanks, Sharon. I appreciate all that. Maybe it could be sold, though.'

'Who'd buy it? Eight bedrooms, only one with an en-suite in this day and age? One bathroom for everyone else? To get any kind of a decent price we'd have to do a lot of work on it. And the site isn't that good either.'

'Well, you're right about one thing. This isn't the time to talk about it. I haven't had time to absorb that Daniel has, had, has . . . Did any of you know he had a child, a son?'

'Jesus!' Sharon's voice faded a little but I could hear her: 'Did you know that Daniel had a son, Ellie?' Her voice then went off completely, as though she had covered the phone. Then, after thirty seconds or so she was back. 'That's not news to her, Marian, it seems she had to keep that to herself as well but it's news to all the rest of us. Look, she's really upset, I'll have to call you back later, OK?'

'I'll talk to you later, Sharon,' I said quickly, before my voice could betray me. 'And please tell Eleanor that there's nothing to forgive. Tell her I'll call her too. Bye!'

Then I experienced one of those brief helicopter moments during which I could see my surroundings and myself as though I was watching from above. On that mild evening of fading blue skies, the birds chirping their little hearts out, trees in full leaf and tiny green blades of new grass coming through shaven lawns, my 'eye' zoomed out, and from on high I saw myself as a big, awkward trespasser in Cindy's environment. Gulliver in Lilliput.

I remembered reading an interview with a famous Irish writer, who was talking about this third-eye business; how, when kneeling beside his mother's deathbed with the rest of the family, he found himself observing and noting the nuts and bolts of the scene – the flickering candles, the room, the bed, the smells and sounds, the relative positioning of the other family members – without any lessening of emotional pain. I think that is what is meant when writers, the good ones, are accused of ruthlessness. I have the helicopter moments but not the books!

Twenty yards away a school bus, trundling into the four-way junction nearby, broke my reverie by braking noisily, then discharging a number of children, who, gym bags and footballs tucked under their arms, tumbled out and then, like leaves on a sudden breeze, scattered in all directions. A junior team, probably, coming home from training, I thought, wondering if, when he was old enough, Daniel's son would be among them.

Don't go there, warned the resident critic at the base of my skull.

Enough introspection. The world still turned. Ordinary people led ordinary lives. Get a grip, I told myself. You're here. Just do this. One foot in front of the other. You have every right to talk to this woman. She invited you to chat.

Cindy's doorbell, attached to an intercom, sounded a cheery but distorted version of the first bars of 'The Battle Hymn of the Republic', and then the loudspeaker beside the door carried two voices, a woman's and a child's.

Woman: 'I'll get it!' Then, cheerily: 'Who is it?'

Child: 'No, I'll get it! I wanna get it! Mom, I wanna!'

The door was wrestled open and the child, his mother behind him, was standing in front of me. He looked around three years old, which fitted with what the legal document had said. Under silky blond bangs, I saw Daniel Lynch's eyes.

* * *

I had remembered uniformed Cindy from her hospital days, but more recently, in my more fervid projections of this encounter, especially while I was sitting on the packed bus on the way there, planning the phrases I would use to her perky little face – 'sexual predator' and others too colourful to reproduce here – I had pictured her as a modern-day miniature Jezebel.

But this tired-looking woman was bare-legged, wearing a shabby housecoat and trainers and her hair was wrapped in a towel. She recognised me immediately. 'Jesus!'

'You did invite me to call? On your sympathy card?'

She touched the towel as though to take it off, then thought better of it. 'What are you doing here?'

'Aren't you going to ask me in?'

Wordlessly, she opened the door wider and stepped aside, pulling the little boy with her. Although I wasn't looking down at him, I was ultra-aware that those eyes continued to regard me solemnly. 'Thank you,' I said, as I passed her and went inside. 'This isn't really a social visit so we'll keep it simple. Okay?' Weirdly, after all the hype and anticipation, even the mental rehearsals, I now felt calm as I followed the two of them down the small hallway to the kitchen-diner at the back of the house. It was clean but cluttered, toys all over the floor, every inch of wall-space hung with childish drawings, calendars and rosters of Cindy's shifts, the door of the icebox bristling with Post-its, gold star charts and reminder notes for play-dates and doctors' appointments.

The space on the small kitchen table was divided into his 'n' hers, paper plates containing half-eaten bologna sandwiches at each end, squeezy ketchup and mustard bottles in the middle, with a container of paper napkins, bills, jumbo pencils, crayons and an open exercise book, in which I could see shopping lists written in Cindy's looping scrawl. There was no trace of any adult male that I could discern.

'Sorry if I'm interrupting your dinner,' I said, searching for a chair, although she hadn't invited me to sit, but there were only two, one at each place setting. Faced with the dimensions of the kitchen and the small stature of its usual two residents, I felt more like Gulliver than ever. 'May I use this?' I pulled out a set of steps, presumably there to help Cindy reach into the tops of cupboards. She had been taking a quick stab at tidying the central heap of clutter on the table but gave up as I perched myself precariously on the upper footpad of the steps and gazed at her.

But she was concentrating on the kid: 'Come on, Junior, finish that sandwich. You have to get ready for swimming.'

Although the pause that followed could not have lasted more than thirty seconds, it felt like ten minutes. The ball was in my court but I wasn't going to serve it to her.

'Well, this is a surprise,' she said then. 'What shall we talk about, Marian?'

'Well, let's see. Men? Treachery?' Aware I was under continuing scrutiny from the little boy, I kept my tone calm, as though discussing ingredients for a nice salad, but she jumped up, so quickly that the sleeve of her housecoat caught the corner of the table, jolting the drinks so that her water and his juice splattered all over the table. 'Junior!' she ordered. 'Go get paper towels.'

Obediently, he complied, trotting across to where the roll was lying on the counter beside the sink. He gave it to her, and as she mopped up, he sat down again and resumed watching me. 'Where do you live?' he asked, in his piping treble.

'Chicago city but, you never know, I might go to Ireland.' I smiled at him.

'My daddy's from Ireland but he's dead.' His tone was matter-of-fact as he took another bite from his sandwich. 'He's living with God in Heaven. He has his own apartment there, with his dog and a big white horsie, and he rides the horsie every day over the mountains. He sees me when he's out and about, and he knows what I'm doing, so I have to be a good boy.'

'That sounds lovely.' My heart nearly broke.

Cindy ceased mopping. 'Go get ready for swimming, Junior! And don't forget your goggles.'

'But, Mom!' he whined.

She glared at him. 'Go! I won't tell you again.'

'Oooo-*kaaaay*.' He did the very adult thing of throwing his eyes to Heaven. Then, as he got off his chair, 'We're going to Disney World for my next birthday!'

'That's amazing! So when's your birthday, Junior?'

'March nineteen. I'm three now an' I'll be four next. An' I'm allowed to brush my teeth now, mine own self.'

'That's wonderful, Daniel. And is that your little dog, Peppy?' I'd remembered the name from the note Cindy had sent me when Daniel died. The animal, a small brown and white terrier-type, was yapping outside the glassed back door, scrabbling at it in an effort to get in.

'Ye-es.' He gave me a pitying look: *Everyone knows that's Peppy*. 'But he's not allowed in when we're eating. It's unhy-...' He looked at his mother for help.

'It's unhygienic,' she prompted.

'Yes – it's that thing. Bye.' He ran out of the room.

'To tell you the truth, Cindy...' I was still looking after him, trying not to think: *He should have been mine*. 'I thought I was ready for this but now I'm not quite sure what to say to you. So it's over to you. I guess I want to hear for myself how you might justify your affair with my husband. And you can tell me what a laugh you had when you thought about the poor deluded wife living in Cloud Cuckoo Land. I suppose she didn't understand him.'

But instead of engaging immediately, she removed the towel from her head, shaking out a haystack of over-bleached hair, obviously home-dyed and almost black at the roots. During our acquaintance, which had been brief enough, I had always pegged

Cindy as stylish, a tiny blonde Victoria Beckham, maybe. Had that been what attracted him to her? Was I too large? Or had he kept the two of us in his stableyard because of the contrast between us?

Don't.

I didn't. Or I tried mightily not to.

'I need to get dressed to get Junior to the pool,' she said. 'And, actually, since you mentioned this, not me, I don't think you did understand him.'

'The pool can wait. You've wrecked not just my marriage but my memories of my marriage, and made garbage of my mourning my husband.' Despite my resolution not to get angry, my voice had risen.

She shook out the towel and folded it into a compact rectangle. 'I'm in mourning too, Marian. And I was with him for a lot longer than you. Have you thought about that? From my perspective, I could accuse you of taking him from me.'

I was stunned. The woman had spunk, I'd give her that. 'You think there's an equality of entitlement here?'

'Isn't there?' Her voice was cool as she started work on her hair, disentangling it almost strand by strand with a wide-toothed comb. I stared at her. This wasn't going the way I had planned it.

'You think,' she went on, 'that a piece of paper from Cook County entitling you to that little ceremony you had in Northbrook gives you more rights than me? I gave him a child.'

I had been waiting for that. 'A pregnancy of deliberate entrapment, I assume.'

'Why would you assume that? And why would I need to? He was with me of his own free will, before and after his son was born. And since we're being so frank with each other, sweetie, Danny was the result of a burst condom. Your beloved husband didn't want kids. My guess is that he didn't want anyone to take the limelight off himself.'

'That's absolutely ridiculous!'

'Is it? Did he tell you he wanted kids? Actually say it?'

'That's beneath answering. It's private.' But she had utterly taken the wind out of the galleon's sails. Because, when I thought about it, Daniel hadn't brought up the subject of our having children. It had been my thing. I had seen our kids, Bobby, Max and Jenna, loyal to the Chicago Cubs, and when they grew up and left us, they'd come back to visit in summertime and we'd go to them for Thanksgiving.

Watching me digest this, she continued to work on her thatch – she was now getting somewhere: the worst seemed to be over. 'Look, Marian, I don't deny that I didn't want him to marry you. That was only natural. There were all kinds of issues there, not least financial.'

'What?'

'You don't think his marriage to you would affect the level of child support he was giving me?'

'He was giving you child support?'

'Marian, Marian – what planet do you live on?'

'Well, considering I didn't know until this morning that there *was* a child, I think I'm doing pretty well to be here having this discussion. What do you think, Cindy?'

'Well, you've no choice really, have you? Neither of us has. I had the advantage, I suppose. I knew what I was dealing with and I knew about you. Where did you come by all this information, by the way?'

'He made a will.'

'Did he indeed? Did he mention us in it?'

'How do you think I found out about you – and about Daniel? Give me a break!'

'I gave you lots of breaks, honey-bun. I didn't go to goddamned

Ireland to make a fuss and disrupt your honeymoon but I could have – I thought about it.'

'So why didn't you?'

'My better nature got me, I guess.'

We stared at one another.

'You threatened my sister-in-law!'

'She was easily threatened. But I didn't carry out the threat, did I? I liked what I'd seen of you, believe it or not. All I was looking for, really, was justice for my son.'

'I'll get the lawyers to write to you.'

'So he's taken care of us, has he?'

'Not as well as you might hope. He's left some money in trust to Daniel for when he gains his majority and you're in charge of that – and before you ask,' I held up a hand to forestall her next question, 'I have no idea how much it is. But whatever it is, that's it. There's nothing else, as far as I know.' I gave her the name of J.L. Ruttger. 'They have all the details.'

'But what you're saying is that we have to wait until Daniel's eighteen? He'd agreed to pay crèche fees and in fact he was paying them – but the reason I was getting angsty about child support was because Danny's got a place in Montessori next semester. How am I supposed to pay for that now? Daniel Lynch's death has been as much of a disaster for me as it was for you.'

'Cindy, I don't know. There's nothing in the will about child support. But what I do know, and it's not going to be of much help in the long term, is that Holy Angels can give Daniel two thousand dollars immediately as an ex-gratia payment for losing his father.'

'I already know that. I've been on to them.' Immediately I remembered Ajay's hesitation when he was asking me if I had any children. He knew about all this. He knew about me, Cindy,

Daniel, the whole schmear. God, I thought, I might as well post it all on Twitter. *@mlesche: Marian is a fool.* But Cindy had gone back to the matter of the will: 'He's taken care of you, has he?'

'Oh, yeah.' Perhaps I was becoming a little hysterical, but to me the conversation was beginning to take on a comical hue. 'I get to be a squatter in a falling-down eight-bedroomed house with one bathroom,' I told her, 'and there's diddly-squat central heating, and it's in Nowheresville, Ireland.'

'That sounds nice!'

'And I'll also be . . .' the laughter was building up '. . . the happy recipient of a pension of – of –' I burst into helpless laughter and, through it, barely managed to say '– a pen-pension of – of tw- *twenty* dollars a *month*!'

I gave in and whooped. Laughter's catching and she joined in. 'A whole twenty?' And, strangely, given the circumstances, we both laughed until the mirth, which undoubtedly was mordant, wore itself down.

Chapter Twenty-nine

Little Daniel came back into the kitchen: 'Mom, I can't find my goggles! It's a mergenty!'

'Hang on, sweetie. I'll go find them.' Then, to me, 'Sorry, Marian, but he has to have them. His eyes suffer with all the chlorine.' She bustled away.

I was still wiping my own eyes. It had felt good to laugh – I actually couldn't remember when last I had let myself go like that. If the situation hadn't been as it was, I thought, Cindy and I could even have been friends. Stranger things have happened. But right now it would be a stretch. We were hardly going to compare notes about Daniel Lynch's bedroom habits over our skinny lattes. But there was, truly, a ludicrous side to all this.

And then, when she came back, Cindy ruined what might have been a Hallmark moment. 'Listen, Marian,' she said, seating herself and resuming work on her hair. 'Nothing against you, honestly, but I'm going to have to fight for child support.'

I was tempted to shrug and say, 'Them's the breaks,' but this was a real dilemma for her. 'Unfortunately, I really believe there's no money to pay it. I'm as bad as you. At least you have a job. I don't.'

'So what you're sayin' is, we're both up Shit Creek? And,' she peered closely at me, 'you didn't even suspect? It never even crossed your mind to ask him what he was up to when he was away from home? Well, that's lurve for ya, and that's certainly our Daniel. Bullshit artist of the century. You take him as he is— Shit! I gotta do something about this hair.' In the last quadrant of her head, she had hit a particularly dense knot. 'He brought you on vacation to Glacier where he died? Well, guess what? I suggested that as a venue.

'The plan was that after you and he made whoopee in the park, he was going to get a call to make another stand-in appearance for someone who'd cancelled at the last minute at a medical conference in Dallas and you were to go home from Denver alone. You had to, unfortunately, as it happened. I was genuinely sorry for you then, but I was sorry for myself too. At least you were the widow and you were getting updates. I had to rely on newspapers. It was a one-day wonder here, but the local rags in the north-west were following the search. I had to get someone to show me how to access local reports online, but they were sketchy at best. They did report on when he was found, though.'

'Denver?' My head was spinning. This was beyond belief. 'We had our tickets – we were going via Boston because it was the cheapest route. And yes, we were connecting at Denver, but—' Words failed me for a moment. 'He was checking in at Holy Angels to sort out a bit of paperwork,' I continued desperately, 'and a few days later he was flying back to Dublin to rejoin the practice in Glanmilish. It was all arranged. You're lying, Cindy . . .'

But was she? I felt ill now. That phone call he'd said he had to make to an 'agency' on the last morning in Glacier when he'd left the van to get better coverage? On top of that so-called private number – or number withheld – when his screen had lit up as it found a sliver of network coverage after we'd just seen the grizzly?

It had been planned all along.

With almost all of her hair now under submission, she stood up and went to one of the kitchen drawers from which she extracted a folded printout. 'Whatever else I am, I'm not a liar. Call me sentimental but I kept this.' She unfolded it and placed it in front of me on the table. It was a confirmation for the Grand Hyatt in Denver.

'We were going to spend just two nights together. I hadn't seen him for ages and I'd been so looking forward to it. I had all my ammunition ready. He'd had his romantic trip with you while I was working my ass off on shift. It was now time for him to get real. I was carrying the can for *his son*! I was devastated on a number of fronts, as you can imagine – at least, I hope you can. We have that in common. We shared him in life, we share him in death.' She refolded the confirmation and put it back in the drawer.

Her expression was almost kindly as she sat back in her chair and, resuming the work with her comb, regarded me. 'Gawd, Marian, isn't life a bitch sometimes? You probably don't want to hear this, and you probably hate me to bits, but I actually do feel sorry for you. You sure didn't get Daniel Lynch. Anyway, he was never going to be the kind of guy who wanted to be understood . . .'

She paused and leaned forward, elbows on the table. Then, the brisk, professional nurse delivering difficult news: 'Look, I suppose it will be little consolation to you, but you can't go beatin' up on yourself about all this. I wasn't the first, and if he wasn't dead, neither of us would be the last. There were others, all the time he was with me, actually, the period he was with the two of us, I guess, which wasn't that long for you.'

'Just months.'

'I've been around the block, Marian, and I figured very early on after he and I got together that no one, not Madonna, not Catherine Zeta-Jones, could have expected exclusivity with Daniel Lynch. He was just that kind of man. So I made a decision not to be jealous or possessive. It was the only way. I don't know how he got away with how he behaved. He did, though, didn't he? Well, until Glacier got him. What actually happened there?'

At that moment, when I was seriously struggling with this latest revelation, it helped my sanity to be asked to reiterate my response to that (now well-worn) question. In some ways it represented a reprieve from taking in the full import of what I'd been hearing. I told her about the autopsy. 'It's a wilderness area, with sparse patrolling and hardly any signage. When you go in there, you're warned about specific dangers and you can get tons of literature and advice but you're almost completely on your own. Certainly we were. And on that day the river was in full spate. Burst its banks, although from where I could see it from our RV pitch, it looked to me that it had just spread over the near bank, the one I could see. The irony was, while I could see how fast it was going, I was just sitting on the steps of the van enjoying the sun on my face.

'There were two volunteers looking after me while I was waiting during those dreadful five days while they were searching, really nice men – I should write to them to thank them but I never got their names. I seem to remember, very vaguely because I was zoned out of it a lot of the time, one or even both of them telling me that stuff like this does happen now and then in the park, where someone, usually a lone hiker, goes missing and no one ever finds out what happened, unless there's something on the body, like signs of an animal attack. But that's extremely rare. Some people are never found. But I do remember they kept reassuring me that they do find people even after six days.

'As for how he got into the water, best guess, the manager of the

RV place said to me that some of the ground around the river was muddy after the overnight rains and Daniel could have gone too close to the water while he was making a phone call or something, wasn't watching his footing, slipped in and got carried away in the current. He'd been wearing rubber flip-flops. Even the area around our van, which was on raised ground, had been wet that morning.

'He survived in that river for five miles or more.' Again, I pictured his struggles in the water, but I wasn't going to show weakness in front of Cindy Kurtz. 'I can't stand to think what that time in the water must have been like for all that distance. He was found a hundred and fifty-four yards away from the bank of a little creek off the main river so what they say is that he got himself to where the water was calmer, got out and then dragged himself there, where he either passed out or just went to sleep because he was so exhausted.' That figure, 154, had seared itself into my brain.

She was holding herself like a statue. And there was something in her expression, especially in the eyes, that disturbed me. 'What is it?'

'Nothing.'

'Please, Cindy.'

'Okay, you asked! That call he made was to me, but the line suddenly went dead when he was in the middle of a sentence.'

There was a long pause. We regarded each other, I trying to regain a grip on reality, where I was. Where she was. What she had just said.

'What was he saying?' My voice croaked.

'Marian, you don't wanna know. You just don't. So don't ask.'

'Please, Cindy. I've been torturing myself. Any little detail will help. Now I know what it's like when someone is killed and the relatives always want to know what he felt, what he said, was he happy in his last moments, what did he look like, did he suffer . . .'

She watched me levelly, still with that expression in her eyes. 'I don't know any more than you do. We were talking, the line went dead.'

'But what was he saying? What was his mood?'

Hesitating, she gazed at me, her face a mask. 'It was just to do with Denver that night,' she muttered. 'I've already told you.'

I didn't believe they had been making travel and meeting arrangements, and my imagination was running riot as to the type of conversation that had engaged Daniel Lynch and Cindy Kurtz on the verge of yet another idyll. But pressing the point any further, I saw, would be futile. 'Did you call him back?'

'Of course,' she said quietly.

'And what happened?'

'Nothing. After a few seconds there wasn't even a tone. I tried on and off for about half an hour, but there was nothing at all.'

'And did you go to Denver?'

'Yes,' she said. 'I figured he'd lost the network or the cell itself had broken down, and until he got back to civilisation, he wouldn't be able to have it repaired or buy a new one.'

And, of course, I had tried calling that phone myself during those waiting days. In that regard, she was telling the truth.

But I couldn't take much more of this. I stood up because I didn't want to keep looking her in the eye at such close quarters. I had come to her with conflict in mind and, while I couldn't admit to having been outflanked, it was the truth, the facts, with which I now had an issue and I was in no position to gainsay them.

I crossed to the window over the sink, which looked out into the small backyard, mostly concreted over, with a swing set as its main feature. From behind me, I heard her say, 'Are you okay?'

I was anything but. I've always prided myself on not being the swooning type, believing that some women affected to faint to gain attention. I was wrong: my face was now covered with cold sweat, so copious that it was actually dripping into my eyes.

'I'm fine!' I tried to turn towards her but staggered – I hadn't eaten anything since that morning. Instantly she was out of her chair. 'Siddown!' she ordered, in her professional-nurse voice. 'Here.' She pulled her chair towards me, and when I stumbled onto it, placed her hand on the back of my neck and pushed my head towards my knees. 'Stay like that for a few minutes.' She hustled over to the sink, filled a water glass, added ice, then came back to me and put her free hand back on my neck as, bit by bit, I began to feel human again, if a little foolish. Not a little foolish. Hugely foolish, humiliated and highly embarrassed. 'Thanks. But I'm okay now.'

'You sure?'

'Yes.'

She removed her hand and handed me the water. 'Drink this slowly. And eat this slowly.' She plucked a banana from a stand on her kitchen counter, peeled it expertly and handed it to me. 'You've had shock after shock after shock. I'm genuinely sorry, but you deserve the truth, and the truth is he was just one of those men who loved not just sex but the hunt. He targeted other men's women just for the pleasure of winning, I guess. I should know. He targeted me when I was with your Peter.'

This was yet another whammy, but I was too punch-drunk to say anything that made sense.

But she saw. 'Dear God, you didn't know that either, did you? Look, are you okay to drive? I assume you have a car – if you haven't, I can drive you to the Metra Line, or I can call you a cab. Me and Junior, we really have to get to the pool.'

Of course I didn't feel okay after that avalanche of disclosures. 'I came on the bus.'

'We'll drive you to the stop.' She gazed at me again. 'Look, I fell for him just the same as you did, and probably for the same reason. He needed sex like other men need oxygen, not to the extent that you could say he was addicted – at least, I don't think so – but outside his work, which genuinely drove him, and you can be sure of that at least, sex would have been very, very high on his list.

'It wasn't just conferences and away days. The hospital shift patterns, the so-called unsocial hours, were always very social for Daniel Lynch, long before you came on the scene – and even before that, before either of us, before he came to America, even. I'm willing to bet there are colleens over in Ireland who could tell you a story or two. But this is America, honey, land of freedom and opportunity, and when Daniel was offered an opportunity he took it.'

Throughout this narrative, while one part of my brain continued defensively to reject it, my sense of Daniel, the husband I'd known, or had thought I'd known, was fading. 'If he was that way inclined, Cindy, why marriage? I just don't get it. He didn't have to marry me. He had me anyway, and it was a surprise, to say the least, when he asked me.'

'You're gorgeous, Marian.' Matter-of-factly. And when I made a face as though to challenge this, 'You don't know that either? Well, take it from me, you are gorgeous, absolutely beautiful, and some men, even our Daniel, like to show off their trophies. It's why men put deer heads and stuffed bears into their living rooms. I doubt he would have paraded me around Ireland and all his relatives like he did you. "Look, Mom! Look at me! Look what I got! Look where I am, top of the heap!"' Then, in response to my look of incredulity: 'Yeah, he told me all about the honeymoon. I heard chapter and verse.

'And you were married to Peter, and Daniel couldn't allow himself to be bested there.' She was watching me closely now. 'I've had a lot of time to get used to this. I made my bargain with the devil long ago. Time will pass and, you'll see, it won't be so bad. Just look on your Daniel period as one of living dangerously. And you did have highs, right?'

I nodded, class clown reacting to the teacher. 'I can do without your advice and consideration, thank you, Cindy.'

'No, you can't,' she said. 'You can do with all the advice and consideration you can get to come to terms with this. It was just sex, honey, nothing to do with love. I guess he was incapable of giving love, just of taking it from saps like us.'

'Whatever.' I fingered his wedding band, which I wore now on a gold chain, but as I did so, I saw that the conversation was over: she was looking towards the kitchen door.

The kid, Junior, was back, swim goggles hanging from a lanyard around his little neck. 'I'm ready now, Mom. C'mon! Let's go! Let's go, Mom! We don't wanna be late.' Singing this, probably mimicking his mother.

'Sure thing, honey! Just gotta pull on my jeans – and, Marian, we can talk again, if you like. But I really have to go now, sorry.' She left the room.

Daniel Junior and I, left together, studied each other, but that seemed to be enough for him, so I let it be enough for me. Despite all I'd heard, I was still not ready to let my Daniel go completely. It was too soon. And I was prepared to believe that this spirited, intelligent little boy was his reincarnation. Maybe . . . maybe . . . In time . . .

Maybe not. This was it. Anything else was pie in the sky. And while Cindy and I, to my surprise, had gotten through our encounter without spitting at each other, this wasn't a movie with a glorious, happy-clappy ending and we weren't going to discover, despite our shared bereavement, we were sisters under the skin or anywhere else.

Having changed into jeans and a sweatshirt, she came back and the three of us, the little boy and two of his father's lovers, left the house together, he skipping happily past the Honda Civic to walk along the short path and onto the sidewalk.

Chapter Thirty

Almost two months later, I was thinking ahead to another trip to Ireland, this one for Rose Marian's christening. For my gift, I'd had Daniel's wedding band remade into a pair of ear studs, each with three tiny diamonds taken from the six in my eternity ring. In the card with them, I had written:

> *These are very special, and when you're old enough to wear these, Rose, we will go out to dinner and I will tell you all about where they came from and answer all your questions about your amazing, very talented uncle Daniel. I'm so excited to meet you on your christening day and I hope we will be very good friends. Much love, your godmother, Auntie Marian.*

I was now regarding the trip as a tentative trial run to see how I would cope if I did move to Ireland. Ajay's ten thousand dollars had dwindled quite a bit since, true to his word, he had gotten it to me from Holy Angels. What with rent, modest though it was, and bills, I'd been drawing on it quite a bit and although I was still able to manage, the day was perhaps not far off when that wouldn't be the case.

The *Tribune* had accepted my piece on the nun (edited down by seventy-five per cent, I reckoned) but had passed on my IT millionaire. 'I'm sorry, Marian,' said my contact on handing it back to me. 'These guys are ten a penny now. You're nobody in the IT sector unless you're about twenty-four and have sold your start-up to some huge corporation.' Then, echoing what Mollie had said: 'It's beautifully written, though, Marian. Have you anything else in your bottom drawer? If you have, we'd be interested in looking at it – about fifteen hundred words, maybe?'

'Perhaps I could work up that interview with the attorney I mentioned to you before?'

'Maybe . . .' But she didn't sound all that enthusiastic.

I hadn't anything else in the journalism line to offer. I considered whether to bluff, but it's not in my makeup. 'Nothing else right now, Kelly, but I'll work something up and see if you might be interested. I'll give you a call. And thanks very much.'

I'd managed to place a few other pieces in local papers, and my nuns, God bless 'em, had asked me to work on a publication to celebrate the centenary of their order, but that was for the following year. So I wasn't destitute, there was money coming in, but it was tough going. And I was still struggling, hard, with Daniel's betrayal. It might have been 'normal', in Cindy's view, for him to pursue sex so vigorously, but it wasn't so in mine.

I was lonely too, and the lure of Ireland, with a readymade, open-armed family I could easily slot into, was growing. They were very good to me, perhaps out of guilt that I'd been had by one or other. What had really happened, though, was that while I was driving through Winnetka or Wilmette – I couldn't remember which – I had seen a sign, pointing west, indicating various suburbs, including Skokie, and, without a moment's hesitation, I had turned in its direction. Nothing to do with Peter, I told myself. But I really did long to see his mother again. I know this is going to sound really, *really* schmaltzy, but I needed a hug.

She mightn't give it – she would be perfectly entitled to slam the door, hard, in my face on first sight, and if she did, I'd just have to suck it up.

I could turn around right now and safely head back to the city, thus avoiding what was probably going to be rejection.

But she wasn't that type, was she? Without further hesitation, I got out of the car and went towards her house. One good thing, I thought, I was wearing a dress.

I straightened my shoulders. *You can do this. You rang Cindy's doorbell, you can ring this one.* Firmly, I depressed the button.

She came to the door wearing slippers but dressed, Letty-style, in a pale blue buttoned-up sweater and navy skirt. Behind her glasses, her eyes widened when she saw me. 'Marian! I – I—'

'I'm sorry, is this a bad time, Letty?'

'I didn't expect—' She stopped, her face exhibiting, after the initial surprise, an expression of horror, clearing then to what I can describe only as 'qualified gladness'. I focused on the latter. 'If it is a bad time, I can go. I just wanted to say hello. I was in the neighbourhood . . .'

While I fought tears, she was still gazing at me, transfixed, as though I were a visitor from some really weird planet. I had really loved Letty but she was so taken aback that it was clear I had shredded our (former) relationship so comprehensively that there was now nothing but resentment and understandable well-deserved of their own. For whatever reason, they all continued to call me regularly, particularly Aoife and Sharon, the former with news of Rose Marian's progress, Sharon for a gossip.

One evening, I was struggling for something original to write about Millennium Park to fill out an article about how the more modern of Chicago's attractions dovetailed seamlessly with older ones, like the Museum of Science and Industry, when Sharon's number flashed up on the cell beside my laptop. When I picked up, she was breathless with Glanmilish news. The village was in shock because there had been a burglary – 'A really bad one, Marian,' she said. 'Remember poor old Billy Murphy? You might have seen him doing his thing in front of the supermarket, and he was at the funeral for Daniel with two men from the Vincent de Paul. Well, a gang of thugs broke into his house some time last night. They beat him up very badly.'

'Is he okay?'

'He's dead.'

'Who found him? Do they know who did it?'

'No. But there's a lot of that going around. Gangs use the motorway to do this kind of thing and get out fast. But it's the first time something like this has happened in Glanmilish. The house is isolated but the poor man was found by one of the local farmers who was passing and saw the front door stove in. He was still conscious. They had tied him to the flue pipe of the wood burner and . . . Well, you can imagine what they must have done to him. Before he passed out he managed to tell the neighbour that they kept shouting at him, "Where's the money?" You know that Da left him money, Marian?'

'Yes.'

'Well, we're all sure it was because of that. So there had to be someone who blabbed to an outsider.'

'You obviously knew him, Sharon?'

'Everyone in the village did,' she responded, 'and everyone knew about the money too.' Then, echoing her brother-in-law, 'Billy was harmless. The funeral is tomorrow, and we're all going, of course. We need to show those animals we aren't afraid.' It was expected to be huge, she told me, with the entire population of the village and hinterland turning out to show solidarity – with whom, exactly, I couldn't quite work out, since his mother was dead and the Lynches' relationship with him was peripheral at best. With each other, I guessed.

'Listen, Marian,' she changed tack, 'I hope you don't think we're a pair of interfering biddies, but Eleanor and I are going up to the house to stay there tonight. Is that all right?'

'It's not my house!'

'You know what I mean. Anyhow, after Jerry gave us the date of the christening, the two of us went up last weekend and did a bit of work on it. Nothing much, mind, just freshening it up, making beds with clean linen, letting a bit of air in, that sort of thing. We spent all day Saturday, then went back on Sunday morning, overhauling the front room, the kitchen, a few of the bedrooms, the hall and bathroom.

'We managed to find someone to jumpstart the Camry, too, and gave the whole thing a bit of a wash and polish. You couldn't see out of the windows.'

'Sharon! That's fantastic. Thank you so much. You must tell me how much the mechanic cost.'

'What mechanic?' She seemed genuinely taken aback. 'It was just a kid from the village. Wouldn't take any money. It was only a jumpstart from my car. Took about four minutes. Anyway, we didn't realise we might be using the house ourselves so soon. We did it because we were hoping you might go there to stay for a few days after the christening. And that we might stay with you, all get to know each other a bit better face to face. Would that be on the cards? Could you stay a few days? We know you're probably very busy.'

I looked at my dad's kitchen table, which, apart from my laptop and the bumph on Millennium Park, had one file on it – the one containing my 1997 piece on an invasion of locusts in Northbrook. I'd been hoping to rejig it a little and place it in a nostalgia slot in one of the north-shore locals. 'I'm not so busy that I can't take a week off.'

'That's brilliant. We'll have a great time. I'll tell Eleanor, and Aoife's still on maternity leave – maybe she could come down too. We'll have a girly couple of days, drink gin, listen to seventies music, our own little party. It'll be fun.'

'How's Eleanor?'

'Flying! She's joined a golf club, believe it or not, and is having lessons. Boring for Ireland about it. How're you, Marian? It's still very raw, I'd imagine. I think you're great, the way you've coped with everything – my blood boils every time I think of what that shyster did.'

'I know what he did was awful, Sharon, and I don't know, really, whether or not I actually miss him – some things, maybe.' It had been on the tip of my tongue to say that I missed the sex but I managed to switch just in time. 'Fun. I do miss the fun.'

'You know what, Marian? If you put that whole thing in a book, who'd believe it?

'Anyway, we're all looking forward to the christening. It'll be nice to have something cheerful to go to rather than funerals. I'm not looking forward to tomorrow. Poor old Billy. I was in that shop to get a few supplies that day we were doing up the house and he was in full gear, the crathur. Wished me a happy Christmas when I was going in. You never know from day to day, do you?

'Anyway, gotta dash. I'm meeting an old pal of mine for lunch and I'm late already.'

After we'd said goodbye, I sat looking at the cell for a long time. Thinking.

* * *

I still hadn't been able fully to process Cindy Kurtz's revelations. I no longer despised her – in fact, I even thought, a little grudgingly, that I could have done with some of her pragmatism. I'd gone into her house all guns blazing – but she had turned my guns on me.

When I unscrambled the series of shocks and placed them in an orderly line, her main point, it seemed to me, had been that there was no point in hating Daniel for his nature, as she had described it. It would be as silly as hating a shark for going after prey because it's hungry, or a cheetah for running fast. Anyhow, there is very little satisfaction to be gained, however grim, in carrying on a vendetta against a dead person who won't fight back because he can't. A one-sided fight is no fight at all.

Thinking back over our short time together, I guess I'd had inklings about at least some of what was happening in the background of my marriage: those mood swings, plus the barely concealed 'my way or no way' I had detected in him from time to time, but, glorying in my new physicality, I had chosen to ignore them.

If I had known then what I know now, would I still have married him?

I'd like to think I might have been a bit more judicious, but that's self-delusion born of hindsight because 'yes' is the honest answer. In the Irish vernacular, I was (literally) mad for him.

Cindy had been right in one respect: if I was not to drive myself actually insane with analyses and endless why-why-whys, I would have to work hard on remembering the highs Daniel and I had had together. And, of course, I would have to put even more of an effort into repairing the big hole in my own judgment of men.

All that being said, I could not stop memories of the man I had first married, Peter Black, rising from the ashes of that marriage to reproach me. Peter could not have been a more sincere and admirable candidate for wedlock. It wasn't his fault that I'd thrown off all the shackles of decency to follow primitive drives I hadn't even known I had until Daniel Lynch hove into view.

We are mobile, we Americans. We move homes quite a lot, and it's hard to travel on any highway without encountering a car towing a U-Haul trailer bristling with furniture, bikes, bags and cardboard boxes. I could go anywhere, I thought now, I could go west, find a job in a Wal-Mart or a Walgreens somewhere and start my life, a different life, all over again in some place like Boise, Idaho. No journalistic deadlines, no bringing home the job in your head, just do it, be pleasant to the customers, collect your earnings, and in your free time go fishing, take in a movie, catch up on Netflix, whatever turns you on.

I was sure someone would give me a job. I was reasonably intelligent, single, with no baggage now . . .

After a bit more of this, I put the Millennium literature aside and opened the file cover containing the locusts article. Bearing in mind it had been written eighteen years previously, I'd read it critically, I decided, judging it as an editor or a sub would, to see if anything could be done with it. If not, well, I'd think about it.

I still remembered how jubilant I'd been when it had been accepted by the *Chicago Sun-Times*, my very first article to be published by a major outlet. I was twenty-four years old and still cutting my journalism teeth.

The article was an account of an 'emergence' as it was called, of the species of insect called, popularly in Chicago, the 'thirteen-year locusts', actually a species of cicada wonderfully named 'magicicada' that rise in their billions, even trillions, to feed and mate from development underground for a few weeks every thirteen or seventeen years, depending on the specific sub-species.

At the time, my parents still lived in Shangri-La, the Northbrook ranch-style house where I had grown up, and were delighted to have me home over the weekend the emergence was expected. The house was set on a large, grassy, wooded lot and that weekend in 1997, as expected, the little bugs came up overnight, swarming onto trees, completely stripping any young foliage in the vicinity. Even the density of the noise they made almost defied description. With windows and doors shut tight, and with window air-con running at full blast, it was still like having an aircraft engine revving right outside.

And when you went out in the morning after the mating and feasting, most of the tree branches were bare and you crunched, literally, through ankle-deep piles of brittle little corpses to get to your car.

The bonus for me, journalistically, occurred when I was driving back to the city to write the piece. On the expressway I had to slow my little Renault to a crawl as, with other motorists, I encountered a swarm so thick, that even before the wipers had completed one sweep, the windshield was again thick with thousands of the creatures. The swarm was on only our side of the expressway, but so big that it took at least three or four minutes to get through it. For that time, it was like driving in the dark with no lights. Honestly.

I wrote my report that evening, a thousand words, laying on the atmospherics. Throughout the narrative, I scattered the information I had gleaned about the basic entomology of the creatures, along with a few quotes from the citizens of the Greater Chicago area, weaving them through the descriptive passages. (One guy moaned about having to use a snow shovel to clear a path from his front door, although most were surprisingly affectionate with a weird sort of proprietary pride. Many said something along the lines of 'After all, we won't have this again for another thirteen or even seventeen years.')

The piece was good, I decided now, well written, as everyone kept telling me about stuff I submitted, but it wasn't, unfortunately, exceptional. I knew that would have been Mollie's take on it. Even in a nostalgia slot, it wouldn't have cut it, not to her standards.

I put the pages back into the folder. Some day, I thought, when the next emergence was due, I could revisit it.

But unless someone died as a result of it . . . *So what's new about this, huh?* I could hear Mollie's grating, honking New York voice.

Nothing, was the answer.

I'd had one further commission. I had contacted the editor of a local weekly paper in Portlaoise, the *Sentinel*, who had been delighted to agree to my offer of a travel piece about Chicago. 'From the Windy City? That'd be great – any idea what you might do, what angle?'

'How about "The Chicago I Love"?'

'Brilliant. A thousand words, Marian, but all we can pay is fifty euros, I'm afraid. I know you're probably used to a lot more.'

'Fifty'll be fine,' I had agreed brightly, but as we said goodbye, I was thinking ruefully about what little consideration I had given to taking an 'attitude' with Mollie Lehman as she and I had parted company and I had stomped off. Not that it had made any difference in the end, of course. And she had really come through for me. The piece for the County Laois paper didn't need research. I was able to write it in a couple of hours and send it off. The guy was delighted. 'Any time, Marian. Anything else you want to send me . . .'

And the cheque for fifty euros had arrived within two weeks. After commissions and currency differences, it had bought me almost a week's worth of breakfasts in my local diner. Not bad, I thought, and had immediately cobbled together a piece on Navy Pier, writing as though I were a three-year-old boy. I'd titled it: 'Through the Fun of the Child'. The editor had loved that, too. The next cheque had arrived just as promptly as the first. Then I got another series of breakfasts – and another commission, this time for a trip to the Museum of Science and Industry: 'And don't forget the U-boat, Marian. That's important.'

'Sure.' At the beginning, it had been a mystery to me why those little commissions continued to come but, apart from the hassle of regular visits to the currency exchanges, they were great fun to do. My pieces had now morphed into a column, which even had a title – 'A now and then letter from the Windy City'. Ours not to reason why, I told myself, because although it wasn't lucrative I enjoyed the work. I loved my city and it was nice – rather easy, too – to share its attractions. Daniel had always said that because Ireland was an island, and County Laois was an island within it, its people were always interested in reading about different, faraway places – and many, while continuing to harbour misgivings about its gun laws and insularity, retained a fascination with the US. 'It's to do with TV and American movies,' he'd said. 'We can all pick out significant landmarks and buildings in the cities, or the redness of Arizona, and we loved the big American fridges in people's kitchens and their breakfast counters. We all grew up with America in our living rooms.'

I had no illusions that I had the gig because it was about Chicago. It could have been about anywhere in the States. But it kept my journalistic hand in and, from the *Sentinel*'s perspective, I came cheap and, the editor said, I was 'classy'.

So here I was, I thought, finding more and more reasons to underpin my decision to go to Ireland. I was a widow with a twenty-bucks-a-month pension, scraping around for work, savings eroding largely because I was paying rent for a worn-out apartment with worn-down furniture and very elderly neighbours. When I wanted a chat other than about the weather – or with the super of the block concerning plumbing – I had to call a country thousands of miles and six hours away.

I was almost half there anyway: in my parents' bedroom my bags were half packed for yet another short trip to Ireland to become a godmother. And Ireland was where my relatives lived, the only ones I had, apart from the two distant cousins I had never met and heard from, apart from an annual Christmas card.

Very little in my current situation made sense, did it?

Chapter Thirty-one

Next morning I woke to a bright blue sky and decided not to hang around in the apartment because what was in prospect was another long, empty day. Even if I went downtown, I was in no financial position to go shopping, and I didn't have the energy for the museums or galleries. I would have felt conspicuous walking alone in any of the parks since I wouldn't be jogging, skateboarding or riding a bike.

But this, I determined, would be a good day for me. I was going to take a day off – but with a purpose. Even though it would make me only fifty dollars, I would research the famous Ravinia Festival of Music, at which, all summer, you could hear any form of music from the Chicago Symphony Orchestra to Taylor Swift, a local band on the rise, or a jazz great, all in the lovely, opulent surrounds of the North Shore suburb of Highland Park. I had decided to rent a little car for the day. Highland Park was twenty-six miles north of the city centre and for once, I wasn't going to rely on public transport.

First, though, it was such a wonderful morning that I was going to take an actual *walk*! I had been so miserable I had been living like a hermit.

I'd got to know Oak Street Beach because the apartment in which I'd lived with Peter, seemingly a hundred years ago, was close by. It's a small beach and just to be beside the lake on a sunny day would be a privilege and, hopefully, would give my head some respite.

After breakfast, I took the L downtown, then walked along Michigan Avenue to the pedestrian tunnel that took me under Lake Shore Drive and straight onto the beach, clean as a whistle, its sand, originally imported from the Indiana Dunes, as pale and reflective as any I've seen in brochures for Greece. And on that calm day at least, I would guess that the translucence of the water could also compare.

There weren't many people about, a few joggers, a handful of tourists taking photos of the skyline, which from there is truly spectacular. An elderly couple, well wrapped up in blankets and woolly hats, had brought their own beach chairs and were sitting right at the water's edge, staring, contentedly, I hoped, towards the horizon. Dogs aren't allowed on that beach but, it being Chicago, one man was walking his cat – it was padding along beside him at the end of a pink lead, fake diamonds on its collar flashing intermittently in the sunshine.

Yet, for the second time recently, I really didn't know what to do with myself. Although no one was paying me any attention, I felt self-conscious, as though I didn't belong, as though I was a character in a film, wearing my clothes and shoes; the effects man on set was feeding in the low sound of water lapping, while I waited for an unseen director to shout, 'Action!' But I had no script and when the director did call on me I feared I wouldn't know which way to walk, what action to take. I was a performer completely adrift.

I left very quietly, back the way I had come. I was heavily tempted to walk by my former home on Oak Street, just to take a look at it, but I wouldn't get further than the concierge so what was the point of that? I heard Mom (again): when I had done something stupid and was trying to cajole her into helping me avoid the consequences, she would say, *You made your bed, now go lie in it.*

I went in search of coffee, and ten minutes later I was in a Starbucks. Again. My diet had gone to hell lately. I couldn't remember when last I'd cooked.

And possibly because of my proximity to Oak Street, while I was sitting there I thought about Letty and her cooking: what would she have made of the crumbs and dustings of sugar on my plate, the dregs of my coffee? She would have been appalled.

Letty had been a cook in the solid tradition of the Midwest. Spaghetti bolognese, lasagne, meatballs with red sauce, casseroles, cottage pie, Irish stew, chicken in all its guises, roasted, fried, Maryland, Kiev, and, of course, steaks or pork chops with mashed potato, broccoli, and don't spare the catsup. I smiled. It was a Monday. As far as I remembered, Monday was shepherd's pie day in the Black household.

It was only eleven thirty but by the time I got to the location of the car rental company, I would be bang on time for my pickup at noon.

My plan was to drive slowly along Lake Shore Drive and up into the northern suburbs, taking my time, ogling the mansions and simply making like a tourist, until I got to Ravinia. And then, ninety minutes later, I was parking the rental, a little tin can that buzzed loudly, like a bee, at any speed above thirty miles an hour, less than fifty yards from Letty's house.

I tried to lie to myself that this was a coincidence, that during the trip north, confused, I had taken a wrong turn at some junction

cold judgement on her side. 'I'm sorry. I shouldn't have come. Sorry, Letty, sorry for everything.' I turned and had taken a few steps down her little driveway when she called me back: 'Marian! Wait!'

I went back. 'Letty, if this is too difficult for you . . . The last thing I'd want to do is to upset you, of all people.'

'You'd better come in.'

'Letty.' I stayed where I was. 'I mean it. If this is awkward . . . I was on my way to Highland Park for various reasons, but I wanted to thank you in person for your letter and that gesture with the Mass after – after . . .' like her, I couldn't say his name, not in front of her '. . . after the death. I truly appreciated it.'

'Come in,' she repeated, opening the door wider.

I followed her along the short, narrow hallway I remembered so well, and into her kitchen-diner. 'So how've you been, Letty?' I asked, as she went straight for the coffee pot .

'Fine, we've been fine,' she said noncommittally, her back towards me, concentrating, it seemed, on measuring the grounds. 'And you?'

'Managing,' I said.

'That's good.' She added the water, put the pot on the stove and turned it on. 'There. That should be ready in a few minutes. I'm sorry I've no cookies or anything to go with it,' she added, coming back to the table. 'I should have some—' She stopped, then sat heavily on her chair.

'So what's this all about?' She gazed at me with unflinching eyes. 'What's really happening here, Marian? I thought we agreed we couldn't be friends. That upset me at the time but I got over it. You do get over things when you're my age. You've no choice but to let things go. Otherwise life would be one long series of disappointments.'

'Good advice, Letty, thanks.'

'So why?' Her gaze didn't waver.

'I'm not a hundred per cent sure. As I say, I just wanted to see you again. That's being totally honest. I hadn't intended to come out here – I was on my route to Highland Park—'

'You've said that. But you're a little bit off course, aren't you? Skokie is not quite on the route to Highland Park.'

'I just needed to see you, I guess. That's the best I can do.'

'And what about Peter? Did you need to see him too?'

'I'm all over the place, Letty.' I evaded the question because I didn't know the truthful answer.

She was still looking at me.

'I can't stand myself when I examine in detail and ask myself – as I do frequently – what happened to me that I behaved as I did.'

'We've been asking ourselves that too.' She dropped her eyes to examine the back of her left hand with its worn wedding band. 'He's still very upset. I'm sure he'll survive, he *is* surviving, but that's what people do.' Her tone was sad now. 'I guess it's going to take more than just a few months, but it's water under the bridge, ain't it?' She looked up again, challenging. 'But I don't want you to think I'm scolding you, Marian. I can see you're doing enough of that for yourself without me adding to the voices in your head. I've had a pretty long life, and if I've learned anything it's that human beings aren't predictable. They do funny things, out of character . . .' She trailed off, then added suddenly: 'Did you love him?'

'Peter?'

'No, the other guy.'

'I thought so,' I said slowly. 'He triggered something in me I didn't know I had – he snowed me. But I don't want you to think I'm not taking responsibility for my actions, Letty. I think I went a little insane for a time.'

But I could see from her unspoken reaction that my renegade tongue had run ahead of my brain. Briskly, she changed the subject: 'What's ahead for you, Marian?'

'I don't know. My future is slightly off the map right now . . .' And then, while I knew it was entirely inappropriate, it all came pouring out: Cindy, my blindness concerning Daniel, my treachery, his treachery, my dad's death, my guilt about Peter, guilt, guilt *guilt*. 'I was such an idiot, Letty,' I cried. 'Peter's a lovely man and I was out of my mind to do what I did to him. You too, Letty. I'm so, so sorry about what I did to you!'

But her eyes had widened. And, distressed as I was, I could see the cogs turning behind them. 'I'm not here to try to patch things up, honestly. My coming here was just . . . an instinct.' I stopped.

Why exactly was I there? For comfort? For forgiveness? To share? To be *mothered*?

'I don't want you, or Peter, to think I'm here to try to . . .' I began. 'Ah, shit! I'm making a complete mess of this.' I put my hands over my face.

'Lovely language, I must say. You were never a cusser, Marian.'

'I had my moments.' I looked up at her dear, kind face. 'I just wanted to see you, Letty. I've missed you.'

'So, that it, then? Gotta see the old gal 'cause she mightn't be here all that long, eh?'

'Oh, Letty,' I said, 'I know what you must think of me. I've just given you the bare bones of what happened. If I needed punishment for what I did to Peter – and to yourself – you can consider it done.'

'I don't think you needed punishment, Marian,' she said quietly. 'We all make mistakes. I have to say, though, it was particularly hard for us, you know, that it was Daniel Lynch and that Cindy was Peter's girlfriend.'

'I know – I mean, I know now.'

'She was here a couple of times and I didn't really take to her, although I did my best. They weren't suited. Not like I figured—'

'Oh, Letty, I'm so, so sorry.'

'So are we,' she said, 'but, look, some things are just not to be. Well, *maybe* not to be.'

I looked at her, at her sensible sweater and her flat shoes, ankles bulging a little over the side of the foot. But as I tried to figure out how to respond to her, I saw her surreptitiously check her watch, the way people do when they don't want you to see you've outstayed your welcome or they've somewhere else to be, letting the eyes fall a little to take a brief glance. 'Do you have to be somewhere, Letty? I should go.' I made to get up from my chair.

'Did you get Peter's letter as well as mine?' She answered my question with another

'Yes, I did. Will you thank him for me, please?'

'I will.'

But then I heard a noise from the hallway, the sound of the door closing.

Letty sat straighter. 'I forgot to tell you that Peter was coming to visit me this afternoon after work. He always has Monday afternoons off.' Demurely, she lowered her eyes to the table and swept away an imaginary crumb.

Of course I'd known about Mondays. He'd visited my dad Mondays.

And then he was in the kitchen, carrying a paper sack from Cinnabon. 'Oh, hi, Peter,' said his mother, artlessly. 'Guess who came to see us? I didn't get a chance to warn you. She's just arrived.' She lumbered to her feet. 'Oh! You remembered my cookies!' She grabbed the sack from his hand and went to the stove where the coffee pot was now stewing. She opened it and looked inside.

'It's cinnamon rolls today, Mom.' Peter, shocked initially to see me, had quickly gathered himself. He fetched a stool from a corner of the kitchen and sat at the table, which was small, maybe three feet by three, so I could smell traces of his cologne, Dunhill for Men.

Seeing him, smelling him, created a renewal of longing for what I had lost by throwing away this man, the mutual, steady affection, the stability and sheer good living we'd enjoyed together.

I quashed those feelings. I had caused him so much pain that I couldn't open any doors to a renewal of our relationship: it would be too crude and self-serving, and he was so decent he might even agree to take me back if, out of loneliness, I made a good enough case for it.

But it wasn't just loneliness. It wasn't until I actually saw him that day that I fully realised I had loved him, in however measured a manner, for who he was, not for what he could give me. And for his sake I couldn't afford him an opportunity to get together with me again. It would be too crass. It wasn't even that I simply didn't deserve him (although that too), and whatever about a blessed renewal of my relationship with his mother, I had to stop thinking about myself in all of this and put him first.

'This has gotta go.' Letty took the coffee pot over to the sink and threw out the contents.

'This is a surprise, Marian,' her son said tonelessly, watching her. 'How've you been?'

'Managing.' I repeated what I'd said to Letty, adding, 'Up and down, I guess.'

'That's understandable.'

I joined him in looking towards Letty at the sink. She was still tending her coffee pot . 'I need to make fresh,' she said.

'I'll get plates, shall I?' Without waiting for a response, her son got off his stool and went to a cupboard, where he took quite a while to select three plates, although from where I sat, the top three on the stack seemed as suitable as any of the others. He coincided his return to the table with his mother's.

'So here we are,' she said then. 'Coffee won't be long now. I had to throw the last lot out.'

'You said that before, Mom.'

'Oh, did I? Senior moment – *another* senior moment.' She opened the sack and distributed three of the rolls. 'Just like the old days, eh?'

'Hardly, Mom!'

'I've just remembered.' Peter stood up again. 'I got a call from work on the way here.' He, like his mother, glanced at his watch. 'I have to call back. It's a bit complicated but it won't take long.' He left the room.

'That went well,' said Letty, and the atmosphere between the two of us, at least, eased a bit as we smiled at her mordancy. I could tell, as we sat waiting for him to rejoin us, that he was now his mother's major concern, and she continued to look towards the door he had closed after him. 'He works too hard,' she said. 'But I guess most doctors do.'

I could think of nothing that wasn't controversial to add to this. We both turned to watch the coffee pot, and when its belching died down, I said, 'Let me.' I went to the stove and, as I had so many times before in that kitchen, poured the coffee, black and aromatic, into our cups. I was about to add sugar to hers, but she waved a wallet full of minuscule tablets.

'Had to give up the sugar, like half the population. The usual. Type two diabetes.'

'Well, should you be having coffee?' I looked dubiously at the cups.

'I have to die of something, Marian,' she said. 'Coffee's the last vice standing. Unlike you, I had to give up sex long ago!'

I was floored.

'What's the matter, Marian?' she asked innocently. 'Surprised?' I had always known that, along with her warm, nurturing nature, Letty Black had a surprisingly offbeat sense of humour. But just then Peter returned. 'Sorry about that,' he said.

'Want coffee?' I said.

'It took longer than I thought,' he said.

'No problem,' I said. 'So, can I pour you a cup?'

'Sure,' he said.

'Sit down and I'll get another mug,' I said.

A little gavotte.

His presence had put a brake on the growing ease between Letty and me. She sensed this and, when we had barely begun to consume our cinnamon rolls, got to her feet. 'I need the bathroom. I may be some time . . .'

Left alone, Peter and I looked at each other. 'This is difficult, Peter,' I said.

'Yes, it is. But, look, Marian, there are things I'd like to say – not in front of my mom, though, if that's OK. Could we go out somewhere, or are you stuck for time?'

'I'm under no pressure at all today.'

'Right. I'll tell her.' He got up again and left the room. I heard him tap on the door of the guest WC. 'Mom, if you don't mind, Marian and I are going out for a spell. That okay?'

Her reply was muffled so I didn't get what exactly she said, but the tone was high. She had clearly given her approval.

Chapter Thirty-two

'Could we not have coffee or, more especially, doughnuts, please, Peter?' We were walking towards Lincoln Avenue where there was a cluster of middle-ranked restaurants, including one called Sweety Pies. 'After my diet for the past few days that place would probably finish the job and kill me.'

'Fine,' he said tersely. 'We'll go to Libertad. They serve what they call "small plates", salads, hummus, tempura, things like that. I take it you haven't had lunch?' He was using his professional-doctor voice.

'I know Libertad.' I was finding it hard to keep up with him. 'We were there a couple of times.'

'Were we? I'm afraid I don't remember. But I have brought my mother there for brunch on Sundays and I can recommend it. I like the beet salad.' He increased his pace so I had to break into a semi-trot.

Even though it was a Monday, the place was humming, and because of the nice day, many people were eating outside, so there was no problem getting a table – in fact, once inside, he immediately spotted two people leaving one in the corner and a bus boy, obviously on alert, zipping over to clean it.

We ordered. I hadn't even looked at the menu. 'If you like beet salad, Peter, that's what I'll have.'

'In that case I'll have the hummus and we can share.' He gave the order, then didn't waste any time with trivialities. 'So, Marian, here we are, after all these years.'

He was being sardonic. My sojourn, as he probably saw it, with Daniel had lasted only a matter of months – and the big question now was how long it would have survived if he hadn't died. I'm not unintelligent or unaware, as I've said, and sooner or later I would have figured out what he was at with Cindy, not because of my capabilities as an investigative journalist – sadly lacking – but possibly because, in the interests of her son, she would have declared her hand.

I doubt I would have discovered for myself that there had been not just her but a congregation of 'other women'. It was probably a blessing, I'd thought, on my way home from Cindy's house, that his funeral had been held in Ireland. Otherwise I might have been wondering at the unusual presence of so many women. What would they have been like? Diminutive like her?

'Yes, here we are, Peter. I'm really very sorry for what happened. For what I did . . .' I managed to keep my cool. 'I hope that at least you now have a girlfriend who treats you better than I did.'

'You're fishing. I don't think you're entitled to ask that, Marian. Do you?'

'You're right. I was fishing. But I am really, really sorry,' I said again. 'If I had the time back—'

'But you don't, do you? Neither of us has.'

'Sorry.'

'Please stop saying that, Marian. It's getting a bit repetitive, don't you think?'

'But I can't think of anything else to say – and I really want you to believe me.'

'Water under the bridge,' he said, echoing his mother. How many times had they discussed me? I could barely imagine. But whatever they'd said would not have been unfair or undeserved. Or had they swept me under their carpet? My name taboo and never to be mentioned?

Our food, obviously pre-prepared, arrived and he seemed to relax a little. 'Nature will out. I'm dull. You're not. In one respect I understand. I'm too dull for someone as . . . as vivid as you.'

I was astonished he thought of me in that way. And had he shared the blame for the break-up? That had never occurred to me before. Those wounds I had inflicted were very deep. When, back then, I'd been rationalising, trying to justify my behaviour and defend the indefensible, while simultaneously being fair to him, I had described him to others and to myself using words such as 'decent', 'articulate', 'honest', 'kind', all of which qualities I admired. Throwing caution to the winds, I said this to him now, but again he interrupted: 'It wasn't enough, though, was it, not when that Casanova turned up? You do know that he took Cindy away from me before you? How do you think I felt after *Rejection, the Movie, Part Two*?

'Dammit,' he lowered his head. 'I swore to myself that I wouldn't get mad.' He would have thumped the table, I think, if his hummus hadn't been in front of him.

'I didn't know about you and Cindy. Not until she told me yesterday.'

'You went to see Cindy?' He was startled.

'Yes, and she was full of news.'

'What kind of news?'

'Well, she told me about you – which Daniel never saw fit to do, but neither did you. I met the kid, really nice boy. The image of his father but blond.'

'Daniel's, I assume?'

'Yes.' And then I told him about Ajay and that side of things.

He had been gazing at me but I hadn't been able to read his expression. He let silence develop for a few seconds while dealing with his food. Then, without raising his eyes from the plate: 'You had quite a day yesterday, didn't you?'

'I'm having quite a day today, too. But I'm glad we're at least talking to each other again, Peter. And in case you think I came out here to Skokie to try to ambush you, that's not the case. I figured you to be at work. I was on Oak Street beach, and I realised I had literally nobody to talk to in Chicago about all of this and I have this rental car and . . .'

'And?'

'It seemed to develop a mind of its own and drove me here.'

'Really?' His tone was mocking. This was a hard-shelled Peter, unfamiliar to me but, truthfully, I was surprised but happy to find myself there with him having a conversation. He was still furious with me – seeing me had, no doubt, reignited those feelings – but, being Peter, he was, I could see, exerting iron control. The last meeting we'd had had been in the atrium of John Berchman's Hospital – his anger that day, his distress and shock, still haunted me, as did the image of his shoulders drooping as he walked away from me. 'I'm not feeling sorry for myself, Peter, or at least I'm trying not to. I know I brought this all on my own head and shoulders. I'll take what's coming.'

'Like the early Christian martyrs, eh?'

'Yes, that did sound self-indulgent and self-serving. But I was desperately lonely on that beach, and so near where you and I had lived together, and I had the car. I knew Letty wouldn't kick me out. Or I hoped she wouldn't. She didn't, and then you came in, and, as you say, here we are. You wanted to say something to me in private by the way. Isn't that why we're here?'

He looked at me, inscrutable. 'It'll keep.'

I had imagined a meeting like this one very differently. 'It won't. Go on. I insist. You can't say anything I haven't said to myself. I deserve your anger, your condemnation, all of it. If I hadn't . . .' I hesitated.

'Yes? If you hadn't . . .?'

'If I hadn't had a rush of blood to the head that time. I can't think of anything more appropriate to say than that. There's no excuse for what I did – that sounds feeble. It *is* feeble. I'm repeating myself now, I know, but if I could turn the clock back—'

'You'd probably do the same.'

'I can't argue with that because I don't know, do I?'

'And here we are, talking about him. The guy won't let us alone even when he's six feet under and four thousand miles away.'

I took another deep breath. 'Will a time come when you forgive me, Peter?'

'That's asking a lot. It hasn't been that long. It's still raw.'

'I guess I'm asking.'

'I don't know the answer to that yet. I could see that my mom was delighted we were in the same room. I can't be, Marian. Not yet. Maybe not ever, although Mom, I know, never gave up hope, no matter how often I've told her there was none. For me, I'm sorry to say, the hurt is too deep. Really, Marian, can you see us together again? With a potential avalanche of bad feeling always poised above our heads, even if we don't talk about it?'

There it was, the potential opportunity – but I drew on all my resolve. 'No, I can't. Not really. As you say, it would be the bloody elephant, not just in the room but following us around everywhere, even individually. For you, it'd be *Is it happening again with this guy or that?* You'd probably never be able to relax to trust me. On my part it'd be, because I'm only human, *How long more do I have to pay for my sins?*

'Very astute.'

He opened his mouth to say something else but I cut in hastily: 'I'm talking theoretically, of course. We've probably said enough. Well, I have.'

He didn't answer.

'Too much, maybe?'

He didn't answer that, either. He seemed to be fascinated by a frond of rocket garnish on his plate. So I answered for him: 'You're agreeing, aren't you, that you can never see yourself trusting me again?'

'Not now, I can't.' At last he raised his eyes, freshly shaming me with the hurt they showed.

'Of course not now,' I said. 'That's obvious. But some time in the future?'

'Is that all you're asking for, Marian? For forgiveness?'

One of the traits I had most respected in Peter Black was his direct honesty. He showed it now, but not in a way I might have expected. 'We can never be just friends, Marian.'

'Of course, of course, I understand—'

'If you'd stop talking for a minute, please, and just listen?'

'Sorry. There's that word again.' I made a zip motion across my mouth.

He waited a bit. 'I get it. I get how sorry you are, and how ashamed and guilty and all the rest of it. But friendship with you is not on for me. And, of course, forgiveness would have to be part of that from the get-go. But I could never be a friend of yours.'

Again he looked down at his plate, pushing the rocket against a small slice of bell pepper, precisely aligning them, yellow beside green. 'It wouldn't be enough. That's what I was referring to when I said I wanted to talk privately to you. I figured it out when I left the kitchen to make a call. I wasn't making a call. I was up in my old bedroom, thinking.

'But there's something else I should say, too. I thought you were the best thing that ever happened to me, Marian, especially after the debacle with Cindy Kurtz.' I opened my mouth to speak again but he raised a hand, like a cop, to prevent it. 'Just stop being abject for two minutes, please, and try to take on board what it was like for me to have that bastard target first Cindy and then you. At least I hadn't been married to her. But you – I suppose snatching a second woman from me, especially one married to me, gave him extra status in his own eyes. When we got together, I couldn't believe my luck. I didn't want to couch it in those terms to you, because I didn't want you to believe I was weak.'

'Weak? You? Wea—' The server had come to ask if we were finished. We were, I thought, surprising myself with how sad that made me feel.

'Desserts? Madam? Sir?' He looked from one to the other of us.

'No, thank you.' I'd had enough sugar in the last three months to last me a lifetime.

'I'll have the key lime cheesecake, please.' Then Peter turned back to me. 'It's very good here. It comes with coconut ice cream and a mango salsa – you won't change your mind, Marian?'

'Good choice, sir.' The server smiled. 'You're sure, madam?'

'I'm sure.' The guy was great, a credit to the restaurant and his profession, but right now, I wished he would just go away. He eked out another couple of seconds, though: 'I'm making an executive decision here, folks. Two spoons. You won't be sorry.'

When he had gone, Peter smiled wryly. 'We were all young once. He'll calm down.'

I waited a bit, and then – what the hell? 'I'll just say this and then I'll shut up, Peter. For good, if you want me to. And I don't know whether I should say it but . . . it feels good to be here with you, talking about ordinary things like key lime cheesecake. I didn't think that would be possible. I won't go into the "sorry, sorry" routine again, I'm boring even myself at this stage, but you do know I mean it?'

'Of course I know you mean it. I was married to you. You do get to know a person during that time, no matter how it ends. And what you want now is for us to talk of ordinary things. That's it?'

'It's something to take away with me. You have to admit it's a positive development. We meant a lot to each other at one time and, you won't believe this, I know, but even at the time of my madness, I realised what I was letting go. Daniel took the ground from under me in every sphere. I'm at sea, and I've been drifting, but I've decided to put an end to that. And to tell you the naked truth, I'm leaning towards going to live in Ireland. I love Chicago, I'm sure you gathered that somewhere along the way, but I don't think Chicago loves me. I've been finding it hard to make the smallest decision lately – but I think Chicago is making it for me. I've no job here, no permanent home – I'll have to leave Dad's apartment because, right now, I can't afford the rent because my finances are a mess. This isn't a whinge and I'm not seeking sympathy, it's just factual. And to know that I can leave with you not actually hating me, Letty too, gives me an immeasurable boost.'

'Why would I hate you? Resentment, regret, sadness, all that sort of stuff doesn't congeal to become hatred. It might feel like that at the beginning, but as time goes on . . .' He stopped as his dessert arrived, the young server, with a flourish, placing the extra spoon in front of me, adjusting it so it was exactly vertical.

'He'll go far – maybe!' Then Peter, instead of digging in to his key lime cheesecake, said, 'Listen, Marian, that guy, Lynch, was an unstoppable force, like, I don't know, a charging rhinoceros or a hurricane, clearing everything that impeded the way forward. I'm not as good as you with the similes. But I'm sure you recognise what I mean. And this is going to sound awful but I can't mourn his loss even though underneath, like us all, he was a human being and I can't hate any human being. But I don't shed tears for him. It's the first time I've ever said something so terrible about the death of anyone. I had a hard time writing that note to you after he died. There were many drafts!'

'Remind me. Why didn't you tell me about him and Cindy, or even you and Cindy, when we were together?'

'I did try to warn you but I guess I was too subtle.'

'I guess you were.' I could feel the air crackling with words unsaid. I was glad I'd decided not to push for any meeting with Peter other than this one. It had been the right decision, for him at least – although his sitting opposite me had renewed the pangs of regret about what I had so quickly let go.

Perhaps it was because I had been to two funerals recently, but there was a funereal sense about that meal with Peter. I was reminded of Daniel's wake in Ireland, the mourners raking over his life – but joyfully, recalling happier times. 'We were happy for a while?' I said suddenly.

'We were. At least, I was.' He couldn't look at me.

'I have a godchild in Ireland now,' I said quietly, to fill the vacuum. 'She's called Rose Marian and she's only a few weeks old.

I'm going there shortly for her christening and I've been given the opportunity to live there. I might take it, although all I know for sure is that I'm going to stop drifting. Daniel took me, causing mayhem in your life, then died, leaving me rudderless. Now I'm taking control.'

'I'm glad to hear it.'

'It's a big tumbledown old house with eight bedrooms.' I was gabbling because I could see his pain. But something about being there with him had made me focus: like the lemons or cherries tumbling in the fruit machine, something had clicked into place and I knew. I was going to live in Ireland. 'I don't know how long I'll stay,' I said, 'but I do know I've not finished totally with Chicago, and I don't think I ever will, but right now there's little purpose to my life here. Maybe we could meet again for a cup of coffee when I visit.' I made sure I sounded absolutely neutral.

But he was puzzled: 'An eight-bedroomed house? I thought you implied money was short?'

'You should see it. "Darkly romantic", I think it would be called by a realtor, meaning it's falling down, but I've never been afraid of hard work.'

'I remember that.' Seeing the hint of a smile, I opened my mouth to reminisce, but closed it again. We had gone, I believed, far beyond mutual reminiscence and I had to face that. But, swiftly, I went for broke. 'I don't mean now, or even in the near future, but obviously I'll have plenty of room for guests,' I said. 'That's an invitation to you and your mom, and let's leave it at that. There are *no* strings attached, Peter, and *no* expectations, if you take it up. I promise.'

'But even by inviting us you're creating expectations, Marian. Certainly in my poor mom's heart.'

'I'll talk to her nearer the time. She might enjoy it even without you. I'd sure enjoy having her! Think of it as respite from caring for her. You could go off to the Caribbean or somewhere. Christmas is coming. I'd take care of her, the way you did my poor dad – and I don't think I ever got the chance to thank you for that.'

'It was no trouble.'

'It was, and I appreciated it all the more for that, so thank you very much. Where Letty's concerned,' I was warming to this, 'I'd show her a good time. And if she came alone, she wouldn't have to lift a finger. Of course, if you came with her, the same applies.' I stopped. I didn't want him to get the impression I was working on him through his mother.

'We'll see,' he said. 'I'm not sure I'd want her travelling all that way on her own – but we'll see.'

'We'd meet her at the airport. She wouldn't have to worry about a thing.'

'Mmm,' he murmured.

I sat back, studying him as he toyed with his ice-cream spoon. 'Thank God for my little tin can.'

'What?'

'My rental car. It has a mind of its own and got me here with you.' I'd meant nothing intimate with this, hoping merely to lighten the conversation, but he immediately called for the bill.

'I promised Mom I'd do what I hope will be the last grass-cut of the summer this afternoon. I'd better get back.'

As we left the restaurant and he walked me back to my car, my feelings were bittersweet: I had assuaged my guilt, however temporarily, but by far the stronger emotion was of regret for my enormous, self-generated loss. I had to take that on the chin. We shook hands as we said goodbye.

Chapter Thirty-three

Just under three weeks after that meal with Peter, I went to Ireland, travelling in mid-October when the weather report from my new country was, unbelievably, of an Indian summer. 'You could be in Tenerife, Marian,' said Sharon, excitedly, when I called to give her the date and time of my arrival in Dublin. 'It's magic.'

We're three weeks into November now, the Indian summer is just a memory and it gets dark very early. I'm told that in December I can expect to put on the lights as early as three thirty in the afternoon.

I continue to miss my city, which is hard to explain to my Irish neighbours. 'Great place to visit, America, but I wouldn't want to live there,' was a common response to the news that I was a Chicagoan. I was surprised to find how many people I encountered had travelled to the States and had cousins or even closer relations there.

For me, it's relatively easy to describe the physical environment that in retrospect seems very attractive: the great suburbs, my parents' neighbourhood in Rogers Park, with its Jewish delicatessens and venerable apartment blocks, the Loop, Oldtown and Michigan Avenue, the laid-back vibe of the city.

I miss the customer-service ethos – not just the formulaic *have a nice day now* but the security of knowing that if, in the morning, you order a repair from a utility, the guy is on your doorstep sometimes as quickly as that afternoon. I miss the humongous steaks, the breakfast pancakes, the smiling pizza-delivery kid with his chatter, professionally focused on guilting you into a bigger tip. I miss the many parks and outdoor sculptures, the winter ice-skating on rinks created by the fire department with their hoses, and the vendors selling hot chocolate and roast chestnuts beside them. I miss the poor old Chicago Cubs, who can't win anything significant, and the Art Institute. I even miss the scruffy old – but constantly reliable – L.

And, of course, the lake. In one sense, Lake Michigan defines the city, which runs along its shoreline and beaches.

But one of the most vivid memories is recent – that of my last sad morning in Chicago. Having lived in Dad's apartment after his and Daniel's deaths, I was moving out permanently.

I had hired a home-clearance company (Alljunk Removal – We Even Take the Dust!), which also ran an auction facility and believed that some of the better pieces of my parents' furniture might fetch a few dollars. While the men got busy, I salvaged not just Mom's percolator and her Sacred Heart picture, but those precious family photographs.

During the clear-out I had been jolted to find Mom's wedding ring and her tiny diamond ear studs wrapped in tissue in Dad's sock drawer: immediately after her death, he had insisted he couldn't find them and had accused the hospital staff of theft or, at best, carelessness. His deceit cut deep as I stared at the modest little pieces in my palm. Had he not wanted me, his only child, to have them? But who to fight with now?

One of the Alljunk guys had been watching me. 'Even if you're not the souvenir type, have a look around – apart from the stuff we'll auction, there might be a few dollars in some of them older bits and pieces.'

I glanced at the scuffed brown furniture in the bedroom, at the stripped, sagging bed, its linens and comforters in a neat, dead heap on the floor, now bare of its rugs. 'I'm leaving for Ireland this afternoon and I'll be travelling light.'

I was taking a last look around the kitchen when the same Alljunk guy came towards me, holding out a thick envelope, A4, the kind with a gusset, used by lawyers but so old that the paper was well on the way to returning to its cotton origins. 'You might want to take this,' he said. 'It was under the bed in the bedroom when we pulled it out.'

'Thanks.' I took it from him. I had brought a large shopping tote with me and, with some difficulty, shoved the envelope into it with the other mementos. I'd open it later. Dad had been a hoarder of receipts: 'You never know, Marian, if things break down or prove to be faulty you might need 'em. These little bits of paper are valuable documents. You should remember that.' I'd probably find that some of the contents of the envelope dated back to the seventies.

I was just about to leave when there was a soft tap on the apartment door, which the guys had left ajar. Our old neighbour, Mrs Feinstein, was standing there, holding out a small package. 'This came in the mail for you this morning. I was down at the mailboxes so I signed for it. I hope that's okay?'

'Sure.'

'I knew you were busy.' She plonked her walking stick in front of her, holding it with her two hands as though settling in for a chat.

'Mrs Feinstein,' I said, 'I hope you won't think I'm rude, but I'm under time pressure.'

'Of course, darling, of course. It's the end of an era, though, isn't it?'

'It sure is – hang on there a moment.' I hurried back into the apartment and did a quick scan, then seized a cushion from the living room, its faded tapestry cover having been painstakingly worked by my mom over a couple of months. I went back to the front door. 'Here you go, Mrs Feinstein.' I held it out to her. 'I'm sure Mom would have wanted you to have something to remember us by.'

To my horror, her eyes filled with tears. 'Thank you so much. I still miss her, you know.'

That was the last thing I needed because, suddenly, I felt emotional, too. 'I understand, of course I do, but I really do have to hustle.'

'Of course, Marian. Goodbye, darling. *Lech l'shalom.*'

'I'm sorry, Mrs Feinstein?' I didn't get it.

'Go towards peace, my dear. Travel safely.'

As I watched her hobble away from our door and down the corridor I realised, I had never known her first name – even Mom had always referred to her as 'Mrs Feinstein'. It hadn't seemed important until now – but she was a living link to Mom and Dad. In the same context in which I had undervalued poor Luzveminda, I had also underrated Mrs Feinstein's role in the day-to-day life of my family.

I looked at the package in my hand. The return address was Peter's Oak Street apartment and he had registered it. I took it into the bathroom, away from the prying eyes of Alljunk.

It was the gold locket I hadn't been able to locate when clearing my stuff out of Oak Street. And there was a note.

Marian –

Before you go to Ireland, I want you to have this back. It's been on my conscience. Before you came to clear your stuff from the apartment we'd shared, I had removed it from your bureau. Because of what I had thought it represented, continuity, family etc. I didn't want you to wear it for him. It was petty of me, I know. And it was equally petty of me not to mention it during the lunch we had in Skokie. I'm sorry. I'm sending it back to you now because if I didn't I'd feel that even the five good years we spent being married would not count for much. And to me they do.

I genuinely wish you well in your new life. I know you're in touch with my mother and she is delighted about that. She, I'm sure, will keep me updated on your progress.

Peter.

I didn't want to dwell on this because between the decimation of my parents' belongings, poor Mrs Feinstein's emotional farewell and the return of the locket, I was getting upset. I came out of the bathroom, stowed the little box safely in my purse and trashed the torn envelope.

Then, having settled my bill and left a forwarding address in Ireland, I deposited the relevant keys in the mailbox for collection by the rental agency, glad that I had held myself together pretty well.

Nevertheless, when I was placing the well-stuffed tote into the trunk of the rental I had taken for my last four days in the city (public transport hadn't been adequate for carting stuff to the civic-waste facility or Goodwill) I had to try hard to keep the waterworks at bay. The car was due back at the depot in less than two hours and I had booked a cab for early afternoon to take me directly from there to O'Hare for the overnight flight to Dublin.

As I set off along Devon to turn southbound on Sheridan Road, I knew in my heart that I was relinquishing my American life. Feeling obscurely that such a significant moment should be marked, I pulled in just before the corner of Devon and Sheridan to probe what I actually felt. Sadness? Apprehension?

Engine idling, I looked back to where the removal truck, doors open at the rear, dominated the kerb outside my parents' block. Mom's chiffonier was already inside, along with the mahogany sofa table that had belonged to her mother and to her mother's mother, both shrouded in dirty grey blankets. In the auction room, her treasures would be pawed and finger-marked, which would have driven her crazy. All that polish and effort, the caring, storing and minding, to end up in the dingy hold of a removal truck. Aside from the paltry array of items in the trunk behind me, I was sweeping my parents' intertwined lives out of sight.

Those tears again, dammit. What was happening? What was all this mush?

Going to Ireland had turned out to be my only option. And the good news, I told myself, was that I was going to join a ready-made family, new and fresh life with in-laws, kids, even a baby, all of whom were ready, they had intimated in words and deeds, to welcome me into their circle.

My parents' interaction, always spiky although never breaking into outright warfare, to my knowledge, had become so familiar it had served as a background hum to my life with them. And quite early on, with more and more of my school compatriots' parents divorcing, the virtually permanent state of skirmish between mine represented a kind of security. Catholics did not divorce. Or, at least, the more committed ones did not, not then.

At some level I always knew that neither could have lived without the other and, indeed, after Mom died, Dad had curled inwards, a snail into his shell, quite literally because he suffered from mild scoliosis, but also emotionally and psychologically. He gave up going for a beer to Eddie's Tavern, and until Peter Black had come into his life, he had more or less given up talking. Hard to be an only daughter then.

As I turned south on Sheridan I saw that the lake, a dark, slaty grey, shivered with little whitecaps while the sky above bulged with what looked to be the first snowfall of the winter. And, indeed, I had driven just eight blocks when my windshield was spotted with the first soft traces of sleet. Two blocks later, against the heated glass, the spots had grown to full-sized splodges. In Northbrook, my family had always marked the first morning of 'proper' snow with the donning of parkas and rubber boots and had gone outside to make snow angels.

As I coasted along Sheridan through the rapidly thickening snowfall, I realised there had been an advantage to that type of childhood. I had become self-sufficient emotionally, and in almost every other way, at a very early age. I didn't need anyone. Until I met Daniel Lynch.

When that happened, an overwhelming and astonishing desire for him had instantly routed every other feeling, physical and emotional. I knew that guilt about how I had treated Peter, Letty and my marriage would continue to haunt me, and it did, despite my trying to reassure myself with glib magazine aphorisms, such as

The heart knows what the heart wants and all that stuff. It had not been my heart that was involved.

Belatedly, I had fallen hopelessly, helplessly – and, yes, mindlessly – in love for the first time in my life. Within an hour of meeting Daniel during that initial interview, Peter had receded into blurry black and white in comparison with the widescreen technicolour of that extraordinary man, who radiated a life force I had previously only encountered in fiction. Daniel Lynch, so powerfully dynamic, seemed to be as attracted to me as I was to him. I was ecstatic. That's the only word for it. Like the saints we had been taught to revere in our all-girls elementary school, St Teresa of Avila, St Bernadette of Lourdes, St Thérèse of Lisieux, the Little Flower, I had fallen into a state of irrational transcendence although, naturally, I didn't see it as the delirium it was.

From that first meeting, nothing else mattered, not my work, not my poor dad, not Peter or the plans we had made together – not even my obsession with having children. I would have them with Daniel Lynch, I'd thought, and what kids they would prove to be! But even that became secondary to my fever to be with him at all costs.

During his father's last illness, Daniel had left Chicago to go back to Glanmilish as principal of the medical practice and had stayed after his father's death. I hadn't been able to go with him because of my own dad's incremental frailty. All medics involved with him, however, said that his heart was 'strong' and that his illness could be long drawn out.

Right now, cocooned in the warmth of the rental car, I realised I had to stop wallowing in nostalgia to focus on driving through what was a rapidly thickening blizzard. As fast as the windshield wipers swished away the snow, which was as fat as cotton wool, more continued to replace it and by the time I got close to the city, traffic along Lake Shore Drive had slowed to a crawl in both directions. In the northbound lanes beside me, the white swirl was pierced with butter-coloured headlight cones a few feet long in front of my hood, while the brake lights of the vehicles ahead showed powder pink through a coating of white.

With the exception of the wipers' swish, it was quiet both in and outside the car, not just because the traffic had slowed to a hush, but because snow had covered the city with a soft acoustic blanket. Less than a mile away now, the skyscrapers north and east of Michigan Avenue seemed to float in the whirling flakes, flirting – now you see me, now you don't – while from my current vantage point, lake and sky had merged into a single, dove-grey fleece. I would miss this too, I thought. I had been told that it hardly ever snowed in Ireland.

I braked just in time to avoid crashing into the car in front. Luckily we were all going so slowly that the one behind me also managed to brake in time and not hit me – although that driver was not so lucky: he, in his turn, was struck – and then there was a chain reaction, with six or seven vehicles involved.

There must be something similar up ahead, I thought, but the snow was so thick that when, like everyone else who had stalled, I got out of the car to take a look, I couldn't see for more than ten or twelve feet. In my immediate vicinity, we all performed that 'What can you do?' shrug at each other while standing helplessly on the roadway.

I decided to tidy up the trunk. I had too many pieces of luggage, two pull-along suitcases, a very large one and one only slightly smaller, a smaller one still as hand baggage, my purse and my tote. There was probably space in the smaller of the two pull-alongs for the tote. Checking ahead – where there was still no sign of any movement and no flashing lights of the emergency services – I pulled the drawstring of my hood tightly around my face and went to the back of the car.

The tote, with its mementos and Dad's thick envelope, wouldn't fit. I took out the Sacred Heart, then figured I would look pretty eccentric carrying it on board in my hand so I put it back in. Then, by removing Dad's bulky receipts envelope, I managed to squash everything else into my carry-on. If the glass broke over the Sacred Heart, it could be repaired, and as for the envelope, I could dump it at the airport, I thought. Who needed a bunch of old receipts? Why had I not dumped it already?

The answer, of course, was that it had belonged to Dad. Almost every other memento I had with me had belonged to my mom.

As I got back into the car, there was still no sign of a breakthrough in the traffic chaos. I might have persuaded myself that I was going to Ireland on an Awfully Big Adventure but Chicago was not easily letting me go.

Epilogue

We, my willow tree and I, survived yet another storm last night. It was one of the follow-ups, really, to the one I described at the beginning of this memoir, the one that had brought down those two slates and had reminded me of how lonely and sad I had been following the death of my husband and the leaving of my city. The gale is still blowing outside but the rain has stopped. I think the worst is over; and through the French windows in the kitchen, I am again watching the willow flail, hoping that, very soon, observing her struggles will be like seeing her on TV with the sound turned low. I'm planning to have the doors and all the south-facing windows in Glanmilish House replaced with double-glazing.

How?

Well, remember Dad's envelope? The one the Alljunk guy had handed to me, saying he had found it under my father's bed?

Having unpacked and distributed around the house the small collection of souvenirs I had taken from the apartment – photos, Sacred Heart picture and so on – I finally opened it.

Inside it, I had found a snapshot gallery of Dad's own family, all his union membership cards, a small envelope marked 'emergency' containing five hundred-dollar bills, a mixum-gatherum of bank statements and – yes – receipts. Lots of receipts. Poor Dad – but we all have our foibles . . .

I was astonished and gratified, however, to find that he had also stored what seemed to be a comprehensive collection of cuttings from newspapers and magazines: everything I had ever published, right back to articles I'd written during the journalism course at Loyola. I hadn't had any idea he'd been doing that. For the professional stuff, he would have had to go specifically to newsagents, hunting them down. But as I thumbed through the collection, I remembered that now and then he would ask casually, 'So what are you up to these days, Marian?' Which of course would supply me with a few minutes' conversation. While Mom and I could jabber together, I had always found interaction with my father quite stilted.

Ironically, the last piece was a computer printout from the internet of my interview with Daniel Lynch. I would probably never know how he'd got his hands on it, I thought – he didn't even have a computer. But then it occurred to me. Luzveminda had found it for him, probably by using the facilities in the local Rogers Park library. But he – and she, when he was no longer mobile – must have been on an almost permanent trawl. This absolutely floored me.

And all Luzveminda had received for her devotion had been an old walker. I put aside the envelope containing the hundred-dollar bills: morally, I owed her at least that amount.

I sure was glad I hadn't dumped that envelope, even more so when I found an insurance policy, issued by Mutual of America, with Mom as beneficiary; if she pre-deceased Dad the benefit passed to me. He had never mentioned it to me – and I had never asked, although I enquired after Mom died – when a 'suitable' interval had elapsed – if there had been one on her life. There hadn't, although I had remembered, as a child, the 'insurance man' calling at Shangri-La every Friday evening and Mom giving him money. It was just something that happened on those evenings, like having fish for dinner. But it appeared now that she had taken it out on Dad's life, thinking it was more likely than not that he would die before she did. He had simply continued the contributions – for me – for the rest of his life, latterly by direct debit.

I can't tell you what that meant to me as I read the policy. It wasn't even the money, welcome though that was, it was that he had done it for me.

I wrote to the company, attaching Xeroxes of the document, of Dad's death certificate and various bits and pieces identifying myself. There was a bit of to-ing and fro-ing but then it became clear that, yes, I was entitled to the payout, which would be substantial: a hundred thousand dollars. Not a fortune in this era, but enough to get me started on fixing up Glanmilish House, beginning with the double-glazing. If I was to survive there, leaving journalism aside for the moment, I had to reinvent the place as a little business, make it pay its way.

Irish newspapers had contained lots of articles about how people had become creative in making a living, outside the traditional jobs: setting up little pop-up shops, trading on eBay, letting spare bedrooms, which, because of Ireland's housing crisis, could earn quite a substantial amount tax-free.

I had discovered that the local Enterprise Office was actually to hold a two-day course in the new year on 'how to run a business on eBay', designed for those who had at least dipped their toes into those waters.

Well, I had done that. Before coming to Ireland, I'd got

myself registered with the company – and with PayPal – and had successfully sold Daniel's banjo, his Gladstone bag, and my two silk dresses. The fee for the course, heavily subsidised by the Irish government, was only fifty euros. I was looking forward to it.

There was a further opportunity based around the house, if I could get my act together – and, of course, the agreement of the family. Airbnb was the new kid on the block, earnings-wise. It hadn't been on my radar in the States but, from reading accounts of how it worked, I decided it was a distinct possibility – *if* I could persuade people to come off the motorway and stay in the house, which stood in a largely deserted village! I would have to come up with some gimmick, I thought – journalism workshops? Offering writing residencies – *Come to Glanmilish House for peace and tranquillity. This historic house is in the quietest part of this wonderfully serene county. Enjoy the incredibly green countryside of Ireland – walk the Slieve Blooms* . . . Not until the bedrooms had been renovated, of course – and a couple more bathrooms put in. Nevertheless, I could already see the blurb . . .

The more I thought about it, the more positive I felt about it all.

In the meantime, I've joined the local bridge club. I had never played any card game, with the exception of Go Fish as a child, but with Mom's blood in my veins, I thought, maybe I would have some aptitude, and it was a way to socialise and make friends. The members of the club had been delighted to have new blood and two of them, a farmer and his wife, who rejoiced in the names of Prudence and Jonathan Entwistle, had volunteered to teach me the game.

And a lot of my time has been taken up with getting down the words of this . . . what? Memoir? I've been calling it that in my own head, but it sounds a little fancy (yes Mom!), as though I'm big-headed. As long as I'm alive it will probably remain in one of the many file-boxes I now have piled in the dining room. I'm a great one for buying storage and leaving it empty!

Jack Cantwell had called at the height of last night's storm. Divesting himself of his dripping raingear, he had come into the kitchen, accepted a cup of tea, then produced my document wallet, out of which he had taken four, not three, of those buff envelopes. 'I hesitated to bring this last one,' he said, 'but I hear you know about it, so I just thought just for completeness . . .'

Sharon had called me in Glanmilish the previous week, again with Eleanor in the background. 'You've been getting hate mail over the past few weeks since you arrived here?'

'How did you know? I didn't tell anyone except that cop.'

'I found out.' She went off the line and Eleanor came on, sounding far less shaky than she had at any time previously. 'Finn, my son,' she said, 'you know him?'

'Sure I do.'

'Well, he got two things into his head. He thought he heard something in a conversation at home during the tail-end of the recession – the recovery hasn't reached us yet, by the way. Anyhow, what he heard was a discussion about how you might be coming to live permanently in Glanmilish House by yourself and we were going to be homeless when we could easily have moved in there, at least temporarily. He blamed you for influencing Daniel to organise it – and, of course, he didn't know anything about his grandfather's will.'

'Oh, God, Eleanor, that's so far from the truth . . .'

'I know, but it gets worse.' Her voice was strengthening by the second. 'This is awful, but it's what he thought. Because you're an American, you support killing people in Iraq and rendition flights by your government through Shannon airport. He was absolutely convinced that certain flights are carrying not just weapons but hooded men and women being transported for interrogation and torture. He was caught last year trying to saw his way in through a fence with a small hacksaw to get at one of the US war planes, as he called them.'

'What? Did it make the newspapers?'

'It did, but just a few small paragraphs. Because he was underage at the time he wasn't named. Somehow we managed to keep it under wraps, although Martin had to get really tough with him to stop him boasting about it publicly on Facebook. It's partly my fault and I take full responsibility. He'd heard me going on at Martin about how poor we were and how we might lose our home, and how it wasn't fair that you had all that space for yourself. I'm so sorry, Marian, it was just silly talk and I didn't really know you until recently, did I? And if I'd thought he was going to terrorise you . . .'

From behind her, I heard Sharon's intervention: 'You didn't send those letters yourself, Ellie!'

'I know,' Eleanor sounded utterly miserable, 'but I might as well have. I'm not excusing Finn. What he did was awful, really awful, and very cruel, no matter how you look at it, and none of it actually makes much sense. Apparently there were four of those letters.'

'Three, actually.' I wasn't enjoying the notion that out there an eighteen-year-old believed I was the type to condone hooding, waterboarding and any other nefarious actions the US government allegedly took against its perceived enemies, but it wasn't the end of the world. Those letters had been annoying, even sinister, but set against the tragedies I had endured in recent weeks, they didn't rate.

'No, there were four. Maybe he didn't send the last one and that's a small mercy. It was really dreadful, scurrilous. I'm so sorry. I can't say how ashamed I am, Marian. That young fella's going to apologise in person. I'll make sure of it. I don't know what got into him. But he'll regret it. Martin and I will make sure of that. He'll be sorry he ever thought about doing such a thing.'

'There may be one complication, Eleanor. As I said, I took those letters to the police.'

There was a short pause as she took this in. 'Fair enough. It might teach him a lesson.'

'How did you find out?'

'He was away for a couple of days. I was cleaning his room and saw that he'd left his computer on. I went to turn it off – and I know I shouldn't have, it was just out of curiosity, the snooping-mother thing, I suppose – but when I clicked on it, it opened up with all the document files listed. The names seemed mostly to do with rock bands and school essays, things like that, but I did see a folder called "Fuck Marian". Of course I opened it. Sorry, sorry . . .' again, she blew her nose '. . . that sounds really desperate when you say it out loud.' She blew her nose again. 'To make sure he learned his lesson, I sent that last, fourth message to that Garda sergeant Portlaoise – he was at both Dad's and Daniel's funerals, do you remember?'

'I remember him at Daniel's,' I said quietly, 'but I wasn't at your father's, I'm afraid.'

'Anyhow, I sent it, and a copy to you, with a letter explaining and apologising, and I made him watch me when I posted them.'

'He's just a kid. If that were to be the worst thing that ever happened to me . . . Look, Eleanor, I'll have a word with Jack Cantwell – I have his number somewhere. I'm sure he'll understand. He'll probably just caution Finn about wasting police time. Honestly, it's not that serious.'

'And now you know about Daniel too. What you must think of this family – of me, dripping around, afraid of my shadow. I shouldn't say it, but it's a real relief to get all this off my chest. I was so ashamed and guilty – but how could I have told you? The only times I saw you were at the wedding party and then at Daniel's funeral. Neither was suitable for laying all that on you. I can't apologise enough for all of us, Marian. Can you forgive me? Forgive us, I mean.'

'Of course, Eleanor.'

'"Ellie", please. "Eleanor" sounds like I'm in a fantasy film or something.'

'There's nothing to forgive!'

* * *

'How did you hear that?' I asked Jack Cantwell now as he sat comfortably in his chair. 'How'd you know that I knew all about it?'

What is it about sitting snugly inside when the wind is howling? Is it a throwback to the womb when, no matter what is happening, nothing much can interfere with that intimate and secure environment?

'Sources!' He winked. 'Lookit, Marian, people talk. There was a funeral for Billy Murphy. People were there. We hear things. And before you ask how we got this last letter, we were watching the house, as I told you, and one of my colleagues found it sticking out of your postbox and took it.'

'You stole my mail? That's a crime.'

'Indeed it is,' he said agreeably. 'Now, do you want this or do you not? And there was this with it.' He gave Eleanor's letter to me.

Silently, I opened it. The first thing I noticed was that we were back to magenta for this one. Now that I knew who had written the damn things, I was able to read it with a slight twitch of amusement: 'WATCH YOUR BACK, AMERICAN NEOCON BITCH!' And that explained the tenor of Finn Lynch's letter of apology, the writing of which had probably been forced on him by his mother:

Dear Marian,
I'm sorry. I was wrong to do that, and I don't
think you're a neocon at all. Sorry.
  Yours truly,
  Finn Lynch.

I gazed at Jack Cantwell, who was wearing a look I can only describe as amused. 'Are you going to follow this up?'

'Are you going to make a formal complaint?'

 'I thought I had.'

'Well, are *you* going to follow *that* up?'

'Of course not! The kid is family.'

That had felt good. I got up from the table and threw all four of the stupid letters, with their envelopes and the document wallet, into the trash. They now seemed faintly sad. 'Will you have a real drink? I have gin – or there might be some whiskey. Are you on duty?'

He shook his head. 'A whiskey, a small one, mind, would be very acceptable. So have you plans, Marian?'

He stayed for almost an hour and I enjoyed his company. I gave him the gist of what I was going to try to do, he told me all about Billy Murphy's funeral: apart from the two Lynch funerals, it had been one of the biggest seen around these parts.

The perpetrators of the poor man's murder had not yet been identified, he told me, 'but we have a good idea. We just have to be fairly certain before we arrest them, these days. Thugs have access to the best briefs in the business and they don't have to put their hands into their pockets. "Legal aid", they call it because they claim not to have a bob and yet they're driving around in massive four-by-fours and top-of-the-range Mercs and Audis.'

Then, in the middle of his story about their hunt for Billy

Murphy's killer or killers, he remarked, without meaning to, I think now, 'Of course, we can't say this publicly, certainly in this town, but poor Billy was a by-child and—' He stopped.

'A boy-child? Of course he was. So what, Jack?'

'No,' he said slowly, 'a "by-child". Illegitimate. That was the term they used around here traditionally. Still do in some places, even in these more enlightened times. I didn't mean to let that slip. Some of us, the older ones, have been aware of this in the force, but it's not generally known and if the media get hold of it . . .'

'Who was the father?'

'If I tell you, you must never say it. Especially not to the family. I don't think they know.'

'What family?' I was bemused.

But he was reluctant to say more.

'Look, Jack, right now I've given up journalism except for a few little feature pieces for the *Sentinel*, and I'm hoping to be able to afford to give even that up, temporarily anyway. I expect to be busy with other things.' I didn't mention my little vanity project – the 'memoir' so-called.

'Well, if you promise . . .'

'My lips are sealed. I promise.'

'Your family. The Lynches. He was Daniel Senior's son. His wife knew, I think. It was probably why she doted on your Daniel when he came along. And in fairness, the man looked after Billy and his ma all their lives.'

'And that explains the twenty-thousand-euro legacy?'

'Of course. Sticking out a mile. But you mustn't tell them. There's still a lot of conservative opinion around here. The Lynches'd be very keen on their reputation. They might find out eventually but that's up to them.'

So – like father, like son, I thought privately, but with no relevance now to anything important. I didn't say it. 'Another whiskey, Jack?'

He refused, and then, 'Ah, sure what harm? A very small one. Have you a slice of bread by any chance? Soak it up?'

'I can do better than that, Jack. Hang on a sec.' I went to the refrigerator and took out an oven dish. Living alone, I tended to cook large and eat small, which usually meant I had something for dinner that involved only the microwave. 'I can offer you spaghetti bolognese or beef casserole – today's edition.'

'The beef'd be great, Marian – all I had since lunch was a Crunchie. But are you sure I'm not depriving you of your own dinner?'

'No. Because I'm going to eat with you.'

'Fantastic.'

* * *

'You've had a rocky few months, Marian.'

'It's not over yet, Jack.' I was feeling no pain. I had treated myself to a second gin and tonic, although he'd refused a third whiskey – 'The last thing I need is to be stopped by a patrol. The new guys are fierce quick to whip out the Breathalyser.'

'God, you were hungry, Jack.' He had wolfed the beef casserole. 'Could you handle seconds?'

'If it's going, Marian.'

He actually stayed until midnight and we conversed easily. He had a general degree in arts, but had applied to the Guards, as he called them, because he'd got married when his then girlfriend got pregnant. The force offered a steady income and 'At the time, Marian, we felt we could actually make a difference to society. I couldn't have faced a job in a bank or an insurance company. I like being out and about and I like dealing with people.'

He was now separated from his wife, and that baby was a son

at college in Dublin and living there. 'Has me crucified. I didn't have a clue about the price of renting in Dublin. He's in a five-bedroomed house with four other guys – I really pity the landlord!'

All in all, he was a lively dinner companion with a store of local lore and an unending fund of gossip about people and politicians, some entertainingly scabrous: 'Of course I'd have to murder you if I told you about him' – and then he'd tell me.

There was a serious side to him too. Over coffee he told me about the break-up of his marriage. 'You'll probably hear about it anyway – it's great craic for some people.' Apparently his wife of twenty-four years had gone off with a carpenter who had come to fit a floor in their house. 'She's forty-six, like me, and he's twenty-five.' There was real pain in his voice and his expression when he told me, haltingly, that the two of them were 'swanning' around the Portlaoise bars and eateries 'in full view of everyone. It's very upsetting because, as you know, Marian, that's where I'm based. Sorry for going on about it. You have troubles, real troubles. Mine pale in comparison.'

'You knew about Daniel all along, didn't you?' I remembered the little flash I had seen in his eyes when he was dealing with me, just before he was interrupted by his female colleague.

'I didn't know you, Marian. I'd seen you at the funeral, of course – you were so stressed and so dignified at the same time that I really admired you. And when you came into the station a few weeks ago with those bloody letters in that little pink folder, I nearly told you. I could have killed that fella all over again, you know. But it really wasn't my business, was it?'

'How did you find out?'

'I've a pal in the force in Limerick. Lynch's sister was living there. She confided in someone who knows the pal and they advised her to tell you, or at least one of the Lynches, but she couldn't. That's how it works in Ireland, Marian. You won't be familiar with it yet, but if you don't want someone to know something, you just have to keep it to yourself. Real tight. You can tell no one, not your best friend, your accountant – nobody. Certainly not anyone who swears to keep your secret safe. Maybe your confessor, but they're *really* out of fashion.' He grinned. 'I knew a priest once – he's dead now, Lord have mercy on him – and he confided in me that when he was chaplain to a convent he dreaded Saturdays. Saturday nights were confession nights and he said he was bored out of his skull. Hearing nuns' confessions was like listening to a crowd of quacking or whispering ducks, depending on their ages.'

'That's awful.'

'Of course it is – that's why it's so funny.'

I found that almost for the first time that year I was enjoying myself in someone's company without some complication muttering at me in the background – there was nothing of which I had to be watchful.

'It was a lovely evening, Marian,' he said, when he was leaving. 'I'll return the compliment soon. I might be out of line here, considering you must be still in mourning, but would you like to come to dinner sometime? There're a couple of nice restaurants in Kilkenny.'

'Sure,' I said. 'That'd be lovely. I'll look forward to it.'

'You're sure you'd be up to it?'

'I'm up to it, Jack.'

'Right, that's great.' He smiled. 'I'll be in touch.' Then he repeated the farewell that seemed to be a mantra around these parts – 'Don't be a stranger, now, Marian' – and went out into the night.

* * *

When I read back through this account, a few things strike me. The most telling – and ridiculous – aspect of the story, I suppose, is how a person's life can change completely in two seconds. While I was working on how to get pregnant with my first husband, I had heard an Irish accent in the background of our living room on Oak Street. On looking up, I had seen Daniel Lynch on cable TV. And my world had turned on a dime.

For the first few decades of my life I was, I think, a reasonably positive person, always going to sleep and, like Scarlett O'Hara, believing that, no matter what had happened that day, tomorrow would be better. My experience with Daniel had *almost* turned that on its head, plunging me into a period where very little in my life could be fully trusted, certainly not the future and least of all my own instincts.

I'm in the process of climbing out of that chasm now. And positives emerged in the interim, anyhow, thanks to the generosity of people I hadn't known before my second husband came into my life. His family, largely, but others too. I have learned what the phrase 'profoundly grateful' actually means and, in many ways, this addendum to the story could be taken in the same spirit as the Acknowledgements pages at the end of a book. (I confess that I actually turn to those before starting on the book proper.)

The second thing that strikes me, reading back, is how we are all subject to influences, whether we know it at the time or not.

I might have imagined that when I grew up and left home, my mother's presence in my life would fade, like the flowers on old wallpaper. But now it seems that was not what happened. It surprises me to find how active she still is in my inner life, and how often she has appeared in this text, Dad too, I guess, but to a lesser extent.

I hope Peter comes well out of this account, and Letty, Aoife, Sharon and even poor old Eleanor, whom I had virtually dismissed as odd, eccentric or damaged, until I learned *why* she had behaved as she did – and that was yet another lesson for me.

Daniel's two brothers helped to rehabilitate my faith in human nature, as did Ajay from Holy Angels, who went the extra mile for me; Luzveminda was a stalwart for me in Dad's last months, while even Mollie Lehman and Cherry at *Femme* played their parts, although I hadn't credited Mollie at the time, far from it.

And here I was, finding myself in Glanmilish as a (very) minor celebrity. I had been astonished to find that my pieces on Chicago had been a hit with the *Sentinel* readers, and I'd even featured in a few Letters to the Editor. In addition, because of the prominence of the Lynch family, I was recognised around the place, in shops and walking along the street. It was a strange feeling.

As for journalism, 'Good but not exceptional' is no longer enough for me, and on the flight to Ireland, I had decided I had been aiming at achievements above my talent grade. That's an uncomfortable place to be. I might get back to it seriously some time in the future, just not now. In the meantime I'm enjoying the daily scribbling.

Then there's Jack Cantwell, who, with far better things to do, didn't dismiss my concerns and is now a friend. We're going to Kilkenny for dinner next Saturday, which marks the beginning of the Christmas festivities. I'm looking forward to that.

So what happened between that lunch with Peter Black in Skokie and today, here in Glanmilish as, with Christmas not all that far away, I write this?

Events continued to move pretty swiftly.

I arrived back in Dublin with just a few thousand dollars in my purse, along with a note from Cindy:

Marian, I just thought I'd write to you. I guess you're probably still very upset? Don't be. The past is the past and we all have to get on with our

*lives and you will too. You have to believe that he
was worth it. He was for me anyway and I hope
Junior will too. Think so, I mean. Cindy.*

I don't know why I kept that. Perhaps as proof, to myself, that when
all this fades into memory, as it inevitably will, I will remember that
there was a time when I was a passionate woman.

The downside, of course, was that I caused incalculable hurt to
a blameless man and his mother. I'm repeating myself here, I know,
but that betrayal continues to produce four-o'clock-in-the-morning
moments when I wake up filled with such shame that I cry out.

I can do that because there's no one to hear me now.

On the Saturday of the week after I came back to Glanmilish,
there was a family meeting in the little hotel in the village where
everyone (except Aoife, who didn't want to leave Rose Marian)
gathered to talk through the rather awkward situation in which
the other three owned everything and I owned nothing but was a
sitting tenant in the house.

I had decided what I wanted. Subject to the legalities, I was
accepting custody of the house, for now, because I had nowhere
else to live. Also, I had, I thought, figured out a way it could
provide me with an income until paid work came my way; they
all understood that, and although Eamon broached the possibility
of selling the place ('Of *course* you'd get Daniel's share, Marian,
regardless of what any will says') the idea didn't get much purchase
and he withdrew it, gracefully, accepting Jerry's assertion that it
wasn't worth much in its present state. I explained my plans for
gradual repair and refurbishment and for making the house work
for its keep. There was a little hoo-hah about that, with Eamon
and Eleanor asserting that if I was to use the place as a business I'd
probably need planning permission – but Jerry and Sharon jumped

on them. 'She's not planning to run a hotel – are you, Marian?'

'No.' I shook my head. 'And it'll all be above board. I'll pay any taxes due *if* there's any profit.'

'And there are grants for upgrading the insulation – like the double glazing you're thinking about.'

The more they talked, the more the whole patchwork of small schemes, which had seemed a little too piecemeal, now seemed a coherent whole. And they hadn't objected seriously to any of it. In a way, I felt that by improving the house, I was investing in my future, and also, importantly, paying my way into the family.

We had a few drinks afterwards, and Jerry whispered in my ear that he thought I was 'doing great, after everything you've been through, Marian. That brother of mine had to be a fecking brainless idiot. And I can't imagine how he managed to keep the existence of little Daniel from us all – although I gather from my sister that she's known for ages. He's just a year ahead of our Tom.'

'Yes,' I whispered back. 'But I guess they won't be sharing their toys any time soon.'

'Stranger things have happened. It's not the kid's fault that his father was a flake—'

But then Eamon interrupted: 'My round. What are you two hugger-muggering about?'

'Nothing!' Jerry and I spoke simultaneously and I have to say it was a lovely feeling. Just like we were two kids in the same family denying a misdemeanour.

Then there's Peter. I haven't worn his locket. I can't really explain why, it just didn't feel . . . appropriate. I think that's the right word. He hasn't engaged with me, hasn't replied to my carefully worded thank-you note for it, but then I didn't expect him to.

These past few weeks have felt a little like an interregnum, if you can understand that.

Letty and I are regularly in touch – she has learned to Skype and we communicate at least once a week – she has seized on this new source of entertainment. She's been hinting about coming for a visit – her son had obviously told her of my invitation – and I would love to have her (I think she'd love my new family) but I haven't encouraged her in any but the most general terms since I'll be away from Glanmilish for Christmas and, anyhow, it's going to take more than a superficial tidy-up and paint job to get the bedrooms up to scratch. One room at a time, is what I plan and, as a matter of urgency, to replace those rattling windows. 'So when the weather is warmer, Letty,' I said, to be told that she had survived seventy-four Chicago winters so 'a bit of Irish drizzle is nothing.' It's as though age has given her permission to shrug off the niceties and get straight to the point.

Do I forgive Daniel?

Actually, in my own mind, like karma in a way, his betrayal of me balances out my betrayal of Peter, which is why I understand my first husband's reluctance to have anything to do with me still.

It's relatively easy to forgive intellectually, less so emotionally, I find. The scars, sense of failure, diminution in self-confidence, the humiliating sense of having been duped are harder to forget. But Daniel is in his grave and I'm not. Using his purview of life, that's a win for me.

And there is a positive outcome. Would it have occurred if he wasn't dead? I don't know. But from having been an orphan with no siblings (and no close friends) I now have a genuinely loving family and a little goddaughter, who bears my name and whose christening is being held, deliberately, on my birthday, Christmas Eve. Taking it in its generational sense, I now have a mother (Letty), brothers, sisters and a child in my life, and that's pretty impressive. And I'm on course, I hope, to make a circle of friends here. How many people get a chance to start afresh, not just in a new country but in a new family?

Regrets? Well, of course, and they have been well covered, but there is no point in dwelling on them. I've apologised. Reading through these pages, I feel I've actually wallowed in apologies, so I'm trying to train myself to get out of that mode.

In my head, and maybe in this account, I had been treating Daniel's betrayal as though it was Wagner's Ring Cycle or a ten-volume Icelandic saga, but it would take only a few seconds to relate this plot: *Daniel Lynch, an Irish doctor, has died, and after his death his wife, Marian, learns that all along he'd had a long-term mistress, and had bedded many, many women before, during and after his relationships with both wife and mistress. The end.*

Put like that, I can see the whole show as the everyday soap opera it actually was. Mrs Feinstein had always been an avid daytime TV story-viewer, and in our corridor, or at one or other of our open apartment doors, she was wont to regale Mom with the latest twists in the plots. She would have regarded mine as tame.

So my Great Adventure closes as it began, with a storm. Outside the wind is howling, the slates are rattling, my lovely willow is flailing. In here, I'm happy to have made a start on putting this house in order, starting with its most egregious flaws, and happy too that the end of these scribbles about my life is in sight.

Maybe journalism didn't suit me. Maybe I don't have the ambition for it. (Finn Lynch was highly impressed that I 'knew' Tim Cook, so much so that he has agreed to create a website for when the Airbnb is up and running at Glanmilish House. Says his mother, anyway!)

And Christmas is coming. After the christening on Christmas Eve, we're having a party in Jerry and Aoife's house in Dublin, a double celebration for Rose Marian and me. I'm staying over afterwards and we're assembling again on Christmas morning for presents, then

Christmas dinner. I've already arranged a Skype call with Letty – I want her to meet everyone.

Burdens are for shoulders strong enough to carry them, wrote Margaret Mitchell of her (and my mother's) heroine, Scarlett. That's something to live up to now. I'm a Chicagoan and my city, as Cherry had pointed out to me on one famous occasion, is known as the City of Big Shoulders.

In the meantime, I'm looking forward to having dinner with Jack in Kilkenny, our neighbouring county. And guess what? He'll be in Dublin for Christmas with his son and we'll probably meet up and go to a movie – or even something called a pantomime. I've never been to one and I gather they're great fun, an amalgamation of a fairy tale and humour. Apparently, they all have happy endings.

Acknowledgements

First of all, gratitude to Ciara Considine, Breda Purdue, Ruth Shern and all the team at Hachette Ireland for their concern and hard work in getting this book onto the shelves; major gratitude too to Hazel Orme, copy-editor, for her skill, encouragement and kindness.

I have a small family by Irish standards, but without them I'd be lost. So thank you sons Adrian and Simon and brother Declan; thanks too to my sisters-in-law Mary and Rosemary, daughter-in-law Catherine, granddaughter Eve, stepdaughter Zoe, stepson Justin, his partner Ciara – and Zoe's husband Claus, niece Gillian, nephews John and Paul, godsons Stephen B and Ross, cousins Barbara, Laura, Philip and Stephen K. All of these people, with their own children, partners and extended families, have been wonderfully supportive, as have Declan's in-laws the Quinns, especially Mag, Larry and Pauline.

Thanks Frances (Fox) for your unstinting support – and thanks, similarly, to all the other 'Aer Lingus girls' who've been so patient with my no-shows at the celebrations and theatre gigs! And to all my other terrific friends, recent, lifelong, and genuinely too numerous to name here, but they will know who they are and I hope I've shown them how much they mean to me . . .

Thanks, Eithne Healy and Mary Sheehy for all the breakfasts – and to my RTÉ colleagues on the 'It Says in the Papers' roster: Valerie Cox, Clodagh Walsh, Fiona Kelly, Caroline Murphy and John S Doyle, all of whom have been very generous.

Thanks to Anne Carmelita O'Connor for propping up my spirit through the year – the same goes for Patricia Scanlan whose trenchant advice and humour is always a bulwark against the inclination to run for the hills! And thanks to my friend of almost seven decades Patricia Byrne and her husband, Frank.

Huge thanks to the exceptionally diligent Dr Karen Aylward, her colleagues Doctors Sinead Morgan, Robert Scanlon and Cathal O'Sullivan – and to Dr John Burbridge, who leads them at the Griffith Avenue Practice in Glasnevin, Dublin. Thank you for taking care of me. And, in that context, thanks too to the 'front of house' staff at the practice, and to Therese, its nurse, all of whom could not be kinder (or more patient!).

Thanks to Patsy McKeon, helper and friend through all.

And most of all, profound gratitude to my husband Kevin. Through thick and thin, Kevin, for better for worse! I hope you know how much I appreciate you – because I sure do . . .

> "I can no other answer make but thanks,
> And thanks, and ever thanks."
> William Shakespeare *Twelfth Night Act 3 scene 3*